LADY JAIL

LADY JAIL

John Farrow

This first world edition published 2020
in Great Britain and 2021 in the USA by
SEVERN HOUSE PUBLISHERS LTD of
Eardley House, 4 Uxbridge Street, London W8 7SY.
Trade paperback edition first published
in Great Britain and the USA 2021 by
SEVERN HOUSE PUBLISHERS LTD.

British Library Cataloguing in Publication Data
A CIP catalogue record for this title is available from the British Library.

ISBN-13: 978-0-7278-9073-3 (cased)
ISBN-13: 978-1-78029-742-2 (trade paper)
ISBN-13: 978-1-4483-0470-7 (e-book)

All Severn House titles are printed on acid-free paper.

Severn House Publishers support the Forest Stewardship Council™ [FSC™],
the leading international forest certification organisation.
All our titles that are printed on FSC certified paper carry the FSC logo.

MIX
Paper from
responsible sources
FSC® C013056

Typeset by Palimpsest Book Production Ltd.,
Falkirk, Stirlingshire, Scotland.
Printed and bound in Great Britain by
TJ Books Limited, Padstow, Cornwall.

The author thanks the women he met
at the Joliette Institution for Women
for their cake and candor,
and dedicates this novel to them.
Be free.

PART ONE

Abigail

They heard murmurings. Tales of allegiances and alliances, rumor of war. The year was 1994. They spoke in whispers and did the laundry.

Over sandwiches one time, they played a game. *Let's say one of us gets snuffed. OK, who did it?* Everyone wanted to be mentioned, to be in on the action, to be considered the killer at large. Everyone was. They laughed and laughed. They howled. Nobody asked who the victim should be. To say that out loud might be sufficient cause for trouble. Or murder.

On Monday mornings the women met in the communal kitchen for a practical discussion. They ordered groceries. Each inmate was allocated twenty dollars a week; a total of one hundred and sixty dollars for a house-unit of eight prisoners. Overspend on meat, go without vegetables. Add a cake mix, request Kraft Dinner to stay on budget. Plan carefully. Be disciplined. Eat through the budget in five days, skimp for two. Go without whatever spoiled or burned. They had to be smart and cautious. By necessity they had to co-operate. That was the general idea: cooperation aided their progress toward that magical realm known as rehabilitation.

'Get this, if we swing along, we get along. Nobody's eyes get gouged out. I know, right? They think that way. Like, insane or what?'

Reaching consensus, they marked their selections on an order form.

Spuds and beans. Steaks. Chicken wings, legs, breasts. Chops. Go easy on the candy bars.

In the Joliette Institution for Women – Lady Jail, they called it; by any name, a penitentiary – the women were segregated into group quarters rather than individual cells. The framework was considered experimental, an attempt at prison reform. Anyone wishing to be returned to the regular system with cells and steel bars and crappy food needed only to put in the request to be transferred within the week. Rarely did anyone do so and the waiting list for female prisoners in traditional penitentiaries hoping to arrive at Joliette was lengthy. The criteria for admittance basic: a prisoner had to be eighteen or older, as in any pen, and have two or more years remaining on her original sentence. That part was easy. The more critical requirement was difficult to achieve: an official's signed stamp of approval.

Once admitted, prisoners were given latitude to adapt. Second chances were permitted. Florence was back in solitary for the fourth time, yet as long as no convict was beating up bunkmates on a regular basis and she wasn't caught with a shiv and didn't topple a guard with a frying pan she could stay. *Do the work. Get along. Stay*. Pretty much everyone's mantra.

Each prisoner managed the life differently.

Recently transferred to Joliette, Abigail was figuring out how things went down. She was struggling to adjust. When she first learned of her transfer, she was super-duper excited but also scared. Being delirious with joy was something she kept to herself, while also letting no one detect her fright. Moving through the system meant landing with a whole different slew of inmates, none of whom she'd know. No one could project how that would pan out. She had to give up the few close friends she'd made at the Nova Institution for Women – a pen by any other name – in Truro, Nova Scotia, and that was hard. Joliette was seven hundred miles away and most prisoners there spoke French, although they lumped English inmates together in the same house-units. She wouldn't have family visitors. Too far away. Pretty lonely. Old friends in Montreal might visit, but who among them would want to associate with a convicted felon? They probably couldn't get past the sniffer dog or the mass spectrometry machine anyway. Abigail was excited, though, and not because she'd be preparing her own food and baking cakes, although she loved to bake cakes. And eat them, too. The biggest deal: wearing her own clothes. Out of prison garb and, within reason, into her own togs: worth any sacrifice. She wasn't prepared for communal living and shy to get started, but wearing her own get-up for the next six years? For that she'd accept any adjustment or hardship ten times over.

'Abigail? Seriously. Order something. Everybody eats it anyway. Order for you, so long as you share. It's your twenty bucks.'

'Yeah,' she agreed. She had something she wanted to order.
'What?'
'Carrots.'
'Carrots are on the basics list. Kinda automatic.'
'I mean the baby ones. The tiny ones.'
Courtney checked the list. 'Yeah,' she said. 'They got those.'
They agreed. They'd order baby-sized carrots.
'With dip!' Courtney suggested.
They had a choice of three kinds. Onion, dill, or roasted pepper.
They argued over that and chose the roasted pepper.
'We could pretend we're having a midnight snack.'
'They're cheap. You know. Just saying.'
'Not the dip.'
'Who cares? More KD, less pork.'
They ordered more baby carrots and dip, this time the onion.
They were looking forward to that midnight snack-fest, although it
could never take place at midnight. They'd pull solitary for a stunt
like that.
'We'll be the first to OD on baby carrots.'
'Abi! Good idea, girl.'

ii

Two days after Abigail arrived, she found out why each of her
housemates was doing time. A way of opening up the conversation,
the getting-to-know-you aspect. She told them what she was in for,
too. Only fair to tell them, since they were willing to share their
own stories.
'Fraud,' Abi admitted. 'Eight and a half.'
'Months?'
'Years. Six to go.'
A silence.
'Fraud,' Temple repeated. She chewed on the word. 'Fraud.' As
though fraud was a wad of gum. Temple, the only black woman
among them, was in for smuggling, although she didn't let on what
she smuggled. Just as Abigail didn't say whom she defrauded or
how she did it or for how much. Abigail figured Temple's smuggling
came down to the usual: drugs, most likely, or perhaps jewelry. She
realized later that everybody gave out only the bare bones of their

crimes; that they held back on the critical details. Instinctively, she did that, too.

Quite the roll call. Even when limited to the bare bones.

She didn't know how she could fit in here.

Doi was the eldest. Abigail didn't want to ask her age. Late fifties, early sixties a reasonable guess. Doi was Polish and a mother. She was still a mother, she said, even though she had slashed her daughter. Cut her up pretty good with a hatchet for staying out late at night. At least the teenager survived. It seemed like the right thing to do, Doi said, to attack her daughter with a hatchet for staying out late with a boy.

Right. The thing to do. Take a small axe to your own kid. Abigail had been inside with rough people in Nova, but she never had to sleep in the same dorm with them or bake cakes alongside them.

The next oldest was Malka. Early fifties, give or take five years. Hard to tell with her, too. She'd been a minor politician. A city councilwoman, and previously a small-town mayor for a decade before losing an election. After her defeat she ran again and made it back onto council. That was before she was convicted of murdering her own husband.

A band of killers, Abigail was thinking. *Christ!*

Florence – who told Abigail she could call her Flo most of the time as long as she called her Florence once a week and warned her to keep track – had thrown acid in the face of a rival. 'Don't worry, I didn't mean to, but she was asking for it,' Flo said, although Abigail couldn't imagine anyone alive asking for that, and someone who threw acid had to mean it. Her blood chilled inside her and she made up her mind to give Flo miles of personal space. She wondered if she shouldn't ask to go back to Nova immediately and she'd only just arrived. The clothes an old friend from school sent to her hadn't passed inspection yet – they were being checked to make sure she wasn't smuggling in a pistol wrapped in her panties or a shiv in her socks – and already she wanted out.

Temple, the smuggler, was in her mid-to-late-twenties like her, and Rozlynn was early twenties although she'd been inside since she was eighteen. The two kids, Jodi and Courtney, were both nineteen years old and seemed to be virtually inseparable, though not, as far as Abigail could tell, as lovers. Big-time friends, though, and she envied them that. Jodi had shot a man in a convenience store robbery while providing cover for her boyfriend – she didn't elaborate on the victim or on the damage done. Courtney had stabbed her best friend to death with a kitchen knife. She did elaborate on why – the girl had flirted with Courtney's boyfriend.

Rozlynn was very quiet overall and said nothing herself about her crime. She was First Nations. Doi spoke for her. 'Can I say?' Doi asked her.

Rozlynn nodded.

'She killed her father on her eighteenth birthday. What does that tell you? I know what it tells me: He deserved it.'

Unlike, Abigail was thinking, your daughter, hey?

iii

Abigail spiraled into a sinkhole of depression. She'd been through this before. The episodes were never welcome. Wearing her own clothes once they'd been inspected – no hidden weapons, no weed – helped her out for about an hour. The novelty faded. Reality walloped her mood. The group voted for Temple to speak with her, partly because Temple volunteered, and mostly because they were similar in age.

'It's like you're not happy here, Abi.'

'Who is?'

Temple chortled. She found that very funny. 'So right,' she said. 'So right.' They sat together in their dorm. They had deliberately been left alone. For several minutes they sat in silence, separated perhaps by culture and race.

'Where is everybody?' Abigail asked.

'Don't worry about it, OK? I'm not making out with you.'

'Then what?'

'Part of the thing here, right? We can't let nobody go down a rabbit hole in the dark. Not by herself. Find out why first. Find out what's up. Keeps the morale high, you know? Supposed to work that way, anyhow.'

'Some idea.'

'I know, right? But look, everybody can tell you're freaking out. I get it. You're a fraud artist. You're in with a hatchet-wielding mom and a daddy-killer. We got a shooter and a stabber. You're peaceful. All you do is bilk people. Malka used poison to finish off her old man. She did it slow. Like she wanted him to feel the worst pain for the longest time, then die in pure misery. We won't even talk about Flo. Let's not. She throws acid. Who does that?'

'I thought we weren't talking about it.'

'I know, right? But me and you, we have this thing in common. You're not in here sitting with a fencepost halfway up your butt all by your lonesome self. All right? We're sitting on the same fucked up fence, me and you.'

Abigail had to work through that image. Then she said, 'In common? How do you figure that? You mean like we didn't kill anybody?'

'I mean like we're the real criminals in here, right?'

'Wait. What?'

Temple's hands were expressive. 'Think about it. Everybody else is nothing more than a fuck-up who didn't control her temper. Me, you, we had our own purpose. We knew what we were doing. They didn't. We're legitimate crooks, right? These others? Fine ordinary upstanding citizens who lost their shit for a few seconds. Except for Malka maybe, because she took her time. But it was only her husband. It's not like she's a homicidal maniac. Just don't marry the woman. All these others, they have regrets. Me and you, we had ambition, right? We had our plans. We were in the game. We got caught is all.'

'Jodi was out robbing a variety store,' Abigail pointed out to her.

'You're right about that, you got me there. Except I think it was a convenience store, but what's the difference, right? Still, it's like she was having an experience. Adolescent bullshit crap. Nothing more. She got stoned. She got pissed. She was on some kind of mind-fuck drug. Like meth. She was handed a gun, told to stand beside her idiot boyfriend to look tough while he emptied the till. I know, what? Like she could look tough. That one looks like an angel on a Christmas card. Fairy dust falls off her back when she walks by. Jodi, she was starting in the life – first time out she panicked. Blasted away for no reason. Tried to shoot her way out of what she was doing, maybe, or tried to shoot herself. Who knows? Really, it's pathetic if you want to know the truth. She panicked and now she's inside. Everybody else here, except us, same thing. Spur of the moment type horseshit. You and me, we were in it for the long haul. We were in the life. OK, Flo was, too, but same as the others she just lost it. We got busted for one crime only but got away with a ton of others, am I right? Tell me I'm not wrong.'

Abigail said nothing, never wise to admit to anything, but her nod conceded the validity of the argument. She had been committed to a life bilking the hapless and the banks, some thought, although those who were plugged in probably knew by now that she'd bilked the mob. Word gets around and that kind of news never stays tight. Mob women were on the inside. Inevitable, and it scared her. They'd still be following orders. Temple was mobbed up, she could tell, so she only pretended to trust her.

'One more thing we have in common. I'm guessing, but fraud artist? You know what that makes me think?'

Abigail waited to hear.

'Tells me you weren't working alone. Plus, you got a whack of years for only fraud. Like, Jesus, must've been some kind of scam. Other people in it with you. A man, I bet, maybe more than one. Maybe a gang. Like me. Part of a gang.'

She sure sounded as though she was digging for deeper dirt. 'What did you smuggle?'

'You really want to know?' Temple asked her back.

Abigail shrugged. 'Sure.'

'Some don't.'

'Don't what?'

'Want to know. I mean, after I tell them, they wish they didn't know. Or they don't want to know me.'

'You have to tell me now, after that intro.'

'Weapons. Ammo. Heavy caliber horseshit, baby.'

Abigail stared back at her.

'I know, what? Now you're thinking you're *really* screwed. Just remember, you're the hardened criminal in here. And yeah, that would be me, too. Us, and that's it. The rest of these chick-a-roos? Amateurs. They couldn't control their own shit. So buck-up, Abi-girl. You belong here. We respect. Even look the fuck up to you. To do what you did? You had to be effing smart. To get that many years for white-collar horseshit? Wow. Not like the rest of us dumb asses. Don't worry that you never killed nobody. Me neither, though who knows maybe a few took it in the ear from the ammo I supplied

and the quick-loaders. The thing is, nobody expects you to kill
nobody. You paid your own dues.'

Abigail took all that in. She said, 'I was in with weird ladies in
Nova. But behind bars. At night, anyway. Separate cells.'

'Stop being so scared. It's not so bad in here. It's not like any
of these killer-broads made it a habit. For them, it was a one-off.
One and done. And Flo don't have no acid supply.'

Abigail felt better after talking to Temple. Her status had been
pointed out to her, and she needed that. 'Flo scares me, though.
Even with no acid.'

'You and me both,' Temple admitted. 'I stay real kind to Flo. Do
that yourself. Don't never cross her. While you're at it, don't cross
me neither.'

'I don't plan to cross anybody,' Abigail said.

'More than I can say for myself,' Temple said, and laughed at
her own joke, as though it wasn't a joke. 'But. Good plan. Good
plan. And look, I know what you're worried about. Don't be. Not
going to happen. I'm not making out with no chickenshit fraud-
artist, no matter how cute you are. You're pretty damn cute, too.
You know that, right? I know all about you slick white chicks.
You wake up in the morning, somebody's goddamn life savings
went missing.'

'Yeah, like you have life savings to worry about.'

'I know, what? Anyway, if I did, you'd be the last to find out.
So fool, we're cool?'

Abigail nodded. Then she said, 'You're wrong about one thing.'
'What's that?'

'No man. I worked alone.'

'No shit,' Temple said, in wonderment.

iv

After that fine discussion, Abigail got along with the other women
more easily. One by one, in different ways, she connected. She and
Doi talked first about their affection for the color blue. The day
that Abi's clothes had been cleared she was a trifle disappointed
with a friend's selections for her prison wardrobe. Then an understanding dawned. Her friend loved pale blues and robin's egg blue.
Abi appreciated blue herself, many of her clothes expressed that

inclination, but in selecting what to send her, her friend fixated on her own preferred palette and ignored the variety of colors Abi typically chose.

Still, at least they were real clothes – skirts, dresses, blouses, pants – not convict jumpsuits. The first time she'd pulled on a jumpsuit she thought she'd shrivel up inside it like an old cob of discarded corn, chewed on by raccoons and ants.

Abigail iced an Elizabeth cake while she and Doi talked. Courtney requested the cake, but she couldn't crack an egg and frequently burned toast. The girl insisted on crispy bacon for herself but ended up with blackened leather. She'd not be allowed near batter. So Doi baked the cake and sat in the kitchen while Abigail beat the icing then lathered it on.

'The two of us, we're alike,' Doi decided.

'How so?' Abigail didn't mean to challenge her, she just couldn't see any similarity.

Doi had prepared a list. 'We're traditional women. We know our way around a kitchen. We're happy to have nice clothes. And we like the color blue.'

Doi's preference for darker blues went all the way to navy. Within the blue spectrum, they were opposites. Abigail let that go. She accepted that blue was still blue no matter the pigment.

She wholly objected, though, to the remark about being a traditional woman, whatever that was supposed to mean, and the bit about kitchens. She didn't abhor kitchens, but she wasn't into them. Rebellion against traditional family values had probably started her on a downhill slide into crime. She let that go, too. Like Doi, she was happy to have nice clothes, although she wouldn't classify Doi's as nice. More on the frumpy side, even matronly. Total lack of style. The older woman wore a slip some days, which Abi couldn't fathom. Her mother had worn slips and she never understood why. But in the 1990s? Who knew they still existed? Knowing that she had taken a hatchet to her daughter for staying out late, she doubted very much that Doi would approve of her delicates, beginning with how delicate they were. In any case, she wasn't going to let her catch a glimpse. Who needed the grief?

'I can ice a cake. Bake it, too. But I'm no cook.'

'See? That's what I mean. You're modest.'

Abigail was introduced to crime and criminals stripping in a highway bar, so she wasn't all that modest. She guessed what Doi really meant was that she was shy, a trait that had dogged her throughout her days. People mistook her shyness for passivity; and, apparently, the quietude of her nature for a love of kitchens.

'We're genteel women. That's the proper word for us two, don't you think? Sure it is. We don't belong in here. That's all I'm saying.'

That was it, then. The crux. Doi didn't feel that a disciplinary outburst inflicted upon her daughter, that admittedly got out of hand in a hurry, warranted incarceration. A reprimand should have been enough. An apology should have ended it, and after that she could have cared for her daughter during the girl's convalescence. She'd make it up to her over time somehow. Doi was thinking that Abi also did not belong in a penitentiary. She was too bright, too pretty, too classy, too well-dressed, too sophisticated and too capable in a kitchen to be stuck behind walls topped with barbed wire. That was supposed to be their connection, then, their bond. Here, visitors were greeted by sniffer dogs who took a whiff of anuses and vaginas to detect whatever might be stuffed inside and that was simply too undignified to contemplate. Not that she had visitors. Family and friends had abandoned her. She was still waiting for the day when her daughter might show up. Abigail, though, carried herself like a proper lady, unlike the others, so that Doi built her up in her head as being traditional and sophisticated, as a worthy prospect for friendship.

Abigail got that part and understood that every attribute Doi saw in her was connected to how and even why she'd been such an outstanding – some might say, upstanding – fraud artist. Uncanny, how well she fooled people. She hardly had to try. Deceit came so naturally to her that she even deceived herself.

v

The second of the two older women befriended her next, although Malka painted similarities, and the concept of women's work, differently. 'We both know how to cook,' she assessed.

'I'm just average.'

Malka wore a broad smile.

'What?' Abigail asked.

'I mean, we cooks the books. We both know how.'

That would be the basis of their association. If nothing else, they were colleagues in deception. Abi would distance herself from Malka because she was into slow-poisoning anyone who annoyed her and she could not imagine doing that, whereas Malka seemed fine with it. Unlike Doi, though, Malka owned up to her crime and was at peace with her choice and the consequences.

They were peeling spuds and carrots and washing mushrooms together. A beef stew demanded the participation of the entire house-unit. They were supervised, of course, and if they wanted to use a knife or a fork, they had to shout it out. Shout again when they were done.

'You're not in for cooking the books,' Abi said, in a tone that did not confront Malka or contradict her. Merely a comment.

'Course not. I was a politician. What crooks never go to jail? Almost never, anyhow.'

'Politicians?' Abi asked, to see if that was the expected reply.

It was. 'If I didn't kill my husband, I wouldn't be here.'

'If Doi didn't hack up her daughter she wouldn't be here. If Courtney didn't off her best friend. If Rozlynn didn't murder her dad . . .'

'You know what I'm saying.'

'I guess so,' Abi said, but wasn't sure.

'We're the sophisticated ones, you and me. We work with our God Almighty brains. We cooks the books. The rest of them in here? *Pfft.*'

Abi was catching on to the lay of the land. Everyone was elevating themselves by virtue of her company. She wasn't sure how she was going to play this, or if there was anything to be played. At dinner, she cottoned on to another aspect of Malka's offer of friendship. Malka had detected Doi moving closer to her. The two older women considered themselves a pair thanks to their ages. They both settled down together for chats that left others out. If Abigail, shy, smart, and mature, was going to be admitted to their clique of two, making it a clique of three, Malka wanted to solidify the relationship first. Abi suspected that Malka might be annoyed that someone else held Doi's confidence, so slithered in on that connection, asserting her presence and, slyly, her authority.

Abi accepted the desire to include her, while doing very little to endear herself to either one.

vi

She did take the initiative to befriend one woman: Rozlynn. A girl who killed her father on her eighteenth birthday had a story to tell, although that's not the story she was after. Abi wondered about the girl's life in Manitoba, way north in the wilderness on a reservation. She dreamed about a solitude that deep; free in the depth of a forest with nothing to know except the earth and the sky. And maybe the snow and a cold north wind.

She knew better than to ask questions or to probe. Abi and Rozlynn were drawn together by their mutual quietude. With Abigail it was a practiced condition; with Rozlynn, it was her nature. The two could spend hours in each other's company and not say a word and not consider the silence a strain. They even met one time to sit and read side-by-side and as she arranged her legs under her Rozlynn offered a slight smile. Abigail grinned back. That communication was huge, and when Temple came by and warned Roz about her, 'You gotta watch out for these slick white chicks, Rozzy, they can rob you blind,' Rozlynn smiled, ever so slightly, again.

She spoke at length – for her. She rarely went beyond two or three words. She said, 'I got nothing to worry me about.'

That could be interpreted a lot of different ways.

Temple wondered about it. 'How do you mean that exactly?'

She shrugged at first, then she said, 'I got nothing worth stealing.'

That was her strength, and perhaps Abigail alone understood that it did not refer only to material things. There was no piece of her anyone could extract.

Cooking or baking together, sweeping up or mopping up, changing sheets and making beds, they could say nothing to each other, yet they were growing closer. The others noticed despite the absence of conversation between them.

'Abi's gone native.'

'I bet she thinks Indians have a gold mine hidden away in the back woods. She wants to check it out. Steal the secret map.'

They spoke intending Abigail to overhear them. She did, too. But she did not respond in kind. If Rozlynn could stay quiet amid the noise and clamor of a woman's prison, then so could she.

vii

The teenagers, Jodi and Courtney, were encountered as a pair. They seemed inseparable, as if Siamese. Abigail considered it a defense mechanism and presumed that they felt safer paired-off than alone. Especially with tough ladies around, like Flo and Temple. The younger ones worried they might be prey and their best hope for survival was in numbers. They may have had a point. Generally, the two were agreeable and most of the time they were irrepressible. They loved to giggle and whisper and be silly laughing themselves sick. They imparted the impression that it was either that or weep, that deep down they were irrepressible because they were inconsolable. True for Courtney. She'd killed her best friend. She wrote daily to her mom, not sending a letter a day but adding on to one until she had enough pages to make the postage stamp worthwhile. That seemed her critical connection in life, and from what she shared with others she needed to know that her mom still loved her and didn't think badly of her. She accepted that what she did had been wrong. She had known it was wrong even while plunging the knife, again and again, into the other girl's chest. Her best friend. She just didn't want her mom, or herself, to believe that her sentence was a permanent condemnation. She wanted her mom to believe that she was still human, a human, worth something, that someday she might still have a life. If she could convince her mom to believe it, she might believe it herself one day.

Abi felt sorry for her. Like Temple said, she'd gone nuts for a few minutes and now had to live with that ballistic moment, and the punishment, forever.

Jodi had also gone ballistic and while she tried to paint herself blasting away in a convenience store the same way Temple did, as 'losing her shit', and she portrayed her crazy minute as being similar to Courtney's, Abi wasn't buying it. Something about her. She was pretty but Abi thought of her as difficult and dark; complicated. It's not as though she hadn't come across the type before during her life of crime. Jodi, though, could be funny, and could not only make Courtney laugh, but the lot of them, including Abi, and including – not insignificantly – Flo. That was a good thing.

The pair stood out like skid row neon. Courtney preferred bright yellow to be included in her tops and in the prints on her dresses. Jodi opted for a spectrum of reds, from the rusty and the maroon to barroom lights. Once or twice a week she wore a crimson bandana in her hair. A brunette to Courtney's blonde, Jodi's selection of colorings was generally more muted than her pal's, yet they seemed to blink in the corner of any room, where invariably they huddled.

They approached Abi, interested to learn what she knew.

'Wait, what? You want me to teach you how to what?'

'Rip people off,' Jodi said. 'Put it that way. The way you do.'

'Tell us how you got caught,' Courtney said, 'so we won't be.'

'You'll wind up back in Lady Jail,' Abi cautioned. 'You want that?'

'Maybe, but not for murder or assault with a weapon.'

'I think if you're not too greedy and you know what you're doing, you can get away with fraud,' Jodi maintained. 'Don't people get away with it all the time? Teach us.'

'Think about it,' Courtney tacked on. 'We don't got all that much to look forward to once we're out.'

Abi knew better than to teach them her tricks. She also knew better than to ostracize anyone, no matter how benign they might appear. You never knew who you might need in your corner someday. She laughed and strung them along.

'We'll see. I'll think about it. Let's face it. We got time by the truckload.'

The girls giggled. They held hands. They figured they were on their way in the life at last. Courtney appeared nervous about that, though, while Jodi seemed thrilled.

viii

Flo looked like scrap iron. 'I got tats on my tits,' she told Abigail when she caught her gazing at her one afternoon. 'Wanna see?'

Abi learned her lesson quickly and turned her head away.

After that, she looked down if Flo walked by. Not always easy. She usually had on a favorite orange sweatshirt that she matched with a clash of colors. The colors varied from day to day and from mood to mood. She walked with a gait that suggested she was wearing medieval armor. While Flo was flagrant in her expressions, they could be difficult to discern. One minute she was speaking in a high octave with a gentleness that disarmed her listener, emerging from that gruff demeanor, the next she turned ferocious at the slightest and often imagined provocation. Her pleasant high octave abruptly grew shrill.

The corrections officers gave her an abundance of latitude until she went a step too far, then rounded her up and escorted her to solitary.

Without making it look obvious, Abi endeavored to be friendly with Flo. Her ultimate goal was self-preservation which made any real connection difficult. She had something to gain; Flo did not. She set about to uncover how Florence might benefit from being on good terms with her. That took time before a perception, and with it a strategy, arose. Flo's burden in prison and in life derived from loneliness. A great yawning cavity inside her that stretched from one horizon to the next and left her bereft of relationships. It instigated her spurts of violence, impregnated her periodic malevolent tone, imbued her snarky disposition, and defeated her. She pushed people off, hating that she was desperate for their company. She smacked people around because they weren't her friends; she wanted to confirm to herself how much she was disliked by being unlikable. That helped fill a vacant void, as did her rage. Abi's plan, then, carefully thought out, hinged on ignoring the aberrant hostility that determined Flo's interactions and instead be uniformly on her side. She'd be quiet about it, without fanfare and without reservation. What Temple said – 'I stay real kind to Flo' – would be her guiding principle, with a difference. Temple's approach was defensive, and that only caused Flo to be more guarded. Abi's plan was to undermine Flo's antagonism with calm, her vitriol with concern, be simply there, undeterred and un-wavering, to never be sullied or complaining, to nod in the face of consternation, to become as perfectly attuned to Flo as her own shadow, and like a shadow never impose her will or buttress her intentions.

Fool her the same way she fooled the rest of the world.

Others noticed.

'If Flo says, "Wipe my butt," will you give it a swipe?' Temple wanted to know.

'She won't ask,' Abigail replied.

'She might. Anyway, I'm being whatchamacallit, metaphoric.'

'Metaphorical,' Abi corrected her, then immediately regretted doing so. Not that it mattered. That cat had long been out of the bag. She was not highly educated but had more schooling than the younger residents of Joliette, and during the time she was in school she'd been a good student. The others didn't mind for they assumed it took a certain amount of learning to be a fancy-dancy crook, to get away with high-stakes fraud. Abi's crimes had to be high-stakes because her prison term was lengthy.

'Metafuckit,' Temple said, not with any major scorn.

Abigail never explained why she believed that Florence would never ask her to do anything vile. She would not explain that she had made strides. Flo had too much to lose to risk doing something mean to her one and only secret buddy in the world. Wisely, Abi kept knowledge of her newly emerging power, and what she might do with it, to herself.

ix

The unit was getting on with their afternoon clean-up. Everyone pitched in. Abi joined Flo in the galley, doing up the dishes and drying the cutlery, which meant an extra guard until they were done putting away what had not been consumed. The couple of knives they'd used, which were as dull as toast anyway, were counted then tucked away with the forks and spoons. Padlocks on the drawers were snapped in place, then that guard departed. Lunch had been pea soup and salmon sandwiches. The bread still fresh so the sandwiches were good. Cheeses, crackers, and a few grapes were left over. Flo had a habit of picking at the food they were putting away and Abi let her, voicing no complaint. Like a shadow.

The fridge was locked again once they were done.

The last that Abi saw them, Courtney and Jodi – commonly referred to as 'the kids' – were sweeping out the ward. The unit C.O. was with them and on occasion Abi heard her bass-level laughter while the kids squealed with the giggles. Everyone looked up when they burst out like that, then shook their heads, then smiled to themselves a little. Temple and Malka were doing laundry; they'd already announced they were doing only their own clothes today. No community wash. Abi considered Doi and Rozlynn, who were together in the utility space, an odd and potentially difficult pairing. Doi had taken a hatchet to her daughter and Roz had murdered her dad. Abi thought that they shared each other's familial dysfunction, each as the other's victim, each as the other's perpetrator, although none of that seemed to come up as they sorted the garbage, dry from wet, stinky from benign. When that job was done, they were to take an inventory of supplies to prepare for the next shopping spree. Everyone liked to call the meetings where they ordered food a shopping spree although it was nothing like that, it just made the tedious sound fun. Even, now, to Abi.

Given that once a food order was submitted it could never be revised, the work of detailing the inventory on hand and what had been consumed or deficient was critical. Rozlynn and Doi had a routine, where Doi held up an item, read the label for contents and size, enumerated the quantity, and Roz found the item on her chart and jotted down the details. Boring work, but they did it harmoniously and accurately. As they seemed to enjoy the task, they were often chosen.

Overall, a quiet, orderly machine. A few were finishing up and starting in on personal tasks. They thought about taking a bathroom run, or picking up a book, finding a cranny to tuck themselves away for an hour. Naps were boring but comforting. The day both routine and tepid, typical that way, with every stomach full and everyone sensing the lassitude of a long afternoon with little to do. Abi was undecided. She wished she had something to work on, a project, not wanting to lose herself in useless daydreams. Maybe she could plan an elaborate cake and see if she couldn't swing the ingredients. That would take some planning, and then some persuasion. More KD on the menu to help defray the cost of her cake.

A shriek suddenly pierced their quarters.

Jarring. A shock, to her, to everyone. Heads spun around. The corrections officer who was off on her own at that moment must have triggered the alarm she carried in her fist. What followed was a cacophony of heavy doors raging open – Abi jumped in her skin – then slamming shut again as more guards burst in. A stampede of heavy running steps followed and a lot of shouting as the guards tried to discern what the disturbance could be and where it had transpired.

Their regular corrections officer, a robust twenty-something Haitian woman named Isaure Dabrezil, was the first to enter the toilet chamber. She emerged and commanded, 'Don't nobody move not one fucking inch from where you stand right now, you fuckers!'

The inmates understood that she referred to them only, although they did not know why. Without speaking, they searched amid the flurry of guards to see who among their group was missing. Abi caught each woman's eyes, nodded, then resumed her count. When she spotted Doi being led out of the toilet room she realized that the hatchet-wielding mom had emitted the scream. That left only one person unaccounted for. Flo had to be in trouble again. More days in solitary for her, most likely, for whatever she'd done now.

Then Doi made the sign of a slow knife-slash across her throat. They guessed that the missing Flo – 'Florence' as she liked to be called on occasion – was worse off than being in solitary.

They remained shocked when she emerged in a body bag.

Doi whispered to Abigail that she'd come upon her face-down in a toilet stall, a strangulation wire around her neck.

Trouble ahead.

Émile

D own the hall from the warden's office through an ochre steel door Abigail waited in a small anteroom. Locked in. A guard outside. She had hoped for a window; she always did when being shuffled within a penitentiary. Something to see to buoy her spirits, a tree leaf, a bird, an aircraft in flight, a cloud. Finding no window was no surprise, yet a disappointment as always. This particular room felt more like prison than everyday life in her new prison.

Sightings out a window lifted her, and she wouldn't want to go through life without them, although inevitably, in the quiet of her night, the memory of such sightings made her sad.

She anticipated being interrogated. No worries. Everybody was going to be questioned and while it was disconcerting to be called first, she had nothing to hide. She was feeling a trifle glum – then quickly became excited, and agitated, when the policeman stepped into the room. She recognized this detective in an instant. He'd arrested her. What on earth was he doing here? He was a Montreal cop who investigated fraud, among other crimes, not murder. Why him? Here? Now? For this? Questions of that nature smacked her one-by-one as her chin precipitously dropped. Was he not outside his jurisdiction by a long shot?

That was not her only concern and she knew it.

Stepping around a small table and facing her, he smiled, perhaps taking pleasure in her shock of recognition. Behind him, the guard who had stood outside now stood inside the locked door.

'Hello, Abigail. Good to see you again. How's it going?'

'How's it going? What the hell, March Five?'

'You may call me Detective Cinq-Mars in here, if you like.'

'Why? What happened? Were you demoted? You used to be a Sergeant-Detective, no?'

'Still am. It's easier to say. Detective rolls off the tongue. If you prefer formality, Sergeant-Detective is fine.'

'I'd rather call you March Five. Or Émile.'

He smiled as he sat, taking no offense. 'Detective, for short, Abi. Protocol. It's how we'll do things in here.'

'As opposed to someplace else? I don't get around much anymore.'

'Not entirely true. I thought you were tucked away in Nova Scotia. Surprised to find you in my backyard.'

'Were you?'

'Quite amazed, really.'

'Oh yeah? Were you flabbergasted, Detective?'

Cinq-Mars cracked a smile. He was not the cheery type in her estimation; a curmudgeon, really, a grump, although even-tempered, she'd give him that. She had found him severe and unflinching when accumulating evidence against her, and intractable. Back then, she tried every which-way to get around him, to no avail. Of course, he'd had good reason, then, to seek a conviction. Now, he didn't, yet she'd not want him lined up against her even if innocent of a charge. As he had once noted to her in the midst of a robust exchange, being innocent of a specific action did not, by itself, make anyone wholly innocent. She got that part. Back when he was nailing her to the cross – how she preferred to describe their talks and her ordeal – he proclaimed checkmate to her every move, rather easily, too. Although he was always slow, turtle-like, and seemed always to prolong things. In this instance, having in her mind the truth on her side seemed a frail defense if Émile Cinq-Mars sat opposite her in an adversarial chair.

'I wouldn't go that far,' he admitted. 'I don't flabbergast that easily.'

'No kidding.'

ii

No less than Abigail, Sergeant-Detective Émile Cinq-Mars was taken aback to find himself inside these prison walls. He had endeavored to adjust to the idea on the drive out from the city. That took an hour and twenty minutes out of his day and he had that same commute to *not* look forward to going home. Next time, he might be quicker finding his way, but to do this drive daily was an unwelcome sortie.

'How does this make a minute's sense?' he had asked the Chief of Police. Receiving orders right from the top was strange in itself; to be assigned a task which no Montreal police detective in the normal course of events had any business being assigned provoked the question. Unfortunately, the top cop's explanation sounded viable. This was more than a bureaucratic shuffle; serious thought had gone into it. He was afraid of that. His shoulders slumped. No getting out of this one, not when the Chief himself gave the order and it held valid rationale. A final, rather desperate plea, 'Why me?' had again been countered by a logic he could not refute.

A further contribution to his reluctance was irrelevant to the commute to the Joliette Institution for Women or to his general disinterest in the project. He had recently fallen hopelessly in love, which, as far as he could decipher, was what had been going on with him in recent weeks. Not that he was certain. He decided that that's what must be happening despite foreseeing his interest in the lady as ultimately futile. She lived across the border, in New Hampshire; she was nineteen years his junior; he was a cop and she was a breeder of horses with no interest in a life in the big city. Pretty clear that the man who married her would be marrying a stable, and he had no room for horses on the back porch of his tiny apartment. Yet his infatuation lingered and over-ruled his synapses a whole lot more on the drive out to the women's penitentiary than did a nasty murder involving a young woman he'd sent up in the past.

Still, duty called.

iii

'Seriously, Detective, what are you doing here?' Abigail probed again.

'Abi, how about I ask the questions, as has always been our routine, then you reply?'

'Didn't do me much good the last time, did it?'

He laughed. She did, too. It brought back memories. They'd had a good time during their weeks of interrogation together. They both knew that she'd been losing their joust and didn't have a prayer, but she made him earn every tick on his ledger. Also, he never got everything he was after – principally, the money she stole. A victory for her.

'How did you wind up here?'

'You should know.'

'I mean here, in Joliette.'

'Beats me. I was told about the place, for sure. Communal living. Sounded all right. A step up. My name goes on a list. Fat chance, right? That chance came around. Quicker than expected. Figured I was chosen because I'm white collar, not considered a violent offender. Then I arrive and like, I expect a certain kind of inmate, right? What do I get? One old gal hacked up her daughter. A First Nations girl did in her old man. One kid shot up a corner store and this other one stabbed her best friend to death. Whoa, Nellie, was I wrong. I thought Temple was in for peddling drugs, something like that, turns out she hustled firearms for the mob. Give me a royal break – please. I have no clue why I was sent here. You'd think they'd want to keep non-violent girls like me away from these lumpy hard asses.'

Cinq-Mars sat back in his chair, crossed his arms over his chest, and considered her response.

'Sent,' he quoted her. 'You didn't apply?'

'I applied. Encouraged to do so. So I did.'

He scanned the first pages of her file, searching for verification.

'Seriously, though, *Sergeant-Detective*. Montreal Police Service, that's still you, right? That hasn't changed?'

'Can't say it has, no.'

'We're out in the boonies. I don't know exactly where Joliette is on a map, but it's not in Montreal. This is a federal penitentiary. Maybe the feds can't investigate a homicide in their own institution, is that it? Doesn't that leave the SQ? They handle murder in Quebec outside Montreal as I recall. Yeah, they do, everybody knows that. So how do you get to butt in? Émile, Detective, March Five, Sergeant-Detective, whatever I call you, if that's the case my question stands. What are you doing here? Did you miss me that much?'

'It's a long story, Abigail. Maybe someday I'll tell you. For now, it's partly your fault, I'll say that. The fact that I booked you in the past has something to do with being selected to interrogate you now. People think it gives me a head start.'

She let that notion sift through her, then asked, 'How so?'

'You're the prime suspect and we have a history. The slow wheels of justice might speed up if I interview you about the murder.'

She stared back at him. The fun she'd enjoyed meeting him again dissipated. Her pleasure in combating an old foe with whom she had tangled in the past vanished. 'Émile – and never mind that you never speed up – why am I the prime suspect? *I* didn't kill Flo.'

'I've given the file a glance, Abi, nothing more. It says you were in close proximity to the victim when she was discovered.'

'Not only me. We were all in the vicinity.'

'You were closer than others. You were doing clean-up duty with her after lunch.'

'We finished cleaning up. Doi screamed when she found her. That makes her a whole lot closer than me. Anyway, what does closer have to do with the price of cocaine? If I killed Flo, wouldn't I stay as far away as possible afterwards?'

'Mmm,' Cinq-Mars murmured, neither agreeing with her nor disputing the argument. 'That's what I'm here to find out.'

'Come on, Detective. Seriously. I mean, it had to be one of us, but why start with the assumption it was me? I don't like that. We got axe-wielders in here. Knife stabbers. Poisoners. As one of my housemates put it, I "cooks the books", that's all. Flo was the type to throw acid in the face of somebody she didn't like, that's what she was in for. In her words it was cool because her victim was asking for it. If you pushed her, she'd probably tell you her victim was begging to have acid thrown in her face. Acid, Émile. In the face. I should be the last person in here you should think about for strangling Flo with a wire. God. She was twice my size. Three times my size? How could I take her on? How could I be stupid enough to risk wrestling a woman who throws acid in people's faces when she could take me out with a hand strapped behind her back while hopping on one leg?'

Good point. 'It says here that you were the last person to have clothes delivered. Some think that that's how the strangulation wire was smuggled in.'

'Does everyone walk around naked? We all wear clothes.'

'Yours arrived last.'

'So? Somebody else stored a wire for a while.'

She had always defended herself well. Cinq-Mars appreciated that. In part, for the challenge. Abi was smart.

'Don't worry,' he said. 'I'll consider everybody else, too.'

'Good! But here I am, the prime suspect. Jesus, Émile. That makes my day.'

'The investigators first on the scene fingered you. I'll make up my own mind.'

'Thank God for that.' She slumped down in her chair as if depressed. Then straightened her posture again, growing comfortable with her new situation. 'Actually, Detective, really, I'm glad you're here. That it's you and not the bastards who fingered me for no reason. You're a smart cookie. Smart enough to figure out it wasn't me. I empty bank accounts. I'm not the Boston Strangler.'

iv

On the cusp of his retirement, a new Chief of Police had rescued Émile Cinq-Mars from the purgatory of the suburbs and brought him back downtown. Previous administrations thought it comical to keep him away from any case deemed interesting, although he managed, while assigned to humdrum felonies, to solve a few murders and disrupt significant forays by organized crime. The new chief, Alexandre DesSaulniers, and Cinq-Mars remained on amicable terms although at arm's length, so that being called in for a meeting with the boss was a rarity and defied explanation. He expected a demotion while, as always, fearing a promotion more.

'I'm assigning you to investigate a murder, Sergeant-Detective, that took place at the Joliette Institution for Women.'

'That's SQ, sir, if it's in a prison, if not the Mounties.'

'Normally. Not this time.'

'Ah, I'm not following you, sir. I'm not in Homicide. How does this make a minute's sense?'

'When the murder took place, Sergeant-Detective, eight inmates were locked in their house-unit. That leaves us how many suspects?'

He assumed it was not a math question, so it must be a riddle. 'One dead inmate leaves seven and however many guards were with them. Unless you also want to consider suicide, in which case it's the full complement of prisoners, all eight, plus the guards.'

'I've never heard of a suicide by strangulation, have you? Let's rule that out. You're right. Seven inmates and one guard only. Her name is Isaure Dabrezil and this is where things get complicated.

She happens to be an SQ officer currently serving a year-long suspension. I don't know what it was for and I hear that I should not expect to be told. Suspended without pay from the SQ, yet they arranged work for her as a prison guard. Part purgatory, while helping her survive her exile with an income.'

'Sounds irregular.'

'Doesn't it? Now, suspended or not, she is still officially a member of the SQ.'

'They're not permitted to investigate their own for murder.'

'Precisely. It's either us or the Mounties, but since it's a Federal Institution—'

'They're not eligible, either.'

'It was the Mounties who advised the SQ to bug out. Otherwise, they might have gone ahead without us.'

'Is the guard a suspect?'

'Everybody is until you eliminate each woman, one by one. We've decided to keep them together until you do. Makes it easier on you. Easier on us to keep tabs. And, who knows, they might decide on their own form of justice, if they have an interest.'

'Irregular, sir,' Cinq-Mars interjected.

'Highly,' the chief agreed. 'We have other reasons to keep them together.'

'Such as?'

'Other objectives. The dead inmate spent time in solitary. More than once. That tells me she had disciplinary issues, which tells me she had run-ins with her guard. So, until you say otherwise, the guard's a suspect. But if she's guilty and reassigned, how will pressure be brought to bear? I agree with keeping her in place. See how the dynamic plays out among the eight.'

'I still have a question, sir, if I may. Why me?'

The chief's chuckling caused the man's jowls to quiver. 'You seem reluctant, Cinq-Mars. I thought you'd welcome the change of pace. Life in the countryside. Not to mention that it's a murder case. Not to mention the opportunity to spend a few weeks among a bevy of women.'

'Weeks!'

'However long it takes. Maybe months.'

'Months. Ah, thank you for giving my leg that tug, sir, it was cramping up on me.'

'You're welcome, Sergeant-Detective.'

'Sir? Come on. Why me?'

'I know you love working with gang members.'

Another leg tug. He hated any involvement with gangs, and they both knew that.

'The dead woman was associated with the Hells.'

'A moll.'

'Not the moll type. More like an unofficial associate. Unofficial due to her gender. OK, you hate the gang stuff, but you're not without experience and knowledge there. Also, Sergeant-Detective, I mentioned another objective. You might like this one. Some of us are worried you might like it too much. You will recall an embezzler by the name of Abigail Lauzon.'

'Of course. She's in Nova Scotia, no?'

'She's since been transferred to Joliette. And yes, she's one of the seven. In fact, she's been identified by the first SQ detectives on the scene as our prime suspect. You two have a history together. That's one reason I thought of you.'

A bit of a shock, that one. 'Is there another?'

The chief had a distinguished look to him. He filled the uniform well. Thin on top, gray on the sides, the naturally chiseled features to his facial bone structure had been softened by time and weight, yet he carried himself with a countenance borne for the position: upright, calm, and superior in a manner that did not give offense. Cinq-Mars had noticed that his desk and office were tidy to the brink of being spartan.

'Cinq-Mars, as you know, the SQ fought hard to get the Lauzon case for themselves. We fought them off. You helped convict her, but the money she embezzled went unrecovered. A feather in the cap of an officer who finds her loot.'

'You're saying I'm getting a second kick at the can.'

'What I'm saying is, an officer willing to compromise his ethics might suggest to an innocent Ms Abigail Lauzon that he can put her away for life on the murder rap unless she tells us where the money is hiding. Do you follow?'

Cinq-Mars wasn't sure how serious he was, or if he was serious at all. 'I don't. You're either hoping to corrupt me or you're saying she's innocent of the murder but deserves to be bullied. What am I missing?'

'This. If she's as guilty as the ten deadliest sins combined, an ethically challenged officer might suggest that he can get her off, if only the money were to resurface. That resurfacing might benefit those she deceived, or, who knows, the officer himself. Or both. Who could not use an extra million or two in his or her retirement fund? Who would not be tempted?'

'I'm sure a lot of guys would not be—'

'Rose-colored glasses, Cinq-Mars. Love that about you. Still, I have never perceived you as being ethically challenged. Even with thirty-six million dollars at stake. I'm less certain that I can say the same for others. Now, some say you took a little too much of a liking to our Miss Lauzon.' The chief threw up a hand to stifle his officer's immediate protest. 'Never mind the smoke: Where there's fire, there's truth, I always say. Doesn't matter to me. It can work in your favor if you handle this right. Just another reason I chose you. Only, you will keep it zipped.' He raised that threatening hand again to stymie objection. 'Hey, you're still single. I get it. Just don't let me down on this one. Go straight to jail, Cinq-Mars. Do not pass *Go*. While you're at it, do not prove me wrong. Oh. The murder? Get to the bottom of that, too. Of course. Keep your ethics. Why not? But also, you know how it goes. For God's sake find the damn money.'

v

Émile Cinq-Mars offered Abigail a ballpoint pen and slid a single sheet of yellow legal-sized paper across the table to her.

'What's this for? I'm not confessing.'

'I wish you would, Abi. Failing that, draw a diagram of your house-unit for me. You said Doi cried out or alerted you in some way when she came upon Florence. Show me where you were within the compound when Doi cried out. Then position everyone else at the time, to the best of your recollection.'

Abigail picked the pen up then put it down. One fist supported an elbow, the other tucked under her chin. A thoughtful contemplation. 'Not so easy,' she determined.

'Why not? You don't live in a mansion. It's a limited space. We know where Florence was found. Doi must have told you. Start there. Draw the bathroom, then scribble in Flo's name.'

Abi sighed, and did that. She had a careful hand. Not surprising, given that she'd been known to forge a signature on occasion. She drew three toilet stalls and three sinks, then wrote Flo's name in the uppermost corner, the furthest stall from the doorway.

'Where's Doi, when she screamed or shouted?'

'More like a shriek,' Abi informed him. She performed her best imitation of the call, without raising her voice.

'You sound like a trapped rabbit.'

'Doi sounded like a trapped rabbit, if the trap was in my ear.'

'Where was she?'

'Also in the toilet, obviously.' Abigail wrote her in. 'Near the door.'

'Two accounted for. One-quarter done. Not so hard. Now, where were you?'

She scrunched up her face. 'This is where it gets tricky. I mean, we were doing our chores. Then we were finishing and moving around. So we were in motion. When was Flo killed? Before or after we started moving around? Only the killer knows. All we know is, Doi screamed and the guards burst in. At that moment we were moving around. Then Isaure – our guard – told us to stand still. I can probably tell you where everybody was at *that* moment, if I think about it. Where they were for every minute that they were milling around, see, that's tricky.'

Cinq-Mars was pleased that she was working with him on this, rather than fighting against the project. 'I understand. That makes sense. Let's do this differently. We know where Doi and Flo were when Doi screamed.'

'Shrieked.'

'Shrieked. Can you draw a rabbit?'

'A rabbit?'

'A bunny with big ears. Draw one in the toilet space with little arrows to Doi and Florence.'

Abi had fun with that and created a cute bunny, one ear straight up, one flopping over. She took longer than Cinq-Mars would like, but he wasn't going to press her on that.

'The rabbit indicates that Doi is shrieking. Now write in where everyone was when they were doing chores. Put a little dark cloud over their names to indicate they were working.'

'How about I draw something else?'

'Why?'

'In here we live with permanent dark clouds over our heads. I hate those.'

'Fine. Then draw what?'

'How about . . . a hammer. Us girls will be the nails.'

'Do it.'

Florence's name showed her in the galley, in the lower right corner of the page. Doi was to the left of that area in the pantry. Abi drew the dimensions for those rooms and inscribed what they were.

'Let's do you next. Where are you with a rabbit and where are you with a hammer?'

Abigail moved her rabbit-self in a central position in the common area, with a bias toward the right-hand side of the room. She was halfway between the washroom and the galley, in front of the pantry. Then she stopped writing.

'What?' Cinq-Mars asked her.

She didn't answer. Rather, she sighed, and wrote her name in the galley next to Flo and drew a hammer over her head.

'So you were with Flo,' Cinq-Mars concluded.

'For chores, yeah. That doesn't mean I killed her. I didn't.'

'Doesn't look good, though, does it?'

'Not great. But you knew that.'

'Let's keep going,' he said.

As best as she was able – 'I was in the galley, it's not like I could see everybody' – she drew everyone in their work area. Courtney, Jodi, and the guard were sweeping up: 'They could have been just about anywhere.' Temple and Malka were supposed to be in the laundry. Doi and Rozlynn were doing inventory in the pantry. That room was drawn at the bottom center of the page.

'Now, where is everyone when the guard told you to stand still?'

The young woman drew clever stick figures for each person, and had them standing on their names, as if hammered in, like nails. 'Best as I can recall,' she said.

'This is very helpful, Abi. You can do me a favor – and if you believe in your innocence, do yourself a favor, too – if you tell no one what we've done here. It'll be interesting to see how drawings from each of you compare.'

Abigail gave her drawing a final look, then shrugged. 'Best I can do,' she said. 'Can't say it's perfect. We finished our chores and moved around.'

'I understand. Now, before this happened, when was the last time you used the bathroom?'

She stared at him without responding.

'Abigail?'

She seemed catatonic for the moment.

'Did you go while you were still working?'

'All right. Yeah. Sure. Why not?'

'Well, did you, or didn't you?'

'I did. I told you. Yes.'

'The truth will set you free, Abigail.'

'Oh bullshit. The truth might put a noose around my neck.'

'We don't hang people anymore.'

'Figure of speech and you know it.'

'Did Flo?'

'Go to the bathroom? Yes. Maybe. I mean, she said she was going. Does that set me free, too?'

'Why the antagonism all of a sudden?'

'I don't like this. She went to the bathroom. I went to the bathroom.'

'Did she come back?'

'Yes!'

'Then what's the problem?'

'People were still working. Probably nobody saw.'

'One step at a time, Abigail. We'll figure this out.'

'If I get a life sentence, I swear, I'll find a way out.'

'Out? Escape, you mean?'

'From life, yeah. Wait. Do you think it's possible?'

'To kill yourself?'

'To escape.'

'Not my department. I don't imagine you can, but I know nothing about this place. I suppose if anybody could find a way out, it would be you. I'm not recommending it. I think you're better off doing the time.'

'I'll do my time. As long as you don't make it for fucking life.'

Cinq-Mars signaled the corrections officer at the door. Abigail thought Cinq-Mars was leaving. Instead, it was the guard who departed.

'What? We're alone now? You beat me up now? Or worse. Really?'

'Abigail, we'll be talking again another time. For now, there's just one more thing. The C.O. is out of the room because no one but me can know how you answer my next question. You'll know why in a minute. Let's say you didn't nab Flo in the toilet and strangle her with a wire.'

'Yeah, and let's say she didn't reach down my throat and pull out my lungs while I was trying to do that.'

'Right. So if you didn't do it, who do you think did?'

They both knew the situation he was putting her in. Snitching was not a good thing in a penitentiary. It's why the guard had been dismissed. A crime, in the culture. At the same time, self-preservation was involved. Abi understood that every prisoner would be asked the same question, and who knows what the others would say, or not say.

'If I had a clue, Émile, I probably wouldn't tell you. Since I don't have a clue, I'll keep it to myself.'

Her words weren't quite making sense, except as a kind of joke that he wasn't getting. He remembered how she used to try to evade him by twisting logic. A memory that provoked a smile.

'Good talking to you, Abi.'

'Same. Let's do this again soon. Trust me, talking to you beats the daily monotony all to hell. By the way. Speaking of monotony.'

He waited on her to continue. She looked impish.

'How's your love life, March Five?'

Something she had needled him about in the old days. Cinq-Mars closed his file folder and called out, 'Guard!'

'Oh yeah? Really? Something's going on! What? What?'

He didn't know what 'tell' he'd shown her, what infinitesimal twinge gave him away. She had probably intended to flirt, but he'd given something away that she'd caught. He was reminded of how accomplished Abi could be at reading others. She could have been a detective herself. With that in mind he considered, if she was innocent of this crime, she might prove useful to his investigation of the others.

'Abi. Out,' he said, and she smiled, flashed her fingers across an eyebrow, a half-salute, half wave goodbye, and stood up to leave. 'Guard!' he shouted again.

Doi

i

P aper was so damn precious. Doi retrieved an unlined sheet hidden near the bottom of her basket of towels. She plucked a pen from her pants pocket. She'd been busy sorting and folding laundry pulled from the dryer when Malka stopped by for a chat, but as Doi appeared to be in a mood, Malka moved on. Her back to the room, Doi wrote on the paper in careful cursive that invariably slanted upward on the right, and she checked often to confirm that no one was noticing. She re-read what she put down, then more quickly added lines. Finally, she squirreled her sheet of paper away amid the towels – under the mauve one and above the pink so that she could locate it quickly – and packed them alongside her clean clothing in the laundry basket. She scooted back to her bunk.

Her nest, she called it.

Put her stuff away. The basket needed to be returned to its proper place. An imperative that everything, once moved for a purpose, is quickly returned to its assigned spot.

With enthusiasm, Doi obeyed the rules.

More than anyone she believed in rules. Still, she had her secrets. And her paper.

She dutifully wrote letters to the daughter she'd maimed.

She wanted to convince her to visit.

The outside door opened with a grating clang. As always, the inmates looked up. They had a special reason to be interested this time as Abigail was returning from her interrogation. She'd been the first. The door clapped shut behind her, bolted and locked, the last of the sounds like a hammer's stroke. *Like a nail in my coffin*, Doi thought sometimes. She wanted to talk to Abigail, but she wasn't the only one and the others gathered around the young woman before she could get close. Doi hung back then, for she really only wanted to talk in private. She desired to know how everything went.

She needed a heads-up on what questions had been asked of Abi
that would also be asked of her. More importantly, she wanted to
know what to say, how to answer those questions when her turn
came for the third degree.

Abi would know.

Only Abi would know.

Among them, she was the smart one.

They didn't call her an artist – a fraud artist – for nothing.

You could talk to Abi. She could, anyway. The young woman
was quiet and possessed a sympathetic nature. Everybody could see
that. Not like these other killers and misfits. Doi didn't belong in
their midst and she knew that Abi didn't either. They had that in
common. They were separate, in every way that mattered, from the
others.

Having missed any chance to catch her alone, she tagged on to
the fringe of the group, listening in. They were working their way
toward the octagonal table for lunch, then she took a seat there.
Temple and Rozlynn were responsible for lunch today which meant
it was likely to be edible. Not that it was hard to screw up soup
and sandwiches, although somehow Courtney and Jodi managed the
feat on a regular basis.

Tomato, the soup. Hot, with soda crackers.

She added butter and pepper.

The sandwiches were salmon. Leave it to Roz to choose one kind
of fish or another.

Good, though. So good. She liked how Rozlynn added chopped-
up green onions and just the right amount of mayo.

They all wanted to know how the interrogation went. What was
it like being grilled by a visiting detective? The women no sooner
fired off their questions than they proposed varying and differing
opinions on the subject before Abi had the chance to answer.

'Let her speak!'

Doi rarely jumped in like that. She never asserted herself. This
time she did. She couldn't stop herself from blurting out her decree
and then Malka backed her up. 'Yeah. Let the girl speak.'

'I know him, the detective,' Abigail said. That astonished them
all. 'Get this. Get this,' she said, and the women leaned into her.
She dropped her voice to a conspiratorial level. 'He's the one who
arrested me.'

A couple of mouths dropped open. A hush crisscrossed the table, like a wave in the air.

'Whoa. Wait. What's going on?' Temple asked.

'You *know* him? What's he like?' inquired Malka.

That's what Doi wanted to know, too, but she wanted to hear the answer in private, not in this public gabfest. She sipped soup from her spoon.

'His name is Sergeant-Detective Émile Cinq-Mars.'

'Sank-what? Like the planet?'

'French. Fifth of March, it means. He's French, too, but his English is not so bad. Better than he thinks.'

'What's he like? Good-looking?' Jodi wanted to suss out.

That's what everybody was hoping to hear the most, how gorgeous he was. Except Doi. She didn't care. At least the others were giving Abigail the time and space to formulate a response. 'He's tall, ladies, he's dark, he's handsome.'

Temple feigned a swoon. Malka laughed at that, then tried to do the same, although she couldn't pull it off as naturally.

Abigail had more to say. 'He's got this huge nose on him.' She spread her hand wide in front of her face, as if her entire palm was needed to cover that nose. 'What a honker. Jesus. You can't help but stare. He can slay you with *his* stare, though, his deep glare. Like an eagle's. He glares at you until your arms fall off. I'm not kidding. He reminds me of . . . I don't know.'

'What?'

'What?'

They so wanted her to say, expecting to hear the name of some movie star dreamboat.

'Of like a mortician. You know? Sort of. Like he's come to collect the body.'

This time they groaned. They didn't enjoy hearing that so much, but they could picture it.

'The thing is, there's one thing you gotta know, then never forget it, not for a second.'

'What's that?'

'Abi, what?'

Doi was interested in her message, too, but these others, they were hanging on every word. Hanging on her words without truly realizing their importance. They were forgetting the context. In her mind, they weren't asking the right questions.

'He's crazy smart. Trust me. If he blew his nose, extra brains would come out on his snot.'

The image made them laugh like crazy, but her words also scared them, more than they'd expected. They had prepared stories and responses to the questions they anticipated, but they hadn't prepared themselves for a smart inquisitor. They didn't know what a smart detective might mean. Each inmate solemnly believed she'd had been incarcerated by a nincompoop. None had had to deal with smart.

Merely the thought of it had them feeling stupid and afraid.

Doi was gauging Abigail, and in that instant saw through her. This young woman knew what she was doing. Now that Flo was gone from their midst, she was almost imperceptibly, step by step, assuming control over them. The detective might be just as smart as she said, but Doi was betting that Abi was way smarter.

Warning them that the detective was super intelligent made herself necessary, given that she was the brilliant swindler among them. From now on, everyone would bring worries about all of this and about everything else to Abigail. Whatever the cop told anyone, Abi would hear it next. They'd all confide. Doi saw that. She saw it happening right before her eyes. She, herself, would do it that way.

ii

'You were real quiet,' Abi said.

'Was I?' Lunch turned out to be festive. The talk gregarious and at times quarrelsome but always animated. The ladies laughed a lot. Tears rolled down their cheeks. When they were about to break up for their post-lunch chores – clean the table, the floor, do up the dishes, put away the supplies which required a guard to unlock then lock the cupboards again and the pantry – Corrections Officer Isaure Dabrezil was called to the front door grill. She received a message there and afterward sought out Doi. She informed her that she was next. At one o'clock sharp Doi was to wait at the front door to be escorted to the interrogation room.

'You didn't say boo,' Abi pointed out.

'With that bunch? It's hard to get a word in edgewise.'

'That's true. So what's up?' Abi asked. She took out a small nail file from the shelf by her bunk and Doi's eyes grew to the size of tablespoons. Doi was standing over her by her bed.

'What?'

'Where'd you get that?' Doi asked.

They both looked at the file.

'My business. Just don't tell anybody.'

'Tell me,' Doi begged.

'I bought it off a French girl,' Abigail whispered. 'Caught her in the yard doing her nails. Bought it off her. That's all. A simple transaction.'

'How did you buy it? With what?'

'Money. Not much.' A bit of cash on the outside helps her to get by on the inside.

Their eyes met again, the tablespoons seemingly expanding before they relaxed.

'There's a reason I was quiet,' Doi said.

'So why?'

'We're all forgetting something. Hard for me to forget it.'

Abi waited for her to finish. When she didn't, she filled in the blank for her. 'One of us must've killed Flo.'

'I can't forget that.'

'Me neither. Still, you know, life goes on in the meantime. Your turn next, huh?'

'Yeah. Abi, tell me, what's he going to ask me? I need to prepare. You said he's smart?'

'He is. You can't prepare for that kind of smart. I mean, it's simple. He'll want to know who you are, where you're from, what you did to end up in here. I'm only guessing, of course. He already knew all that about me, so he didn't ask me that. He will you. We only reminisced a little.'

'Doesn't he have my sheet? He must.'

'Sure. He probably knows your jacket by heart. He'll want to hear it from you. Don't lie. He'll catch any tiny fib and walk it back with you down a corridor straight to the back door of a dungeon in hell.' Abigail said that then put a hand over her mouth and laughed.

'Don't say that,' Doi objected.

'He's investigating a murder, Doi. No stone unturned.'

'But *I* didn't kill Flo.'

'Who did?'

'I don't know!'

'He'll want to know that and a whole lot more. Just make sure that when you lie you can back it up until the cows come home.'

'I won't lie!' Doi declared.

'Don't be silly. Of course you will. Everybody fucking lies. *Especially* when somebody like Cinq-Mars puts you through the wringer. You'll get scared for no good reason. You'll get frustrated. You'll panic. You'll lie. Then try to worm your way out of it. Really, don't bother. Whatever you hide will crawl up to the surface, you know, like worms in the rain. By the time he's done, if you didn't kill Flo, you'll wish you did. You'll be dying to confess, Doi, just to get the pressure off you. Just to get those squiggly worms out of your hair.'

Doi felt herself reeling inside. 'You came back so happy, so flip. You seemed that way.'

'That was me. Him and me, we have a thing. We've been down that road. You and him, you're starting out. Be prepared.'

'Oh shit.'

'Feel that way. Oh shit – you said it. There. Now you're better prepared.'

'But what's he going to ask me exactly?'

'Did you kill, Flo? Why did you? He'll ask you that.'

'I didn't!'

'Why did you hack up your daughter?'

'He won't ask me that!'

'You wanna bet?'

Doi knew better than to argue with Abigail about anything. 'No, seriously, Abi,' she said, worrying about the nail file again, 'how'd you get that thing in here?'

'Doi, Doi, I told you that already. It's nothing. It's not like I can saw through bars with it. We don't even have bars. We don't have a window. You can't pick a lock with this thing. I would've tried if that was true.'

Doi could never tell when she was joking.

'You're still not allowed. Why do you have it?' She wanted to remind her that there were other things she could do with a nail file. Poke an eye out. Slice an artery. Someone else's or her own. More reasons to prohibit the file than could fit on a list.

'Doi, get real. You don't want to know. If I told you that, I'd have to strangle you with a wire just to keep you quiet.' Abigail laughed at her friend's evident consternation. Then she implored her, 'Doi, I'm kidding. God. I have it to do my nails. I like nice nails.'

'You shouldn't joke about that, strangling,' Doi admonished her.

'Come on! You know I wouldn't hurt a fly. But! I'll swat you dead if you squeal on me.'

Doi believed her. 'I know,' she said.

'Good,' Abi said. 'Now get ready. Remember, like I told the girls, it's OK to ask this cop for a smoke. If he gives it to you, it means he thinks he's getting somewhere with you. So enjoy the smoke, at least. It's one minute to one, Doi. Do your lipstick. You'll feel more confident that way. You won't look so guilty like you do now.'

She still could never figure out when and if she was joking.

She guessed that that was Abigail's way.

iii

Doi had to wait more than five minutes for the detective to arrive after she was deposited in a room that felt cold and alien to her. The delay increased her fret. When he arrived, he was exactly as Abigail had described, so tall and with a nose that made her want to stare. Abi had warned her that he might look as though he expected to take away a body. She was right about that, too. Maybe Abi only put the idea in her head and it wasn't really true, but the impression stuck. *Back door parole*, a phrase she'd learned at her previous institution; if she was to die in prison, if that fate awaited her, this one might as well collect her now.

She was impressed that everything Abi remarked about him was confirmed as true. She could see it for herself. A good indication that everything else was true, too. Such as, he was smart, he was going to ask tough questions, and she had no hope of holding her own against him.

Then he smiled. That knocked her off-kilter.

'Doi Katowski,' he read from her jacket, then looked up again. That stare. 'How are you today?'

Tongue-tied for a moment – she hadn't anticipated the smile or the greeting, and the way he stared was disorienting – she nodded. She cleared her throat as though that was her only problem. Then managed to smile back. She'd already forgotten his question.

'I'm Sergeant-Detective Émile Cinq-Mars. Pleased to meet you.' He leaned back in his chair on the opposite side of their little table and folded his arms across his chest. She was expecting him to glare down at her with eagle-like eyes; instead he smiled a trifle, and glanced at her and at his papers repeatedly. She was cross with herself that somehow, he had made her feel more comfortable. 'Any questions,' he asked, 'before we start in?'

'Abigail said,' she began, then thought she shouldn't say.

'You talked to Abigail,' Cinq-Mars confirmed.

'I did. That's allowed, isn't it?'

'Perfectly natural. What did Abigail say?'

'I could ask you for a cigarette.'

He took a deeper breath, and looked away, perhaps to spare her his eagle glare.

'You gave Abigail a smoke,' Doi told him.

'Why would I do that when Abigail doesn't smoke? At least, she never has. Since inmates are not allowed to smoke in here, I assume she still doesn't.'

Doi stared back at him, confused. Finally, she contended, 'We can smoke in the yard.'

'I stand corrected. Still, not indoors. And Abi doesn't smoke.'

'She said she had a smoke.'

'Of course she did. Now you think that I'm a liar and that Abi told the truth. Isn't that right?'

Her head bobbed down, then back up again.

'Abi didn't bum a smoke off me,' Cinq-Mars repeated. 'She never asked for one. The subject never came up. Not that it would've done any good, since I don't have any. I quit. Trying to, anyhow.'

'She says she asked you,' Doi maintained, 'and you gave her one. She told everybody that over lunch.'

'Why would I lie to you? I didn't do that.'

'I don't understand.'

Cinq-Mars explained it to her. 'Abi said she smoked. She said you could smoke. She said everybody could smoke. All you have to do is ask. The problem with that, it's a big fat lie. But now we have a bigger problem. Do you know what it is?'

She didn't.

'You believe her. That's the larger issue here. Not that you can't smoke, but that you believe Abi was given a cigarette. Tell me, who do you think is in charge of this investigation?'

She was feeling hopelessly confused again, as if they were talking through a wall. Doi spoke quietly. 'You are, of course.'

'No. I'm not. I mean, I should be. But Abi is in charge right now. She's in charge because you believe her and not me.'

Doi remained at a loss. 'I don't know what you're talking about. Abi can't be in charge.'

'Who do you believe, her or me?'

She hesitated long enough, and she knew that, to suggest her reply had not been honest.

'See what I mean?' he asked.

She didn't.

'Why would Abi lie?' Doi put to him.

'Why would I?' Cinq-Mars asked her. 'That might be the better question. But we'll start with yours. Off the top of my head, Abi has a few reasons to lie. She might want to play me, hoping I might get irritated if women come in here, one after another, expecting to smoke. Or she wants to conscript you. Make you believe in her and not in me. A third reason for her to lie is that she plans to use you in some way that neither of us can figure out. Only time will tell. She figures she might need to use you someday if she's not doing so already. It's worth thinking about. Abi might be setting you up for something.'

'For what?' Doi asked. She couldn't follow the conversation and felt that she was spinning.

'If she killed Flo, for instance, she might need somebody to take the fall. You never know. She could be setting you up for that. Of course, I'm not saying that she killed Flo. Did you?'

'Did I what?'

'Kill Flo?'

'No! Of course not!' Abi had said he'd ask her that, only natural that he would. She just didn't expect it to be so abrupt. That not only caught her off-guard, but as Abi forewarned it almost made her feel guilty.

'Hmm,' Cinq-Mars murmured. Then he asked, 'Why not?'

'What do you mean why not? Why not what? That's a crazy question. Why would I kill Flo?'

'That's a good question. You found Flo. That means you were in the toilet room with her. Tell me about that. Why did you scream when you found her? How did that happen anyway? How is it you were in the toilet room with Flo, that she was dead, and you were screaming at the top of your lungs? Tell me how everything happened, and please, I'll ask you not to leave anything out. It's important that you not do that.'

'Of course I screamed. Flo was dead.'

'You've been in violent situations before. Your daughter was a bigger mess. Were you screaming then? I bet your daughter was.'

'Don't ask me about that,' Doi said, sullen.

'That's not how this works.'

'How what works?'

'This. I ask. Whatever I want. You answer.'

They stared across the table at each other, and Doi saw that it was true, that he had an eagle's glare. Like Abi said, she felt as though her arms were going to fall off.

iv

Day into night had been exceptionally hot and muggy. She passed the time at home wearing only a slip over her underwear as she lived without air-conditioning. Mopped her brow with a towel. The house felt airless, the air close. Her husband had stayed out late with the guys, then come home surprisingly sober and gone straight to bed. She tried to sleep next to him. The heat stymied her. His skin emitted heat and a strong scent of old sweat and pizza fart. And Katarzyna had not come home.

Doi got up and waited in the kitchen.

She lived in the far-flung suburbs of Toronto, in Burlington, Ontario. Middle of the road everything: class, money, advantages. Not the big houses, not the small. Not the newest, not the old. While the homes all looked the same at first glance, they were not identical, unlike in some areas. She could point out the differences to anyone who couldn't see it for themselves, how each house was unique. She could be proud. Her man was a decent man. Not her first

husband, hopefully her last. Katarzyna was not her first daughter
either, but the only daughter anyone knew about. The only one of
her daughters she knew. She wondered where the others went, if
they were alive.

She considered her husband, Dawid, to be a good if imperfect
man. What blemishes distorted him, and his general lack of interest
in her and in their marriage, did not compel her to think poorly of
him. He worked dutifully, if not hard. He helped build and repair
homes. Never the contractor himself, always the contractor's laborer.
His bosses, and there were several, appreciated his worth and were
also infuriated by his peccadilloes. He did not work in heat. He did
not work in the cold. He did not work in the rain. He did not work
one job if he was offered another that was less physically demanding.
He did not work on his knees. He had to be standing or sitting to
put in the hours. If not, if he was asked to parget a foundation or
dig a ditch or get on his belly and squiggle into a crawl space, he
went home for the day instead. His bosses complained to her about
these things, although they still hired him for what he was willing
to do and for how well he did it. He made a living, he paid his
bills, and at work his assistance was appreciated when the job was
not too demanding.

Better if he was his own man, a contractor himself, and she had
pushed him in that direction, but he always declined.

So they were not rich, or richer. They got by.

Not strict with himself, he was not strict with Katarzyna either.
Not strict enough by half! Dawid did not understand what can
happen to a girl lacking the proper supervision. She tried to explain
it to him, but he dismissed her worries the same way he dismissed
her entreaties to work harder. Her daughter assured her father that
she could take care of herself and he, the easy-goer, the don't-work-
too-hard nincompoop, the relax-it's-not-a-problem decent man of
the house went along with everything his daughter desired. He didn't
understand and she could not explain it to him. She could not explain
it to Katarzyna either. To do that, she would need to explain about
her other daughters. Her unwanted daughters. And she could never
explain that. Not to anyone.

The night stayed hot and muggy. Katarzyna stayed out late. And
she remembered, Doi did, how she bent over at her kitchen table,
while waiting, bent over with both her arms across her belly, bent

over and she moaned, the pain there, that memory of pain there and still Katarzyna was not home. Then she arrived. It seemed like the middle of the night. Later, she'd admit, not that late. But it seemed like the middle of the night and Katarzyna and her boyfriend kissed in the car in the back lane, then they both got out. They kissed outside the fence to the backyard and came into the yard and kissed again. His hand on her behind. Doi must have left the house by then for she was already in the backyard with them and yelled at the boy and her daughter screamed back at her. The boy laughed. He thought it was funny. Funnier when she shoved him away, funnier when she punched his shoulder, his arm. He was laughing even as he was leaving and Katarzyna, huffy, angry with her as if she was the one with the laughing boyfriend in the middle of the night, as if she was slamming the door in her mother's face going into the kitchen. Doi, in a rage then, to have that boy laughing like that other boy laughed when she was sixteen and he was done with her and she would be disgraced in the city, handed over to the nuns there, until the birth. That child, that daughter she was told, taken from her and only then was she returned to her family and to her disgrace. Yet a soldier still married her only to die on maneuvers. In a war game, dead. A game. And Katarzyna, now playing her games, her anger as if the mother was to blame for ruining her night, her life, her chance at love and where was her bra? That smile. That coquettish smirk she had. Doi had left on her own for her second disgrace, she would not be sent away that second time, she went on her own, back to the city and to the nuns and when that child was born she would not take it, and left the world she knew for a world she did not know, walking across the border in exchange for a certain kind of sex that meant nothing to her, but not nothing, but *nothing*, what mattered was escape, leaving Poland, and Doi, was she screaming now? Perhaps she was screaming now, the daughter screaming back, the daughter saying, 'Mom, he likes my titties, so? Live with it.' Then the blood, the slashing, a real and different screaming now, more blood, the husband awake and wrestling with her but he was too lazy and she slashed again, the daughter screamed again, the blood, and finally the husband got her on to the floor and while she begged him then he did not let her up like those others had not let her up. So much blood on the floor she wanted to mop up. Then the neighbors came.

And the ambulance came. And the police came. The trial after that.
Then prison.

v

'A question, as I see it,' Émile Cinq-Mars said to her, his voice soft
and slow and deliberate; she had been forewarned that he was smart
and that he would ask questions that she did not want asked, and
say things that she did not want heard, 'has to do with how the
small axe, the hatchet, the one you injured your daughter with, came
to be in your right hand, Doi. It did not suddenly appear there. Did
you pick it up in the backyard? Or on the porch? People don't
usually leave a hatchet just lying around. Had you already brought
it into the kitchen with you, while you were waiting, so that you
were waiting there with the hatchet at the ready?'

'What?' Doi asked. 'What?' This made no sense. He was wrong.
The axe. It was in her hand. She admitted that. But it was not like
he said. It just appeared there. What else?

'That's one question. At what point did you pick up the axe so
that you could attack your daughter?'

'Just to scare her, maybe. Only to show her that she was wrong.
Her father didn't care from nothing about the trouble she was in.'

'Some would say she was in love, not trouble, but when and
where did you pick up the axe?'

It just appeared. It was in her hand. It was not in her hand. Then
it was in her hand.

'The other question that I'd like you to take back to the dorm,
to think about, is why you looked into the stall where Flo was killed.
You told the police that you urinated in the middle stall, that that's
the toilet you used. But Flo was out on the end. Why did you go
down to the last stall and look in there? Do you usually look in on
other people doing their business?'

'There are no doors.'

'I know there are no doors. All the more reason to respect someone's privacy, no?'

'I looked in her stall.'

'I know you did. Why did you? When and where did you pick
up the axe, and why did you look in Flo's stall? Can you think
about those two things?'

'Why?' Doi asked.

'You're wondering why I want to know about the axe?'

Doi nodded.

'That's a fair question. I want to understand your anger. What is spontaneous with you? What is planned when you go off the deep end? I think it's fair for me to know that. That we both understand it. That may help both of us to understand what happened in the toilet.'

'I didn't kill Flo.'

'But you attacked your daughter with an axe, and I'm told that you still don't believe it was all your fault.'

'She was out so late!'

'Why did you look in on Flo?'

'Flo?'

'Wasn't that rude? Are you a rude person, Doi?'

'I'm not. I'm not rude.'

'Then why? For now, just think about it. You can tell me what you discover the next time we meet. The issue with the hatchet helps me to understand you. I'm interested to learn why you screamed, after you found Flo, when you didn't scream when you slashed your daughter. Or did you? I also want to know what you did between the time you came across Flo in her dreadful state and the moment when you screamed to alert the others.'

'What?'

'It's in the guard's report. You were standing right at the opening to the toilet room when the guard located you. Flo was in the stall at the opposite end. You found Flo, then went to the doorway so that people could hear you better when you screamed. That's what it seems like. Then you screamed. Strange delay. Why? But that's a question for another time. In any case, I think you understand me. I'm quite sure you do. Time now to do your maps. Do you know what they are? Did Abi tell you? I bet she did. The maps, then that'll be it for today, Doi.'

Understand him? She didn't understand a damn thing. He didn't seem so smart to her. Maybe Abi was wrong. No, not smart, not smart at all.

She diligently, angrily, sketched out the stupid maps.

Rozlynn

i

Within their quarters, Rozlynn strode back and forth like a caged animal approaching its wits' end. Never a good sign. She walked a straight line across the room, a straight line back. Abigail joined her for a minute in each direction, keeping silent the way Rozlynn preferred, then whispered, 'Roz, Rozlynn girl, we got word, you know? He's gone home, the detective. Is that what's bugging you the most? You don't have to talk to him, not today, nobody does, so don't worry.'

Roz did not ignore her yet neither did she respond. She stopped walking for about twenty seconds, which indicated to Abigail that she was mulling the news. Then she returned to methodically pacing once more. Across the room and back to her bunk. Across the room and back to her bunk. Not looking to either side. Facing forward to the floor. Abigail waited; with a gesture she warned others not to intervene. Then she sat on the end of Rozlynn's bunk and continued to wait. Not looking at Roz, not signaling to her, just waiting. Finally, Roz sat down at the head of the bed, and folded her pillow onto her lap.

Doi had upset her. Nobody knew that, and if they did, they wouldn't know why. The way that Doi returned from her meeting with the cop disturbed Rozlynn. The woman's evident distress affected her. She normally didn't have much to do with Doi and if the truth was told – she would not herself say it – she didn't like her. That's not what mattered. Doi was distraught as though she'd been beaten up on the inside, which was always worse than the bruises a person might show on the outside. A bruise on the skin vanished over time; those on the inside hemorrhaged and hung around forever. They never healed properly. Forever tender.

Abigail let her settle. Even after Rozlynn had done so, placing the pillow behind her back and holding her head up, her hands relaxing on her lap, she didn't press for a discussion. She waited on Roz to say what she needed to say, if anything, and if she said nothing that was fine, too. She wanted Roz to know she could count on her silence in their interactions. They could both stay mum, or not, as she wished.

She chose to speak.

'How come he bugged out so soon?'

'Lazy, maybe. I don't think I wore him out. Maybe Doi did.'

'Maybe,' Rozlynn said. 'She wears me out sometimes.'

Abigail gave her a look. That was a lengthy statement for Roz to make. Lit by humor, which was rare from her as well. She didn't challenge her on it. She said, 'I hear he has a girlfriend. Maybe he was missing her. Went to see her.'

'What are you talking about? How'd you hear something like that?'

'I asked him. He didn't give me a straight answer. Not quite anyway. That's not like him. I don't know for sure, but I think he's in love. Are you worried about talking to him?'

Rozlynn didn't usually care about how things looked but she knew how this must look and it wasn't good. She was afraid to talk to the police. She saw how Doi came back, wretched, forlorn, ready to pull her own hair out. Doi was on the verge of tears and at times she was obliged to dab those tears away. Talking to the cop had caused Doi grief and that's what Roz didn't want, that's what she feared the most. More grief.

She could not explain it, to Abigail or to anyone else, because people never understood. It made no difference that it was a simple thing. When she'd been arrested for the murder of her father the cops brought her into an interrogation room and asked her questions she didn't answer – she didn't refuse, she simply chose not to answer, she didn't feel like it – and then one detective put a pad of white foolscap down in front of her and plopped a pen on top. He said, 'Write up your confession if you don't want to say it out loud.' So she did.

She wrote, 'I did it.'

The detective looked at what she wrote. 'You could add a few details,' he suggested, but she did not do that.

He asked her to sign it, so she did.

When they asked her in court if she did it, she said, 'I did it.' That's all. Then they sentenced her.

Talking with this cop wasn't going to be the same. She could tell that by the way Doi came back and the shape she was in. With this cop, she'd write down 'I didn't do it,' and then she'd really be in trouble. No one would believe her. No one would accept her word. They'd twist everything she said, and if she didn't speak they'd put words in her mouth. They'd drill down into her. If she insisted that she didn't do it, they'd kick her around the room then stomp on her properly until she changed her mind and saw everything differently in a new light. They'd force her to sing a different tune, one she didn't know. That would happen. She couldn't win and she accepted that. If she protested her innocence, she'd be found so guilty she'd scream.

'I did it,' she said.

Abi looked at her 'Did what? No. You didn't kill Flo.'

'I didn't say that.'

'I didn't think so.'

'I killed my father. I did that. That's what I did when I said I did it.'

'Tried and convicted, Roz. That goose has been cooked. And eaten. The bones tossed. No need to chew on that carcass anymore.'

She couldn't say to anyone, especially not to the cop, 'I didn't do it.' He'd be on her then. She couldn't explain her dilemma to Abigail. This was the kind of deal where it's better to keep your mouth shut and fret about it on your own.

Abi let her keep her silence. She knew that that's why the two of them got along so well.

ii

When she was small her father was ending his days on the trapline in winter. Fox pelts and ermine, wolf and beaver. He got by for decades. As he grew older the work became increasingly more difficult for him, the results less encouraging through no fault of his own. She helped out by walking the trapline with him. Those days were the best. She didn't mind that he took her out of school. She loved being with him in the woods, on the snow, under the stars, in the silence of the cold where all you could hear on a windless night were the trees crackling and the wolf howls. She understood why wolves howled in the dark and in their torment.

She'd howl too if she had the ability. The crackling trees confused her. She asked her father once if it was the bark of the trees that barked in the night, if that's how bark got its name, but her father said that tree limbs went *crack* because the cold was so cold.

'Bark is English word,' he said. To him, that mattered. 'Trees don't speak English.'

'Do they speak Cree?'

'Sure.'

Sometimes she found herself in trouble when she came home from the trapline because she had skipped school, but mostly the teachers only hung their heads. Or they sighed, their hearts heavy. As though a transgression had occurred and no hope existed to undo the wrong. Her girlfriends were unhappy with her also because they thought she was as snooty as a white girl after she'd been out on the trap, but the boys were the worst. They were so jealous! She didn't care that the boys were mad. That was their problem, she said. And it was.

Her father was going out for longer times and returning with fewer pelts. Then he started getting paid less for each pelt. Then he went out for shorter times on shorter traplines and came back with fewer skins than ever. And got less money for them, too. Then he went out less often and stayed home and played cards. He played solitaire. Their cabin was two miles outside the village, so she walked to school although sometimes in winter her father took her on the snowmobile when he had money for gas. In the spring and the fall she could ride her bike. Walking in the winter was fun on snowshoes but she didn't like to walk to school in the spring or in the fall because coming home she passed near her uncle's place and he would talk to her, not in a nice way, or one or two of her boy cousins would talk to her, also not in a nice way. Or the boy cousins would yell at her sometimes. In the summer she could speed away from them on her bicycle until that time they put a wire across the path which sent her flying and the boy cousins were on top of her then. They never could do what maybe they hoped to do because she could fight back, and even though they pulled her skirt up and grabbed her there she still got away when they both decided at the same moment to pull down their own pants. She bolted away and got on her bike and she was gone before they got their pants back up.

She watched for a wire after that.

The boy cousins were not good. Her uncle was also not good, but he was a man, not a boy, and too strong for her to handle. She said she'd go to the Mounted Police. He said he wasn't stupid. She didn't know what that meant at first. Then he explained one time when he was drinking – and when was he never? – that he was waiting for her to turn eighteen. He'd have her then. She didn't know what that meant, and he explained, 'When my dumbass brother-in-law is shit-faced and you're pissed too I'm gonna take you out on the grass, you bet. You won't forget it. You wait for that. When you're eighteen. The Mounties won't say nothing then. You'll be too old.' She didn't know what that meant either, but time went by and then she did know. She was ten the first time he said something like that to her and eighteen seemed an eternity away, as far away as the stars in the night sky in winter while the wolves howled.

He said it for years. Then the time wasn't so far away, and her uncle kept reminding her that she had a birthday coming up real soon, and on that day, he planned to visit.

She thought it was him on the night of her birthday, creeping around in the dark outside. She'd been expecting him, not her father. She'd gone out to sneak a smoke, heard him, or heard something, then went back into the kitchen and crouched down. Nobody came in the back way, and they didn't have lights, no electricity, and when he stepped through the back door, she slammed a knife into his chest. She thought it was her uncle, her dead mother's brother, but it was her father who came back late from playing cards and had gone around back to pee in the woods maybe, probably, and fell down dead at her feet. She didn't mean to kill her loving father, the man she adored, but she did.

How could she explain to anyone that she'd been so scared she couldn't think? She could scarcely breathe.

'I did it,' she wrote on the foolscap pad, and not a word more.

Why explain what no one would understand or believe?

iii

'White people never understand,' Rozlynn said. 'Basically, they're stupid in the head. They don't believe me.'

'I'm white. Don't I understand?' Abigail asked her.

'Probably not,' Roz said.

'OK,' Abi backed down. 'I don't. Tell me anyway what I don't understand.'

Rozlynn remained quiet for a long time. Abigail never knew if she was thinking when she went that still, or if she drifted off somewhere, or if she fell asleep on the inside while appearing to be wide awake on the outside. She could never figure that out. She didn't know that on this occasion Rozlynn was thinking about white people. Eventually, she put it to Abigail this way, 'Take my name.'

Abigail waited some more. Then she prompted her friend, 'Where do I take it?'

'It's Rozlynn.'

'I know that.'

'With a zed. The Americans call it a zee. I don't know why. Isn't it the same language? I don't write my name with an S; do you know why?'

'It's your prerogative, or your mother's if she named you.'

'My what?'

'Your— Never mind. She could name you whatever she wanted.'

'She tried to. Name me. I was supposed to be Ozlynn, no R, that's really my name but it's not, know why?'

'Nope. Still don't.'

'She was in labor she told me, and it was on the TV.'

'Her labor was on TV? Your birth?'

'No. You know, the movie? The wizard and the scarecrow and Dorothy and Toto and them. The Lion and the Tin Man. She could've named me Dorothy from that movie, but she chose Ozlynn. Lynn was my aunt. So Ozlynn. An Oz Lynn, that's me. Except when she went to register me in for being born, the white man at the office put an R in front. My mom, she had to be fierce to keep the S out and the zed in, and keep an extra N, but she lost on the R in the end. They put it in. She didn't fight that hard about the R.'

'What you're saying is, white people didn't let you be Ozlynn. I can see that happening. It's not right, but I can see it happening.'

'Doesn't matter. I'm Rozlynn now anyhow. How I grew up. At school and that, I tell the teacher or the nurse or the doctor, don't spell it with an S, please. They think it's a white girl's name. It's not. It's with a zed. They think I got it wrong. I didn't. How many times, you think? Millions. Millions. Always it's white people who won't accept that what it is, is what it's supposed to be. Why are they like that? White people always want to take the second N off my name. There's two! N, N. Why is that so hard?'

'I understand. You have a case.'

'I'll tell you why.'

'Why?'

'Because they're white.'

They both broke up after that. They had a silly laugh. But Rozlynn still couldn't explain to Abigail that she couldn't write 'I didn't do it', because no white cop alive over the next one or two hundred years was going to believe that, and she didn't have time to wait that long. She'd stay silent forever instead.

iv

In summer she'd shoot with her dad. He didn't call it hunting, he called it shooting when she went with him. Hunting is what he did on his own or with his buddies and usually in the fall for moose or caribou. With her dad she'd wander into the woods and pick on an old birch and be mean to it, or the two of them would pick out a hole a woodpecker pecked and see if they could shoot the hole. She was never good at shooting. Neither was her dad. She thought there was something wrong with his eyes. At noon, they'd unpack a lunch and he let her snap the cap on her first beer one time, but she was permitted only a sip. 'Eighteen, you can drink. A little, not a lot. Before that, you don't drink.' She went along with that. Everything, it seemed, was going to happen when she turned eighteen, when everything was going to change. Rozlynn had not been in a hurry for that day to come. She'd rather wait forever and go shooting with her dad in summer and snowshoe the trap alongside him when the snow flied. She was starting to drink, though, and take pills, as that time drew closer. Not at home, but with her friends in the woods or behind the old school. They'd share gin or beer or pills or everything together and talk about the boys you could talk to and the boys you had to watch out for especially when they were drunk. Her boy cousins were on the watch-out list and her uncle was considered the worst of a bunch of bad men. 'He's got no conscience.' He'd tried something with every one of them except Roz and they agreed it was because he was her dead mother's brother. 'That only means he'll wait, because he's my uncle,' Roz explained, but nobody knew what she was talking about or, if they did, they didn't believe her or understand. Her uncle wasn't going to bother her like he did the others, they were sure of that. He was her uncle.

Which meant that even her girlfriends didn't believe her when she told them something that was true.

At night in the prison, and often during the day in prison she thought about those best days in the woods with her dad, and she thought about him often and she daydreamed about walking the trapline with him even while sitting down beside the other inmates. At night, especially, she could smell the piney forest and hear the brook's chitchat and the wind fluttering the leaves. It's not like she forgot the tougher times, either. Like when they were out on the trap, and the blizzard was worse than the one they expected and they had to huddle up for the night, she and her dad, and in the morning, it was so blindingly bright in the fresh snow and so cold your limbs crackled. You couldn't hear that sound but your bones felt like crackling, for sure. Or the time a wolf ate through his own leg to get out of a leg-hold and they had only the leg to see. Or when small animals, sometimes ones nobody wanted to catch, were caught but they weren't dead yet. Her father didn't like to use a knife or use a gun because it might score the pelt, at least that's what he said when he was teaching her to use the wire to slip over their necks and then twist because he didn't like to do it himself. Not close up. So she learned how while he walked away a short distance and then came back to do the skinning.

She saw that he was a gentle man because he didn't like to strangle an ermine. She loved him for that.

When she thought back and relived those days, she could say that the duck hunting was tough, because she was always cold at that time of year and she wasn't allowed to do any shooting herself because she'd been brought along with the men and the boys, too, so she had to help with the other chores. Which was all right except that she was always so cold and damp and usually bent up in a tiny wet blind waiting for ducks to land. Those might be remembered as difficult days and sometimes maybe she was sore about how things were then but thinking back she'd give anything to be there again, to be bunched up under pine boughs waiting for shotguns to blast away.

She liked it, especially in memory, because her father was there and she was with him.

What she hated about being on trial for his murder is what they did to him, what was said about him. Everybody assumed something terrible. He drank too much, they said, even though he didn't, not really, and he played cards badly, but he was a kind man and a gentle man who would never harm his daughter. In court they said he kept his daughter out of school and forced her to sleep beside him on the trapline and in the duck blinds, that that was unnatural, and one day, they said, it was inevitable, her own public defender said, to help get her less time, the girl just snapped. Then she'd said, 'I did it,' but instead everybody involved in her case went around saying that her father was guilty. She hated that part.

He wasn't guilty. He was dead.

He didn't harm her. She killed him.

She devised a plan because of it. One day she'd be released. She'd go home. She'd kill her dead mother's brother. Her uncle. To take revenge for her father being dead because of him. Then people would know that it wasn't the father who was to blame. People will believe the corpse when they see one. Even white people. She doesn't want to spend one more day in prison than necessary, especially not because of Flo because that will prevent her from finishing her job – clearing her father's name by killing the man responsible for her killing her father. People will know then who was the guilty man, who was the innocent victim. She might even say so right out loud in court. But day-to-day, you can't tell people those things. They'll think you're only talking. You have to show them first. Then they'll listen.

After that, she will happily go back to prison, or go back and not worry about being happy, even if it's not to Joliette, and dream her life away remembering her dad in the woods in the winter in the cold with the wolves howling and the tree limbs barking, partly in Cree like her dad imagined and partly like wild stray hungry mutts as she first imagined.

v

Late in the afternoon Doi and Rozlynn talked. They rarely chatted to each other without other people being included in the conversation, and of course Roz rarely chatted at all. They started out by washing their faces over the sinks across from the toilet stalls and Doi just kept going with whatever she was saying. When they left the room they stayed together and when Rozlynn sat down, Doi served her a coffee and sat down beside her.

'I think she'll come see me now,' Doi said, which caused Rozlynn's ears to perk up. Usually, Doi yammering away was nothing more than background noise. You got used to it like you got used to so many things. But her ears perked up. 'Don't you think so?' Doi asked, as if Roz might have an opinion that mattered to her. Then she answered her own question because in the end only her own opinion counted. 'I think she'll come.'

'Why now, you think?' Roz asked her back. She assumed that Doi was talking about her daughter again, but she had never before suggested that she might show up someday.

'Because I wrote to her.'

'You always write to her.'

'No, but this time—' Doi started to say something when she stopped herself. 'What do you mean I always write to her?'

Roz didn't feel like having that fight. She said, 'I thought you did.'

'I write to lots of people,' Doi said.

She didn't believe her but didn't care either.

'This time I wrote to her, I said we were eight in here. Now we're only seven. I told her it's dangerous in here. That Flo was killed. I could be next. That could happen. I won't know why. Somebody, I'm sure it won't be you, will strangle me with a wire around my neck if I don't look out.'

'Why won't it be me?'

'Don't joke.'

'Who said I'm joking?' Rozlynn asked but Doi didn't take her seriously, probably because she wasn't really listening.

'When she knows how dangerous it is, that I could die any day, she will come see me. Maybe. I thinks so, don't you? When I write again, she'll come see me, don't you think?'

They were silent together because Rozlynn thought she'd better not say what she wanted to say and Doi wasn't listening anyway as far as she could tell. Doi had said what was on her mind, that her daughter was coming because the mother might be in danger and her daughter of course loved her, so to her that made sense.

Rozlynn finished her coffee and then she said, 'I did it.'

Doi wasn't listening or maybe she didn't want to hear.

Roz meant something by that. She meant that she had stuck a hunting knife into her father's heart and that Doi had done what she was in here for, too. She had hacked her daughter with a hatchet. They weren't ever going to be friends was what she really meant to say.

Doi said, 'You and my Katarzyna are about the same age.' Somehow, making that statement gave her the right to reach across and touch the hair on her forehead a moment. The touch of her fingertips felt so light. Hard to imagine, Roz was thinking, how someone can be so softly gentle one minute then go wield an axe. Although she could imagine it, and that was the hard part, why she and Doi could never be friends. She could imagine doing what Doi had done because she had done it, too. In her own way. That's what she wanted to say to her, 'You did it, too.' But they were in a prison. In prison, you didn't pick a fight unless you had a chance to win it. You watched what you said, even when you were someone who said hardly anything ever.

The guard was too close for her to have a chance of winning any fight anyway.

Rozlynn didn't say out loud that Doi's remark was true, that she and Katarzyna were about the same age. She just warned herself to be careful.

vi

'You came back today at night,' Rozlynn said.

In silence, they had sat in the interrogation room for five minutes. The guard inside the door made the only sounds, shuffling her feet from time to time and when she did that, both Roz and Émile Cinq-Mars looked up to see what was going on. Nothing was going on. Otherwise, Roz looked down at the desk and from time to time pawed the surface gently, then stopped abruptly, as though suddenly conscious of the motion, while the policeman in the room sat side-ways to the table with his legs stretched out and seemed to stare at his shoes. Only that.

She wanted to stare at his shoes, too, his gaze that prolonged and intense, to see what was so special about them.

Then she spoke, stating that he'd returned, and Cinq-Mars straightened himself up, as if suddenly aware that she was in the room. Or that he was.

'I did,' he said. 'I came back.' Returning at night had not been a strategy. He had decided that commuting back to the city every day would be a drag. It would wear him out. He called the Chief of Police to coax him into springing for a motel room, then drove home to pick up extra clothing and things he'd need. Five nights a week at a minimum he'd sleep out in Joliette to save on travel. Established in his new digs, he went for dinner, then returned to the prison. His intention was not to keep the inmates off-guard, although that proved to be the result. 'Don't worry. I won't be coming in around the clock, but we want to get this resolved fairly quickly.'

They sat quietly again. Cinq-Mars had yet to ask a question. He simply sat there and waited for her to talk. In the interim, he had a lot on his mind and matters to work through, so he wasn't bored in the least.

The first question was posed by Rozlynn. 'Can I go now?'

'What do you think?' he asked her back. His first question.

'About what?'

'The murder.'

'I don't think nothing about it.'

'That's unusual,' Cinq-Mars said. And asked, 'Don't you think?'

She didn't understand the question. She answered, 'I think.'

'But not about the murder.'

'Nothing to think about.'

'How come?'

'What do I know?'

'You tell me.'

'Tell you what?'

'What you know.'

'Nothing.'

'You didn't do it, I suppose. You don't have to answer. I wouldn't want you to lie.'

'I'm not lying.'

'We can agree on that. You're not lying. How can you be if you're not saying anything?'

'You're not neither.'

'That's true. But we know I don't know anything. I wasn't in the room. Why not tell me where you were when Doi cried out.'

'Do a drawing, do you mean, like Abigail said?'

'Abigail talks to everybody, I guess.'

'She talks to me.'

'Sure,' Cinq-Mars said, 'do a drawing.'

He waited while she sketched a map of the situation from her perspective the moment Doi cried out. It looked familiar.

'Now show me where you were after Doi cried out, but after all the guards arrived and the corrections officer ordered everyone to stand still.'

Roz pointed to the stick-person representing herself on the page. She had drawn everyone with short oblongs around their waists to depict skirts.

'That one is you,' Cinq-Mars confirmed. 'When the officer ordered that no one move—'

'I still didn't move.'

Cinq-Mars said something she did not expect. 'That's what I thought.'

They were quiet for a while. Then she said, 'Can I go now?'

'If you have something to confess,' Cinq-Mars advised her, 'now would be a good time for that. If you don't, then sure, you can go now. Just one more thing.' He looked at the guard by the door and she left the room. The two of them in the room waited for the door to click closed. Roz looked up at him, really for the first time. 'Who do you think killed Flo?'

Rozlynn shrugged. 'I dunno.'

'Who do you think?'

'I dunno.'

'You can stay here a while if you want. Just sit here. Or you can go now. Up to you.'

She sat there a while not really knowing what to do. Then she said, 'I guess I'll go.'

Cinq-Mars walked her to the door where Rozlynn said, 'Abi says you got a girlfriend. Abi thinks you're in love.'

'Abigail thinks a lot of things.' He rapped two times on the door and the guard opened up. 'It's nice to meet you, Rozlynn. We'll

talk again sometime if you don't mind too much. Good to talk to
you today.'

He had listened to her breathing while they sat together. He
didn't think she exhaled a single guilty breath. Not that he could
go by that. But he considered it a start.

Cinq-Mars decided to pack it in for the evening.

Rozlynn went back to her bunk and didn't say anything to anybody
about anyone. If she was still upset, she didn't let on.

Sandra

Detective Émile Cinq-Mars would not acknowledge even to himself that he chose his motel due to its proximity to a liquor store, but upon spotting the outlet he booked into the first accommodations that came up along an industrial and retail strip. Set back from the road, frontage for the premises included a communal porch, each unit outfitted with a pair of plastic Adirondacks. He could see himself taking his ease in the evening – and a good whisky, sipped slowly, might help the time slip away. A Laphroaig, being on sale, was selected. He was not always one for peaty, yet the peat-smoke of the brand suited his loner's mood. A wee dram in the cooling night air was a welcome companion in this far-flung town called Joliette where he knew no one, and where he wanted to keep it that way.

Company arrived despite his wish. Uninvited. Unwanted.

A biker roared in, the so-called muffler on his hog calibrated to awaken the comatose. In case anyone had hit the sack early, he gunned it repeatedly after coming to a stop, then finally shut the motor and dismounted. He looked the part of an incendiary figure, beaded, bearded and shaggy-haired, large of belly and littered with metal. Cinq-Mars had a mind to go over and kick in his testicles, to see how much he enjoyed having a peaceful evening disrupted. Merely an idle fantasy, of course, as he'd not do that under any circumstance – a good thing, as another four bikers arrived out of a cloud of dust a short while behind the first.

This second wave was either less loud or the first guy had deafened him. As the bikes went silent the riders slapped each other's paws and beer appeared out of their saddlebags. One in their number lumbered over to the office to book rooms.

Not next door, Cinq-Mars was thinking. He might revive his thought about kicking testicles if that happened.

Like a hefty rock rolled down a hilltop into a pond, the bikers' arrival produced a swift rippling effect. Others who'd been out on the porch returned indoors. Lights went off in at least three rooms, the curtains closed. Teens smoking between this property and the next chose to split. Cinq-Mars remained seated, and four of the five bikers, just one with a girlfriend, tramped past him after their rooms were acquired. The clerk apparently had a brain, sending them down to the far end of the building. In a mood, the policeman expected a confrontation, however mild; surprised, then, when the group proved courteous. One excused himself as he went around the seated man.

'No problem,' Cinq-Mars replied, and pulled his feet in.

'That's good shit,' the lanky biker added, indicating the bottle and raising his own. He walked on.

Perhaps they were happy not to have been treated as vermin. Yet these few were not benign. Their colors declared them to be members of a criminal gang, a Hells Angels satellite. Their turf was outside Montreal; Cinq-Mars knew of their violent reputation.

Which signaled that their good manners might be fleeting.

The fifth, the guy with the outrageously loud Harley, sauntered by, his steps heavy and jangly on the porch wood. Chains on his boots. He nodded as he went by, yet something in the exchange alerted him. He stopped, came back. Leaned against the porch rail. It noticeably yielded to his weight. He put his beer bottle down, stuck one hand into the front of his jeans, and buried the other in an armpit. Overall, not a menacing pose, which belied his general look and attitude.

'How's it hanging?' he inquired in French. He had a tiny mouth, virtually invisible under facial hair.

Cinq-Mars found the accent difficult to distinguish, new to his ear. 'Not so bad. Nice evening.'

'What I thought,' the biker said.

'What? That it's a nice evening?'

'That you're doing good. You look it. You with that bottle.' He took out the paw from under his belt to lift his beer and enjoy a thirsty swig. 'From around here?'

'What do you think? It's a motel.'

'Yeah. Me, too. On the move. You got a big nose, anybody ever tell you that?'

'Nope. No one. I never noticed.'

'That's a lie and a half. I got a nose on me, too.'

Cinq-Mars looked more closely. If anything, it was diminutive for the scale of his visage. 'Looks normal to me,' he said.

'*Looks* normal, you bet. But it don't smell normal.'

'Oh no? How's that?'

'I can smell a cop a mile away.' The man was pleased that he got him to walk into that one. He added, 'No offense.'

'None taken,' Cinq-Mars said right back, 'given that you're rather odiferous yourself.'

Cinq-Mars let his left arm fall to his side and found the neck of the Laphroaig bottle. He lifted it off the floor of the porch and shifted it to his right hand to be in his swinging arm and lowered it along his right side. The biker, after all, stood above him, and that beer bottle looked dangerous.

Whether or not the biker noticed or cared could not be discerned, but a chuckling emerged from deep within him, rising up through his chest to finally be emitted along with a smile.

'Like I said, no offense.'

'We both know it's how I signed in,' Cinq-Mars pointed out. Weary, he hadn't been thinking, and had inscribed his name in the register the same way he signed in at the penitentiary. *Sgt.-Det. É. Cinq-Mars.* 'Nothing to do with scent.'

The man chuckled some more. He seemed to genuinely be enjoying himself. 'I'll see you around,' he said.

The old comeback, *not if I see you first*, was considered, then rejected. 'Have a good evening.'

'Always do, Sergeant-Detective. Count on that.'

'You don't mind,' Cinq-Mars spoke up after the man had turned and walked several paces, which caused him to stop and return once more, 'if I check out how you guys signed in.'

The biker seemed to think it over, perhaps casting his mind to the names he'd scribbled down. Having done his mental tally, he said, 'Feel free, man. That ain't no sweat off my balls.'

He should kick them in anyway, Cinq-Mars mused. Curious, he thought, how that was a thing with him this evening. Perhaps it stemmed from some reflex, or weariness of mind, or an intuitive response to danger beyond his knowing.

He might choose to sleep lightly, just in case.

ii

Before contemplating dinner, Cinq-Mars telephoned Sandra Lowndes in New Hampshire. Younger than him by nineteen years, the woman was the apple of his eye these days and he'd been alone in the orchard for some time. He'd fallen in love with the lady, instantly and perilously, which he recognized as a hopeless venture. He shouldn't bother. Yet his customary discipline had deserted him around her.

'Are you in your tiny monk's cell?' Sandra inquired, teasing. He had told her that that's how he'd been living for years now, in a miniature Montreal apartment. If he considered his digs to be some kind of penance, he didn't know what for. Unless it was for becoming a cop when he thought he'd be a priest. He'd revealed all that to her. With her voice on the phone in his ear, her eyes, her lips, her hair, her sensible nose – their children might stand a chance at normalcy – formed in his head. He'd called with nothing to say and now the news of the motel's biker inhabitants and charm-free rooms gave him something to relate. Which led to the obvious question of what he was doing there.

'I'm spending my working hours in prison.' More news to relate. Sandra was eager to learn about the women in the Joliette Institution and Cinq-Mars obliged her curiosity. Grand to be talking to her.

'Who do you think did it? Do you have a suspicion?'

Normally he'd curtail such talk. Not now. This was a woman for whom he'd taken a major tumble. He'd been out in the desert so long that an oasis – perhaps real, perhaps a mirage – exploded across his senses.

'Way too soon to say. I have about half the suspects still to meet.' That was too dull a comment to offer up to the woman who enchanted him, so he carried on. 'It's a David and Goliath thing, in reverse, in a way.'

'No David. No Goliath,' she pointed out. 'They're all women.'

'A few, shall we say, are larger and more physically endowed than others. The dead woman, Florence, she was powerful. Thick. Very muscular and imposing. Tough and rough by all accounts.'

'A Goliath.'

'That's it. So far, anyone who identifies as a David – small, frail in comparison to Flo – plays that card. The improbability of taking down a Goliath. But David had his slingshot, didn't he? Florence's killer used a strangulation wire. A wire around a neck can incapacitate a victim very quickly. If the victim tries only to defeat the wire, which is a typical reaction, if she doesn't strike an effective blow or kick behind her back, she dies. That's my only conclusion so far. Essentially, anyone could have done it.'

Time flew by. The long-distance charges would be something, probably eclipse the room fee. The two had met in New Hampshire when Cinq-Mars was taking time off to run an errand for his dad. His father raised horses and relied upon his son's expert eye to select new ponies when demand eclipsed what his mares produced. He had stepped into a barn and seen her – had she been shoeing a horse or merely cleaning its hoof? He couldn't recall, so taken was he by the image of her in a sliver of natural light through a notch in the barn's wood. Nothing could remedy a sudden swerve off his axis.

She had looked back at him. Swiped the back of her hand across her cheek, muddying it. Which only enchanted him more.

Sandra caught his awkwardness in the moment and sensed its provenance. She put him at ease, helping him land gently. They discussed horses. Including their purchase. While he was seeing her for the first time, he had evaluated her animals earlier and ably wheeled off a comprehensive summary of their merits and demerits. She disputed none of his opinions, only what value he assigned to each horse. A discussion, Cinq-Mars suggested, that might best be resolved over dinner. Sandra emitted then a ghost of a smile, which indicated that she knew what was going on but also that she did not mind. 'I could eat,' she said.

The subject of food came up again over the telephone. Both admitted to being famished; they'd need to break off for dinner, and finally said goodnight. Cinq-Mars walked down the road to a restaurant he'd noticed, his spirits buoyed, his pulse quick. He didn't know how a relationship with Sandra could ever evolve but at the same time he had no idea how it could not. Even the realization that he had selected the same restaurant as the bikers he'd met earlier failed to undercut his upbeat mood.

He was falling in love.

Fallen, he corrected himself, over dessert.

Once he got the proper tense in his head, he knew what he should do.

Isaure

i

The warden's secretary took the morning off, giving Émile Cinq-Mars the opportunity to use her office to interview Corrections Officer Isaure Dabrezil. Arriving, the woman's walk was heavy, augmented by her large steel-toed work boots, although she countermanded that abrasive presence with a full, bright smile upon entering the room. The boots were a choice, not part of any uniform, for as the inmates at Joliette wore street clothes, most guards did too. At a glance, they were indistinguishable. The guards, though, always chose jeans or pants, never skirts or dresses. The Haitian woman held out her hand across the desk and Cinq-Mars returned a gentle smile of his own. He gave her muscular mitt a solid shake.

'Have a seat. How's everything going?' he asked.

'Good. How goes it with you, Sergeant-Detective Cinq-Mars?'

He did not reply, not being inclined to answer questions, even though his mood this morning was buoyant. He had wanted to interview Isaure Dabrezil in a different room than the one where he sequestered inmates. The interrogation room's atmosphere felt automatically adversarial, judgmental, and by virtue of her job, the corrections officer deserved differential treatment. He wanted her to feel relaxed, despite an intention to challenge her.

'I'm glad we could pull you away from your duties, Officer Dabrezil. It took some finagling, as I found out.'

'Visitors' Day today. Inmates, we move back and forth. Busy-busy. Not like in a regular girl-jail, these ladies, they have their privileges. They need time to do their make-up, you know, fix their hair. Look tidy. They do it, then at the last minute go look in the mirror again. A big to-do.'

'Yes, if loved ones are showing up, it must be a big to-do.'

'A bigger to-do when they don't show up. Then comes the sadness, you know. Sometimes trouble follows after that. The lashing out. Things have turned that way.'

Cinq-Mars took that in. He spoke thoughtfully. 'Not hard to see how that could damage an inmate's morale. In your group, we've had a murder. How are your ladies coping in the aftermath? I can't imagine it's business as usual.'

'Oh, on edge, on edge,' Dabrezil confirmed. 'Nasty work. I don't think anyone was so sorry to see Flo go, not deep in their heart, but the way it happened is bad. Under their noses like that, a murder, and by who? Difficult for everybody. Then comes the investigation, you know, everybody questioned, that makes them tense, too. Nobody knows who done it, for sure everybody's jittery.'

'Is it difficult for you?'

'Sorry?'

Corrections Officer Isaure Dabrezil was a thick-shouldered woman, broad through the hips and thighs, with a ponderous bosom. If a female prisoner guard was needed in a tough prison she'd be handpicked first. Cinq-Mars pegged her to be equally capable among rough men. Few would try anything. He had been a breeder and trainer of horses, and within that field was known for feats of natural strength, but he wouldn't want to tangle with her.

'The murder occurred under your nose, Officer Dabrezil.'

'Please, call me Isaure.'

He did so, and said, 'Keeping the peace is your responsibility. A murder violates the trust the institution has placed in you.'

She crossed her heavy arms, as a way to fortify an implicit barrier between them.

'Who can be everywhere at once? Tell me that. It's obvious the killer picked her spot when I was someplace else. Nothing I could do. No one knew it was happening. Even when it was over no one knew. That came later.'

'We presume so. In any case, tell me about the day's events. Any clues or suspicions, now would be the time to share.'

The woman sighed and mulled it over. 'Clues, I have none. Florence was a big rough woman, her. Tough as nails. Do you know why she was inside? Throws acid straight in a person's face. She looks another woman in the eye then throws acid. That's a mean one, in her heart, who does something like that. That's Flo. Not

your average alley cat. I think you have to be almost crazy to take on Flo. Almost fearless, I would say. You make a mistake, it goes the other way.'

'The other way?'

'Flo would kill you if you tried killing her but failed.'

'I understand. No one wanted to mess with Florence.'

'Who would dare? For me, that's the one question. The bigger women might stand a chance, so that would be Temple, of course, or Malka. Doi is like a housewife, but she's not small, and we know what she did to her own daughter. She can fool anybody with that way she has, like a little old housewife. Like I said, Temple is strong enough. Also, she comes from a hard background. Malka is big, not necessarily so strong. It's not like she worked at hard labor in her life. She was a mayor in her town, she'd didn't mix concrete, you know. Still, big enough. And like I said, Doi. Now, if you're looking at crazy enough, that would be the kids, Jodi and Courtney. But they're so small. Hard to imagine. They were with me most of the time anyway. Not all the time. It's possible it's them. It's possible it's anybody.'

'What about Abigail?'

'That's who the police think, isn't it? I mean the police who came here first. I don't see it in her personality, do you? I don't see her strong enough neither.'

'That leaves only one woman you haven't mentioned.'

'I know. The best to last.'

'Best?'

'My best guess. Only a guess. Who knows what goes on in her head. Rozlynn, I'm talking about. She murdered her dad. She could do anything. If I was marking the odds, it's her. But I don't know why I say that. I could be dead wrong.'

Cinq-Mars leaned to one side in his chair. The backrest yielded to him. He intertwined his fingers, then separated his hands and with the thumb and forefinger of one outlined his lower lip repeatedly. An attitude of concentration. He looked across at Isaure Dabrezil and kept his gaze on her a while, then asked, 'How did you get along with the dead woman?'

The officer crossed her thick arms again, erecting that barrier.

'Me? You mean with Flo? Nobody got along with Flo.'

'No reason why you should. She was a prisoner. You were her

principal guard during the day. Still, you packed her off to solitary a few times. You had those interactions.'

Isaure Dabrezil raised her eyebrows – they jerked upward suddenly, scrunching her brow and seemingly pushing back her hairline, as if she'd suddenly been struck by a bolt of insight as swift and as bright as lightning. 'You're thinking of me for this? Because don't. Just because I do my job that don't mean nothing. I didn't have it in for Flo.'

'She gave you a hard time?'

'Me and most of the universe, so what? Why would I strangle her with a wire when any day I want I can stick her back in solitary? It's not hard to get her out of my sight.'

'Is that why you put her there? To make her disappear?'

'For her violence, I put her there. What she deserved. For her threats, you know. Refusing to cooperate, to get along, to stay calm. She could be one huge aggravation on a person but I can deal with that. She pissed me off, but I never felt the need to terminate her existence. That's going too far. That would not be very Christian of me. One thing I am, it's Christian. I go by that.'

'Good. We have that in common.'

The remark brought her up short again, only this time her brow unfurled, and her eyes squinted as if she'd lost her light.

'Why did you put her in solitary, Officer Dabrezil?'

'Misbehavior.'

'Specifically, I mean.'

She mentioned that Flo would insult her. Isaure would laugh her off and advise her to mind her tongue. Then the woman would insult her race, and Isaure would demand that she take that back, but Flo would use the foulest language to insult the color of her skin. Isaure deposited her in solitary. Freed, Flo would then compliment her race, as if she'd learned her lesson. 'Black is so beautiful, it's gorgeous! You, too, Isaure!' She'd go on like that and be irritating. Isaure could not put her away for antics like that. Then the next day, she'd insult her island.

'"You don't talk to me about Haiti like that," I'd tell her.'

But she did anyway, her tongue becoming increasingly vicious. 'Black is beautiful, but Haiti is dog shit piled on—'

Another round of solitary.

'On we go that way. Then the last time, that was different.'

ii

'Isaure! Help me wring the neck of this here chicken.'

'That bird already dead, Flo.'

'Aw, but I need the practice, Dabby. Don't you do this with your Haiti Voodoo shit? Wring chickens' necks? You castrate goats, right? Make a stew of cockroaches and rat cocks.'

'Don't you get into nothing with me, Florence, not today.'

'Anytime you're mad at me, you call me Florence. Not Flo. You should call me Florence some time when you're not mad, just to confuse me.'

'You talk that crazy talk again. That gets you in big trouble.'

'You think? I'm making sense to me. All that matters.'

Suspicious that something was brewing, C.O. Dabrezil walked away, hoping her nemesis would chill.

Flo continued to prepare chickens for the evening meal.

iii

'Why do you think she did that?' Cinq-Mars asked.

'Coated the inside of chicken breasts with enough cayenne pepper to kill a grizzly bear. She did it because she was Flo. Understand me. She hated people. She wanted to show it.'

'Mmm. Almost as though she wanted people to hate her. Strange behavior.'

'I think so. You know what happened. More solitary.'

Cinq-Mars wrote down a few notes. Then changed the subject.

'Do you mind detailing for me, Isaure, your history in the *Sûreté du Québec* leading to your suspension?'

The woman stared back at him, not hard, and in a way that seemed vacant, as though she was suddenly absent from herself. Then she answered, 'I mind.'

'Why's that?'

She took her time before answering. 'It's a condition of my employment.'

'With the penitentiary?'

'With the SQ.'

'Why is that? Forgive me, but it sounds strange.'

'Not for the SQ. They don't like to be embarrassed.'

'You're saying that if I learned why you are under suspension from your force, the force would be embarrassed.'

'Humiliated, frankly.'

'So you've been told to keep quiet.'

'Quiet, I'm worth something. Talk, it's good riddance to me.'

Cinq-Mars paused to study her. She was resolute in her body language, argumentative, defiant. 'Did you commit a crime?' he asked.

'Some say.'

'What do you say?'

'I did the right thing.'

'Were you charged with a crime? Bear in mind, if it's a crime, that's something I can find out. It's not confidential.'

'Not a crime, no,' she stipulated. 'So it is confidential.'

'They suspended you for cause. For what reason? They didn't say it was for doing the right thing.'

'They called it insubordination. I'll say no more.'

An insubordination that, if revealed to the public, might embarrass the provincial police. Yeah, he could see that.

'Do you know why I was chosen for this investigation?' Cinq-Mars asked.

'Because of me?'

'Yep. The SQ can't investigate. Potentially, you're a suspect, and you're one of their own.'

'Seriously, you don't think I'm a suspect. You can't!'

'Imagine, if you're guilty, how embarrassed the SQ will be then. They'll be humiliated.'

She wasn't sure if he was mocking her or not. Then decided not. 'Let's make sure that never happens. I do not want to embarrass my department.'

Now he wasn't sure if she was mocking him. 'First,' he said, 'tell me, as the others have, or they will if they haven't had the chance to do so yet, that you didn't kill Flo.'

'I didn't kill Flo.'

'Where were you—'

'I was on the other side of the room.'

'The farthest away. That's true. When Doi screamed. Before that—'

'I didn't move around much,' Isaure Dabrezil claimed.

'Ever go to the bathroom?'

She thought about it.

'Remember,' Cinq-Mars said, 'seven surviving witnesses are recording where everyone was standing for me.'

'Every one of them a criminal.'

'Except you.'

'Let's hope.'

'The bathroom?'

'I sure was peeing a lot that day. One of those things. I went in a few times. I wanted it to look like I was checking things out, to make sure no one was goofing off in there. No one was. But really I was pissing a lot.'

'Sorry to be personal, but can you define "a lot" for me?'

'Four times. Maybe one more.'

'When you were in the toilet room, did you look in the other stalls? Were you in there alone?'

She had to think some more. 'I kind of glanced in them the first time. The second time, when I was washing my hands, I could see in the mirror they were empty. After that, don't remember. Lost interest maybe. I do not recall doing a serious check. Sue me.'

Cinq-Mars wrote down a note, then entwined his fingers on the secretary's desktop. He gazed at that woman's family photos and did a reconnaissance check on the desk clutter. He wasn't being judgmental, as his desk at work habitually succumbed to chaos. Once a year, not more often, he'd clean up.

Officer Dabrezil was waiting for him to speak, and finally he obliged. 'Please understand, Isaure, that I'm hoping you will be a critical component of my investigation.'

'You mean as a suspect?'

'That, too, but only if you're guilty. Otherwise, I was thinking along the lines of being kept informed on how the group behaves. Whatever comes up that's within your purview. We are on the same side of the law, are we not?'

'Let's hope. But sure, I'll help. Even if I am a suspect.' She was beginning to feel that she wasn't. 'In that case, it's better to see that the real killer is caught, no?'

'That makes sense. Anything and everything that comes up, Officer, I'd appreciate timely reports. Including minutia. It doesn't matter if your information seems to be irrelevant. You never know what will help me paint the bigger picture.'

'Fine with me. Like you say, we're on the same side.'

'Let's hope,' Cinq-Mars said, echoing her own words back to her.

iv

After Isaure Dabrezil's departure, Cinq-Mars crossed the floor and knocked on the warden's open office door. He was invited in. She was a handsome woman of sixty or so, with greying hair worn in a bob, dark-rimmed glasses that perhaps made her look too severe for her expressive eyes. He presented Warden Agathe Paquet with a plan that had ticked his interest during his talk with Dabrezil – one he kept from the guard – and he was well pleased that the warden acquiesced. Of course, she could say one thing and do another, he was not naive about such behavior, yet after this opening volley he felt optimistic.

His plan would also need to pass muster with the Chief of Police. Undoubtedly the more difficult sell, given that he'd already ordered up a motel room and a *per diem*. He'd be adding to the expenditures of his investigation without a resolution, or even progress, in sight.

Still. Worth a shot. And it might be fun.

He then departed the building, a confounding labyrinth of locked doors and different guards with separate keys and code words. No one person, including guards, had the capacity to exit the building on his or her own. That process served as an additional protective layer, so that merely seizing a guard or her keys provided no one with a way out. As well, every guard walked with a warning device in her palm. A press of the thumb: A thunderous, instant response.

Outside the penitentiary, Cinq-Mars immediately wanted back in. He returned to speak to the people who had just opened the outer door for him.

'There are bikers in the parking lot – did they just leave?'

'Yeah. Visitors' Day. They were visiting.'

'Who, specifically, were they visiting?'

'I can find out for you.'

'Please do.'

He waited. The woman inscribed names off a ledger. Then she returned.

'Did they get past the spectrometry machine and the sniffer dogs?'

'They didn't have to, sir. We don't allow them direct contact with inmates. They converse through a glass shield. We confiscate their metal for the visit, of course. Guns. Knives. Weapons.'

'They don't have to pass the tests, but do they go through them anyway?'

'They do.' She shrugged. 'They're bikers, they failed the mass spectrometry. What else is new? They handled drugs in the recent past. The dogs indicated they had none on their person. The metal detectors went off, of course, they always do with bikers, but once we got the last of their rings and chains off them, they were admitted.'

The names of the inmates being visited were unknown to Cinq-Mars, all French. None from among his murder suspects.

'Tell me, inmates in each house-unit have contact with all the other prisoners, correct?'

'Sure. In the yard. The library. The workshop. The gym. Chapel. Therapy. Everybody runs into everybody else sooner or later.'

When he returned outside, the bikers were gone. He knew where to find them if he wanted to, unless they'd checked out of his motel in the morning. He didn't really want to find them.

Lunch was next. He drove away from the prison, across a rural landscape back into town.

Malka

'You won't give away my secret, will you?' Malka urged Cinq-Mars upon arriving for her interview, mid-afternoon. 'Keeps me alive in here.'

On the spot, he determined the remark to be a ploy to control the conversation. He knew better than to bite. Still, he was intrigued by the notion that her life was bound by a secret to which he unknowingly had access. Her file did not allude to any big secret, and yet asking her to explain it to him would weaken his position. He postponed falling for her game. The maintenance of authority was critical to any endeavor to unmask and hollow out an individual.

If one inmate among the few he'd spoken to wore a mask, it was Malka Hayer.

Her look differed from the others. She arrived in a tailored suit, as if on her way to a consultation with her accountant. She'd been a politician – a minor one; a large coy swimming in a municipal wading pool, was Cinq-Mars's evaluation – and she appeared not to have relinquished the privileges of her office. He guessed that she wanted his vote and was willing to pay for it. Whatever it might cost.

'Before we go there,' Cinq-Mars countered, 'remind me, what chore were you doing when, or just before, Florence was killed?'

'Oh my goodness,' Malka demurred. She placed the tips of the fingers of her right hand between buttons on her blouse and caressed the skin between her breasts. 'The way you say that. Killed, that word, the way it comes off your lips, so naturally. To think of Florence – I mean, she was an odd creature, we all know that, she scared the living daylights out of me – but to think of her face-down in the john – I won't use that stall now, I just won't – *strangled!* Killed! Murdered! This is what my life has come to, living among people who talk about murder with no more concern about it than if they were reading the funny papers on a Sunday afternoon.'

Quite the speech. He was willing to give her a lengthy measure of rope, to see what she might do with it. 'Living among criminals is a strain on you.'

'It is! I see that you appreciate my situation, Detective. I see that. Thank you. It's true what they say I did, I killed my husband. You've read my file. But it also tells you there that I did not inflict the greatest agony possible on the man I deeply loved and cherished.'

Her file told him the story. Malka had killed her husband because he was dying horribly. A mercy killing. The courts were not being lenient in such circumstances. A move afoot to revamp the law had not come through soon enough to help her, although she was counting on a change of law and heart to secure a release long before the full length of her sentence expired.

Cinq-Mars latched on to her secret then. 'To other inmates, you say you murdered your husband . . . not out of mercy? What do you say? Revenge, blind hatred, a lover's quarrel? A crime of passion? Self-defense? What do you tell your housemates?'

'Not much. Only that he died slowly, thanks to me, and deserved it ten times over. In truth, the poor dear man did not deserve to suffer. That's what I alleviated, and the courts know it, the police know it, only I don't say that in here. My Roy pleaded with me over months to end his life. Love made me a killer, Sergeant-Detective. I'd rather people within these walls never hear that truth. To them, I'm as malicious as they come. It's best if they think that way. Self-preservation, I call it. If they think I'm just a nice old lady I'm in deeper trouble than I can handle.'

He caught on to the scheme. The sort of ruse that transpired in a jailhouse. The meek pretended to be vicious; the frail, manic. On the other hand, Malka was making a case that, not being a willful killer, except as an act of mercy, she should not be considered for the murder that occurred within her prison family. That opinion might be valid except for the overriding fact that one of eight women killed Florence and she was one of those suspects. No one escaped scrutiny.

'In case you've forgotten the question, what chore occupied your time when, or just before, Florence was killed?'

'A woman's work is never done, Sergeant-Detective! Are you

aware? I was doing laundry. Not the general laundry, which *is* a chore. Temple and I were doing our personal clothes. Just us.'

Cinq-Mars was confused. He misheard her words. 'Justice?' he asked.

She looked curiously back at him. Of course, he was French. Pronunciations could be missed. 'Just us,' she repeated, more slowly. 'Temple and me, our clothes only.'

Cinq-Mars pushed his pad of foolscap across the table and asked her to do what others had done. Where had everyone been at the moment when Doi cried out? Where when Isaure Dabrezil ordered everyone stationary? Where had she been, and where were the others, before all that? Malka's drawing skills were the best of the bunch and the information close to what others recalled. No one drastically contradicted anyone else. He could not believe that they were all in cahoots with the murderer, but they could be pooling their resources with respect to these maps. Which raised the specter that they all might know who committed the crime, and together worked to obscure the truth. Cinq-Mars stood up to stretch while Malka labored over her diagrams, and he realized then that he had neglected to ask Officer Dabrezil to do this simple exercise. And Doi. He'd have to get a map from Doi as well.

Time for that in the days ahead.

ii

Group laundry sanctioned a chaos of sheets and towels to be cleaned, but not personal items. Lumping everyone's general laundry in together created its own quagmire to sort through and it wasn't done. Instead, personal clothing was undertaken by two inmates at a time. Never individually, never more than two. Given scheduling requirements and restrictions, over time the same pairs did the job together. Temple and Malka, then, were doing their personal laundry the day Florence was strangled.

Most of the time, the task meant observing the washer turn around and around, then spin, then do the same with the dryer. The most boring of duties within an environment that was interminably boring made the task a grind. Minutes barely ticked by. Malka, the small-town, small-time socialite and politician, and Temple, a black woman mixed up with gangs who smuggled both light and heavy weapons, grated on each other's nerves.

'Gotta go pee,' Temple said.

'Break out the champagne,' Malka shot back, before she could censor her own tongue.

Temple rose quickly to any challenge. 'What's your beef?'

'I don't have one. Why should I?'

'It bothers you if I piss in a hole?'

'A simple observation, that's all. You pee often.' She realized that she ought to diffuse the situation. Temple was not a woman anyone wanted to fight. 'It's the washer, isn't it? I think so. All that water sloshing around. Makes a girl want to pee.'

'You want I should piss in your ear?'

'Temple, I'm sorry, there's no need for hostility. I take it right back. I promise. I won't notice again how many times you rush off to the can.'

'You want to keep track of something like that?' Temple asked. 'Do you? You'll wake up one morning, your life is the shits. It's one thing when you don't want to live, everybody feels that way sometimes. A different thing, when you're wishing with all your heart and with all your wretched soul, if you still have one, that you never was born. You're wishing your own mommy had such a powerful orgasm when she was doing it in some backseat of some Pontiac in some back alley somewhere that she dropped dead before you got conceived. That's what I say anyhow.'

'Probably I agree with you.' Malka went along with her. She hated the reference to her mother, yet her death-wish was not strong enough to give voice to her objection. Backing down helped moderate their dispute, although Temple continued to burn as she trundled off to the washroom to relieve herself, for neither the first nor the last time that morning.

Each time she returned, Malka said, 'Oh hell, me, too,' and walked across the common room to the washroom herself.

'You mocking me?' Temple asked after her third trip.

'I don't get it either,' Malka replied.

Temple mulled that over before asking what she meant.

'I have to go, too, today. Often. I don't get it.'

'Like you said, maybe it's the sloshing around.'

They made peace that way, and sorted through their things,

separating shirts and undergarments. They jerked to attention when
Doi let out her high-pitched scream.

'Jesus!' Malka exclaimed, spinning around for a look.

'Trouble,' Temple said. She was calm. She was expectant. The
voice of experience. 'What the hell did Flo do now?' Which was
interesting, Malka would think later, because who knew at that
moment Flo was central to the matter? It wasn't Flo in full scream.
She wasn't anywhere in sight.

iii

'How did your husband earn his living, Malka?'

Cinq-Mars sympathized with her situation. Hard to lose a
husband; harder still to take his life when that was the only remedy
to his suffering. Equally hard to be incarcerated for an act intended
as mercy. He did not necessarily envision her as an ally, or as
someone who could be conscripted to become one. Aloof, in his
estimation, possibly an antagonist, in civilian life she held positions
and had had standing in her communities. She'd known real local
power, which even on a small scale meant deflecting the slings and
arrows of others and imposing her will where it was both warranted
and resisted. Yet the toughness she'd displayed and depended upon
on the outside went only so far locked up in a penitentiary. Different
rules applied. Her public service steeliness was outstripped by those
with dark alley experience, by those who bent others to their will
through violence and fear. She was savvy enough to know the
difference. Cinq-Mars's expectation, then, was to gently guide her
into opening up about her life on the inside to see what glimpse
that might provide into recent events. If she remained a closed shop,
his interest would only perk up, and he'd find other ways to hone-in
on what made her tick.

'Roy split his working life between two separate careers. Twenty
years in the military. Sounds rough and ready, doesn't it? His title?
Financial Services Administrator. A captain in the army. When he
left, he taught high school math. He enjoyed both careers. He was
good with others. Hard to believe I became the politician in the
family when he could've excelled at it. At least, he'd excel at getting
elected, which is not the same thing.'

'What got you elected?'

'I'm no-nonsense. I let people know. Sometimes they responded. Once they didn't. If the citizens wanted an efficient administrator, I got their vote. If they preferred a mangled hubcap who'd fallen off a dump truck with shit for brains and grease in his ears, they went with that guy.'

'Tough decision, those two choices.'

Malka managed a brief laugh. She showed a little sparkle. Time to ask a more penetrating question.

'Who do you think killed Flo, Malka? Hold on.' Cinq-Mars looked over at the guard, who took her cue and exited the room.

'Impressive,' she noted. 'You don't trust guards?'

'I don't expect you to. This way, whether you do, or don't, doesn't matter.'

'I don't know who did it.'

'Hmm,' Cinq-Mars murmured, and appeared to be mulling her reply. Then he asked, 'How many women do you think will suggest to me that it was you?'

'Oh, get off the pot. Nobody will say it's me!'

'Why not?'

'Because I didn't do it!'

'They all say that.'

'But I'm not a killer, not like some of them, you know that!'

'I might, but they don't.'

Malka was shocked into stillness a moment.

'You see the problem,' Cinq-Mars stated.

'Yeah. I killed my husband to get rid of him. Did it slowly to watch him suffer. That's what I let them think anyway.'

'Makes you as badass as the rest, which was the idea behind that plan, no?'

'Why would anybody say it was me?'

'Did you use the toilet that day?'

What did other people remember? What had they said?

'We've established that. A few times, I guess.'

'Suspicious, no?'

Malka declined to treat the remark as a question.

Cinq-Mars had been developing a technique over the years where he'd continuously change the subject while conducting an interrogation. This interview was meant to feel cordial in Malka's mind, even friendly and sympathetic, but in his own mind it was an interrogation, right from the get-go. He changed the subject frequently which made him appear to be disorganized but he never relinquished his objective to lay bare the truth.

He altered course once again. 'How did it go, the laundry, with you and Temple?'

'What do you mean? It was laundry. We watched the washer go around and around.'

'Were you talking? Laughing? Having fun? Were you at each other's throats?'

What had the others reported? What had they said to him?

'Maybe there was some bickering, I don't know.'

'About what?'

'I don't know. Bickering. You know.'

'I don't. Tell me.'

'I don't know. Peeing. We bitched about peeing. I said she goes too often. She wanted to punch my lights out. I mean, she's a violent person, right? She sold guns to fucking bikers, for God's sake. I picture her walking around on the outside with a grenade in her purse and a bazooka up her butt.'

'She probably did.'

'Why do you say that?'

'You have every right to fear her, that's all. She's tough.'

'Did she do it, do you think? Temple went to piss a lot.'

'You didn't?'

What had people said?

'I might've. I guess I did.'

'Does that mean you're guilty?'

'No. Of course not!'

'Does it mean Temple's guilty?'

'I get your point. I was only answering the goddamn question.'

'If you could talk to Flo right at this moment, and you asked her, "Who did it?", what do you think Flo would say? Who would she name? This is only speculation. Nobody but me will ever hear your answer unless you repeat it yourself. What would Flo say?'

The query took away the imposition of asking a suspect to finger one of her fellow inmates. In absentia, Flo would be casting the aspersion, not Malka herself.

Malka introduced a wrinkle to his game. 'Let's say Flo never knew who did it. Somebody caught her from behind let's say and she never saw who. So, if I'm talking to Florence and she's still a dead person, her answer would still only be a guess.'

'Fair enough. What does Flo guess?'

'I think Flo would say Temple.'

Cinq-Mars rocked his head a little, skeptical. 'I put that idea in your head. What's really in *Flo's* head? That's what we're after here.'

Shot down once, she was willing to try again.

'Flo still thinks it was Temple. Strong enough. Tough enough. Taller than Flo, she had leverage over her. That's important, I think. Flo thinks so, too. Also, they didn't get along so well.'

'OK,' Cinq-Mars said and scribbled a few notes. His handwriting upside down gave Malka no clues, although not for a lack of trying to read it.

'Temple's tall enough that's true. It's also true for you, too.'

'Oh God. I didn't do it. I didn't!'

'We'll find out, one way or the other. Depending upon your guilt or innocence, you can take that as a threat, or as reassurance. Up to you.'

'I'm not all that reassured. Innocent people get found guilty, you know. A woman can be sent to prison because she loved her husband. Don't talk to me about justice.'

'We'll both guard against mistakes. Let's leave it at that.'

'Nothing else?' she asked him. To her mind, they'd run the gamut.

'One small thing, Malka. Who do you get along with in your group? Who not? Who do you like? Who do you hate?'

'No way is that a small thing,' she said.

iv

'I look at it this way if you want to know the truth,' Malka interjected into the discussion. The other women were listening. Paying attention was required in Group Therapy, and GT was on the docket that day. 'It's not unlike being stuck in the army. The same. My husband was in the army. A soldier. Put in twenty years. His best buddies in his life were the ones he made in the army. The things they went through. Slogging through the mud and all that. He was in war zones. He shot people. I presume so anyhow. Aimed at them anyway. Not sure he pulled the trigger. He just didn't talk about it

much. That's an army thing. Then he taught school. He didn't have
buddies there. Acquaintances, that's it. People he socialized with,
just not people he shared his life with. In the army, you're thrown
together for weeks or months at a time. You get down to it. See
people for who they really are, you know? Like in Group Therapy,
like us here, only more intense. There's good and bad. I see the
good in people, even in you guys. I mean some of you, you've done
bad stuff, but you're OK, you know? You know? With me you're
all right.'

She seemed to expect an ovation. People didn't disagree with
her. Similar remarks were spoken in response. Yet Malka felt
emotionally drained as she came down after her sermon-from-the-
jailhouse speech. Part of her trepidation afterwards came from
knowing that she'd lied – again. Her husband had not seen battle,
not when his job was in Financial Services. No one had to know
that. The greater fuel for her consternation though, her sense of
having her grand speech rejected, came when other women said
similar things in a casual, off-hand manner, as if it was no big deal.
She felt that she'd been snooty. Her tone, she didn't get that right.

The one thing she'd not want to be accused of inside a woman's
penitentiary was being snooty.

That would not help with anything.

Returning from GT, she remained grumpy. Others noticed but
didn't care. What she hated in the end, that little guttersnipe Jodi,
who had shot up a convenience store for God's sake like it was a
video game, had finished up the meeting with a speech of her own
and the others preferred the guttersnipe's nutty spiel. Jodi said
that you only made friends in prison for life if you were sentenced
for life, otherwise no. 'I got eight. Years. Out in six for super
excellent behavior, right?' Already the other ladies were chuckling
away, repeating her words about super excellent behavior. 'I love
you all to death but only until parole sets us loose.' More laughs.
'Then it's a clean break the hell out of here. If I know you after
prison, that's associating with felons. It won't happen. Does nobody
no good. In here, I love you to bits. Don't take that the wrong
way. Once I'm outta here, I don't want to see your ugly pusses,
pusses. Take that any way you want, just stay the hell away from
me. Got it?'

Laughs.

That concluded their talk on friendship for the session.

Guttersnipe Jodi won the day. Malka was supposed to be the politician, an elected leader. Not the guttersnipe. But in here, Jodi's sass trumped her wisdom. What a pathetic little bitch. To hell with jail anyway. She wanted out. Now. She'd do anything to get the hell out. Now.

When the detective asked, she didn't say who she hated more than anyone else. She loved everybody, period. Liked them the same anyway. She never mentioned the guttersnipe. That was not really another lie. The guttersnipe did not deserve a mention.

Cinq-Mars pressed her on it, though, the bastard. Finally, she told him, 'I'm not so keen on Jodi. There. I said it. But I don't *hate* her.'

She could tell that he could tell that she was lying. That she absolutely loathed her. She wanted to lie about it some more but thought she'd better shut up while she was still ahead, if she was ahead in the slightest. Malka was expecting him to come down hard on her, to press his advantage, except that she was saved by the bell. By bells. Alarms resounded throughout the penitentiary.

A red light above the door throbbed like a heartbeat.

The guard burst in.

'We're in lockdown,' she declared calmly.

'What's going on?' Cinq-Mars demanded and shot up from his chair.

The guard didn't answer and instead ordered Malka to put her arms on the table. She complied and accepted being handcuffed to the tabletop with the set already in place there.

'What's going on?' Cinq-Mars asked more gently, relying upon a different tone to receive an answer.

'Trouble. Red fucking alert.'

'Which means?'

'You got five options. A sixth, that would be the unknown.'

'What five?'

'In order of frequency? A catfight. An escape or attempted escape. A hostage-taking. A riot. Or . . .'

'Or what? The fifth?'

'What you're here for. A murder, or an attempted. Usually a stabbing. Shit happens.'

'Can I go see?'

'You're locked down, too.'

'Come on—'

'Sir, relax. You're not going anywhere. I'll cuff you, too, if you object.'

She was serious. Protocol, damn protocol. Cinq-Mars sat.

'Would you like a cup of coffee?' the guard offered as a form of compensation.

Although the alarms went quiet, the red light continued to pulse. The guard said they'd have to wait for an all-clear siren. Cinq-Mars declined the coffee.

'I'll have one,' Malka piped up.

'Who asked you?' the guard taunted her.

v

A siren did not resound but Cinq-Mars was summoned to the scene of the action. The warden sent for him. That left Malka alone with the guard, her wrists fastened to the tabletop.

'Oh shit,' she said.

'You said it.' The guard, a tall thin woman with a long skinny nose and a tiny mouth with her hair pulled up and bobby-pinned under her guard's cap – she was one of the few who wore a uniform – loomed over her. She drew her baton from her belt.

'Oh fuck,' Malka said under her breath.

'Something wrong? You don't feel safe around me?'

Malka cast her eyes down, as if not looking up helped her be invisible.

'Hold this. Like it's a millionaire's dick.' She put the baton in Malka's hands, not that the woman could swing it. She could barely balance it upright with her wrists cuffed. The guard went around the table and sat in the chair Cinq-Mars had occupied. 'Suck on it,' she directed.

'Please. No. I didn't say anything to him. Please.'

'Butch bitch. Shut up. And suck away. Put your heart into it.'

Shaking, Malka put her mouth over the end of the baton.

'Even a teen boy won't come that way. Get busy.'

She performed reluctant fellatio on the baton.

'Now take your head away.'

Malka was grateful to do so.

'It's a microphone. Talk to it.'

'What?'

'Tell me everything you said in here after I got booted. Don't leave nothing out. Then tell me what anybody else said in here you overheard you found interesting.'

'I didn't say anything! I never heard much. Honest.'

The guard removed her Taser and put it down on the tabletop. Malka quavered.

'That's another thing,' the guard commanded her. 'There'll be no more fucking lies out of you. You know who killed Flo? Tell me. You think you know? Tell me. You did it? Tell me. From now on, anything you hear comes to me first. Not that guy. Now talk. Hold up the fucking microphone!'

The baton was drooping. She raised it. Malka had heard of good cop, bad cop. She didn't know if this was that. She only knew that she wanted her good cop back. She'd tell him anything he wanted to hear now. She'd speak the truth to him now.

Instead, she arranged her lies and talked to the guard.

The red light above the door continued to pulse.

Marie-Philomène

É mile Cinq-Mars was briskly escorted to the yard. Doors buzzed open ahead of him, slammed shut behind, a cacophony of steel-on-steel and the echoey trammel of feet. Going outside to a level one story high, he stood next to the warden on a broad balcony. Below, rival combatants had been separated. Guards formed a line between two groups as if trying to decide which contingent to pummel first. The physical fracas had concluded, reduced to heated intermittent cursing, yet trouble remained volatile. Menace underscored the yard's atmosphere. Not explosive in the Montreal cop's estimation – the guards ruled – yet still dangerous.

Men and women with rifles rimmed the perimeter.

From a distance, the warden oversaw a return to normalcy.

'Your girls were involved,' she said. 'I thought you might want to see this.'

'My girls,' Cinq-Mars repeated. A surprise. That she had said *girls*, not women, was a note that caught his attention. Not a reference he could justify voicing himself, but he supposed that the warden was entitled. He was taken aback that any of 'his' inmates were involved. He had expected the women to be on their best behavior given the attention focused on them recently.

The melee had been a decent dustup. Abigail bled from her nose and lip and the frock she wore was seriously ripped. She needed to cover up to preserve her modesty but didn't. A prisoner unknown to him displayed claw marks down one side of her face – deep fingernail cuts, Cinq-Mars assumed. Battles among women were commonly disparaged as 'catfights' – the guard by his door used the term and Cinq-Mars had disrupted a few such altercations in downtown bars as a beat cop. He had labelled them as exactly that. Brawling men, as a rule, punched, then kicked if they got a man down. Most women didn't practice punching well enough to make the assault worthwhile. Their kicking lacked force if they'd never played soccer as kids or weren't wearing boots. Instead, women who snapped who were also inexperienced in battle resorted to hair-pulling and scratching and biting – *catfights* – their fury a match for any legitimate feline joust.

This had been all of that.

A shiner blooming around the eye of one combatant indicated that at least one solid blow had landed. Among the scratch marks and bites, a few deep cuts were indicative of a makeshift or contraband weapon.

Isaure Dabrezil stood in a line that separated inmates barking intermittent verbal abuse. She'd exerted herself in the middle of the fray and was now taking a breather. When Cinq-Mars snagged her attention with a wave, he signaled her up to his landing. Given that he stood next to the warden, she obeyed.

She came through a locked gate topped with barbed wire, then up steep metal stairs. Her immense weight lumbered along. Her steps heavy. Through another locked gate, jangling her keys. Upon her arrival, the warden lauded her good work, then moved along to address matters with other guards and officials.

'Who were the main combatants?' Cinq-Mars inquired.

'Abigail for the English. You talked to her, right? You know her? French side, Marie-Philomène. She used to be Flo's enemy. Maybe now she's looking for a new one. It looks like the fight broke out along language lines.'

'Who else from our group?'

'Temple jumped in quick. Probably to save Abi. She walloped a couple of ladies good. Jodi, she was scrapping away, that girl. I got to hand it to her. My respect. She fights above her weight class. Rozlynn was in the mix, too, but more like she was pulling people off her friends. She helped me out when I got in a jam. I will remember that, you know. The rest, mostly cheerleaders.'

'What started it?'

'We'll find out. All ladies cooperate in the hole.'

'Should I wonder why?'

'Don't.'

'I thought you were a Christian lady.'

'That does not stop me doing the job I do.'

Cinq-Mars had his eye on a young inmate – who looked no older than fourteen although that was impossible – moving among the inmates gathered on the French side of the battle line. She kept her eyes down, looking for something, then stooped to retrieve an item off the ground. The girl – Cinq-Mars felt comfortable thinking of that one as a girl – passed by a bleeding woman and surreptitiously slipped the item into her hand. Cinq-Mars judged the older woman, who had a hardened look even without the blood, to be a principal battler.

'That one,' he asked Dabrezil, 'bleeding out of one ear and her nose, is she Marie-Philomène?'

'That's who she be.'

The very young one moved to the edge of the inmates and guards – no one said boo to her – and idly slipped along the prison wall, shadow-like, over to the English side. An impossible transition, really. Somehow, she crossed from one side to the other without incident and without being noticed by anyone on the ground. Cinq-Mars was puzzled at first, then corrected himself. She had not *not* been noticed, for that truly was impossible. She had been ignored. Which was different. And that had been deliberate.

'Who's she?'

Once Officer Dabrezil figured out whom he meant, she said, 'Courtney. One of ours. One of yours.'

'The one who stabbed her best friend to death.'

'Her, yeah.'

'Don't send Marie-Philomène to solitary right away. For now, skip the infirmary also. I'll clear it with the warden. Send her straight to me. And listen, be careful with her. Don't let her ditch anything. Nab her by surprise, then search her thoroughly. Bring me what you find.'

'What will I find?'

'When you do, we'll both know.'

Dabrezil consented. She required an official order, and yet proceeded to do his bidding in anticipation of it coming through. Cinq-Mars went across to interrupt the conference between the warden and her people.

ii

Request approved, although the warden tacked on a stipulation. She required a representative in the room. Given that Marie-Philomène was not party to his murder investigation, the demand was deemed appropriate.

The infirmary visit would wait, yet Marie-Philomène was patched up on the fly. Her wounds cleaned and bandaged, she was given a cold compress to hold against her welts and a small towel to sop up blood. A split lip. A severe cut on her ear, probably caused by teeth. Her wounds did not amount to much, but she looked a sorry mess. Cinq-Mars couldn't imagine that Abigail had been responsible for that much carnage. Temple jumping into the breach was the more likely culprit.

They were both French but didn't speak as she came into the room, nor after she sat down and shot him a glance of casual contempt. Cinq-Mars, arms folded across his chest, stared at her as if, oddly, he wasn't seeing her. Once, the prisoner made a sudden gesture with her hands, as if to jump him, hoping to make him flinch. Cinq-Mars didn't budge. After that, she looked away, offering a full dose of her disinterest. To no avail. Finally, she shouted, '*Quoi!*' What!

The policeman still did not respond. He sat up only when a guard knocked and entered, pulled back the seat beside his, sat, and passed him a plain brown envelope. Cinq-Mars peered inside. Then tilted it upside down and let a thin silvery object slide out.

A nail file.

Marie-Philomène shrugged. No big deal to her. Except that she put her elbows on the table and leaned forward, ready to joust.

'Why is she inside?' Cinq-Mars asked the guard who was representing the warden.

Marie-Philomène answered first. 'I burned a guy alive. A long time ago. If you want me to apologize you're wasting your fucking time. I'm so reformed now, it's unbelievable. I burned nobody alive since I got here. You can release me now. The worst I'll do out in the real world is go piss on that dead man's grave. Maybe that'll help put out the fire in the hell where he lives. See? I don't hurt nobody.'

Cinq-Mars caught everything she said but her delivery was so rapid-fire it took a moment to interpret the spiel. Her French he understood, yet the speed was unprecedented, all her sentences sounding like a single syllable.

'Tell me,' he asked, speaking ten times more slowly than his normal speed as though to offset her mercurial rate, a three-toed sloth to her cheetah, 'is this what you were fighting over or what you were fighting with?' He moved the nail file an inch forward. 'Or' – he paused as if out of breath – 'or both?'

'Who knows?' she asked him back.

'The next time you ask me a question, it's an extra week – a whole extra week – in solitary.'

The threat meant something. Her eyes shifted over to the guard by his side to check if this outsider possessed that kind of authority. The guard played her part, staring back at the inmate without blinking.

'Maybe things started that way, could be,' Marie-Philomène conceded.

'Whatever the warden gives you for the fight,' Cinq-Mars let her know, 'I'll cut a day off it for you. Do you see how this works? Your part is to tell me who was filing her nails in public. No big deal. So, who was filing her nails?'

The inmate's eyes wandered between the two of them, as though trying to anticipate where this line of inquiry might go, or why it mattered. A major brawl in the yard, yet she was the only person taken aside so far, and the subject of conversation was about nothing more than a nail file.

'I was,' Marie-Philomène admitted.

'You were. To be clear, if we find puncture holes in an inmate, you'll be the one to charge for the stabbing?'

'Didn't say that. I was filing my nails. Abigail attacked me. Said it was hers. What do I know? I found it. Soon as she attacked me, it's gone. Then I found it again after the fight.'

'Who's Courtney to you?' Cinq-Mars asked.

She shrugged. 'A cute chick. One of the Anglos. Why?'

'She lives in an English dorm. She walked on the French side after the fight. She found the nail file on the ground, then passed it to you. Then she wandered back to the English side with impunity.'

'With what?'

'People let her do all that.'

'Maybe everybody knows what I think.'

'And what's that?'

'I think she's cute.'

'I see.'

'Good that you're not too blind.'

'Not why I called you in,' Cinq-Mars said, throwing her attitude out the window, if they had a window.

'For the fight, no?'

'I don't care about the fight. Not interested.'

'Then why? You think I'm cute?'

'Think I do?'

She was caught in her sass. She retreated. 'Doubt it.'

'Who came to see you today?'

'See me?' Marie-Philomène stalled.

'You had a visitor.'

She didn't want to say although it was obvious that she understood the question.

Cinq-Mars helped her out. 'It's not something to confirm or deny. It's on the record. I've already seen your name on the list of prisoners who had visitors. I know who came to see you, and that's why you're here now. You met with a biker named Paul Lagarde. A man who's done time himself.'

'So?' the woman asked.

A good question. Private conversations were none of his business. Still, he had forbidden all questions.

'I've let you get away with several questions already. I've been generous. I've been kind. I can still impose an extra week or two for insubordination. Or, I can let that go if you become more co-operative. This point forward. Tell me, do we blame the prison fight on you, Marie-Philomène, or on Monsieur Lagarde?'

'What? That's crazy. Abigail started the fight. Blame her.'

'You were filing your nails, no?'

'That's my business.'

'What prisoner, in her right mind, would take out a nail file in the yard, an item that could land a prisoner in solitary if found on her person, and then, in full public view, proceed to file her nails? Bad enough under any circumstances. You must really have meant to provoke someone. If the nail file didn't belong to you, but belonged to someone you were trying to provoke, what did you think would happen?'

'You can't prove that.'

'I have no interest in *proving* anything. I'm only interested in

why you started the fight by provoking Abigail. How much of a
hand in this do I attribute to Paul Lagarde? I'll ask him, of course.
I'll be talking to him shortly.'

She didn't like the sound of that, he could tell. She tried to
conceal her reaction.

'Abigail started the fight. Snarky bitch – nobody likes her. Word
is, she did Flo. The day she's roadkill, I bet you anything, buzzards
will yell at her to fuck off. They'll watch her rot in a ditch, not
even go in for a nibble. Go talk to her, if you want. I got nothing
to say.'

'You weren't friends with Flo?'

'Who was?'

'Then why do you care?'

'I don't.'

'I see. Thanks, Marie-Philomène. You've been helpful.'

'Shove it, copper. Want I show you where?'

The guard purposefully cleared her throat and said, 'Respect.'

Marie-Philomène clammed up then. Airtight.

iii

Late afternoon. The wind was picking up. Swirls of dust gyrated
crazily around the parking lot. The World's Loudest Harley
roared in and Cinq-Mars cupped both ears. He sat on the porch
like the monkey who could hear no evil until the motor was
switched off.

He smelled French fries even before Paul Lagarde pulled a bag
from his rear saddle. Cinq-Mars discerned a hot dog scent as well.
As the biker passed him on his way to his room, he tucked his feet
in, said, 'After you eat, come see me.'

The biker stood still. 'You got a warrant, *flic*?'

'No, but I have some decent whisky.'

'Even better. See you soon.'

Cinq-Mars had been eating well, but he could put a stop to that
and renew bad habits. The wafting scent of the French fries was
fiercely tempting.

When Lagarde returned they drank out of water glasses the motel
supplied wrapped in a film of rip-away plastic. The whisky offset
the lack of ambience or decorum. Rush hour; traffic was constant.

The porch the preferred place to be, not for the unsightly view of the road, but to be free of the stuffy rooms.

'Good shit,' the biker said of the whisky. He held his glass up to admire the color. Asked, 'Something on your mind, *flic*?'

'Who is Marie-Philomène to you?'

Lagarde thought through the question, which was unexpected and required consideration before a reply was offered. Cinq-Mars took his silence to mean that his answer would be complicated. The biker resorted to the whisky first, swishing it around like a mouthwash before he swallowed.

'She could be my sister.'

'Why not lay out all your fibs at once? Get them out of the way, then start over.'

'She could be my moll, but she ain't that interesting.'

'You can do better than that.'

'Never met a woman with a meaner streak. She's all right though. I like her. You? What's your interest? Whatever it is, she didn't do it. She's in jail.'

'That I know.'

'Why waste your time?'

'Why visit her? What does that do for you? How is that not a waste of your precious time? Not even your moll, you say?'

The biker was quiet again, wishing he grasped the dimensions and ramifications of their conversation.

'What's your interest?' Paul Lagarde asked again.

'Big fight at Joliette Pen today.'

'Was there? Marie-Philomène was involved? Any dead? She survive?'

'Interesting, you're more interested in a body count than the well-being of your friend. If she is a friend.'

'All right. I'll put her first. How is she?'

'A little the worse for wear. Nothing serious.'

'Good. She can handle herself. Any dead?'

'Nope.'

'Not much of a fight. What's your interest?'

'Anything happens to Abigail on the inside, I put my shield in a drawer.'

That brought another silence to the conversation. Cinq-Mars appreciated the consideration. Respectful, not to have denials or feigned ignorance to contend with. Paul Lagarde might be a lout but he was a mature lout who possessed a brain.

'The circumstances won't interest me,' Cinq-Mars said. 'Not too much, anyway. I won't ask anyone to bring me up to speed. I'll put away my shield. We'll pick this up right where we leave it off tonight, only I won't be restrained by the law. Or, given that I'm a peaceful man at heart, I'll work within the law to make absolutely certain that the consequences for you will be unpleasant. Either way, I'm game.'

'You'll choose the weapons for our duel. You're saying that.'

'Exactly that. Yes. Good way to put it.'

The biker held up the last drops in his glass, then downed them. 'Laphroaig,' he said. 'Peaty. I could develop a taste.'

'Beer can put a belly on a man. Whisky keeps you thin.'

'That don't bother me none. Thanks for the drink.'

'You're welcome. Whisky, I find, keeps the mind clear. It can elevate a man's thinking, in the right circumstances, of course.'

'What's your interest, Cinq-Mars? I'd like to hear.'

'The girl stays safe,' he said. He knew that *girl* may not be the right word for him to use, but it suggested a familiarity that in this case might help indicate, and solidify, a protective barrier that could prove necessary.

The man put his glass down on the porch floor and stood, which required a good push with his arms. He tapped his nose, the sniffer he'd been proud of a day ago. 'It's not the money with you. I'd get it if it was that. It's not the sex. No possibility for years. This jail don't do conjugal. I know. I've asked. Leaves me only one thing. You're a dedicated whack-job, Cinq-Mars. Like they say you are. One of those.'

Cinq-Mars smiled. He was pouring a second glass for himself without offering another to his guest. 'Once again,' he said, 'I hear a reference to your nose. We both know you looked me up. That's how you know what you know. I looked you up, too.'

The biker tugged his beard, a form of tacit agreement. 'Be seeing you, I suppose.'

'That's not a threat, I suppose.'

'Let the future decide. It always does.'

'The girl stays safe,' Cinq-Mars repeated.

'Heard you the first time, bro,' Paul Lagarde said.

'Worth repeating. Now, before you go, there's one more thing,' Cinq-Mars said.

'Don't break my balls, all right? You are who you are, you're carrying a shield, but I got my limits with you. That will always be true.'

'This is an easy one. Where'd you get those French fries?'

The biker happily gave him detailed directions and a five-star recommendation.

Jodi and Courtney

i

É mile Cinq-Mars called in Jodi and Courtney to be interviewed together. They were reported to be inseparable; he wanted to see how that played out, how they connected. If it unnerved one or the other to be treated as part of a pair, rather than individually, that might also suit his purposes.

From the outset Jodi proved mildly antagonistic, ready to snap back, while Courtney came across as fearful and timid. Each shot glances at the policeman then over to her pal. The detective surmised that Courtney looked to her friend for necessary support, while Jodi checked to see that her best friend was keeping herself together.

'Interesting day,' Cinq-Mars remarked.

'Oh yeah. Breaks up the monotony, say that,' Jodi pointed out, a comment that caused nervous giggles to sputter through her pal. 'How come you're talking to us anyhow? I mean together, not separate?'

'My prerogative, don't you think?'

'What makes us so special? Or don't we count like everybody else?'

'Jodi, if it's all right with you,' Cinq-Mars let her know, 'I'll ask the questions. For example, tell me how you did in the fight? Win, lose, break a nose? You look bruised.'

A purpling cheekbone, a puffy lip. Her nose had been bloodied but was fine now.

'This ain't nothing. I did all right.'

'Better than all right. I heard you kicked ass.'

Jodi was not expecting that. Unaccustomed to praise, she was unsure how to respond.

'Took my lumps, too,' she murmured.

'Courtney, what about you? Brawling or egging others on?'

Jodi answered for her. 'Come on, she's like the smallest person in Lady Jail. Except for a couple of Chinese squirts. What do you think?'

'You're not much bigger.'

'I'm physical, man. I'm like an athlete. Maybe I'll be a boxer when I grow up.'

Courtney giggled again.

Cinq-Mars kept his gaze on her until she stopped. At least he understood the humor this time, as Jodi might come across as a too-skinny fashion model before anyone could picture her as a boxer. 'What's your perspective on the brawl, Courtney. The two of you, closely knit pals, they say, you do everything together. Big fight in the barn and Jodi's caught in the middle of it, whaling away on somebody. What did you do?'

'I was her back-up, I guess. Reinforcements, like. Call it that.'

This time, Jodi found the notion humorous on various levels.

'Fair enough,' Cinq-Mars said. 'I'll put down that you were watching and waiting.' He appeared to make an official note of it.

'Sure. Why not?'

Cinq-Mars put his pen down then, cocked his head from one side to the other. 'It makes sense to a point. Here's where things don't jive. How is it possible that by the end of the fight you wound up on the French side? We have a clear battle line. You're watching and waiting, yet end up on the French side, the enemy side. How come you didn't get your head kicked in over there?'

Courtney shot a look at Jodi, seeking help with her reply. Yet her buddy deflected that appeal and kept her gaze fixed to the floor. Keen on their interactions, Cinq-Mars remained patient, curious to see how they'd muddle through the question.

Hesitant, Courtney protested, 'I wasn't on the French side.'

'Sure you were. I saw you.' Her first instinct, then, was to lie.

'She meant—' Jodi butted in.

'Let her tell me.'

'I meant,' Courtney continued for herself, 'that during the fight I wasn't there, on that side.'

Jodi agreed. 'She wasn't.'

'I only went over there after the guards broke up the fight.'

'That's right,' Jodi said.

'You were in the middle of some pile,' Cinq-Mars reminded her. 'How do you know where Courtney was?'

'That's true,' Jodi admitted.

'How and why did you cross that line?' Cinq-Mars pressed Courtney, as much to see how she'd react to pressure as to hear her reply. 'You were welcomed among your enemies. How come? That seems strange to me. When you came back, your friends also accepted you. Even stranger, those two things together. Nobody said a word to you, it didn't faze anyone.'

Courtney again appealed to Jodi to bail her out.

'Go ahead,' Cinq-Mars invited the second young woman. 'Answer for her just this once. I don't mind. Tell me what Courtney was doing on the wrong side of the battle line.'

'How much do you know already?' Jodi inquired.

'No questions, please. I'm the one looking for answers.'

Reluctantly, Jodi accepted that proviso. She'd been slumping down in her chair and now slithered further. In another half-hour she might be on the floor.

'Court didn't fight. You can see that for yourself. Not a mark on her. If somebody clocked her, she wouldn't be sitting here now, would she? Too small. In a fight she'd be yesterday's lunch.'

'Why's that? Do you think she's delicate? You're not much taller. You're thinner.'

'Yeah, but inside I'm as cold as ice, see. Like cold steel when it's twenty below out.' Courtney giggled away for some reason, or for no reason. 'Makes a difference,' Jodi continued. 'Anyway, after the fight, when it's almost over, the screws got between us, right? Then Marie-Philomène and Abigail came to an agreement. They made a pact and the whole thing was over.'

'The two principal combatants shook hands and formed an alliance? What kind of fairy tale are you spinning for me, Jodi?'

'A surprise when it happened, that's true,' Jodi admitted. 'I get why you say that. But it wasn't no fairy tale.'

'I understand. Tell me about the pact, then. Explain.'

ii

'Finders keepers,' Marie-Philomène taunted Abigail. She blew on her fingertips, flaunting her possession of a contraband nail file.

'Give it back. Now,' Abigail demanded.

'What, Abi, you don't know the law? You? A fucking fraud artist, you're supposed to be the brains around here. Possession is nine-tenths of the law. I am, like you can see here, in *possession* of this motherfucking nail file. *Capeesh* in your English?'

'Who the fuck stole it for you? Anyway, that's Italian.'

'Abigail, get a fucking life. I found it in the dirt. You dropped it? I'm so fucking sorry, but I won't take your word for that, in English or in fucking Italian. Too bad, so sad, and piss the fuck off already. I'm doing my nails. Reminds me, what colors you got for polish?'

Abigail turned away from her antagonist, her position a lost cause. She heard the mocking laughter from a few French women behind her. Jodi saw Abi's mouth crack, the faintest of smiles. That told her everything she needed to know so that she was ready when Abi bent low, then swung around, then charged. Abi plowed straight into Marie-Philomène, her shoulder square into the woman's middle. Instantly, they were rolling on the ground, hands in each other's hair, kicking with their knees. Other women tried peeling them away from each other, a hopeless task, and before they gained much traction those who were not interested in breaking up the fight assailed those who wanted to do so. In her rampant fury, Jodi had two women by the hair and was trying to butt their heads together, a doomed enterprise. They took her down with their elbows and knees. They turned the tables yet had no idea whom they were fighting. Jodi was a dervish of writhing limbs and flashing nails, elbows and knees and eye-poking fingers, and when the opportunity presented itself, down on the ground, a thigh across her face, she bit, wildly and deeply. The scream for mercy thrilled her. She bit down harder. Ten fists walloped her to get her to stop. Someone dragged her off the other woman by her ankles.

She saw blood and the bite mark on her victim.

She liked that.

Rising again, bloodied, scuffed up, she looked around. Abi had Marie-Philomène squirming in the dirt, lifting her head and slamming it back down with rhythmic intensity. A woman from the French side of the conflict who had tried to tackle her was being pummeled by Temple, who had joined the fray, while the next ones to jump on Abigail's back were peeled off by Rozlynn. Roz didn't hit anybody but kept the odds fair whenever one of their group was outnumbered.

The bells were resounding, guards charging in, whistles shrill.

They were swinging batons indiscriminately and a Taser dropped a pair of combatants in a millisecond. Both women, a moment earlier entangled in a wrestling match to the finish, moaned on the ground in mutual dismay and agony. Jodi saw somebody get to her feet, half upright, and charged, stepping on bodies then leaping through the air and slamming into her victim in full tilt, rocketing her back to the ground. She then tried to pull the woman's ears off before a guard intervened. The woman on the ground yelled, 'Fuck fuck fuck,' in English with a French accent, twenty times before becoming aware that no one was on her anymore and that her ears remained securely attached.

Jodi was shoved next to Abigail and her rival. She overheard Abi hiss, 'Find it, dumb fuck, then hide it.'

'Your ass,' Marie-Philomène shot back.

Both women had guards holding them.

'You,' Abi whispered to Courtney, 'go find.' The girl knew what she meant. Abi then directed Marie-Philomène, 'Let her.' Both women understood the significance of a weapon – what could be construed by the guards as a weapon – to be found on the premises. Good for no one. Mean as they were to each other, the screws were both a mutual and a greater menace. Marie-Philomène nodded acceptance of their pact. Before Courtney crossed over the line – having been a cheerleader she was ignored by the guards – Abigail whispered further secret instruction in her ear.

iii

'We expected Court to bring the nail file straight back to Abi, right?' Jodi said. 'Except Abigail's too damn smart. She won't let her do that. She whispered to Court to give it back to Marie-Philomène, put it in her hands instead.'

Courtney nodded. This was true.

'In the moment, it's not like Marie-Philomène could argue. She was caught holding the merchandise, right? Court put it in her hands, and she didn't know it then, but Abi stuck it to her. Does she get extra time in the hold? Hope so. Me telling you the story doesn't get her off, right? Trust me, she deserves it more than anyone. Well, maybe not more than Flo, but pretty damn close, and anyway, Flo's dead.'

'You didn't like Flo?' Cinq-Mars asked.

'Who on this planet did? If she had a buddy on Mars, I dunno. Even the sniffer dog didn't sniff Flo, I bet. Flo was an acid-in-the-face bee-itch.'

Courtney chortled, then caught a glance from Cinq-Mars and suppressed her titters.

The pad with a horizontal spiral binder that Cinq-Mars used for his notes covered a pair of yellow foolscap pads. Sliding them across the table, he passed one to each of the young women.

'Oh goodie,' Jodi exclaimed. 'Maps!'

'Not yet,' he cautioned. 'First, I want the two of you to sit apart. Stay on your side of the table; move your chairs down to opposite ends.'

With some scraping and banging, they did so. Jodi was the real culprit, the noisy one. Courtney, when she did cause her chair just once to scrape the floor, apologized. They sat up straight this time like proper schoolchildren.

'Pens!' Jodi called out.

Cinq-Mars had forgotten. He culled two from his pocket and warned Jodi to return hers.

'What will you do if I steal it? Arrest me?'

A hilarious quip, in Courtney's mind.

'Draw two lines. One that's horizontal across the middle of the page. One that's vertical down the center of the page. You'll end up with four equal quarters.'

The tasks being novel, the women followed instructions with evident care.

'Good. Top left corner, write your name.' They did so. 'Now, at the top of each section, in the middle, I want you to write one word. Upper left section, write "LOVE".'

'Woo-hoo,' Jodi chimed, and wrote the word in cursive. Courtney carved out precise block letters.

'Upper right, "LIKE".' This time the words went on to the pages without commentary. 'Bottom left, "DISLIKE".' The pair glanced at each other at first, both shrugged, then they each wrote the word. 'Bottom right—' Cinq-Mars said.

'Don't tell me,' Jodi interrupted.

'Then you tell me.'

'HATE,' she said.

'Write it down.'

They did.

'Now,' Cinq-Mars decreed, 'think about each person in your dorm. Write each person's name in one of your boxes, depending on whether you love, like, dislike, or hate that person. Ready?'

'Wait!' Jodi called out.

'What's the problem?'

'Who sees this?'

'Only me. It's exclusive. It's why you're at opposite ends of the table. You won't see what your best friend puts down, not even her, nor will anyone else.'

The two looked at each other again, shrugged once more, and proceeded to inscribe their evaluations. They both took time making up their minds.

'Guards, too?' Jodi asked in the middle of her task.

'If you want,' Cinq-Mars said.

Minutes later he took back the pads and examined the results.

He slid each woman's pad back to her.

'Both of you left someone out.'

'No I didn't,' Jodi said.

'I didn't either,' Courtney objected. 'Unless you mean Flo. She's dead.'

'I didn't mean Flo. You can put her in a box, too, if you want.'

'I even put in Dabrezil's name,' Jodi pointed out.

'Me, too!' Courtney trumpeted, and thought it hilarious.

'Quiet,' Cinq-Mars censored them. 'Do not consult with each other. Think about it. Both of you left out a name.'

Jodi ran down her list of names while Courtney did a count on her fingers. They lit upon their error simultaneously. Both had forgotten each other.

They wrote in the missing name, but then went further, writing another name each. When the pads were returned, Cinq-Mars saw that Courtney had added 'My mom', her only entry under LOVE. Jodi had inscribed 'Émile Cinq-Mars' in the DISLIKE box, adding, *That could change, hey?*

While Courtney inscribed her mother in the LOVE category, her best friend Jodi had no one in that box. Both had reduced each other to LIKE. That surprised Cinq-Mars at first, until he realized that any mention of love accrued risk, especially in a same-sex dorm. Courtney gave the identical designation to Jodi as she did to Abigail and, a surprise, Isaure Dabrezil. She 'liked' those three.

The Corrections Officer, relegated to the HATE box by Jodi, was joined there by Marie-Philomène, Doi, Malka, and the deceased Florence. Although Courtney did not achieve the designation of LOVE, she had Jodi's LIKE box to herself. For Jodi, DISLIKE stood as a reasonably high standing, where she placed Temple, Abigail, Rozlynn and, with the qualification for possible change, Émile.

'Thank you,' Cinq-Mars said, and tore off the sheets, folded them, and tucked them into an inner pocket of his sports coat. He passed the pads back. 'Now, the maps. I assume you know how this works. Where you were and when you were there.'

They did know. The maps had been discussed in-house. The two young women busied themselves with their drawings while Cinq-Mars observed them. He devised questions he would ask each woman when he interviewed them alone and not in this two-person setting. Jodi was the first to hand back her maps. They could have been copies of what he'd seen before with the exception of her random heart doodles. For someone who claimed to love no one, she seemed to be a romantic. What Courtney handed in next was a total surprise. None of her illustrations matched what the others had inscribed.

He concealed his reaction, donning an implacable visage.

iv

'Here's a question for the two of you in tandem. I'll ask it again later in private—'

'You're going to see us again, boss?' Jodi inquired.

'I'll be seeing everybody again, as well as anyone I haven't seen yet. For now, I'm asking this one question of both of you at the same time. You're two people but answer as if you're one. Did the two of you, together, kill Florence?'

'What? No!' Jodi was quick on the trigger. Courtney seemed too stunned to form a sentence. Noticing, Jodi tacked on that 'Courtney agrees with me. Totally.'

'Different question,' Cinq-Mars continued. He had wanted to confirm who between the younger women would fear a private session more. He got his answer. 'Did the two of you, together

or with others, have anything to do with Flo's murder in any
capacity whatsoever? Did you conspire? Let Courtney answer this
time.'

'I killed my best friend,' the young woman burst out, but quietly.
'I'm sorry about that. OK? A bad time in my life. I'll never do
nothing like that again. I don't go around killing people. I had
nothing to do with Flo being strangled. My God, that was bad stuff.
I couldn't do that anyway.'

'Stabbing your best friend in the chest over and over again was
pretty bad, too, no? It's on the record that you're capable of doing
that.'

'Shit, now you've done it,' Jodi remarked.

'What's that?' Cinq-Mars inquired.

'She'll be bawling her eyes out half the night. You can't bring
up this stuff with Courtney without like a really huge supply of
Kleenex handy. She gets wound up about it.'

Cinq-Mars checked on Courtney. To him, she seemed on an even
keel, perhaps a little down in the dumps. Nothing more.

'I will bring this stuff up with both of you. One of your housemates is dead. We don't know who did it and if any of you do know
who, so far no one is saying. Expect the question. Courtney, you'll
be hearing it again in private.'

She nodded. She wasn't the emotional wreck Jodi foretold. A
little surprised and reticent, but she seemed stable to Cinq-Mars.
How she'd fare in a more rigorous one-on-one with him might be
another matter.

'What about you, Jodi? What you've done in the past doesn't
bother you? You shoot some innocent guy in a grocery store—'

'It's not like I killed him. I think it was a ricochet. I hit him in
the toe. It's not like I aimed. Anyway, I don't remember what kind
of store it was.'

'That matters?'

'Seems to me. Wish I could remember.'

'You remembered the fight pretty well today. Good details.'

'I wasn't doped up today. Not like back then.'

'That's your excuse? Dope? For being a lousy robber?'

'Trying to get a rise out of me, Detective? What does that do
for you?'

'I'm sure you remember more than you care to admit.'

'I'm thrilled you're so sure. I think it's . . . peachy.'

Courtney laughed.

'It's not that funny,' Cinq-Mars pointed out to her.

Jodi agreed. 'He's right. It's not.'

'Hit my funny bone is all.'

'She's out of whack this girl,' Jodi said. Courtney thought that that was funny, also.

Cinq-Mars gave the guard in the room a glance, and as usual she departed. The two young women grew worried then, and Jodi ceased sliding down in her seat, sitting up straight once more.

'When you talk together, you discuss the murder. Who wouldn't? Only natural. If you didn't kill Flo, who do you think did? No accusations. Just share your speculations with me.'

They looked at each other. They couldn't say they didn't know, because that wasn't the question. Cinq-Mars was betting that Jodi would be the one to wiggle through on this one, and he was right. 'We decided, like, right off the bat, that since we don't know who did it, we shouldn't talk about it because, you know, you can get your head bashed in around here for something like that. I don't know who did it. I'm pretty sure she doesn't, either. Between us, we leave it at that.'

Cinq-Mars nodded with a certain solemnity. 'If you don't talk about it, that could indicate that you're not wondering about it. If you're not wondering who in your group killed someone else in your group, well, that kind of indicates that you already know. Or – that you think you know.'

Jodi considered all that. Courtney only waited for her answer. 'I swear,' Jodi said, 'both of us, we don't know a damn thing.'

The detective nodded again, gave nothing away.

'Do you believe me?' Jodi pressed him.

Cinq-Mars returned a slight smile that mirrored her own. 'I believe everyone, Jodi. Until I don't.' They stared each other down a moment. Raising a finger for emphasis, he asked, 'You tell me. Do you think I believe you?'

Stumped only momentarily, Jodi resurfaced with a reply. 'I'm an honest girl. A regular straight arrow. You're a smart guy. You can see that.'

'I heard you were funny,' Cinq-Mars noted. 'It's true. That's the best laugh I've had in here.'

'Then why aren't you laughing?' Courtney inquired. Her question seemed sincere as though she was genuinely confused.

'I'll explain it to you later,' Jodi promised.

'You should be so lucky,' Cinq-Mars cautioned her. 'You don't have a "later" anytime soon. Last I heard, you're headed for solitary.'

'Oh fuck. I keep forgetting. Sorry, pet. I'll explain it somewhere over the rainbow.'

Cinq-Mars broached a new subject. 'One more thing.'

'We heard that about you,' Jodi piped up. 'You always have one more fucking thing.'

Ignoring that remark, Cinq-Mars asked, 'Aside from battling her gang in the yard, tell me about your relationship with Marie-Philomène.'

'Find out who killed Flo, all right?' Jodi said. 'Then I can go ask whoever that was to waste Marie-P next. I *soooo* hate that bitch.'

Courtney gazed at her but otherwise did not respond.

v

The women talked about being sent *down* to solitary. In reality, the cells were located on the same level they occupied. Yet the chambers *felt* subterranean, as if they were in a cellar below light and sound, removed from the realm of effects and occurrences. An abyss. When conversation was denied, madness spoke up instead. They called it the hole. The few who were outwardly sanguine about solitary were secretly no less terrified than anyone else.

Some could handle it. A few could not. Most survived.

Jodi knew she'd hate it and might come undone. She'd be weak in there. Solitary was an internal nightmare that both attracted her, as a moth to the flame, and repelled her. She wanted to see if she could stand it yet knew that she could not. 'If I come out like a babbling brook,' she told others, making her lips flutter with a forefinger while she moaned, 'throw a few goldfish into me, will ya? Be a pal. Let them swim around.'

Inmates laughed at lines like that. They thought her a hoot.

Down in the hole, even if it wasn't a hole, she'd have no opportunity to make folks laugh. In the hole, life was no joke.

Harder on some than on others. Jodi could intellectually rationalize her situation yet still not bear it. Humans are social creatures; the total absence of others is difficult for most and impossible to tolerate for others. She fitted herself among the latter. Her brittle toughness, her cool social arts, her sarcasm, her edgy rejoinders, all fell away when she was alone. Didn't matter if she was as free as a bird on a mountaintop or down in the hole, she could not stomach being alone. She could not be herself or resemble herself without having others around, as though she did not exist if she had no one to talk to, no one with whom to catch a reflection of herself. She knew herself only when bouncing her personality off others. Whether shooting the breeze or firing a pistol in a mom-and-pop convenience store, making love or smartass remarks, arguing or encouraging, getting ripped or just chilling, she was only up and running when connected to someone else. By herself, she did not know who or what she was or how she could hang on for another minute without screaming.

Some people believed in God. Jodi thought it was because they needed someone to talk to when nobody was around. She figured she was too evil to invite that sort of make-believe companion into her life, no one would arrive, not even a made-up make-believe replica. Anyway, she wouldn't survive with only a monologue or a prayer. She needed a response. A quip, a kiss, a nod, another voice. A fight. A burning bush. Something. Any response. Otherwise, she'd go nuts.

Away from the hole, she could laugh about it.

In the hole, she could not.

For the first twenty minutes after she was thrust inside and the door had slammed behind her, she shut her eyes and breathed through her jumpsuit, using it as a brown bag to keep from hyperventilating. It didn't work. Her lungs cracked open, she felt her spine snap, her eyes popped out of her head, a wonder she was still alive. She only knew that she remained alive because of the pain which zipped through her. Settling down took time and was both a blessing and a curse. She could breathe, she could open her eyes voluntarily and shut them, she could weep, she could sit on the floor and grab her feet and roar. But the aloneness, she feared it so much that she was overtaken quickly and wholly and if one spell relinquished its hold another immediately seized residency.

She was going nuts. Her only hope: she knew what was happening.

The room was narrow. Four feet wide. Six-six long. Six-two high. The toilet built into the floor required a squat to the ankles. It flushed every four hours.

She tried to keep her hands off herself.

Then the door opened, and she had another calamity to confront.

Corrections Officer Isaure Dabrezil was on her in a trice. Seized her by the ankles and lifted her upside down so that her head grazed the floor. The cuffs of her solitary jumpsuit fell below her knees. The guard shook her. She was three times her weight; ten times her muscle mass. Jodi warded off blows to her noggin from the floor with her hands. 'Shaking the bullshit out,' Isaure incanted. 'Shaking the stupid out from you! Shaking the crap from your stupid head! What's in your ass comes out your ears, Jodi! Shaking you! Shaking you, Jodi!'

She flung her down and Jodi landed in a wrecked heap.

At least she had company.

Not the most desirable companion, but they could rant and rail back and forth, which Jodi welcomed.

'What the fuck are you doing?' Jodi objected.

'Watch your language with me! I'm a Christian woman.'

'You swear like a pirate.'

'I'll cut your throat like one, too.'

Jodi suddenly had time to be afraid. She felt her skin crawl, a surge of fear inundate her bloodstream. 'Wait,' she whispered. 'What?'

Isaure grabbed hold of her and turned her on to the floor. She smothered her with her great weight. Jodi struggled to breathe. 'Don't you fuck with me, Jodi,' Isaure whispered in an ear. 'Don't you fuck with me, child.'

'I won't. I'm not!'

'What you given so far? What you given me? Say it out loud.'

'I don't know what you mean.'

'Say it out loud! I want to hear it. What you given me, Jodi? Say it!'

'Nothing, I—'

'Louder. Say it!'

Pinned to the floor, Jodi understood then. She didn't know yet if this attack was sexual or merely violent, but she had an inkling now. She said, 'Nothing. I gave you nothing.'

'Louder, the fuck!' Isaure insisted, her weight like a bulldozer on top of a skinny stick.

'Nothing!' Jodi shouted out. She had no option. She couldn't breathe. 'Nothing!'

Isaure got off her then. She appeared to be satisfied. But she kept one large hand on the other woman's ankle, a threat to upend her again at any moment for any whim that struck her fancy. She clutched that ankle, yet also rubbed the girl's opposite kneecap, gently circling her hand over it. 'What you here for, Jodi? Right here. What you here for?'

'You know.'

'You tell me now.'

'I shot up a corner store.'

'Not that. Not asking about that. What you doing right here, how come you are way out here in Joliette? You don't know? You don't remember? It's not something you want to forget. Do I need to shake you to remind you?'

'You know?'

'What're you here for?'

'You know? You tell me.'

'Why should I tell you what you know for yourself.'

'Could be a trick. I don't know you.'

'I do believe that you are here for Abigail. Am I right or am I never wrong, child?'

Jodi's lower jaw sagged.

'Shut your mouth,' Isaure said. 'What I'm looking at is not a sight to see.'

Jodi did so. Then she said, 'Yeah. Abigail. I'm here about her.'

'What you doing about Abigail 'til now?'

'Gaining ground. We're closer. I got stuff going on.'

'Stuff? You're picking fights in the schoolyard like you're an eight-year-old kid. What's the matter with you?'

'No, see, I was defending Abigail. Right? Right? That gets me closer. You can see that.'

'Were you?'

'I was. I wasn't out there for a fucking picnic. I don't enjoy getting my head kicked in.'

'You did a lot of the kicking yourself, what I saw.'

'Yeah, I did, didn't I? You see? Don't you see? Gets me closer. What counts is the long-term gain. I'm working on that. I'm getting there. I'm closer. I know I am. Is Abi in solitary, too?'

'Walked in like nobody's business, like she was booking into the Ritz.'

'Help me out here, Isaure, please.'

'Nothing I can do for you, Jodi.'

'You can stay. Keep me company in here.'

'They call it solitary. A reason for that.'

'I can't— It's not for me. I can't take it. Stay.'

'That I cannot do.'

'Visit a lot.'

'Oh white girl, I can't do that neither.'

'Help me out here, Isaure. I'll lose it. I'll fucking lose it. I know I will.'

Isaure sighed, and finally took her hand away from Jodi's ankle. She pushed herself up to her feet which took a major effort. 'Tell you what. Let's see what I got here.'

She went through her pockets. She found a small tin container for aspirin. She emptied the few remaining pills into her shirt pocket and handed Jodi the empty little box.

'What the hell is this?' Jodi asked.

'Wait for it.' Isaure went through her pockets again and found a ballpoint pen. She removed the refill and handed Jodi the empty pen.

'What's this?' Jodi asked.

'Tap the pen on the tin.'

Jodi did so.

'Makes noise, right?'

Jodi agreed, nodding.

'Now make music. Find a rhythm. Find a beat. Make music. Dance to your music. You can get through this. You're feeling blue. The lights are on now. You'll be in the dark, too. Tap the pen against the tin. Let the music talk to you. You won't be alone if you're beating on a drum. You'll get through it that way.'

Isaure didn't stand on ceremony. She departed without another word and the door slammed hard shut. Jodi heard the lock wrench into place. She was locked inside – alone – again.

She felt her inner panic raging on.

She listened to that terrifying stillness. No voice spoke back.

She tapped the empty pen against the wee tin box.

She made sound. She tapped and tapped. She found rhythms.

She made sound her trusted companion.

After a while, deep inside her head, she danced.

Lagarde

B ikers in gangs can look a mess, but not their bikes. Pipes shine and tires gleam. Riders won't drive a mile without reaching for a microfiber cloth to polish their hog again. If she fails to sparkle in the sunlight a pressure washer or an air hose is hauled out to correct the blemish. The Harley parked directly in front of Cinq-Mars's motel room door was the exception proving the rule. Its dustiness indicated that it hadn't moved all day with no one handy to give it a loving buff. A brief shower spotted the fuel tank and smeared the road dust on the saddlebags. A light greenish pollen suffused the chrome surfaces.

In biker-world, a disgrace.

Taking his ease on the porch as a few hours passed gently under the lens of his whisky glass, making a few calls on the motel's porch thanks to a long extension cord, Cinq-Mars was adroitly positioned to observe the biker's return. The leader arrived in a taxi without his gang colors. Not quite a suit upon his frame as the jacket and trousers didn't match, nonetheless he was duded up. Burgundy sports coat. Pressed charcoal pants. Polished winged-tip brown Oxfords. An honest to God white shirt. He had drawn the line at a tie, but still, the man turned out as sharp as a mannequin.

Even so, he clunked his way up the steps.

Passed in front of the visiting Montreal detective.

'On your own?' the policeman inquired. One bike only remained in the parking lot.

'I know what you think.'

'Do you?'

'Up to no good, the others, that's what you think,' the biker said.

'Curious is all.' As he spoke, Cinq-Mars realized that he could no longer qualify himself as sober.

'More like suspicious,' the biker declared. 'Stupid way to live.

My friends left. I stayed put. I had work to do. Makes you no safer, if that's what's gnawing on your pecker.'

He was slow to comprehend, an effect of the whisky. 'How do you mean?'

'Don't flatter yourself, Cinq-Mars. We got no interest in you. You're under no threat. But you never know. Things change. So you're no safer, neither.'

'Same here. You're under no threat from me,' Cinq-Mars assured him.

'How come? You wake up in the morning with a job to do. Put the bad guys away. That's me, no?'

'Way beyond my jurisdiction. I have no cause to pinch you.'

'Sounds about right. But whatever you doing here, isn't that outside your jurisdiction?' the biker inquired. He was softening. 'This ain't no place to be hanging out just for the hell of it. Nobody takes a vacation in this town.'

'Same as you in one respect.'

'How's that?'

'Visiting folks in the Joliette Institution for Women.'

The biker gave him a long look, for while he knew that Cinq-Mars had been visiting the jailhouse, it had not occurred to him that his own comings and goings were under scrutiny. He shifted his gaze to the roadway and a moderate bustle of traffic there. The view was not much of an entertainment, yet provided a destination for his gaze as he sorted through his own reactions. He turned back to Cinq-Mars. 'I'll buy the next bottle if you're in a mood to share the one you got.'

'Take a seat,' Cinq-Mars invited.

'What the women say' – he issued a whoop of a belly laugh – 'let me go freshen up first. For me that means taking a long leak.'

'Come by when you're ready. I'll find an extra glass.'

Early in his career, Cinq-Mars had been advised to make connections. As his mentor had stipulated, he was a loner, yet in his profession he could not go it alone. By connections, his mentor meant people of every stripe, including the nefarious. Paul Lagarde, who was suited up today, was a mid-level criminal biker, perhaps with greater ambitions, who worked outside Montreal. They'd have no occasion to run into each other in the normal discharge of their opposing duties. That being true, the day might come when he could be useful. Who could tell what an unforeseeable future might bring?

Nothing to lose. Had the man not offered to purchase the next bottle?

ii

Paul Lagarde reemerged freshened in biker leather, chains, and his usual bling. The Iron Cross that dangled from an earlobe had not been present ten minutes earlier. He accepted a glass of Laphroaig from Cinq-Mars and took it down a few steps to his Harley. From his saddlebag he pulled out a rag and a plastic bottle of Quick Detailer. Spritzed his machine and rubbed her down with ardent enthusiasm, returning his beast to its primal glow. As he labored, the two chewed the fat on their upbringings as farm boys, each curious about how two men from the countryside diverged in opposite directions upon entering a wider, wilder world.

One man stayed righteous, the other chewed on the hard tack of corruption. Which he found tasty. Both were content with their lot in life.

Lagarde put his stuff away and joined Cinq-Mars on the porch. Cop and biker, side-by-side in the shank of the evening, imbibing.

'Cops I know been crooked the day they got hatched.'

'I hope you don't know many like that,' Cinq-Mars responded.

'As many as you, my guess.'

'The wrong ones, then.'

'Your take, not mine.'

'Grant you that.'

Both grinned.

'Consider though,' Cinq-Mars asked him to ponder, 'that a crooked cop can be useful to your needs today, but who knows what's on the news tomorrow? The time comes when the only hope you got left is a righteous cop.'

'Hard to think that.'

Cinq-Mars sipped, then said, 'I've seen it. Crooked cops get sorted out. Either by your guys or by ours, in-house. You live on a one-way street, Paul. Don't get me wrong. I'm not preaching. Just asking. How many bad guys die in old age without losing time inside? Try none. It seems like a good street for a while, yours.

Affluent. Can't argue with you there. Your spare change will outdo my life-long pension. You won't even miss the wad you blow in Vegas. For all that, for what you know and who you know, the card you play can kill you. Hard times require hard measures.'

'Too long a fall for me. I'm righteous in my own house.'

Cinq-Mars rubbed his chin. 'Says to me you lack the imagination to see what's coming.'

'Possible. But I don't see a righteous cop offering me a street I'd walk on. The desperation comes around and goes around, but it don't mean much. I don't feel that way much anyhow.'

'Desperate, you mean.'

'Like that, yeah.'

'Never said it was likely. A last resort if your tank runs dry.'

'I'm no snitch, Cinq-Mars. Only in your dreams, the wet ones.'

'I wasn't asking, Paul. That would be disrespectful.'

They sipped in a convivial fashion. Cinq-Mars had downed several glasses and had lost count.

'I've seen the other,' Lagarde said. 'The good cop who turns bad enough.'

'Seen that, too,' Cinq-Mars agreed. 'But a sad day. How is it a good thing if you take the wind of hope out of the weather?'

'Fancy words. Are you a poet or just drunk?'

'We can always use a sea breeze,' Cinq-Mars replied. Definitely tipsy. Lagarde saw that.

'One man's losing his hope can be another guy's opportunity up in the air.'

'I thought I was the philosopher,' Cinq-Mars said. 'Must be this porch. Or the whisky. Shall we drink to that?'

'To what?'

'Philosophy,' Cinq-Mars suggested.

'Philosophical horseshit!' Lagarde toasted, raising his glass.

They clinked and drank to that.

iii

'What's your end?' Lagarde asked him. 'You warned me off Abigail. For no good reason, I say that. What's your take?'

'What's yours?'

'Didn't I ask first? Some rights in that.'

'I'm the investigator. I got rights, too.'

'We're only drinking whisky. Seemed personal to you, that's all I'm saying.'

Cinq-Mars tapped his own nose with his thumb a moment. 'You knew what I was talking about without my explanation.'

'What's your end, I'm asking? It's not something I can go look up.'

Cinq-Mars thought about it. He had to keep Lagarde aware that his threat to protect Abigail within or even outside the restraints of the law still held, notwithstanding the diversion of their evening. If the man couldn't differentiate sincere threats from idle ones, that would work in his favor. Keep an adversary confused, and never let him think you'll be hampered by the law. Basic alternative police procedure. Force the bad guys to resort to lawyers; better that way for everyone's security.

'My interest is in her protection. I don't consider what she did to be worth a death sentence, I don't care who the victims were. Besides, maybe it's personal. I arrested her.'

'No shit?'

'That was me. And I compiled the evidence against her. She got more prison time than she deserved. Her punishment should end there. If she dies, I won't tolerate it. And you, you're another one after her money?'

'You're right. I have no shame. It's always about the money, Cinq-Mars. Anyway, it's crooked money. We got a right.'

'Sorry? How's that? Money from a trust company?' Cinq-Mars knew better but did not want to reveal the depth of his understanding. Sometimes it helped to play the naive.

'Who made the deposits?'

'Not something I'm aware of.'

'So you say.' Lagarde checked the other man's look. 'Really? You don't know? Good. Tells me we looked after our end. No fuckups. Until Abigail goes and sticks her fingers in the pie.'

'Some pie.'

'Say that. You heard about the hits on LeClair and Fournier, while back?' Bikers both, although no one could guess it from their choice of apparel. Suits and ties, quality cloth. Italian leather for their shoes. They never spent time on Harleys, too difficult to pull themselves away from their ledgers and adding machines. 'Both hits on account of Abigail. She should not feel safe on this planet earth. No matter your threats. I'm not speaking for myself. I'm only the messenger. You might want to watch out for your own threats though. Say it to the wrong guy next time, you can be like LeClair, like Fournier. Respected, but in the dirt. If somebody was willing to do in those guys, then somebody is ready to do in anybody, even an Émile Cinq-Mars.'

'Point taken. Begs the question though.'

'What's that?'

'If Abigail is under so much threat, why is the inmate who is dead not her, but Florence? Did you know Florence, Paul?'

'Not personally. She had a rep. Do you know who did it?'

'Do you?' Cinq-Mars pressed him in return.

'If I did, I wouldn't tell you. No point asking is there?'

'Did you order the hit on Flo yourself?'

'Whoa. No need for that. We're having a friendly few drinks here. I'm not answering to shit like that.'

Cinq-Mars nodded in appreciation of the biker's point-of-view. 'Felons and that, killers, let's say, never rush to confess. I've noticed that in my life. Just letting you know that my brain is on a merry-go-round and somebody in my vicinity is guilty. Somebody has to be. For now, everybody I meet, even the old guy who made my French fries last night, is a suspect.'

'Speaking of – what do you think?'

'About what?' Cinq-Mars asked.

'Fries, man. Poutine. I could kill a half-dozen dogs, too.'

'You bad guys. You always want to tempt us normal folks.'

'You game?'

'Yeah,' Cinq-Mars decided. 'Why not? Another night of fries and dogs. Then I'll have to get back for a phone call.'

'We'll take my Harley. I don't have an extra helmet but you're a cop. You can shake the fine if we get caught.'

'I'll pay the fine. But I will also wear the helmet. You can be windblown for once.'

'Just don't fucking arrest me, Cinq-Mars.'

'Not this once.'

iv

The sun had long set by the time Cinq-Mars telephoned the new lady in his life. Although he was lucid, she caught on pretty quickly that that glass of lucidity was augmented by a decanter's worth of inebriation.

He explained. 'I got home. Felt weary. The room, too oppressive for a nap. I took a bottle of whisky out to the porch. Forgot myself. Mistook the whisky for soda. A couple of glasses went down way too quickly. Drinking slowly after that didn't much help. Then this biker came by—'

'Biker.'

'Yeah. Hells Angels affiliate. Rap sheet maybe not as long as your arm but wrist to elbow, let's say, and we had a couple of drinks—'

Sandra Lowndes was heard to be enjoying herself at any rate.

'What's so funny?' Cinq-Mars inquired. He was not put out, but happy to pretend he was. Her laughter delighted him.

'Nothing. Go on. You and the biker got drunk, you were saying?'

'Not really. We went out for hot dogs and poutine.'

'What's poutine?' The popularity of the dish had only recently taken hold across the Province of Quebec. Its fame had not spread to other lands as yet.

'Cheese curds and gravy on French fries.'

'Oh my God. What? You eat that?'

'You remember your meal afterwards, let me tell you. Washed that down with a couple of beers.'

'I hope you weren't driving, Émile.'

'I was on the back seat of a Harley.'

In this conversation he was not conforming to the man she'd been talking to lately. She'd admitted an interest to herself, although any number of red flags had to be considered. Catholic, and practicing – *where was that at?* – a police detective of all things, older by far, French – *good grief* – from Canada, specifically the French Province of Quebec. His gargantuan nose she'd leave for others to mock. But she'd had to acknowledge a plus side, as well. She knew horses and she knew people who knew horses, and yet he was as knowledgeable as anyone. He had a better eye for foals than she did, and her eye was excellent. He was humble but damn smart. Gawd. And again, looking past the nose, he was good-looking in an aristocratic sort of way. Way tall. Superior build. Maybe softening up a bit. Ox-strong, she'd noticed it around the horses, although he handled them with an adroit tenderness she admired. Off the cuff, not her type, yet strangely and undeniably appealing. Anyway, whatever her *type* might be, no one in that indeterminate bracket had swept her off her feet in the last decade.

Unless this one had.

She admitted she felt herself lift above the floorboards on occasion when they talked. Damn he was smart. You ask a man to enumerate his hobbies and he comes back with quantum physics. Whoosh.

Even a few so-called negative aspects – French, religious, living in another country – created a dash of exotic appeal. She had not thought it likely in the beginning, but had begun to discern a possibility.

Still. She was thirty-one. He was fifty. Cripes.

'How's the work going?' Sandra asked. That was another thing. Unlike accountants and lawyers, farmers, engineers and contractors, among other suitors she'd known over time, his job was an ever-changing topic of conversation.

'In circles,' Cinq-Mars replied. 'The women had a brawl. A big one. If I call it a cat-fight, think lions, tigers, leopards. A few of my suspects have been tossed into solitary confinement.'

Who arrived home from work with stories like that? Who?

'Wow,' she said.

'As for how it's going, I'm getting nowhere. Speaking of nowhere . . .' He took a deliberate pause. Then explained, 'I don't want you to think I'm drunk.'

'But you are.' That was another thing. For all his upright bearing, his moral and religious fortitude, he seemed willing to enjoy himself when the time was right. He wasn't *only* a stick in the mud, although he was that, too.

'Ahh . . . What I mean is . . .' Another pregnant pause.

'What do you mean, Émile?'

She was both teasing him and goading him on.

'I might be in my cups but it's not the drunk in me who's doing the talking. I mean what I'm about to say. The drunk part, maybe that helps me say it, that's all.'

Intrigued. 'I'm listening.'

'I'm stuck in this godforsaken town eating hot dogs and poutine

with a criminal biker when I'm not drinking whisky, but mostly I'm drinking whisky.'

'I feel for you. To the Catholic in you, it must feel like purgatory.'

'Join me.'

Momentarily, dead air was returned. Then: 'What? Oh, I like that, Émile. What girl has ever had a finer invitation?' She switched to a deep, mock-male voice. "Hey, lady! I'm hanging out in a lower rung of hell. Come join me." Who could refuse an invite like that?'

He was breathing a bit easier thanks to her reaction. 'I was hoping maybe you couldn't. Look, I'm living in a crappy motel without air conditioning. It's uninhabitable during the day when it's hot out. But there's a hotel in the center of town that looks half-decent. You could stay there. In town, you can find things to do during the day. Maybe. Not promising. Then at night we can have dinner, get to know each other better. Your folks can look after the horses for a bit, right?'

'My mom can, yeah. So, you stay in the crappy motel while I'm squirreled away in something that's half-decent, like an unwanted mistress in a rundown flophouse? This gets better by the minute.'

'If you put it that way,' he said.

'That's how I put it.'

'It does sound tawdry.'

A pregnant pause from both of them this time.

Cinq-Mars felt that she was waiting for him to improve his offer. Or rescind it.

'I suppose, if you were to come all this way . . .'

'I'd drive. If I went there. It's a long drive. A full day on the road.'

Somewhat encouraging. 'Right. It maybe would make more sense, you know, to just bite the bullet, and say, how about it, would you like to stay with me for a few days? See how that goes?'

'In your crappy motel.' More teasing. More goading him on.

'I could take a room in the hotel downtown. The half-decent one.'

This time the pause felt more serious, to both of them. A line to cross.

'You won't change your mind when you're sober?' she asked. He supposed that that was her way of saying yes.

'Oh God,' Cinq-Mars said.

'What?'

'The biker's banging on my door.'

She ignored that faraway intrusion. 'This hotel, is it right in the center of town?'

'Exactly right there. Restaurant on the main floor.'

'I'll find it. *Joliette*. Almost like Romeo and *Juliet*. Émile, this is almost your lucky day.'

'Almost?'

'Book two rooms. Same hotel, though. I'll see you tomorrow.'

'Two rooms.' One part joy to one part frustration.

'Good night, Émile. Say hello to your biker.'

'Good night, San.'

The man at the door was not a biker. An officer from the SQ, the provincial police, had arrived to pick him up.

'What's going on?'

'The Joliette Institution asked me to escort you to the scene of a crime. Do you know Corrections Officer Isaure Dabrezil?'

'I've been working with her, yes.'

'She was murdered this evening, sir.'

'What? How? At the prison?'

'No, sir. In her home.'

'Take me there. I'll be right behind you.'

'No, sir. I can't let you drive in your condition. I'll drive you.'

Cinq-Mars stared at him a few moments as though trying to comprehend what he could possibly mean. Inebriated, in love, in shock at the news that Isaure was dead, that Sandra was arriving tomorrow, a mix of emotions had him swirling. His brain, he was thinking to himself, being out of sync with himself, emulated the planet's wobble on its axis, and why was he thinking that?

'I'll ride shotgun,' he conceded.

PART TWO

Paquet

' 've had a few but I can still walk a straight line. Won't wobble much.'

Émile Cinq-Mars silently rehearsed the comment to himself to preempt any colleague's potential concerns. He had a buzz on, although not a pleasant one. He did not feel well.

The constable from the SQ was driving him.

'How bad, tell me, how bad do I look?' he asked the junior cop. 'Be honest.'

'You kinda get by, sir. Just don't talk too loud. Don't drive. Don't sing, you know? Try to sit still.'

Excellent advice. He made a note to himself to take down the officer's name. He might want to know him someday, when sober.

'Gum in the glove box,' the younger man let him know.

Cinq-Mars helped himself to a stick of Juicy Fruit.

'It's not what you think,' the SQ cop thought to tack on.

'I have no opinion on the subject. Lots of reasons to keep gum in your glove box.'

'Number one, my partner's bad breath.'

'Works for me,' Cinq-Mars quipped.

'I'm serious.'

'So am I.' He could get along with this guy if ever they worked together. Which he supposed they were doing right now. 'I won't bother to tell you I'm not usually this far gone. But I'm not. Not usually. This intox—' he burped '—icated. Sorry, what's your name again?'

'Dubroc, sir.'

'Émile,' Cinq-Mars stated, either a deliberate choice to be familiar or the whisky was working his tongue.

'Yann,' the cop responded in kind.

'Well, Constable Yann Dubroc, what the hell is going on? Why has a prison guard been murdered? What's up with that? The timing,

I got to tell you, is inconvenient. Although I guess someone might argue that it's not the dead woman's fault.'

'I know exactly zippo about it, sir. Will it be up to you to find out?'

'Can't say. Don't know. Jurisdiction – that'll be a bloody mess.'

'How so?'

'Figure it out. The SQ loses one of their own, what happens? Your guys insist on full control. Can't blame your side for that.'

'One of our own?'

'You haven't heard? The guard, a fly-in. In her regular job she's SQ. I'm already looking into things, so I have a stake. The Mounties will say she's a guard in a federal lock-up – the pen will make the same claim – therefore it's *their* case. Municipal police in Joliette will want a kick at the can, too, but they'll get the boot. They don't have a prayer. Like I said. Messy.'

'Maybe we can all work together. Cooperate.'

'Ah, excuse me? Were you born a month ago? You look older to me.'

The officer possessed sufficient whimsy to laugh at himself. He wasn't *that* naive.

They turned into a community of small cottages surrounded by manicured lawns and tidy gardens. Out-of-the-way Quebec towns, Cinq-Mars had noticed, occasionally went overboard in their zeal to imitate suburbia. Two more turns down side streets landed them on a crescent inundated with police vehicles, cherries flashing, and a burgeoning horde of neighbors and curiosity seekers. Five-year-olds who ought to have been in bed hours ago, and perhaps were, raced around. So many older folks were out with walkers, canes and wheelchairs that Cinq-Mars presumed the existence of an old age home in the vicinity. The elderly were ducking out at night to absorb a glimmer of excitement. He'd have to be careful making his way through the crowd not to knock anyone off their pins. That would be easily done, given that his own balance was imprecise.

Cinq-Mars tested himself along the edge of the cement walkway up to the house. Not too bad. Not quite a straight line. He passed muster, although he'd still flunk a breathalyzer.

The cottage was both small and sparsely furnished. Isaure Dabrezil had rented, he guessed, given the temporary status of her job description. She had furniture better suited to fit an even smaller

apartment, which was probably what she'd left behind in her
previous posting.

The large woman lay on the living room floor. Her final minutes
had not all taken place there. To Cinq-Mars's eye, she'd been
engaged in a battle which had gone from the kitchen by an open
back door, through the dining area and into the living room. A table
was bumped aside. A couple of chairs upended and plates smashed.
Knick-knacks were scattered across the floors. A sofa chair, on its
side, spilled cushions. Gripped in the victim's hand, a fireplace
poker had been seized as a desperate measure, a valiant failed
attempt at self-defense. Blood across all three rooms. Most of it on
the carpet where she died. She'd bled out from several wounds, any
one of which may have been fatal. Knife wounds, obviously, or
from another sharp object. She'd fought, the mess caused by the
fury of her response. A loud, raucous fight. Knowing how robust
and muscular a woman she had been, she'd been met by an over-
powering counterforce. Cinq-Mars computed a minimum of two
attackers against her. Men, he presumed, but no matter the gender
they were probably huge themselves and strong to have taken her
on and survived.

He suspected her attackers had absorbed a few blows from her.
Injuries that might show.

He paused a moment over the body, not as a policeman on duty,
but as a fellow traveler, wishing this one a bon voyage to her next
destination.

An abbreviated silence. 'Sergeant-Detective Cinq-Mars.' His
name spoken kindly. He turned to face the warden for the Joliette
Institution for Women, Agatha Paquet. The severity of her dress and
grooming – hair pulled tight to her head and snapped into a bun
– and her authoritative demeanor were contradicted by an inherent
gentleness to her gaze. Her grey eyes, if not her comportment, were
naturally expressive. 'Thanks for coming.'

'I've had a few—' he started to say, then stopped himself.

'Are you all right, Sergeant-Detective?'

'I'm fine. Bear with me if it seems otherwise. This is one helluva
thing, Warden. Sorry for your loss.'

'It's barbaric. I thought you should be here – in case it reflects
on your current investigation.'

'To be determined, of course.'

'Of course.'

An SQ detective, not knowing him, probably mistaking him for a forensics technician or a morgue attendant, physically bumped him aside on his way back to the body. A solid shoulder thump. Cinq-Mars considered breaking his arm but now did not seem the right time and he considered that it might be the whisky egging him on. Instead, he exercised his position there by introducing his SQ driver, Constable Yann Dubroc, standing beside him in uniform, to the warden. That got the SQ detective's attention; the man gathered that he'd been obtuse. He still didn't know who Cinq-Mars could be, but he was not whom he assumed. He'd be careful next time, perhaps ask permission to play through. Cinq-Mars let him stew about that as he had more pressing concerns.

'Warden, does this connect directly to Flo's murder, do you think? Any reason to believe they're related?'

'It's your investigation, Sergeant-Detective. You tell me. A guard spent five days a week among eight inmates. Nine women in total, now two are dead.' She made a slight gesture to lead him away from the SQ detectives and forensic technicians. Alongside a window blocked off by ceiling-to-floor curtains, she resorted to a husky confidential whisper. 'Émile, I want us to understand each other. It's time for that.'

'Let's.'

'One inmate, now one guard, dead. This is on my watch.'

'It is.'

'I don't have an investigative arm to figure out what the hell's going on.'

'You'd like me to be your arm?'

'I'm left in the dark, otherwise. I don't want that. You've been working on the inside. A head-start over anyone else who's here now. My sense is, until we find out differently, this runs from the inside out. SQ officers will work it from the outside in. They'll consult with me not at all, and if I'm right, that will get them absolutely nowhere. Then what? No resolution. Worst case, another death?'

'On your watch.'

'Yes, on my watch. I won't apologize for caring about the institution on my watch.'

'Sorry. *I* will apologize. I've had a few.'

'Excuse me?'

'I can still walk a line. Don't worry about that.'

'Cinq-Mars, what are you talking about?'

He put a hand up, more to stop himself than her question.

'Pull yourself together,' she advised him, whispering still. 'Nobody says you have to be sober off the job. But if you're a drunk, keep it to your fucking self, all right? Shape up. You're my only option.'

'Not *a* drunk,' he protested quietly. 'Just, you know, at the moment, a little. Tipsy. Listen, if you can use your influence—'

'I have virtually none with respect to these assholes.'

He liked this woman. She understood the lay of the land. 'I might not say this if I was sober.'

'Go ahead. Say.' She was growing impatient with him.

'Finagle. Deceive. Generate a few white lies. Impress upon the SQ that you need to be appraised of every aspect of their investigation—'

'They won't go in for that.'

'Doesn't matter. If you trick them into believing that you will insist on the Mounties taking over the case, and convince them that the Mounties will do so, they will cooperate. With you. A little.'

'After that, you want what they say to me turned over to you.'

'Aren't we working together? I know the SQ. They'll hold stuff back. They might pass along material they assume is irrelevant when it's not. They'll miss things. Screw stuff up. I've learned to count on it.'

'You won't miss things?'

'Let's be fair, being on the inside gives me an advantage.' He seemed to drift for a moment, then come back. 'Trouble is, I need to know about developments on the outside, too.'

Warden Paquet's eyes slid across at that moment to Officer Dubroc, who drove him there, then back again.

'Yes. He represents access,' Cinq-Mars admitted. 'I'll take care of it.'

'And I'll take care of my part,' she promised.

ii

'Who're you?'

The question was inevitable. At least the right man was asking: the Investigating Officer for the SQ on this case.

'Montreal Police Service. Sergeant-Detective Émile Cinq-Mars. How do you do?'

'Montreal?'

'Also, your liaison with the penitentiary, authorized by the warden. I'm conducting a related investigation on the inside.'

'Related how?' The SQ detective was a swarthy, hirsute man, on the plump side although that may have been an effect of his genetic code. He looked fit despite the weight. A big boned, brawny man. Scruff beard. Neck hair poking from his shirt collar where he'd loosened his tie. His bushy eyebrows had been granted permission to grow wild.

'Your victim was a murder suspect. One of many. But one of.'

'Hate to break it to you, Montreal. That's absurd.'

'Why? Because she's one of yours? I know that,' Cinq-Mars told him, which caught the other man off-guard, forcing him to re-appraise the outsider who stood before him. 'Here's the deal.'

'We have no deal.'

'Give it a minute. We will. If you copy me your dailies—'

'In your dreams, Montreal.'

'—in exchange, I'll give back whatever I learn on the inside. Tit-for-tat.'

'How about you keep me informed. Every scrap. Our dailies, I keep to myself.'

Cinq-Mars anticipated he'd offer along those lines. 'The horse-backs will want to take this over,' Cinq-Mars mentioned.

'You're too late. We've cleared it with the Mounties. They agreed to stand down.' Having an SQ officer as a victim was different than having one as a suspect. The Mounties were willing to let the provincial police hold sway.

'No, sir. Due respect. You cleared it with a staff sergeant some-where, or a sleepy lieutenant who couldn't be bothered. I'll be informing the Deputy Commissioner of the situation here, as it stands. He will talk to your Head. Who will then have your balls pressed in a vise while you take a flying fuck off a trapeze. Which has got to be thrilling. At least, I imagine so.' Sometimes he needed to talk in the lingo of other cops to get a point across. He could play that card. 'The staff sergeant or the sleepy lieu will deny ever taking your call. His ass on the same trapeze otherwise. Check me out, Detective. Find the weight on my hip.'

The cop who had bumped hard into him earlier was listening to the talk intently, leaning in as though trying to grasp the intricacies of a chess match. The IO had not made his next move.

'One more thing,' Cinq-Mars added. 'Your sidekick owes me one hell of a motherfucking apology.' He immediately regretted saying that last remark. The whisky kept his tongue too loose.

'Fuck that shit,' the more junior detective declared. Also built solidly, he was the lightest and shortest of the three.

'That doesn't sound like an apology to me,' Cinq-Mars said, not looking at him but at his superior. 'Sound like it to you?'

'What's he apologizing for?' the senior SQ officer asked.

'Slamming into me.'

'It's a small room. Crowded,' the offending cop maintained.

'Next time, go around. This time, apologize.'

The three stood still in stalemate.

'Clock ticking,' Cinq-Mars told them.

'You've been drinking,' the IO noted.

'On my own time. Punched out six hours ago.'

The IO chewed his lower lip a moment, then asked, 'How does this work?'

'We find a way. Let's say that the driver you sent over—'

'Dubroc?'

'Is that his name? Let's say he gives me an hour every couple of days to meet up. Sometimes downtown Joliette. Other times, the prison. I meet him at the gate. We exchange relevant news. What I get, I give back the same. You hold back, I follow your example. You know how it goes.'

The IO was nodding, as if they were coming to an agreement, but still delaying. 'Tell you what. I'll call your bluff, Cinq-Mars.'

'Who's bluffing?'

Turning to his associate, the IO directed him to 'Call Borde. He knows Montreal cops. Ask about this guy. Let me know what he says. You don't mind hanging on for a bit, Cinq-Mars?'

'No problem.' Before the junior detective dashed away, he added, 'Say hi to Gabriel for me.'

The man stopped in his tracks. 'What?'

Cinq-Mars addressed both men. 'You're calling Gabriel Borde? Say hello. One of my closest pals.'

He wanted to qualify his last remark, to tack on *in the SQ*, but didn't. He figured that that quick self-correction indicated he was sobering up in a hurry.

The IO surrendered then, raising a hand to keep his junior in place. 'All right, Montreal. We'll see how this goes.'

'Plus my apology.'

Both men looked at the guilty younger officer. 'Fuck sake, I bumped into the guy. Fine. Sorry. What the hell. A little bump.'

'Good enough?' the IO inquired.

'Adequate,' Cinq-Mars confirmed.

iii

Outside, he arrived at a different conclusion regarding his state of inebriation. No question that he'd been drinking too much, but he had also been eating poorly. The combination had disrupted his inner gyroscope, not strictly instigated by the Laphroaig. He reached that conclusion while stumbling on the walkway from the house when he tried, and failed, to tightrope along its edge. As he righted himself before hitting the ground, his stomach lurched. That wave train of hot dogs, poutine and whisky sashayed through him and was identified as the real culprit in pulling him off-kilter.

'You OK?' Officer Yann Dubroc inquired as he sorted himself out.

'Never better.' A feather might not knock him over, but an old-timer with a walker probably could. Those guys were around, too. He had to watch himself.

The crowds had not diminished, augmented now by broadcast news trucks and the general citizenry. A morgue van precipitated a few parents to gather up their teenagers and beat it home, but they were quickly replaced as word traveled around town even at this late night hour and over the airwaves. Cinq-Mars led Dubroc to a quiet patch. The younger man had no clue he was being led anywhere until the older one stopped short.

Dubroc noticed then their abrupt isolation. He figured out quickly that they were about to converse in private.

'We could talk in the car,' Dubroc pointed out.

'Not ready to leave. I might want to replace you before I go.'

'Replace?'

Cinq-Mars shrugged. 'Depends. Say what's on your mind, Yann. Get it off your chest.'

Cinq-Mars laughed a little at his own fumbled directions. The idea of what was on someone's mind also being on his chest amused him in his current state. Still mildly tipsy.

'What am I supposed to do?' the officer inquired.

'Good question. What you do is entirely up to you.'

'Oh yeah? I don't follow.'

'You and me will talk. Regular basis. Your bosses will not co-operate. That's a given. It's in their DNA. The SQ will pass along as little as they can, pretend to make an effort. I will pass along to your bosses what I think might help them. Still, if I think the SQ will screw up my information, I won't.'

'So really, there's no difference between you. No cooperation.'

'You're the difference. You come between the SQ and me. You will make decisions. If you hear something that you think I should know but your bosses don't want me to hear, you decide to tell me or not. Works the other way, as well. Everything is up to you, Yann. If you have information that serves the cause of justice, but maybe not your superior's territorial gravity, it's your decision to pass it on or not. Good luck with that. Not saying it's easy.'

Dubroc mulled everything over, which required a prolonged scratch to the back of his neck. 'You don't know me,' he said.

'I make snap judgments about people all the time. Most work out. Some don't. For instance, I have recently decided on the woman I want to marry and I scarcely know her any more than I know you. Let's hope it works out. That's a bigger concern for me right now than you are.'

Dubroc was confounded again, until he realized that Cinq-Mars was either sharing a confidence or still drunk. He decided it was the former. 'Good luck with that.'

'Thanks.'

Their solitude next to a brambly bush attracted the attention of onlookers wondering who they might be and what they might be discussing. Warden Agatha Paquet also noticed them and strolled over. Blue and red flashing lights from patrol cars on the street rhythmically illuminated and alternated the color on their faces.

'Warden,' Cinq-Mars greeted her. Dubroc took a step back, a movement that the Montreal detective forestalled by raising a hand.

The SQ officer hung on the periphery of the talk after that, listening in. The warden noticed that Cinq-Mars was admitting him to their chat.

'Something you should know,' Paquet said. 'When you came here, you knew that Isaure Dabrezil was SQ, did you not? That's why Montreal police were asked to be involved.'

'Right. I knew that.'

'You were told a bogus tale.'

He returned his imperious gaze. People usually hated it and he could tell that the warden did, too. He said, 'She was marked up for insubordination, that's what she told me. She alluded to the SQ being embarrassed if the reason for her suspension got out.'

'Straight out-of-the-box bullshit.'

Cinq-Mars and Dubroc exchanged a quick glance and waited. Cinq-Mars dropped his contrary attitude.

The warden said, 'Those are the official stories, that's true, disguised as secrets. If folks get wind of what they consider to be a secret, they'll believe it. What you thought was secret was a ruse. Isaure was a plant. She was never on my payroll. Only on the SQ's. You can guess why.'

'Abigail,' Cinq-Mars concluded in a trice. No other option came to mind.

'Specifically, Abigail's money.'

'You allowed this?'

'Cinq-Mars, we've put cops next to prisoners since the cows came home. The difference this time—'

'Isaure came in as a guard. Not as a fellow prisoner.'

'In place long before Abigail got transferred here. Abigail's smart. She would suspect all fellow prisoners as being potential informants. She would never suspect a guard who arrived months before she did. That was the idea, anyway.'

'It's elaborate, give you that.'

Paquet nodded agreement. 'Not my plan. Given current events, I thought you should know. Powerful people, Cinq-Mars. Every side of the spectrum has an interest in Abigail's money.'

He was beginning to fathom the possible dimensions.

'A word,' the warden said. She meant to speak to him beyond Dubroc's ears.

Cinq-Mars nodded, and the junior policeman walked off a

distance. Grateful to have been included for so long, he didn't resent being dismissed at this stage.

'The plan you spoke to me about?' the warden whispered.

Cinq-Mars nodded, knowing her reference. 'We'll abort, I guess?'

'Too late,' the warden stipulated.

'Why say that?'

'She arrived today. After you left. She's in place.'

'Fuck.' The reaction escaped him. His whisky tongue. 'What happened tonight changes everything.'

'She's in danger. I hope you chose well.'

'We can still pull her out.'

'You convinced me the first time. We need her. Now more than ever. Dangerous or not.'

'Fuck,' Cinq-Mars muttered under his breath again, this time deliberately.

'Language,' the warden admonished him. Then warned, 'Proceed with caution, Cinq-Mars, and goodnight.'

Lagarde

Rain beat down in the morning. Cinq-Mars sat on the motel porch eating an egg-and-bacon sandwich on an English muffin that he'd picked up at a breakfast joint down the road. The joint's coffee was muddy and bitter but doing the trick. He was feeling remarkably spry although by his judgment he looked hungover when he woke up and caught a glimpse in the mirror. He waited. Not for the rains to end but for Paul Lagarde to rouse himself. The man's bike faced his door as biting sheets of rain pelted down.

When Lagarde finally emerged and readied himself for the day, he lumbered down the porch to where Cinq-Mars was sitting and stopped there. Stared out at the torrent and at the puddles surrounding his Softail Harley. 'A man needs a boat,' he said.

'Take a seat,' Cinq-Mars directed him.

'Naw. Starving. I'll catch you later.'

'Sorry. My fault if I made that sound like an invitation.'

Lagarde gave him a look, chose to shrug, then slumped into the Adirondack next to Cinq-Mars. The porch overhang kept them dry.

They gazed out at the day and dark sky.

'Last night, in town,' Cinq-Mars told him, 'a corrections officer was murdered. Tell me what you know about it.'

The gang member accepted the news as serious. Ramifications would have an effect.

'Less than nothing,' he said. 'Why? What should I know?'

'On the radio this morning, she's described as SQ,' Cinq-Mars explained. 'Temporary leave of absence or something like that. That could be heavy news.'

With his massive hands on his thighs the man looked over at the policeman. 'I hope you don't think of pinning this on me.'

'I'll give it some thought, Mr Lagarde.'

'I'm Mr Lagarde now?'

'Sorry. Paul. Look, I spend time thinking things through. It's what I do. I don't admit this too often, but sometimes, it's like I forget I exist. I just sit, and I think. Or lie down and think. It's my worst trait, some say. I'm not convinced, but I get that it bugs people. Paul, hear me out. The dead woman fought back. She fought back hard. She was fierce. I need to speak to your four pals who were in here the other day.'

'Why?' The biker pounded a fist against his own chest. 'Take my word. No way they were involved.'

'Maybe so. I can account for where you were last night at the relevant hour. Also, your face is unmarked. I don't know where the other four were or what their faces look like this morning. Whoever killed the guard had to be big, and I think it took more than one person. Whoever did it last night is marked up this morning, that's my take. Bruises, cuts. I want to see your friends today, before they heal up if they need time for that.'

'Like I said if you weren't listening, it was never them.'

'Now, Paul, can you honestly say that you've never lied to an officer of the law before? In declaring innocence for yourself or your friends, you have to admit, you lack credibility.' He smiled, and the biker did, too. Lagarde gave a little tuck of his head that emulated a tip of the cap. 'Easy to prove, anyway,' Cinq-Mars advised him. 'No point arguing. Show me their pretty faces. Not an invitation. I have their names from the motel register. You don't want me tracking them down. I'll arrive in a mood.'

Lagarde nodded solemnly this time. He seemed relieved. He leaned onto the armrest to bring himself closer to Cinq-Mars. 'They don't live so far away. I'll send them around. Unless they cut themselves shaving this morning – fat chance, they got beards – they'll pass your inspection.'

'Good. Let's say two o'clock. Right here. Constable Dubroc of the SQ will be on hand if I'm not. All we want to do is look at their faces and hands. Check that they're not hobbled. Confirm their IDs. Process of elimination is all.'

'I follow.' Lagarde pushed himself forward to prepare to disembark from the chair. 'Cinq-Mars, get this. I'm not spilling any lima beans here. If anybody in the outer clubs—'

'The satellites, you mean.'

'That's who I mean. If a cop or a prison guard goes down, that's a bigger deal than somebody's got a skin rash. You know? It ain't

no settling of accounts. Something like that? A cop? A guard? If it
happened? Not saying it did. That ain't no minor scratch. Takes
expertise. Experience. Somebody has to sit and think about it first.
To put that on the back of a local chapter – I don't see how that
happens. No, for that, somebody shows up from someplace else.
Always it's an outside job. Otherwise, the local chapter gets shook
down to the ground and how can that be fair? That can't be justified
in the long run. Makes it too easy for you guys.'

Every word made sense.

Still. 'Bring your boys in,' Cinq-Mars insisted. 'We'll check for
war wounds then send them on their way.'

'That's fair. I don't mind fair.'

Cinq-Mars stood before the other man did. He gathered up his
paper coffee cup and breakfast waste. He made it to the top of the
stairs. Before stepping out into the rain, he turned and said, 'One
more thing.'

Paul Lagarde pushed himself to his feet in his black leather jacket
and gang insignia and waited for whatever came next. He may have
been chewing a lip but that was impossible to know for sure under
his overgrown beard, although his jaw appeared to be moving.

'That killing last night?' Cinq-Mars pointed out. 'Total lack of
expertise.' He touched his famously massive nose. Lagarde had
remarked previously on the value of his own sniffer. 'Keep yours
to the ground,' Cinq-Mars forewarned. 'Nobody made it look
like an outside pro rode in. Makes a thinking man wonder: Does
somebody want you shaken down?'

Lagarde took a couple of heavy steps forward, his boots loud on
the wood porch, his various chains tinkling. 'Say this, Cinq-Mars.
You got a wilder kind of imagination in your head.'

'Do I? Ask yourself, how is it you showed up at a pen the same
day a mini riot breaks out? A day later a prison guard is murdered.
Coincidence? Or was it your call? Or were you sent? You know,
sent by somebody who maybe wanted to implicate your Harley ass.'

'Maybe you do think too much,' Lagarde brought up. 'I can see
why it pisses people off. It might do you harm one day.'

'Or you.' Cinq-Mars wanted that last word. Sometimes it felt
necessary.

Quinn

The *hole* was situated above ground. The chambers for solitary were on the same level as the general population. Yet the cells were isolated and the level of silence inside the sector was striking. Haunting for some. Difficult to bear for many. Air was piped in so gently it could not be detected; panicked prisoners often believed they were suffocating. The light was cold, sharp, and could be disorienting over endless hours. Émile Cinq-Mars was admitted to a skinny side room. The door locked behind him. Protocol demanded that he keep a buzzer in hand if he needed help or rescue. He wouldn't. He put the thing in a pocket.

'The outfit suits you,' he said to the woman rising from her bunk. A grey jumpsuit. A prisoner in solitary loses the privilege to wear her own clothes.

'Think of me as Cinderella after midnight,' she remarked. 'I'll think of you as my wicked stepmother.'

'Wrong again.'

The two came together in the center of the small room and embraced.

The hug lasted before they split apart.

Then they both sat on the steel bed with the skimpy mattress.

'You've come way up in the world, I see,' Cinq-Mars mused.

'You should talk. You're still slumming.'

'Can you take this?'

'You mean the décor? No problem. Sixteen hours more. I can sleep the time away. But, you know, this interruption is welcome.'

'How're you doing, Quinn?' Not a casual question. He meant to probe into her state of affairs, her life lately. They hadn't seen each other for some time.

Quinn Tanner had started out as a thief dedicated to a life of

crime when, twenty years earlier, their paths crossed. She'd been
seventeen at the time; Cinq-Mars, thirty. He could not arrest her
back then as an adult for burglary and would have lost control of
her case booking her as a juvenile. He played it by ear. Eventually,
he rescued her from the mob; Quinn saved his life, also. Either or
both might have been killed in a skirmish. Each pulled the other
through.

She quit her criminal escapades after that close call, grew up,
tried school for a while, then traveled, then worked, then did more
schooling. A number of career possibilities were open to her,
though none had the flare and attraction that robbery had held
for her. She finally conceded to her penchant for raw adventure
– of the type she pursued as a thief, and of the type introduced
to her by Cinq-Mars when he was battling the mob. Intervening
on her behalf, Cinq-Mars helped her to join the Montreal Police
Service.

She was entering the Joliette Institution for Women under her
old guise, as a chronic thief, when really Cinq-Mars had
conscripted her with the acquiescence of the warden and the
Montreal Police Service to be his eyes and ears on the inside.
With the death of a guard the night before, the duty was abruptly
more complex and dangerous than first thought. He was visiting
her in solitary to consult but also to let her know how the matter
had changed.

'You're pulling my leg,' she said, stunned by the news.

'Hardly.'

'A guard's dead, too?'

They sat silently under the solemnity of that news. Cinq-Mars
suggested, 'We can call it off.'

'Sure. Send me back to traffic patrol.'

'Is that where you've been keeping? Traffic?'

'A bigger punishment than solitary, let me tell you.'

'*Official* punishment?'

'I might've, you know, pissed someone off, like royally. I'm not
much of an underling it turns out.'

Cinq-Mars laughed. So did she.

Quinn Tanner arrived at Joliette with only the warden knowing
the story. She purposefully contrived to tick off the guard on duty
to draw her stint in solitary. Her way to both make her mark within

the community and to initiate private and secret contact with Émile
Cinq-Mars.

'Wits' end, boss. This is like Disneyland compared to traffic.
Thrilled to get the call, not only because it was you. My boss was
sure pissed. I liked that, too.'

He filled her in on his conversations. He had no conclusions to
proffer except that Abigail was under scrutiny by a variety of forces:
money talks, and she was sitting on a chatty Fort Knox. 'Trust no
one on anything but especially not on that. Biker or cop, warden or
inmate, money warps light. I swear, money is like a planet weighing
down the time-space continuum.'

He seemed strangely angry to her. Unlike him to be that way. 'I
know it's your thing, Émile, but how about you spare me the cosmological analogies.'

'Why do you think I brought you in here? Precisely so I could
bend your ear with a few cosmological analogies.'

She put her dukes up to feign boxing him. They were both
enjoying the other's company.

'I have a new girlfriend,' he confided. 'I think.'

'Émile! About effing time! Oh God, don't tell me she's an inmate.'

'Worse. She's an American who's nineteen years younger.'

'Than me?'

'No, stupid, than me.'

'Which still makes her younger than me. Whoa, Émile, what are
you doing?'

'I don't know. Not sure I have much choice. What about you,
romance-wise? Last time we talked, it was another break-up.'

'You're hoping I'm off your list? I'm off your list. He's a prosecutor who might be heading for private practice soon.'

'A handsome devil?'

'He's so effing hot. Our children, if that happens – I'm running
out of time – will be so freaking gorgeous, Émile, it's insane. So,
how do I get to live long enough to have kids?'

An ex-thief, Quinn was also the daughter of a reformed safe-
cracker. She'd mingled with the nefarious and tangled with evil.
She wouldn't have to fake it too much within the prison population,
although she'd be judged constantly and everyone would be suspicious. She and Émile concocted a history where she'd been a model
prisoner briefly in Alberta, where no one in her group had ever

resided, and before that she'd been clever enough to stay out of jail. So – an experienced crook, but with no hard time as a convict. That should cover her tracks. As well, her evident intelligence might draw Abigail towards her.

'Abigail and a First Nations woman, Rozlynn, are close pals,' Cinq-Mars let her know. 'Try to get along with Rozlynn. Age-wise, you're between the older and younger ones, maybe you can get along with both.'

'Or neither. Should I pick a fight? For appearances?'

'With care. Nothing to suggest in that regard. I'm going hard on everyone very soon to see who's breakable. What I don't get to observe is how they recover once they return to their bunks and hang out with the other inmates again. Keep an eye peeled on that. Who talks to who when they're pissed off? Who retreats? Each of them has gone off the handle in their lives. That could happen again, so take care.'

'Great. You'll crank up violent personalities and leave me to be their punching-bag. I *like* this gig, Émile.'

'I knew you would. Really, you can thank me later.'

'Yeah. If there is a later.'

They laughed lightly, but each knew the situation was dicey and possibly dire.

Courtney

The women were marshaled into the larger kitchen off their dorm. Normally kept locked, the room came into use when preparing meals and for baking cakes, cookies, and pies. None of that was on tap which confused the inmates. Usually they had to pester a guard to have the kitchen opened; they were never herded into the space without explanation. Their best baker was in solitary. Four of their number – Abi, Jodi, Temple, and the new girl, Quinn – were in solitary. That left Malka and Doi, Courtney and Rozlynn, abandoned to the kitchen with nothing to cook.

They felt apprehensive.

The kitchen décor was white on white. Counters, walls, ceiling, even the dining table: white. Small black circles centered white floor tiles. The space might resemble any large home's kitchen if the drawers, cupboards, and refrigerator were not shuttered with chains and padlocks.

Courtney pushed herself up onto the counter and sat there.

Surprised to have been left alone, the four waited without a guard. Their surprise redoubled when Jodi was escorted in, released early from solitary; moments later Temple and Abigail showed up in tandem. The house-unit was together again, although for an unknown reason sequestered in the kitchen.

The guards left them alone once more.

Temple and Abigail were soon gabby. Jodi, withdrawn.

Courtney wondered aloud if the new girl was also going to arrive, then explained to the three who'd been in solitary that Flo had been replaced.

'We have a new bunkmate?' Abigail repeated, her suspicion apparent.

'Her name's Quinn.'

'Wait. She went straight to solitary? What the fuck?'

That had to be explained and the women took turns. 'Quinn seemed OK.'

'Settling in. But then—'

'Somebody told her—'

'That would be me,' Doi admitted.

'—that the last person in the bunk was dead. Killed.'

'Know what she said?' Courtney asked Temple.

'I wasn't here, remember,' Temple said.

'"I'm not sleeping in no dead girl's shit." That's what she said.'

'There's nowhere else to sleep, right?' Courtney pointed out.

'She flat out refused,' Doi explained, with a distinct note of appreciation. 'The new guard sent her to solitary. What happens when she gets out, don't ask me, but I'm betting she won't sleep in Flo's bed. She's stubborn that one!'

'Like she has a phobia,' Malka said.

'I'll sleep in Flo's bed,' Abigail offered. 'Puts me head-to-head with Roz. We can share our dreams. I don't mind. This Quinn-chicka-filla thingee can have my bed.'

That, then, was settled. As she had not been involved in the brawl, the new inmate would be serving her full hours, they surmised. They heard the door unlocking. All eyes turned that way. The next arrival was not the new girl, but their inquisitor, Émile Cinq-Mars, with a pair of corrections officers in tow.

'Can we bake you a cake, Detective-man?' Abi exclaimed, glad to see him.

'That won't be necessary.'

'You don't like cake?'

He looked directly at her. 'Not your conversation, Abi.'

She relented. Took a seat.

'Good idea,' Cinq-Mars said. 'Why don't you all sit?'

Temple and Rozlynn chose to lean. Others sat in chairs around the dining table with Courtney staying put on the countertop.

Abi put her hand up.

'Don't annoy me,' Cinq-Mars warned her.

'Legit question,' she stated.

'What?'

'The ones who just got out of solo, after this talk or whatever it is, do we go back?'

'You're out of solitary,' Cinq-Mars confirmed. 'Up to you to keep it that way.'

The ladies were happy about that, although Jodi aired a note of skepticism. 'So much for the good news. What's the bad?'

They caught on and looked at the policeman. They noticed his reticence, his seriousness.

'Something I need to tell you. A shock. Corrections Officer Isaure Dabrezil is dead. Like Flo, she was murdered.'

News of a guard's death might be greeted with jubilation in some prisons, at worst, or at best with mere disinterest. Here, the shock and a palpable dread glued everyone in place. No one asked the obvious next question.

Cinq-Mars had requested to be the one to share the news, wanting to reconnoiter their reactions. He was somewhat taken aback by their response. Real or imagined, these women were living in fear. That would be his takeaway.

They waited for him to address their unspoken query.

'It happened last night. She was killed in her home. The killer – or killers – has not been apprehended. If any of you has evidence or any suspicion, tell me now, or tell me later in private, as you wish.'

On the spot, no one volunteered.

'How?' Malka asked.

'A knife. Or something sharp. She fought back. Sadly, to no avail.'

They took that in.

'Revenge, you think?' Temple asked.

'For what?'

'Killing Flo, maybe.'

'Do you think that?'

'No. I mean, what do I know? Do you?'

'I've spoken to many of you already,' Cinq-Mars told them. 'I still need to speak to you, Temple; and I didn't get a chance to talk to Jodi and Courtney in private, either, only jointly.'

'They're attached at the hip anyhow,' Malka said, which won a nervous laugh. The news of the guard's murder left them apprehensive.

'They're fucking Siamese,' Temple tacked on.

'They had to be surgically separated when Jodi got sent down to solo,' Abigail said.

Normally, the women would chuckle at that, take up the repartee. Not this time.

'I'll be speaking to everyone, including those I've already inter-viewed,' Cinq-Mars let them know.

'Can I be next?' Abigail put in the request. She returned the blank expression she was receiving from the others. 'What? It's fun. It gets me out of the house, you know?'

'This time around,' Cinq-Mars spoke over a burst of bluster, pulling their attention back to his statement, 'unlike last time we'll get down to brass tacks. Forget the games, the BS, the crap. Each of you knows stuff that can help me out and from this point forward, I'm going to know it, too. We have a dead guard on our hands. If you thought I was soft with you after Flo's death, now that we have a second death, and a guard, everything will be different.'

The women took him at his word. While not contrite, they were solemn.

'At a bare minimum, at least one of you knows who killed Flo. At least one of you killed her. I'm here to find out who and I'm not leaving until I succeed. I intend to find the answer sooner rather than later.'

Abigail put up her hand again. Cinq-Mars gave her a look. 'I think you're forgetting something,' she pointed out to him.

'I presume you want to tell me.'

'Isaure's dead. She could be the only one who knows who killed Flo because maybe she did it. Talking to us might get you nowhere.'

Not only did she have a point, but any lawyer, if representing an accused among them charged with Flo's murder, had the means to fabricate reasonable doubt. What if Isaure did it? The women nodded in unison, clinging to the fresh possibility that Flo's killer might no longer be alive.

'I won't think that way,' he replied. 'Instead, I'll talk to each of you and get somewhere fast.'

Abi did her best to lighten the mood. 'In that case,' she said, 'I don't want to be next.'

She didn't get much of a reaction this time.

Cinq-Mars explained that from now on there'd be two guards in their dorm, not one. He revealed that 'Courtney sees me next.'

The girl's head spun on a swivel for a second. Then she looked away, sheet white.

Abigail made a sound that was barely audible.

Cinq-Mars looked at her. 'What now?' he asked.

She raised and dropped a shoulder. 'You're starting over with the most vulnerable among us. I get it. That's basic.' She had a black eye and a split fat lip from the jail yard brawl. 'Except, Cinq-Mars, you don't do basic. Not your thing.'

'You can shut up now,' Cinq-Mars told her, although the other women noticed that his tone was gentle. He left the room. A guard held the door open only for him, then remained behind.

'So. What now? Are we cooking?' Abigail asked.

'Let's bake!' Doi called out. The locked cupboards were not deterring her.

'Tarts,' Abigail said, 'how about it?'

She was suggesting what to bake, although a couple of inmates wondered if she had just teased them with an insult. After her fight in the yard and her stint in solitary, she seemed different somehow. Rozlynn noticed, and gazed at her, until Abi stared back and Roz looked away. At the same time, Jodi came out of her shell and went over to Courtney, to give her an encouraging hug and tell her that it was going to be OK. 'You'll get through it,' she said, but Courtney sloughed her off and leapt down from the counter. She wandered off a short distance on her own. Everyone noticed.

ii

'You'll fall apart if I get tough,' Cinq-Mars said in his opening volley to Courtney. 'Jodi thinks so. If I'm hard on you, the smart money says you'll disintegrate.'

Courtney managed a shrug. Not one of defiance or disinterest, nor was she inclined to feign boredom when she was clearly wary of how the talk might go. Her shrug conveyed that Cinq-Mars might have grasped the order of things, that she could do nothing to help herself now. She was willing to feebly collapse.

'It's pretty obvious that I can take you apart at the seams.'

She was finally annoyed enough to speak. 'If you say so,' she said. 'I dunno.'

'I say so. I can turn you into mush on the floor. You won't sleep for weeks. You'll need a pack of pills to face the next day.'

She curled in the chair. She seemed to be shriveling up even before he got going.

'I dunno,' she reiterated.

'Don't you? Oh, that is such a crock of hooey,' he said.

'Of what? Sorry?'

'Bull crap. Horseshit. Cow dung. Call it what you want.'

She looked more concerned now. 'What do you mean?'

'I don't think you'll fall apart, Courtney. I'm looking at a girl who stuck a knife into her best friend's belly—'

Courtney inhaled sharply.

'Your friend, what was her name?'

Courtney curled into herself more tightly.

'Tell me her name.'

'Daphne,' Courtney whispered.

'Daphne hollered with the shock of it, she must have, the overwhelming brutality, the pain beyond human belief. She was going to die. She knew it by then. Probably she couldn't believe what was happening to her, that you, her best friend, could do that to her. But the pain was unbearable and then you stabbed her again, Court. And again. And again. And again.'

'Stop.'

'Did *you*? Stop?'

She shook her head.

'Then why should I? Courtney, think of the poor girl you murdered. Daphne could be living right now. Breathing. Falling in love with some new guy. The new guy might be somebody's boyfriend again, but who cares? You're only kids. These things happen. But no, you had to keep stabbing her again and again and again.'

'You're being so mean! Why are you being so mean to me?'

'How mean were you, stabbing your best friend?'

'Stop it.'

'Stop what? I'm not going to stop. You didn't. I'm going by your example.'

'You're so mean to me!'

'Do you know what I'm going to do?'

She had no idea. Tears shone in the corners of her eyes. When it was apparent that he was waiting on an answer, she asked, 'What?'

'Guess who I'm going to visit.'

She shrugged again, largely out of despair this time. 'How am I supposed to know? Who?'

'Your mom.'

'What? Why? You can't!'

'I can. Several reasons why I'm going. Quite a few, actually.'

'Like what?'

'Can't you think of any? Well, let's see. I will read the letters you've sent home. That will tell me a lot, I think.'

'You don't have the right! They're my letters!'

'Courtney, this is a murder investigation. I have a right. What will those letters tell me? Don't answer. I'll find out for myself. I also want to speak to your mother, of course. Give her my report. Let her know what I think of your progress these days, your cooperation.'

'What do you mean?' This mention of her mother had her cracking. She had a weak point, and when it was tapped, even lightly, she was breakable. 'I've been good inside. A model prisoner. It's on my last report.'

'Model prisoner? I saw you pass a knife to Marie-Philomène.'

'You saw that? Did you? I had no choice. But it wasn't a knife.'

'What was it?'

'A nail file.'

'At least you're willing to admit to your crime. So you passed a weapon to Marie-Philomène.'

'A small nail file!'

'A weapon. Do you think that makes you a model prisoner?'

'I had no choice!'

'Didn't you? Explain it to me, Courtney.'

'*I'm human!*' she shouted out.

Silence. The desperation in her voice was utterly raw and stymied the detective's onslaught.

She bunched herself up in her chair, her feet on the seat, both arms wrapped around her knees as though holding on to herself.

'I can't explain it,' she whimpered, answering his question.

'You'd better explain it,' Cinq-Mars said.

She was stuck in her predicament, not wishing a bad report for herself, not one repeated to her mother, yet she needed to adhere to the prisoner's code of silence. Cinq-Mars let her stew.

'I was told to pick up the nail file. To give it to M-P.'

'Who told you?'

'I can't squeal.'

'You can tell me because I already know the answer. You have to tell me to prove you're being cooperative.'

'Tell me who if you're so smart. I'll say if you're right.'

'Courtney, Courtney, I agree with you. You're human. You're not a monster. Although you did a monstrous thing. The issue is – and this is about being human – why do you do what you're told to do in here? If somebody, for example – I'm not accusing you – but if somebody told you to go strangle Flo with a wire, would you do it?'

'That's crazy. She'd kill me first.'

'Who would?'

'Flo!'

'I'm only using her as an example. What if it was someone smaller than you? Would you do what you're told?'

'No. But that's a big, big thing. Smaller things, I'd probably do what I'm told. You gotta get by in here. You don't know that?'

'So who tells you to pick up a nail file and hand it to Marie-Philomène? That's a small thing. Please don't substitute a false name. I already know the answer.'

She considered her answer, then replied, quietly, 'Abi.'

'That's the right answer,' Cinq-Mars said. He slapped his hands against his kneecaps. 'I'm sure your mother will be pleased to learn that you're cooperative. Now, next question, how come you or anyone else will do what Abi says? She just got here a short time ago. How come Abi is at the center of things, in the middle of that fight, for instance, when she only just arrived? Marie-Philomène's a leader in here. For her side. That's not true for Abi who's an outsider. What's going on with that? I'm really interested in your point-of-view, Courtney.'

Having softened her resistance and having touched her core when she protested that she was human, he was opting to be more conversational with her, less confrontational.

'Everything turns around Abi,' Courtney said.

'How so?'

Another of her deflective shrugs. 'I dunno. It just does.'

'If you don't know, then you didn't figure it out for yourself. Somebody else knows the answer and told it to you. Who told you that everything turns around Abi?'

Courtney was not inclined to say.

'Another thing about visiting your Mom. I'm going to ask her why she thinks you stabbed your best friend to death.'

'No, don't. Please,' she begged. Her plea sincere. 'Please don't put my mother through that.'

'I'll bring it up. Maybe I'll talk to Daphne's mom, too. Or – or you'll tell me who told you that everything turns around Abi, whatever that means.'

She hung her head a while, and kept it down when she said, 'Jodi.'

Jodi.

'And what does Jodi mean when she says that everything turns around Abi?'

Her head remained lowered. She hesitated. Then she said, 'I dunno.'

'Shall I ask Jodi? Tell her that you wanted me to explain what she said to you?'

Her head came up this time. 'No,' she said. 'Don't.'

'Well then?'

'Everybody wants to find out what Abi knows. Jodi says it's the only thing keeping Abi alive. Nobody wants her dead, because they want what she knows first. We're supposed to make friends with her, Jodi says. To help find out what she knows. It's not my idea. What do I care? But I have no choice.'

'Are you afraid of Jodi?'

He gave her time to consider her response.

'I'm afraid of everybody,' she said. 'But please, please, please, please don't tell my mom that. I don't want her to be scared, too.'

'Fiddlesticks. What about your father?'

'Why ask me that?' The question didn't bother her. She was merely curious as to why he asked.

'Does he live with your mother?'

'No. They split after—'

'After you killed your best friend.'

'Will you stop saying that?'

'It's true, isn't it? You not only ended your best friend's life, you wrecked your parents' lives too, starting with their marriage.'

'Why are you being so *damn fucking mean*?'

'Language,' the guard said.

They'd both forgotten that she was still in the room.

Somehow it broke the tension. They both laughed a little.

'Yeah, language,' Cinq-Mars said. 'Let's watch out for that. Two people dead, we don't want anyone swearing.'

'Why are you?' she asked calmly. 'Being so mean?'

He leaned in closer to her, which elicited a similar motion from

Courtney, as though they were preparing to speak in confidential whispers.

'Courtney, I can be on your side. I like you. And you *are* human. You're not a monster. But you have to stop playing the little girl card and accept that you're a killer yourself. You've killed. Everybody gets mad like that, but most people have a stopper. Your stopper is weak. If you're going to build it up to a normal level, you have to face what you did. In the meantime, I have to ask myself, could someone push you to kill Flo? Almost nothing, a little spate, a mere misunderstanding, a petty jealousy, that's all it took for you to brutally murder poor Daphne.' She slowly recoiled from him, then curled in her chair, as though curling within herself. 'Don't tell me that whatever she said or whatever she did set you off. She didn't stick a knife in you or threaten you. People here know that you can kill, and I wonder if someone might take advantage of that. You have more of a charge in you than you let on, and too weak a stopper. I think you try to forget what you did, Courtney, but you can't quite believe it. Isn't that right?'

She nodded.

'Believe it. That's my advice. I have no choice but to view you as a suspect. You have it in you to kill, suddenly and viciously. That can't be denied, as much as you would like to. Courtney, I need you to come around. To grow up. Help me on this case. Nothing else will take the weight off your shoulders. I'm talking about the weight I'm putting there. Yes, I will visit your mom. What I tell her is up to you. What's my report going to say?'

'Oh Christ,' Courtney whispered.

'Mmm. Oh Christ? I believe in prayer myself, but it won't help in this case. You have to be truthful to pray and you have to be truthful to me. Otherwise, the weight, Courtney, the weight on your shoulders I guarantee will crush you. Your fraidy-cat-little-girl stunt is not something you can pull off with me. It just – won't – work.'

'What do you want?' she whined, squirming.

'Let's start with this. Tell me who stole Abi's nail file in the first place. Who brought it to the yard for Marie-Philomène?'

He had a good guess in mind if she answered the question honestly. He was betting on Jodi. But Courtney surprised him.

Doi.

Temple

i

Cinq-Mars was reviewing Temple's rap sheet as the woman was brought in and shoved down in the seat across from him. Neither spoke a word for over a minute and when he looked up, she was wearing a venomous scowl. 'Something on your mind?' he asked.

'Speaking only for myself, I'd love to pull it right out your nose. Just saying.'

He stared back at her and waited. Then said, 'I'll regret the question, but what are you talking about?'

'The rebar. The one I stick up your rump. Pull it out your left nostril. I'd love to do that.'

'Respectful,' the guard inside the door forewarned.

'Fuck that kind of shit,' Temple fired back.

'Language.'

'What's the matter? You don't understand English?'

'You're in a mood,' Cinq-Mars noted.

'Don't worry, Mr Man, it's a skinny bar. You can take it. You'll probably enjoy it. Your nose is big enough. It's not like I'm ramming a Douglas fir up your butt.' She leaned over the table to whisper, 'I'd like to do that, too.'

'It's an image,' Cinq-Mars responded. 'Like they say, it's the thought that counts.'

'Fuck you.'

The guard at the door made a move but Cinq-Mars raised his hand. 'I got this.'

'You think? You got fuck all,' Temple disagreed. 'Fucking big man, Mr Man, the Man, pushing the kids around, Mr Tough Guy. You think you intimidate me? Bull-fucking-shit in a bottle. You don't know your dick from your backdoor snatch. You don't know who you're talking to. Ever had cigarette butts snuffed out on your

Dubroc

i

Cinq-Mars had a quick shower and was drying soap from his ear sockets when a knock resounded on his motel door. He'd ordered a pizza, yet this was swift service. He figured they didn't have time to cook it, never mind the delivery. He opened up wearing only a towel surprising his guest as much as he was surprised by him. Constable Dubroc did his best to avert his eyes.

'Come in. I'll be dressed in a jiff.'

'I'll wait out here, thanks.'

He regretted losing the time to himself. He dressed quickly and joined Dubroc on the porch. 'What's up?'

'Overheard stuff. Thought I should share it.'

'Good. Share.'

'I'll be jammed up if this gets out.'

'Gotcha. I will blow no whistles.'

'I overheard a conversation.' Dubroc stalled after saying that, either to review the talk in his head or to reconsider repeating it.

Cinq-Mars gave him time and space and stretched out his legs. Finally, he prompted him. 'Anytime you're ready, Constable.'

'This isn't easy. Never thought I'd be doing something like this. You understand, I'm telling you about a conversation among my superiors.'

Cinq-Mars nodded gravely. 'I understand your dilemma,' he assured the other man. 'Seems to me, if you want to tell me what you overheard, if you feel that it's your duty to go that way, then it must be pretty damn important.'

Dubroc took a deep breath and let it out slowly. 'Yeah,' he agreed.

'Take your time,' Cinq-Mars said. 'Hungry at all?'

'I'll get something later.'

'No need. Here comes a pizza.'

The delivery car drove in and parked and Cinq-Mars signaled

the driver over, who was searching for door numbers. He paid with a bill and held up his hand for the man to keep the change.

'Pepperoni, all right?'

'I can do a slice. I don't want to eat your dinner.'

'Constable, I'm a detective, so trust me on this: I have a very strong suspicion there's more where this came from. Dig in!'

The first slices were all but inhaled, and they slowed down only as they started on their second pieces.

'Who was talking?' Cinq-Mars inquired.

'I won't say. Tell you this. A chief inspector, an inspector, two captains and a lieutenant, all in on it. That's a lot of weight out here in the boonies. I'll keep their names to myself.'

'Fair enough. Quite the rogues' gallery. How did you happen to listen in?'

'They knew I was in the room. Furniture, to them. Probably they didn't think I had a clue.'

In which case, what he had to say could not be all that incriminating.

'I guess they don't know I met you,' Dubroc added.

'How does that matter?'

'They were talking about you, Sergeant-Detective.'

His news might be of interest after all. 'Me, huh? And?'

'They want your ass in a sling.'

Cinq-Mars nodded gravely again. He could always take the high road in any internal battle among cops, but that position assumed a fair fight. An assumption he could never count on.

'How did they word it exactly?'

'"Take him down."'

'That's plain enough. And the man talking had the rank of—'

'Chief Inspector.'

Weight.

'Something about money and a woman in jail,' Dubroc continued. 'Not clear to me, that part.'

'I can guess. Any plan on how to take me down?'

'They seemed to know. Nothing was said about that.'

The two men finished their slices and each helped themselves to another. Cinq-Mars had forgotten to bring anything to drink, so went into his room and returned with two cans of Coke. They swilled them down quickly.

'I'm not sure what I can do with it but thank you f
'No problem.'

'I'll keep the source to myself. One thing, if I may. had to be careful how he broached his query. After Du himself out and taken a risk, he didn't want to imply t trust him, even though he didn't, not fully.

'What's that?' Dubroc asked.

'Why are you telling me this? I asked for your h have no loyalty to me. Going against your superiors, that's a tough nut.'

The way Dubroc rocked his head to one side sugges Mars that the man was comfortable with the question reply. 'Another name came up. One of the captains m

'A name.'

'Yeah. One of our own. The captain mentioned th guy was around. "In the neighborhood," how he put it

'OK. And?'

'No matter what, this other captain could never find talked about you. Almost like they swore to never let

'This other captain, does he have a name?'

'That's the thing. I've worked under him. I know one. If these other guys are telling me that the captai side, and you on his, then maybe that's the side I wa too.'

'His name?'

'Captain Borde.'

Cinq-Mars nodded again, more positively this tir Borde. Good friend of mine. And a damn good cop. He' For the record, Constable, I now know that you are, t

feet? Ever had your toes crushed? Let me introduce you to the pleasure. That reminds me, you got a smoke or what?'

'I don't. If Abigail said so, she was leading you on.'

'Don't bullshit me. Don't even try.'

'I have nothing to say. I ask questions. You answer. That's how this works.'

'Fuck you and fuck your fucking questions anyhow. Fuck!'

'Language!' The voice from the door, strident this time.

'You're in a mood, I'll give you that,' Cinq-Mars said.

'Save it.' Tall and built with solidity, Temple looked as though she could knock an army tank on its side with one swipe. 'You get to give me nothing. Pushing our young ones around, who do you think you are? I'm not afraid of you.'

'Is that your thing? You defend the kids?'

'Why not? Somebody should do that.'

'Did you defend them against Flo?'

'You have big teeth. I'd like to floss them with a crowbar.'

'Are you done?'

'Done? I just got out of solitary! This is what happens. I get to rant against the machine, and you're the fucking machine.'

The guard warned, 'More solitary coming if you don't behave.'

'You guys are a broke record. Solitary solitary solitary. Skip skip skip. Fix your needle. Do you know what I do down in solo, Cinq-Mars? Why I love it? Send me down, I don't give a shit. Why do I love solitary, you think?'

'Like I said, I ask, you answer.'

'Hurry it up, then. You haven't asked a fucking thing. Let me paint you another image. They say you should never touch yourself in solo. You start, you won't stop. I say, bring it on. You can't make out with yourself living in a fucking group. Solitary is my one good shot. I let my fingers do the walking. Can you picture it?'

'Temple, did you kill Flo?'

'What? What the fuck is that?'

'A question. I expect an answer.'

'You can't push me around, Mr Man. Picture it. Me in solitary. Take that home with you tonight when you're dancing with your blow-up sweetheart. Did you bring your favorite dolly on this road trip? Describe her, your blow-up baby. I bet she's a blondie. Real

hair below? I'll get off on the image back in solo, of you fucking
your blow-up plastic blondie.'

'Did you? Kill Flo?'

'I told you, Cinq-Mars,' she said slowly. 'You cannot intimidate
me with that shit! Maybe it works with the kiddies, but you're
talking to a roadhouse motherfucking babe right now, don't you
even know?'

He rocked his head slightly. 'I've read your file, Temple. I know
what you've accomplished in life. Running guns is major dirt for a
loser like you. No doubt about it. You don't care who dies because
of you. Yet you're in here defending the kids. In the yard fight, you
jumped in to defend Abi. What a gal. What a big heart you have.
You're everybody's heroine except we both know you're not.'

She was glad to get a rise out of him, to provoke him into being
combative. It's what she wanted. It's how she'd win the confrontation, by turning it into a shouting match, a contest of recriminations
and bile. She'd shout her lungs out, give voice to her spleen. His
last comment though effectively turned her sideways in her chair.
'What you say?'

'The defender of the meek and mild. Yeah, I'm the bad guy. You
won't be shoved around. Not you. But the others, the ones you're
fighting for so valiantly, what do they say? Who do they say killed
Flo? Who gets a pass for that? You? Do they say, oh, Temple didn't
do it, no way. Leave her out of it. Or do they say, it had to be one
of the bigger women, such as Temple – and name you first – or
maybe Malka or Rozlynn? How many of them give you a free pass?
If your answer starts out at none, you'd be very hot. Right on the
button, I'd say.'

He should know. He'd been the one talking to the others. What
he said made sense. If someone was conjuring who to accuse, her
name was likely to pop to mind. She hadn't thought in those terms
before. Never considered that the very ones she defended might
turn on her when pressed.

All that sifted through her synapses in the stillness of the room.
Cinq-Mars let her mull things over. Then she asked, 'How come
you waited to talk to me? You could have taken me out of solitary.
You should've. Never mind my walking fingers. I would not have
minded that.'

Cinq-Mars flexed his shoulders as though they'd stiffened on him.

'Temple, it's not as though you or the others are ordinary citizens standing around on a street corner. You were in a confined space and knew all the players. Time can go by, but you won't forget a thing about that day. I'm in no rush.'

She took that in. 'Do I draw one of them maps or what?'

'Sure,' he said. 'We can go there. Before we do, tell me about your life in the Hells. In particular, tell me who you were working for running guns. Temple, come clean honestly, or you'll get more time than you need to explore your sexuality down in the hold all alone. If you think I'm trying to intimidate you, I apologize for that. I'm sorry. It's just the way things go.'

ii

She had on a big old straw hat with a rounded tall peak that she adored. A little frayed around the edges. Coming up to the border sometimes she stuck a strand of straw in her mouth. Played the hick card, as she called it. The black gal who lived on the American side, worked on a farm on the Canadian side. A corn field. That sections were devoted to marijuana crops she kept to herself; as far as anybody needed to know she was a working girl, black, living on starvation wages who came across the border on a regular basis. Used to be she was checked. When the guards on both sides got to know her and stopped checking, exchanging pleasantries only and flirting with her a little, men and women both, she kept up her end. She was pleasant, she was flirty. The bales of hay in the rear were present sometimes, then absent, more on some days, then fewer. On occasion she stuffed high caliber rifles, pistols, rapid-fire weapons in the hay, then on weekends rode with her biker buddies, her pockets flush with cash.

She lived the life.

Any day out of prison was a helluva good day.

The irony, her deepest trouble came from going straight, although she always kept rough company. Originally, she'd been a mule out of the Caribbean into American ports of call. Nasty drugs, mostly carried internally. Enough money to mean something for a young girl escaping abject poverty in D.C. The back and forth gave her knowledge, and she had a brain to augment the revelations. She saw how things worked, how things moved, how to get ahead in the game. That she was a large, thick woman had advantages. She didn't receive vile advances often, and when she did she could slam the man against a wall until he backed off. In the meantime, success bred contempt for the process, and she had an urge to settle down, settle in, go legit.

Friends brought her up to Canada. There, she answered a request for farm labor, and took to it, baling hay with the best of the men, threatening to choke the guy with the racist remark. A night of trouble gave her a taste of prison. It felt sour. She made a friend there and, on the street again, she rode with her new biker pals. They had a thing against black, racism was built into the Hells Angels creed, except there was this one dude who had an interest. He was attracted. As they were out in the countryside and she was 'only' a woman, the gang let it go. They let her be and the biker, too. She was nothing more than a road moll, after all, and then a roadhouse agent in a strip club where she took care of the girls who had trouble with the rules, usually due to being bent on cocaine. But she was legit. Clean as a whistle, job-wise.

The bikers in the area roamed the countryside coercing legitimate farmers into leasing fields for marijuana growth. The farmers could agree and turn a nice profit or have their homes torched while their children slept, their choice. A few had their knees busted by baseball bats to coax a prompt decision. She overheard talk in the strip club. Guns needed importing. Their chapter was asked to figure out a solution, since they rode down by the border. Temple had an idea. She remembered her pleasant days on the farm. All she needed was an old flatbed Ford and a straw hat and an apparent job on a Canadian farm. She was still an American citizen, still carried her passport.

That all worked out. Until it didn't.

The judge didn't take kindly to a black lady running guns for the mob. Nobody said it but she could tell: gender and race caused her sentence to expand.

iii

She wound down after her intemperate start. Cinq-Mars saw a different side of her. He let the conversation wander, content to have her settle into herself and grow accustomed to his proximity. As was true with the others, to be in a different space was a pleasant shift to dull routine, and to be in the company of a man, for nothing more than its novelty, pleased her. Mainly, she enjoyed reminiscing about the old days. He began to nudge her away from personal stories to matters at hand, although she resisted when she discerned his intention.

'I could tell you some things,' she intimated.

'Please do.'

She considered if she should. Cinq-Mars assumed that after opening a door, she was not inclined to shut it. He suspected that she had a reason, which she might divulge in due course. She whispered, 'I hear the guard gets to walk out of the room.'

Now would be a good time for that. Cinq-Mars nodded, and they were left alone.

'War,' she said. 'One's coming on hard.'

'Go on.'

'Don't ask me about methods.'

'Methods?' He was already asking.

'Messages came through. For me. Don't ask how. People are consulting me about weapons. Believe that? Mostly about what's a fair price. But more important stuff, too.'

'Like what?' Cinq-Mars probed.

'Sources for ammunition. Heavy weapons. What I don't know about that shit nobody does. The way the times are, I can be useful.'

'What's being planned, Temple?'

'Told you. War.'

'Internecine?'

She scrunched up her face. 'What the hell does that word mean?'

'Biker against biker. Or is it biker against what you call the machine?'

'The first thing. What did you call it? Your fancy word?'

'Internecine.'

'There's been disputes, big time, on the inside. If that means internecine, that's what it is. I'm guessing some mean stuff got out of hand. The Angels want their monopoly, you know, they want it intact. Everybody in the drug world has to go through the Angels, and that includes the other biker gangs spread across the countryside, not just in the city. Some been grouping together. Right now, some call themselves the Alliance, some the Rock Machine. A vote's

coming. Then a name. My money's on the Rock Machine for the
name. Then boys will be boys.'

'What does that mean?'

'The fighting and killing starts.'

Cinq-Mars breathed in deeply. 'You're convinced there'll be a
war? No way to stop it?'

'Folks been gearing up. I mean, what the fuck, they're consulting
me about ammunition! That gives you an idea. The Hells Angels
have their own experts, normally the other gangs work through
them. But the Alliance – or maybe it's the Rock Machine by now,
what do I know, me on the inside – they're trying to put together
their own supply chain. That's where I come in. That tells me one
thing and one thing only. War is fucking inevitable.'

Cinq-Mars gazed at her as he processed the information. 'That's
a big word,' he said. 'Inevitable.'

'I know a few. We're talking about a hundred or more.'

'Words?'

'No, asshole. Deaths. The body count. People figure it might go
high.'

Cinq-Mars sensed a leakage in his stomach lining. Battles had
occurred in the past, but the bikers were always able to keep a lid
on things. They policed their violence to keep it controlled and, in
their minds, justified. This sounded as though the lids were close
to being removed.

'You realize, Temple, that you have implicated yourself today.
Flo was gang. It's on her sheet. And on yours. You're gang, too,
and you've just indicated that that's ongoing. Probably perpetual.
Interconnected chapters, maybe not the same gang exactly, but
ultimately the same headman. Do I have that right? But now you're
on a different side.'

'About the size of it. So I'm not the Easter Bunny. How does
that implicate me about anything?' She had a look on her face
similar to an angelic cherub.

'You've indicated to me today that you still have contact. You
remain on the pipeline. Flo attacked someone in your chapter, with
acid, do I have that right?'

'You don't. Another chapter. Third party, let's say.'

'Still, bikers make it a habit to stick together. Gives you motive
to kill Flo. Or, if it's not your motive, someone on the outside has

motive, someone aware of your proximity to Flo. Someone who saw opportunity in that, then convinced or coerced you to do it.'

She looked very directly at him. 'Why do you think I told you my story?'

'Why did you?'

'Because you're gonna get there anyway. You'll pull it together. Stitch it up. You along with others will think maybe it was me. But this is where I have a say: Maybe it wasn't me. I'm owning up to some things, letting you know that, yeah, it could be me. Only it wasn't. It isn't. Give me cred for that, that's what I ask for here, what I hope from you. A little cred.'

'I see. Tell me about Paul Lagarde. He involved?'

She was mulling over whether she should admit to even knowing him. That she took too long to decide occurred to her.

'Maybe not as much as he should be,' she said.

'What does that mean?'

'Means what it means.' She had crossed a few lines in their discussion. This one was prohibitive enough to go no further. She was stepping away. 'You got to remember,' she warned. 'I'm not taking sides in here. Not as far as anybody can ever see.'

'Appreciate the talk, Temple,' Cinq-Mars admitted. 'I'll keep your cooperation in mind. Now, let's do the maps.'

She drew them up as he suspected, with her and the other larger woman, Malka, doing the laundry.

'You were together the whole time?'

Perhaps the easy-going atmosphere had caused her to be too relaxed. She lifted a shoulder absently, then acknowledged, 'More or less.'

Or perhaps her comment was intentional. If others were willing to consider her as the killer, and say so out loud to him, then she might permit a suspicion of her own to slip past her lips. Either to put him on the wrong track, to divert him from herself, or to put him on a track she considered significant.

Perhaps the right one.

Malka.

Rozlynn

i

A declarative nod of his chin directed the guard to decamp. Before doing so, she challenged him with an acerbic facial expression, then her shoulders slumped in annoyance. The prisoner had arrived that very minute, why should she, the only guard in the room, leave now? Cinq-Mars jerked his chin again. The corrections officer got the message and grumpily departed, leaving him alone with Rozlynn.

Rather than sit, the woman paced. Decidedly uncomfortable.

He let her walk off her tensions, forward and back before the table, forward and back. When she showed no inclination to slow down, he returned to reading a folder of documents until she did.

After she finally stopped pacing, he said, 'You're allowed to sit.'

She neither acknowledged the invitation nor declined it. Three minutes later, she sat.

'You did a good job,' he told her.

Roz was baffled.

'With the fight,' Cinq-Mars explained. 'Pulling people off the pile. Good job. Were you hurt at all?'

She shrugged, which seemed to convey that she was sore.

'Are you always the peacemaker around here?'

She appeared to be mulling that over, which concluded with a shrug of indeterminate meaning.

'I know that you're a quiet person, Rozlynn, but I do have to ask that you answer my questions. Thanks. So. Are you a peacekeeper, do you think?'

Rozlynn thought about it some more, then said, 'I dunno. Yesterday maybe.'

'You did a good job, being a peacekeeper. That doesn't exactly square with the crime that put you here. Murdering your dad. That was not keeping the peace.'

'Maybe not,' she said. Defiant.

'*Maybe* not? Do you think it might? Were you keeping the peace at the time?'

Once again, she reverted to a shrug.

'It's possible,' Cinq-Mars ruminated. 'I mean, I can see where that could be the case. The court documents, for instance, mentioned a few things about your father and your relationship.'

'What documents?' As softly as she spoke, an underlying antagonism was present.

'He took you hunting in the woods, it says. That meant you had to sleep beside him—'

'Not like that!' Rozlynn burst out. 'Not that way!'

He had never heard her so animated. A pent-up emotion let loose.

'I didn't think so,' he said.

He waited. She was calming down as best she could. Not ridding herself of her emotional impetus but concealing it from the only other person in the room. 'What did you say?' she asked.

'Only my opinion, but it seems perfectly natural to me. The way the lawyers were talking, and the social workers in the courtroom, sleeping beside your father while you're out hunting ducks – they made it sound abnormal. What did they expect? That your dad would sleep in the blind and you would . . . what? Sleep in the lake?'

She laughed, just a little.

'They were crazy,' she said.

'The lawyers?'

'Them, yeah.'

'I thought so,' Cinq-Mars said. 'If your dad abused you, you never said so. Their assumption could have been correct, but it was based on nothing. Unprofessional. I could use other words. Anyway, how was your relationship with your dad? You killed him. I don't imagine it was great. Or were you crazy on drugs or something? Or did an argument get out of hand? What happened?'

He gave her time once more, respecting her pace. It seemed necessary. Others he might press for a quicker response, but he was crossing a divide with Rozlynn. Several divides. Racial, gender, historical laments and betrayals. She needed to find her way through this and took time to gaze across the table at him, to study him.

'I killed him,' she said.

'You've been honest about that, right from the start. It's appreciated.'

'I didn't mean to,' she said.

Cinq-Mars took that in. 'That's something you never told the courts.'

'I didn't know it was him.'

Cinq-Mars needed time, and Rozlynn gave it to him.

'That's news,' he said eventually. 'Who did you think it was if not your father?'

'I thought it was my uncle coming for me. He said he would. My dad's brother. I don't like him. For years he said he'd come after me, get me on my birthday when I turned eighteen.'

'Get you?'

'He told me that the first time I was ten. I didn't know what he meant, not back then. I learned. He wanted to throw me on the grass. Do it to me on the grass like an animal. He said that. He was only waiting for the right time.'

'When you turned eighteen.'

'Because I was family. If I wasn't family, he wouldn't wait. With other girls he didn't wait. With me, I was family. So he waited. He is not a good man.'

'You shouldn't be here,' Cinq-Mars stated flatly. 'An accommodation should have been made. Reduced sentence at least.' He believed her to a fault. She had a flat, monotone speech pattern that rarely changed, but somehow, he could decipher when she was repeating what people expected her to say and when she spoke from a depth.

'I can't get out of this place,' she said. 'I'm stuck here.'

'Not saying it's easy. No way can it be quick. We could begin a process. Give you a chance to state the real facts, tell the courts what really happened. I'd be in your corner. You never know, people can be influenced sometimes. Worst case, we'd be ready for the parole board and nail it the first time in. What would you do if you got out, Roz? Where would you go?'

'Go home. Find my uncle. Kill him next.'

Cinq-Mars mulled that over, trying to decide if she was merely serious or dead serious. 'Yeah,' he decided in the end, 'maybe you should stay here.'

She laughed a little. He wasn't sure if she was having him on or not.

'Maybe I won't now,' she said.

'What's changed? Are you more mature? No longer seeking revenge?'

He could tell that she was wrestling with her answer. For some reason this was harder on her than her response about the death of her father. He'd soon surmise that, as the first question was about the past, about everything said and done, it was less of a hardship than trying to discern what was yet to come. His second question concerned the future, and that was a time difficult to fathom.

'Rozlynn, why not?' he asked again quietly.

'Abigail says you're all right.' Another of her prolonged silences. 'Thinks you're decent. You know, for a cop.'

'She should know. I put her in jail.'

'Yeah. She told me that.'

'If I put her in jail and she still thinks I'm all right, you're thinking that maybe you can talk to me. Abigail thinks you should?'

'She thinks that, yeah.'

From what he could determine from her appearance, from how she put herself together, from the clothes she wore, she remained nostalgic for the life she'd left behind. First Nations women did not fare well in prison. Did anyone? he asked himself. Still, First Nations women when among their own were sunk by old problems and perpetual bad habits. Drugs. Alcohol. Wretched stories. Among a broader prison population they were ostracized, kept on the fringe, lacking any cultural connection to the lives of white or black women. An abject loneliness did many in. Rozlynn was a handsome young woman, she exhibited a physical prowess to her deportment, but he could feel the over-arching, aching, naked loneliness rampant in her. He imagined that Abigail had noticed that, too. That in befriending her, Abi had made herself indispensable.

'The two of you are close,' Cinq-Mars stated. 'It's hard for you to trust anyone. Especially a white male police officer. I get that. A lot of history there that nobody wants to talk about. But here's something worth thinking about. Abigail is willing to be friends with you. Even anxious to be your friend. She's close to you. She also can't trust many people in this world. Not in prison, not on the outside, either. Mainly on account of what she's done. If she can trust you, and if she can trust me, then who knows? Maybe you and me can trust each other. Is that possible?'

She wasn't going to answer that question. A step too far.

Cinq-Mars worked from a different angle after that. 'Why did you confess to killing your dad when you didn't know it was your dad you were killing?'

That shrug. 'Because I did it. He was dead. I killed him.'

'I wish all criminals were as straightforward as you. Except I'm not sure it's done you much good.'

She shrugged.

'Why were you pulling women off Abi during the fight? Why get in there like that when you might get hurt?'

'Abi's my friend.' The question felt absurd to her. Of course she'd peel bodies off Abigail's back in that situation.

'That's what I thought. Do you know what I think? That Abi, in a way, wants to peel bodies off your back, too. Help you out that way, the same as you would do for her. Difference is, the bodies on your back are invisible. They're hard for anyone to see. But Abi can see them. Because she's like that.'

If she wanted to ask if Cinq-Mars could see them also, she didn't.

'Everybody wants something from Abi,' Rozlynn said, which for her was a veritable speech.

'What do you want from her?'

'Nothing. I'm the only one who doesn't want nothing.'

'You see? That's one very good reason why she's close friends with you. You're a rare and special person to her. She can count on you not to be out to get her. What does she want back from you, do you think?'

He was expecting her to say 'friendship', or something even simpler, such as 'someone to talk to.' Instead she responded with a more complicated reply. 'I can't tell you that,' Roz said.

'Because you don't know, or because you do?'

A non-committal shrug.

'Now you have to,' he argued back. 'After showing me that carrot, you have to let me have a bite, no?'

'No,' she said. Then she was quiet, and he hoped that she was mulling through her options. He dared not interfere with those internal deliberations.

ii

A different tack.

'Rozlynn, do you think Abigail's life is in danger? This is pretty important, so I hope you don't just shrug it off. Think about it. Is her life in danger? You talk to her a lot. Does Abigail think her life is in danger?'

Cinq-Mars was under the impression that Roz was dwelling on his question in a serious manner, except that her answer dispelled that notion. 'Her life is not in danger,' she said. 'She's safer than anybody.'

He pursed his lips in a way that betrayed his disappointment with her response. 'I'm not so sure about that,' he opined.

'Abi is sure,' Roz said.

That response interested him. 'Why say that?'

'Abi says it.'

'Why is Abi so sure?'

The question provoked her, got her out of her chair. Rozlynn paced again. She settled after about a minute and returned to her seat. While she normally sat as still as stone, this time she tapped the chair's arms with her fists lightly curled, and not with any discernible rhythm. Intrigued, Cinq-Mars leaned forward.

'Why,' he asked again, 'is Abi so sure she's safe here?'

'People want her money,' Roz answered.

'No surprise, but it's not really her money.'

'They want it anyway. So nobody wants her dead. If she dies, her money's gone. Nobody will ever know where it is. Anybody who kills her is in big trouble because of that. Abi thinks so, too. She says so.'

Perfect sense. Abi knew well that she was under threat, that she walked a thin line with dangerous and dedicated bad actors. Connections with those adversarial forces undoubtedly traveled throughout the prison system, high and low, and that worried him, and undoubtedly it worried her. At the same time, as long as people followed orders, she was not going to be killed. Still, how could Abi's issues connect to the deaths of Isaure Dabrezil or the much-disliked Florence? Perhaps Flo was physically confronting Abigail, scaring her, pressing her to reveal her secrets. In which case, Abi may have taken the matter into her own hands and fought back.

Abigail.

iii

'Have you ever discussed getting out of here with Abi?'

Back to shrugging as her primary response.

'Let's say, hypothetically— Sorry, do you know that word?'

Rozlynn shrugged again, yet added, 'Course I do.'

'Yeah. Sorry. You probably speak English better than me.'

'You speak it good. With an accent. Like me. Different accent.'

'There you go. Hypothetically, your uncle vanishes off the face of the earth. He walks off into the sunset, let's say. And you happen to get released. Then what? What would you do? Go home? Behave yourself this time? Or do you want to kill a bunch of people?'

'I'd like to kill my cousins, but I won't.'

This time he knew she was playing with him, and he laughed. She joined in. 'You don't like your cousins. But would you go home, anyway?'

'Nowhere else to go. Abi, she can go anywhere. Maybe she comes to Manitoba, lives there.'

This was a line of demarcation he hadn't expected. Abigail might very well want something from Rozlynn after all. A place to run to. A place to hide. Out in the wilderness, until people forgot she existed. She feared for her life sufficiently to disappear among bugs, bears, trees and moose. She'd probably build a cabin and keep a rifle above the door. Not an easy existence. Perhaps a necessary one. Do time in the wilderness until people forgot about her. If they'd ever forget.

'Would you like that? I guess you'd be helping Abi out.'

'Could be all right,' she said.

'It's a thought,' Cinq-Mars agreed.

If the two women had discussed life after Lady Jail, they may have plotted Abi's rescue in other ways, too. Not beyond the realm of possibility that, jointly, they had dealt with Flo. Rozlynn may have taken Flo off Abigail's back, just as she had hauled others off her back in the yard fight. Permanently, in Flo's case. She had the strength. She'd been a hunter from childhood. Mistaken identity, but she thought she was killing her uncle who intended to do her harm. Cinq-Mars considered that perhaps he'd been too kind, too conciliatory with her. He may have misjudged her, and he should not rule her out as the killer. Given her alliance with Abigail, who possessed an innate ability to fool people, she had to be considered a candidate.

Rozlynn.

Sandra

i

Running late, he hadn't felt this nervous in a decade. Émile Cinq-Mars had started packing that morning but didn't finish before leaving for the penitentiary. The solution was to book for another night and switch from the highway motel to the only downtown hotel in Joliette at the end of his workday. The department could pay for one, he'd chip in for the other. In the office, the motel clerk passed a folded note across the counter to him. Constable Dubroc, reporting in. The arranged meeting with the bikers had not transpired. Dubroc had waited through the day and been stood up.

'Damn,' the detective muttered under his breath. The bikers adding one more irritant – not entirely unexpected – maddened him. In retaliation he'd stick spikes in the spokes of their Harleys – he briefly reveled in that consoling fantasy.

Émile Cinq-Mars finished his arrangements with the clerk and, back in his room, pressed for time, he stuffed his suitcase in a rush. He did take his time with the papers and notes strewn around the room, rearranging them into a semblance of order.

Finally, he was done. He experienced a lurch within himself. A bit like tumbling off a spinning log into a cold dark lake: He hadn't heard from Sandra. He expected her to be waiting downtown, perhaps anxious that he might never show. Wild horses, and he was familiar with the beasts if not the sensations coursing through him, could not drag him away. Super excited to see her again. Yet he had to face it: He was also super terrified to see her again.

Was he right? Was she the one? Or had he concocted a ludicrous notion in his head from the safety of distance? Love had never drawn a simple trajectory for him, the road ahead usually appeared potholed with sharp twists. The priest in him, in part – was he meant for marriage? And Sandra was nineteen years younger! A mature woman of thirty-one, that was true, but – *yikes*. She operated a horse farm. In another country. She was American. She was an atheist amused by his religious bent. How could this be broached, except as a short-term affair? Yet the notion of short-term explicitly saddened him. He felt ruptured when any thought of the two of them added up to nothing more than a fleeting encounter. Ships passing in the night, that sort of thing. Or colliding. When reality strikes, and sooner or later reality will clobber any couple, how would he absorb the blow? How would she? Would they hit the ground running and feel the pain or happily keep falling into eternity together?

He had all these questions. And many more.

He threw his bags into the front-end trunk of his VW Bug. Clambered in behind the wheel. Deep breaths. Pulled out of the motel lot and headed for town.

He soon had company. Two bikers on his tail. They had a few opportunities to kick it and go around but declined to do so. When he slowed, they did so, too. They weren't generic enthusiasts or geriatrics on Hondas. A clear look in his rearview mirror confirmed they were full-patch members of the most notorious biker gang and one of its most deadly chapters on the planet.

Another pair pulled out from a service station down the highway and rode on ahead of him. No coincidence, he speculated. Easy to assume that they meant to be intimidating. They were good at it. They stuck precisely to the speed limit. Traffic was busy enough approaching town that a chance to pass never came up. Usually he had double lines and when he didn't, oncoming vehicles foiled the attempt. The bikers took no obvious interest in him, but two in front, two in back, by design, posed a threat. In the habit of entering the penitentiary in recent days, Cinq-Mars had been locking his service revolver in the glovebox of his car, which is where it was now. Out of reach and locked in. If he was forced to pull over, he'd have to stop, pull the keys from the ignition, unlock the glove box, retrieve his weapon, insert the keys in the ignition again, start up in case he had to step on it, and hope that he did all that at something approaching the speed of light.

Now ten. Six more bikers pulled out and fell in behind. The sound of their engines reached jet-like decibels. A saving grace occurred when the town limits rose up to greet him – he welcomed the safety of population. The bikers slowed to fifty kilometers an hour to suit the new speed limit, and Émile Cinq-Mars slowed his Beetle accordingly.

He parked alongside the hotel in the center of town. All ten bikers did so as well, demonstrating that those ahead and the two groups behind were in this together. He retrieved his weapon, casually, no rush, and clipped the holster to his belt. As he exited his car and heaved out his bags, the others took no interest in him. He found that conspicuous by itself, the way they expressly paid him no mind. Cinq-Mars walked past them to check-in to the hotel where he hoped the love of his life was waiting. *If* she was waiting. *If* she was the love of his life.

And how was he going to win her over with all this scruff around . . .

Checking-in was perfunctory and quick, but Sandra had not arrived. Highly worrisome. He felt his heart lightly pound. He ditched his bags in his second story room, then waited for her in the street-level bar.

The presence of the bikers invoked danger into his liaison. If Sandra did arrive, he should perhaps dispatch her home. That they were ignoring him was no consolation. He knew that bikers didn't threaten. The ride-in aside, they either went after you or they didn't. But what did they have against him, other than his investigation which was going approximately nowhere? He reminded himself that bikers had always kept a victim's family out of their actions. They knew that attacks on family would provoke a more concerted response from the authorities, so they simply didn't go there. All things considered, he and Sandra should be safe.

All things considered, he wanted her to show up.

While he sipped a cold beer – which, after his day, felt miraculous – the bikers in their grungy pose were checking-in as well. The hotel manager came out to assist a disconcerted clerk, and the man's consternation was apparent. He was not going to deny them entry – he was neither that brave nor that foolish. Paul Lagarde was not among the visitors. Cinq-Mars recognized none of the men as having stayed down the road a few days ago. Curiously, they were bereft of girlfriends, which suggested they had an agenda that excluded their molls. Cinq-Mars returned to ruminations aroused by the beer and the next time he looked up Sandra stood before him, three feet

away, all smiles and beautifully brown quizzical eyes, a travel bag
gripped in each hand.

'You're here.'

'You doubted me?' she asked.

She could fluster him so easily. 'No, I—'

'*I* did,' she said. 'I never thought. I got to the border with my
dog—'

'You came with a dog?' He really did not know her well.

'Sandy, my golden retriever. Sandy, Sandra, get it?' She finally
put her bags down. 'Anyway, I got to the border and didn't have
the paperwork for the dog. Her shots, etcetera.'

'Oh no.'

'I mean, Canada really is another country. I don't know what I
was thinking. Then all this talk about the dog among the guards in
French, of course, a language I haven't spoken since university, and
I'm like, what? Am? I? Doing? Here?'

'Do you always take your dog on a date?'

'Stop. This is a trip. It's like a vacation, only not to any part of
the world you'd visit on vacation. I don't mean Canada. I mean
Joliette. What's jolly about it? First impressions, anyway, I can see
why they chose this place for a prison. I mean, you don't need to
do a thing, right? No walls. Just put people here, it's like jail.
Anyway, long story short, I have friends in Vermont, fifty miles
from the border. So fifty miles back there, drop off Sandy, fifty
miles return trip to the border, and here I am, late, and without my
doggie protector and why, tell me, is this hotel *loaded* with bikers
who look like they want to kill me for breathing too loudly? Or
only for breathing?'

He laughed. He loved her spiel. He loved her. He saw that she
was nervous about all this, too, but he was so delighted to see her
and now relieved that, if they slept together, it would only be the
two of them, no dog.

'Let's get your room straightened away.'

'It's reserved, right?'

'Right.'

'Then finish your beer, Detective. Tell me, do you always wear
a gun on a date? I'll have one, too. Not a gun. A beer. I need a cold
one. I passed a dozen *bar salons* along the way and was tempted.
Neon signs advertising naked girls kept me driving.'

He kissed her then. It lasted. Then she laughed and gave him a quick peck back after they broke it off. Everything had happened so fast, but they were in love and both knew it.

They sat together at the bar in their own wee bubble of a world and shot the breeze. All wonderful. Nothing was awkward despite their lengthy separation. Then Sandra checked in and collected her key. She washed away the road dust, changed, and met him again within twenty minutes in the hotel dining room for dinner in the company of ten Hells Angels.

ii

The maître d' placed the gang members as far from the front windows as possible, to conceal their presence, leaving a table by the window as the preferred spot for a couple. Cinq-Mars hesitated.

'What's wrong?' Sandra asked.

'It's not as though there's a view. In this case, we're the view, to anyone outside.'

'It's fine.'

'You don't like the table, monsieur?' the maître d' inquired. The restaurant was not high-end, its menu a mixed fare that catered to a variety of tastes. Yet the maître d' was well dressed, black suited and bow-tied, as though to evoke a former, formal adherence to propriety and glamour. The restaurant was still the nicest spot in town, and the maître d' was determined to evoke a bygone glory day that probably never existed. Not here.

'I'll take that one,' Cinq-Mars said, and pointed.

Sandra Lowndes caught on once they were seated. Émile put his back to the wall to give himself an expansive view of the premises.

He felt more secure that way. She didn't mind. 'Ohh-kay . . .' she said, drawing out both syllables. 'You with the gun on your hip. I didn't know Canada was like the Wild West. You'll let me know if I need to duck.'

'I only have eyes for you tonight. Not them,' Cinq-Mars teased. 'And yes, I just said that. On the other hand, I prefer to keep them in front of me. It's not typical for the Hells to commandeer a place like this while wearing gang colors. It's possible that it has something to do with me.'

'Not to alarm me or anything like that.'

'Not at all. If they're making a spectacle of themselves, they intend no crime. That would be stupid, and unfortunately for me in my line of work, they're not that.'

He wasn't the only one to exercise a speck of caution. The waitress appeared frazzled, making faces to communicate her trepidation.

'Nobody will blame you for leaving,' she let them know.

'Is the food good here?' Cinq-Mars asked.

'The best, but, you know, who can eat?'

Cinq-Mars took her at her word. He was confident the dinner would be an improvement over his hot dog and poutine diet lately. 'We'll stay. They'll behave in public. They look quiet.'

'They do, don't they?' the chubby brunette with an upturned nose and the rosiest of cheeks agreed. 'Let's hope they stay that way.' Her tone betrayed her doubt.

'Have they been by before?'

'Not all at once, not like this. Can I get you drinks? You might need one.'

After she skipped away, Sandra turned more serious. 'That was said for my benefit, wasn't it? About the bikers being polite.'

'I don't always sit with my back to a wall, but honestly, I would get you out of here if I was concerned. I don't expect them to be disruptive.'

'Just sitting, they're disruptive.'

He agreed. 'What they do in secret we don't want to imagine. Still, they're a criminal enterprise. That takes discipline. When they're a public spectacle, they make that work for them, it's intimidating. It lets people know they're present. But they won't give people like me cause to arrest them.'

'That sounds brave, but I think – let me count – yup, you're outnumbered.'

Drinks and menus arrived. Settling into their meal, Cinq-Mars's prognosis proved accurate until another biker arrived. The jangle of Paul Lagarde's boots alerted the detective first despite his back-to-the-wall, eyes-on-the-room positioning. The biker seated himself at their table before the policeman could react. Cinq-Mars shot a glance at Sandra expecting her to be in panic mode, but she clearly thought the intrusion was a hoot.

'Cinq-Mars! You fart!' Lagarde slapped a beer bottle down on the table. 'We meet again. Good looking lady.' He addressed Sandra: 'Me and this guy eat out. I admit, you are prettier than me. I don't blame him not to send an invitation in the mail.'

Sandra raised an eyebrow. She retained more than a smattering of French from university, but the man's dialect was impenetrable. Not receiving much of a reaction from her, he looked to Cinq-Mars, perturbed.

'She doesn't speak French,' he told him.

Cinq-Mars didn't mention that he struggled with the man's unique patois himself, although he was getting the hang of it. Sandra thought to correct him, that she did speak a *little*, but given that she could not comprehend a syllable of their visitor's diction, she explained instead, 'I'm American.'

'Love Americans,' Lagarde announced in passable English. 'I ride in New Hampshire. You know New Hampshire?'

'That's where I'm from.' She glanced at Cinq-Mars, wondering if she should have admitted to that.

'Live Free or Die. The best motto. Mine, too.' He patted her shoulder with his big hand. 'In New Hampshire, no helmets. I like to live free or die when I ride my bike.'

'A private dinner, Paul,' Cinq-Mars commented. 'I'm sure you understand. Sandra, this is Paul Lagarde, who's pretty high-up in the Hells Angels, although he might be splitting with a rebel group. Paul, this is Sandra.'

'You a lawyer? A cop?' the biker inquired.

'I raise horses for a living.'

'Good. Then we be friends. Not like this guy. He might shoot me someday. Or put me in jail with very bad men. Me, I am not a bad man. I am a sheep in the clothes of a wolf.'

Sandra smiled at his inversion of the familiar phrase.

'Don't believe him,' Cinq-Mars interjected, sticking with English for Sandra's sake. 'Paul, your boys were supposed to show their faces to Constable Dubroc today. We agreed. They didn't. That was not an option, Paul. I'll scoop them up. Your fault.'

'No need. They were delayed. Couldn't be helped. I'll get them to you real soon, Cinq-Mars. No problem. No worries.'

'By noon tomorrow.'

'Works for me.'

'What can I do for you, Paul?'

Lagarde tried to explain himself in English but fumbled his words. He apologized to Sandra, then switched to his shotgun French. 'What you told me, Cinq-Mars. Truth in it. Not like you think.'

'What did I tell you?' He and Sandra accepted that the interruption would not soon end so resumed their meal. Cinq-Mars had opted for the prime rib, while Sandra had chosen the chicken *vol au vent*. The fare did not rise to a gourmet standard yet was respectful of anyone's pallet.

'We do business, inside the organization.'

'Have you voted yet?'

That gave Lagarde pause. He stuck his fists on his thighs and glared back at Cinq-Mars with a look that conveyed both mystification and respect. 'Watch out for this guy,' he said in English to Sandra. 'There are different kinds of cops. He's the worst kind there is.'

'What kind is that?'

'He's informed.'

Her mouth full, Sandra suppressed a laugh. The heavyweight tough guy with the Iron Cross suspended from an earlobe and the skull and crossbones in his eyes was not devoid of charm.

Back to French. 'A vote's been taken, if you know what I'm talking about. If you're only guessing, I say nothing more.'

'Are you still a Hells Angel?'

'Don't ask. You know too much already. Not good for your health maybe.'

'Paul, remind me. What did I say before, that now you find true?'

'Not my turf, Cinq-Mars. I did not come here on my own. I'm away for the vote. I didn't know about it at first. When it's discussed, where am I? Not there. Not in the room. I'm out here in the wilderness with the deer and the wolves visiting a ladies' prison.'

'You still get a vote, no?'

'We're waiting on the count. Democracy, man. One jackass, one vote. But I got a rep even you maybe don't know about. Guys call me the peacekeeper in the gang.'

'Are you really?'

'Don't give me that look. My guys know that about me. I can persuade guys this way or that way. Did certain people around the countryside and in the city want a peacekeeper, a guy with a gift to show the blind how to see, did they want their peacekeeper in that meeting, help persuade the vote? Don't think so. Some wanted me out in nowhere-land because they don't want peace. They're itching for war. If I was there maybe I'd find a way to make peace happen.'

'Meaning, you're not for the war.'

'Bring it on. It's coming anyway. You coppers will love it. Dead bikers all around. The streets littered with our corpses. The gutters will flow with our blood.'

Cinq-Mars put his knife and fork down. He was sensing an opportunity, and Sandra's presence was not enough to let it pass him by. For her sake, though, he switched back to English.

'It's done? There's been a vote? The Hells Angels are at war with their own satellites? And you, you've thrown in with the Alliance?'

'I've made progress with the name. The Rock Machine. It's catching on.' He asked Sandra her opinion, in English. 'Do you like the name?'

'Much better than having the word devil or demon in it. Sounds modern.'

'Keep her,' Lagarde said. 'She's a smart cookie.'

'What's true?' Cinq-Mars asked again.

He reverted to French. 'I got played. Out here to visit the prison. That was a play. To keep me away when the big meeting happened. Now I'm on the outside, looking in. And the outside is at war with the inside.'

Meaning, the gangs across the Quebec countryside were going to fight Hells Angels in the cities.

'I wanted to let you know, Cinq-Mars. Guys arranged for me to be here so I wouldn't be someplace else. If being here makes me look bad when a prison guard is whacked, that doesn't make me part of it. Because I wasn't. My enemies used to be my brothers. Look at them for that.'

The man stood, his chains jangling.

'Thanks for the visit, Paul.' He had a thought. 'You've been respectful. That's appreciated. To be clear, I still need to see the four guys who were around earlier this week.'

'Busy voting. A priority.'

'This is my thought, or I should say my suspicion, Paul. I'm being respectful, too. Still, it's my job to be suspicious. If a gang knows a war is on the horizon, then the side in the battle that carried out a killing might be motivated to see the other side take the blame.'

The biker glared back at him a moment; his gaze less friendly than it had been. He looked down at Sandra then, and nodded towards her dinner companion. In English: 'Smart guy, hey? My advice, watch out for him.'

'I promise,' she told him, which made Lagarde laugh. 'I will.'

'See you later, Cinq-Mars.' He picked up his beer bottle, empty now, and departed. He did not join his companions at their tables but vacated the hotel.

'Sorry about that,' Cinq-Mars said.

'I'm not,' Sandra replied, and they both smiled at one another before returning to a different conversation and their meal.

iii

Their joy carried them into Émile's room. The physical had been absent from both their lives for some time. His muscularity surprised her, although it should not have, she realized, this man who'd worked with horses since childhood and had attended to a farm before becoming a cop. For Émile, the electricity on contact with her skin astounded him. Mutual surprise and discovery yielded to passionate intensity, then later, their tender explorations.

They were lying curled and contented, in the shock of love, when the first violent volley occurred outside. The sound was startling, and in their state, disorienting. They did not know that the shattering sound came from a baseball bat missing a head and smashing a car window instead. The night erupted.

By the time he reached the window, peeking around the blind due to his nakedness even though the lights were off, Cinq-Mars saw about two dozen combatants arrayed in the street below. Kicking, punching, swinging chains. Growling and grunting. He felt it prudent to dress. Sandra flicked on a light switch and covered her breasts with the top sheet. 'What's going on?'

'Bedlam. A fight. It's the bikers.'

'Do you have to go?' He was tugging on his pants.

'Their fight. Not my town. But if I'm pulled into it somehow, I'll want my pants on.' He was trying to take the edge off his alarm.

'Should I call the police?' Sandra asked. 'In case?'

'I'm the police.'

'Should I call anyway?'

'Call.'

Dressed, he raised the blind and peered below.

'The front desk won't answer,' Sandra reported.

'Dial nine. Get an outside line.'

'I tried that. Nothing happens.'

'Stay here,' he instructed her. The room's safe was in the closet by the front door. He opened it and extracted his holster and weapon. Cinq-Mars went downstairs where he showed his badge to the biker on-duty. 'Out.'

'You want to fuck with me?'

'Not sure. Maybe I'll kneecap you first, then decide.'

The thug noticed the pistol and obediently slumped out the door.

The night manager was sitting on the floor like a dog who'd suffered a reprimand. Sheet-white but he could still function and was beginning to stir with the biker out of the building. 'Hook up the phones. Call the police,' Cinq-Mars instructed him. The old guy had seen a few things in his day although this night was taking the cake. He made the call. By the time Cinq-Mars stepped outside, sirens wailed. A citizen had probably alerted the police sooner than did the clerk.

His call though put more units on the streets and ambulances as well. The night became a jeremiad of wailing sirens.

Men slammed one another to the pavement. Punched, kicked, kneed, elbowed. More than one combatant moaned in the dirt and held on to his testicles. Blows hit home; jaws popped. Cinq-Mars noticed a telling difference between this brawl and any other he might expect from men like these: the total absence of serious weaponry. A couple of bats and a couple of chains, but even those tools had fallen to the pavement and no one took an interest in retrieving them.

Curious, that.

The lack of weapons made the battle seem benign, and whatever it was about, the fight appeared to neutralize itself. A tussle between four men was being broken up by six, and two guys remained locked on the ground bound by each other's grip. Three men lay on the pavement unable to rise from the damage done to them. Their injuries apparently took care of whatever score needed to be settled.

The first police unit wailed on to the scene and from the opposite direction a pair of ambulances followed.

Cinq-Mars maintained his position on the front stoop of the hotel. He leaned against a post. A uniform suggested he move back as more cops arrived. He showed his badge; otherwise, he did not impose himself on the proceedings. One ambulance peeled away with a victim; a second was loaded and a third showed up. Cinq-Mars displayed his badge again as he strolled through the battalions of bikers and cops right into the rear of the second ambulance. 'Give me a minute,' he told the medic before the next guy was loaded in. 'Put him in the other one.'

He sat down opposite a bloodied man.

'Well played,' he told Paul Lagarde who was holding a towel to his bloody head.

'What you mean by that?'

'I counted twenty guys. Only fourteen were here at first. Then you. That's fifteen. Five more showed up. I presume those five include the men who stayed at our motel a few nights ago.'

'Maybe,' Lagarde submitted. 'In the confusion what do I know?'

'Confusion, my ass. Those four were in the fight and like everybody else, their faces are bloodied and bruised now. That part was convincing.'

'Can't say,' Lagarde admitted.

'The total lack of knives gave you away. But like I said, well played.'

'Something on your mind, Cinq-Mars?'

'DNA. Off the carpets where Officer Isaure Dabrezil went down and from the cuts on your guys faces.'

'Yeah, if it still exists. That DNA, I mean. That sort of thing gets lost or bungled in the system sometimes. I don't trust it.'

'More where it came from.'

'You think? The grapevine – you know about the grapevine, Cinq-Mars? I heard those carpets got removed. Where they are now, you think?'

The man's confidence staggered him. 'So much for being the peacemaker,' Cinq-Mars noted.

Lagarde removed the towel from his head, rested his wrists over his thighs and leaned in closer. Blood popped along his brow, sticking to his long and stringy hair. He needed stitches. 'Like I told you, it comes down from the top, a hit like that. Like *you* told *me*, or you made me think about it anyway, maybe somebody wanted me to look bad for it.'

'You said,' Cinq-Mars reminded him, 'that it had to be an outsider. That could be. But you're an outsider, Paul. Living in a motel. Same with those close pals of yours.'

'Let's say that I didn't like the fucking guilty arrow pointing right between my eyeballs. If an order comes through the door for a serious hit, if an outsider is brought in to carry it out, that don't point an arrow at nobody. Especially not me. I get it now, what you said. I didn't before.'

Cinq-Mars knew that he was catching him at an opportune moment. 'The vote.'

'My buddies are not my enemies. But here we are. At war.'

'This show tonight wasn't war.'

'Tonight was nothing. Wait for what comes.'

'No stopping it?' Cinq-Mars inquired.

'Not by you. Like I said, cops will like it. Lots of dead bikers. Seventh heaven for you guys.'

'And you can guarantee that no innocent bystanders will also be killed or maimed, even accidentally?'

Lagarde shrugged to acknowledge the issue. 'It'll be a mess,' he prophesied.

Cinq-Mars leaned in closer himself. 'You've taken sides, Paul. You were a full-patch member of the Hells Angels yet I see you've torn yours off. You're Rock Machine now.'

'I been moving that way for a while.'

'Take whatever side you're on and help me with my case by giving me something – a truth, it has to be true – give me something that goes against the other side. You'll be protecting your own. Anyway, all's fair in war, right?'

Lagarde nodded and rotated his head from side to side. 'Run down where you're at so far.'

'Isaure Dabrezil is dead. Florence is dead. Why are they dead? That's one question. Here's another. Jodi and Courtney are kids, but Jodi has knowledge of what's happening.' A bluff. But a substantive one. He wouldn't want to be on a witness stand himself. He didn't know it for a fact, but Courtney told him that Jodi had told her that everything turned around Abi. To know that, Jodi had to be in a

loop, and he had assessed her background which had been a revelation. With some confidence he asked Lagarde, 'How come?'

'The Hells sent Jodi in,' Lagarde said. 'My old gang. She shot
up a store, something like that? Not what you think. She didn't
panic. She did it on purpose. The whole point was to get arrested.
The Hells would take care of her in prison. We – they, I should say
– run the prisons, right? Then we – they – worked her through the
system to arrive here. They worked Abigail through the system to
arrive here, too, after her. For a different reason. Follow me so far?'

'I follow. What else? What do you know about Temple? Or
Rozlynn? Anything? How are they involved?'

'Temple's a helper for the new side. My side. Leave her alone
in this.'

'Temple's buying guns for you, or showing you how,' Cinq-Mars
pointed out. 'How do I leave that alone?'

'Don't judge.'

'She's not coming off the radar screen.'

'Temple's invisible. She does what she does. She knows how to
do. She is an asset. Who you call Rozlynn, I know nothing. Anybody
else?'

'A woman named Doi. Another called Malka. Older ladies.' He
expected no reaction. He was surprised when Lagarde hesitated.

'Them I don't know,' Lagarde said, but why so slow to say that?

'I know quite a lot about Abigail,' Cinq-Mars told him. 'I arrested
her. Tell me something I don't know.'

'She made friends with Flo,' Lagarde told him as though that
was a serious matter.

'She did.'

'Some people maybe thought that could be a problem.'

'How so?'

'Think about it. Maybe Flo was supposed to be trouble for
Abigail. Instead they became friends. You see? Somebody somewhere might've figured out that that wasn't right. Not the way it
should be. Not Flo's purpose. If she wanted to get off the hook for
throwing acid in the face of a biker's moll, because she needed to
get off the hook for that, or the alternative—'

'The alternative?'

'Whacked. She didn't want to be whacked, she had to make up
for the acid. Her job? Making friends, not part of it. You follow?'

Sort of. But yes, he did.

'Maybe she was asked to switch sides and didn't. Or maybe she wasn't asked and did. Listen to me, Cinq-Mars, the SQ thinks Isaure Dabrezil was one of theirs. Right? It won't be the first time in history they might be wrong.'

As instructed, he listened. He said, 'That doesn't get your people off.'

'Time will tell. It might. But don't miss the point here. If Flo was in with today's Hells, then Temple or Malka might've been against her. Leaning that way anyhow. If she was in with what is now the Rock Machine, and remember, it didn't exist then, so it's hard to know what side was her side, and which side she was on, then Jodi and Marie-Philomène could've lined up against her. Hard to say. Even for me. Look, my head hurts. Kinda bad right now. I need to get to a hospital. Stitched up to keep me a handsome mother-fucker. Scars, I got enough. If you don't mind too much, time to piss off.'

Cinq-Mars was willing to let him go. He knew that the man had secretly loaded his responses with a clue.

iv

Upon his eventual return to his room, Cinq-Mars found the bed abandoned and a note on his pillow.

> *Émile,*
> *Totally beat. You will be too whenever you're back.*
> *Take care. See you in the morning.*
> *Love,*
> *San*

He didn't know her room number. He resigned himself to sleeping alone again, although he wasn't certain that sleep would come easily given how his head buzzed. He was not long for the pillow – hard to judge as he fell asleep quickly – when his phone rang. He snapped it up, expecting the call to be from Sandra and hoping that she had changed her mind.

'Hi,' he said. A modicum of sexiness infused his tone.

'Sergeant-Detective Cinq-Mars?'

He gave his head a shake. The voice sounded familiar, but in his sleepiness, he couldn't place it. 'Yeah. Who's this?'

'DesSaulniers.' Alexandre DesSaulniers, Chief of Police. His boss.

'Yes, sir?'

'You're still alive.'

'I am. Why? I'm not necessarily fully awake, sir.'

'Maybe my news will change that. I had a hard time tracking you down.'

'Yes, sir. I booked out of the motel for a hotel. Better digs. Eighteen bucks more a night. The department can afford it, I'm sure.'

'Why move?'

'Long story, Chief.'

'Good that you did, maybe. Are you aware? Somebody broke into your old room and shot up the mattress. Twenty rounds. The question is, did they know the bed was empty or did they think you were on it. Either way, a cause for concern, no?'

'Yes, sir,' Cinq-Mars agreed after a pause. Concern was an understatement, but he could not improve on the opinion in his current state of surprise. He had to assume that the assailants believed he was sleeping there. Which meant the bikers who had escorted him into town were not the mattress killers. They wouldn't ask for that kind of trouble.

Still. A chill coursed through him. Never mind that he might have been in that bed. Under slightly altered circumstances, Sandra could have been in it, too.

But no. Thank God. He'd never have the bad sense to take her out to that dump.

Still.

'Very least it's a warning,' DesSaulniers continued, another understatement. 'Take care, Cinq-Mars. I know you're fucking religious. If you say you left the motel on a whim, that could make me religious, too.'

'Yes, sir. Thank you, sir.'

'Strict vigilance, Cinq-Mars.'

'Yes, sir. No question.'

Strict vigilance. Somebody shot up his old mattress. The one he was now sleeping on felt less safe.

He had an idea. Cinq-Mars dressed and went downstairs. He had gained the trust of the night manager by kicking out a biker earlier. He parlayed that connection into receiving Sandra's room number then had the clerk scrub her name from the hotel's register, adding a Mr Alphonse Lemay as the occupant. He'd knock first. She might admit him. Under the circumstances, her bed was the preferred option for the night, not the one under his name.

A preferred option. Perhaps that might be true for the rest of his life.

He went upstairs after talking to the night manager. Went to his room and retrieved his pistol. Then went to her room on the next floor up. He knocked. She admitted him.

He made sure the lock was secure with his pistol on their bedside table.

Doi

i

Their wish for a languorous morning in bed vanished before they roused themselves for the new day.

The telephone jarred them awake.

Startled from his dream state, Cinq-Mars swore under his breath. A call this early meant trouble. Doubly so if someone had taken the trouble to track him down in another's bed.

Sandra lit out for the washroom. Cinq-Mars sat up and answered with a perfunctory, 'Bonjour,' as though warning the caller that this had better be good.

Warden Paquet. The alarm in her voice was unmistakable even as she fought to exercise control. 'We have a situation, Émile.'

'What sort of situation?'

'Whose room are you in?' she wanted to know first.

'I'm lying low.'

Paquet wasn't buying his story. She made a sound similar to a snort that may have been a snort.

'Not low enough if you located me.'

'I live here. I know people in this town,' she explained, then filled him in on her crisis. She didn't give an order, she didn't have that authority, and yet she let him know that he was expected back at the penitentiary lickety-split.

As he put the phone down, Sandra detected his disquiet. 'What's up?'

'A hostage-taking. Inside the pen. I better go.'

'Oh no. Yes, go. I'll be here when you're done. Be safe, Émile.'

They kissed quickly and he rushed out the door, then poked his head back in. 'By the way, you're now here under an alias. You are Monsieur Alphonse Lemay. Just so you know.' Then he headed first to his own room for a fresh shirt and his badge. She didn't tell him that these interruptions, sudden emergencies, and even the ludicrous name-change were intriguing, an add-on to why she was interested

in him. She didn't mind the excitement or the danger. The sense
that critical matters should be at stake in their lives felt about right
to her. Perhaps she'd been immersed in the pastoral ease of the
horse farm for too long. The change was enticing.

When she thought more deeply about it, though, she recognized
that she was romanticizing the risk. To live a life where she did not
know if her man would remain alive come nightfall was probably
too severe a counterpoint to a quiet rural life. She reminded
herself to think this whole deal through, upside down and inside
out, and to permit her persistent doubts a voice.

ii

Cinq-Mars zipped across the countryside in his Beetle. Not the
gentlest of vehicles on a ridiculously rough road. Quebec blames
its weather, cold snaps and sudden thaws in winter for the plentitude
of potholes and ripped surfaces. Cinq-Mars shuns the excuses but
braced himself for the jarring, bone-splintering shocks. He figured
his car's undercarriage wouldn't survive another two weeks driving
out to the prison.

Not at this speed.

He arrived famished and once through the security checks asked
for a donut, a croissant, an Oh Henry! – if they had to choose a
candy bar from a machine – and coffee. He missed his customary
lox on a Montreal bagel. While he was waiting to be led to the
scene of the incident, a guard brought him an egg-and-bacon sandwich on an English muffin. Brilliant. The paper cup for the coffee
was large and full. Sensational.

A different guard took him through the gauntlet of opening and
closing locked doors until he stood at the entrance to the unit that
housed the crew he'd been investigating. Heavily armed guards at
the ready, both men and women, had stood down. The unit guards
had evacuated the premises under threat of a hostage – in the
warden's words as she brought him up to speed – 'being sliced and
diced.'

'Who's involved?'

'Doi flipped a switch,' the warden informed him. 'She has a knife
at Courtney's throat. You understand the dynamic here. A woman
who took a hatchet to her own daughter is holding a girl about her

daughter's age at knifepoint. She's in a helluva state. Both of them are. We're out here because Doi demanded we back off or she'd harm Courtney. Or kill her. Still, I couldn't order a full retreat. Then Quinn, your friend—'

'My friend,' Cinq-Mars said in a hushed tone. This was not something that other ears should be hearing. Too late now.

The warden tried to correct herself. 'You know what I mean. The prisoner you once arrested. She tried to intervene.'

Cinq-Mars looked at her. 'How did that go down?'

'She got hurt.' Quickly, she explained that, 'It's not too bad. We were able to treat her. Doi let us do that. Quinn could have come out with us but said no. She devised some cockamamie excuse to stay behind. She's good, your girl. She didn't leave us any room to argue.'

'Sounds like Quinn, yeah. I'll wring her neck.' He was wolfing down his breakfast sandwich.

Paquet whispered a further explanation: 'I was willing to retreat if I still had one of our own on the inside. Doi threatened serious shit if we didn't back off. I couldn't permit that. An impasse. Quinn had a suggestion, that we back off if Doi agrees to let you come in and update them on the situation.'

'The situation.'

'Who killed who. Hey, Doi agreed to it. Apparently, you're the one she wants to see anyway. This is now up to you, Sergeant-Detective.'

'No hint of pressure, nothing like that.'

Paquet nodded in sympathy with his mood. 'We're right behind you if things go south, although it means a bloodbath if that happens. We can end it fast, but not without serious damage.'

'Lovely.'

'You didn't sign up for this, Sergeant-Detective. I wouldn't be honest if I said I wasn't twisting your arm. But for the record I'm not forcing you. You don't have to go in there.'

'That's not true. I have to go in. Tell me about Quinn. Is she bandaged up?'

'She is.'

'The cuts are serious? Big bandages?'

She jerked her head up with the odd question. 'A fair amount. Why?'

'She's mobile? Maybe limited but mobile?'

'I'd say so.'

'Then bring me fresh bandages, please, and a nail.'

'A nail?'

'Four to six inches long. Whatever you've got. Quickly.'

iii

Cinq-Mars stepped into the house-unit's compound carrying his paper coffee cup. He had never been beyond the segregated kitchen previously, so the layout was new to him. The premises appeared empty and shockingly quiet. He walked through the vacant common area to the sleeping quarters and sized up the scene there. The quarters were arranged as an octagon, except for the openings where he had entered from the common space and the entrance opposite him for the communal showers. With one exception, the women were arrayed around the room on bunks. To his left, which Cinq-Mars designated as twelve o'clock, Doi sat on her bed. Courtney, the exception, was on her knees on the floor facing him, with Doi's shockingly large knife at her throat. The knife was bloodied. Small cuts were apparent on Courtney's chest above her left breast where her blouse was torn. Quinn sat cross-legged, off-center near the middle of the room, also bloodied.

'Quinn, you OK?'

'Peachy,' she said.

Cinq-Mars addressed Doi for the first time. 'I want to check her wounds, see how's she's doing.'

'Her fault what happened.'

'Could be. Not arguing the point.'

Doi considered her options. Finding none that mattered. 'Yeah, sure. Go ahead.'

Cinq-Mars knelt beside Quinn and they shared a glance. He put his coffee down on the floor. Her wounds were more than superficial. 'Really deep' she said of one wound. That one likely required more than stitches, but the bleeding was contained with bandaging and pressure. She was handling the pain.

'I need to change the dressing,' Cinq-Mars announced. 'Will that be all right?'

He requested permission from Doi to let her know that she was in charge, that he was respecting that reality and ceding authority to her. The woman's grip on Courtney was a tight one. He could see in the younger woman's eyes that she feared death as a likely outcome, and before that end arrived, perhaps unspeakable pain. With one hand, Courtney was holding on to Doi's wrist. Her other clutched her own tummy, as though trying to contain the freak-out of emotions seizing her there.

Cinq-Mars set about to change the dressing.

As he did so, Quinn's eyes widened.

She nodded imperceptibly, for his benefit alone. She understood what he had just done.

'I want her to sit up on a bed, all right?' Cinq-Mars requested.

Doi consented with a stipulation. 'Not near me. She attacked me, that one did. She had no business interfering.'

'For your own good, maybe. You're in some trouble now, Doi, isn't that right?'

Cinq-Mars escorted Quinn in the opposite direction and had her sit on the same bed as Abigail, between her and Malka in the next bed over. He again tried to speak to Quinn with his eyes. She seemed to grasp the message conveyed.

Abi may have noticed their silent communication and Cinq-Mars noted that. He looked more directly at her to evaluate the young woman's status. She seemed to revel in the chaos, which would be her way. Her expression confirmed that the situation was potentially dire, that in her opinion Doi may have gone completely around the bend. All this conveyed with her expressive eyes.

'So! Doi!' Cinq-Mars turned on his heels abruptly to confront her. 'What the hell is this about? What's going on here?'

Doi took the knife from Courtney's throat, aimed the blade at Cinq-Mars across the room. 'Your fault, you bastard! We're living here! Trying to. How do we live like human beings – like human beings! – when somebody is killing us? Who dies next? Me? How do I sleep at night when a woman *in this room* killed Flo for no reason and I don't know who she is? Who killed Isaure? Why? You're supposed to tell us that. You. What's going on? Tell us who killed who, so we know. Then get the killer out of here! Get her out now!'

Cinq-Mars returned to the middle of the room, ostensibly to retrieve his coffee from the floor. He picked up the cup and sipped through the small opening in the plastic lid. 'Getting cold,' he said. 'You don't mind, I'm going to polish this off. I'm barely awake. I got a feeling I'll need the caffeine.'

Doi returned her knife to Courtney's throat, so close the girl had to recoil back against her.

'How about you relax your grip a little,' Cinq-Mars suggested. 'If you do that, Doi, I'll go around the room. Talk about everyone. See who might be guilty and why, or why not. See if that helps your mood. Courtney's very frightened, Doi.'

'Like I give a big fat shit.'

'Come on, Doi, you don't talk that way. It's not natural for you. You're a mother. I know, you regret what happened to your daughter. People make mistakes. That was a mistake. You agree, right? You don't want to make the same mistake twice. Did it do you any good the first time?'

'This little *scamp*,' Doi said with bitter undercurrent.

'She didn't put you here, Doi. She wasn't the judge or the jury. She didn't arrest you. You brought that on yourself. Now come on, relax the knife a little. I'm not saying to let her go, not yet. I know you're not in the mood to do that, but how can I talk about my investigation if you're about to slice an artery? You know? It makes me nervous. You can understand that.'

Although Doi took her time, she let the hand wielding the knife to ease off. She dropped that hand to the girl's lower ribcage, and with her free arm maintained her grip on Courtney's neck. The compromise indicated that Doi was willing to negotiate, that she still had her wits about her.

Cinq-Mars surveyed the room. Putting Doi and Courtney at twelve o'clock placed Temple at two and Rozlynn at four. At six o'clock Abigail sat with Quinn. Malka was seated at eight o'clock and at ten Jodi was close to Doi and her captive. His eyes went around the room and paused briefly on everyone. 'Hmm,' he demurred. Then seemed to settle upon a strategy, or at least a way forward. 'OK.'

He was surprised by the quietude of this arena. These were, for the most part, women who'd been through violent episodes as participants and as witnesses. The blood shed by Quinn and to a lesser extent by Courtney did not shock them, yet they were seated apart and compliant with Doi's decrees. She must have ordered them to their beds, and the specter of a young woman having her throat sliced open in front of them made them obey.

'OK what?' Doi disrupted his meditation.

'I'll start with you,' Cinq-Mars announced. 'Why you might be the guilty party, and also why you might not be. Ready?'

'No problem,' she said. 'I'm not guilty.'

'You know if you're guilty or not. I don't. I don't have that luxury. Instead, I'm forced to rely on what I learn and what I put together. I've spoken with each of you, as you know. I've also investigated every one of you, which you don't know. I've talked to your families, to most of your arresting officers, to authorities in places where you used to live. I know more about everyone here than you think I do.'

'Rumor and hearsay won't pay for that coffee,' Abi objected.

'Speak when spoken to, Abigail. Not until.'

'Fascist.'

She garnered a laugh or two. The majority weren't interested in her remark.

'Button it,' Cinq-Mars warned her, and for the moment she did.

'Doi, try not to take it personally. I will be equally hard on everyone. I approach my investigation with the advantage of knowing that one of you did it.' He deliberately built drama in his movements in the center of the space, for an aspect of his strategy was to keep the women in general and Doi in particular attentive, if not entertained. At that moment he could not prevent her from harming Courtney, so needed to distract her from that rash impulse. 'Quinn wasn't here then. Otherwise, one of you, or more than one, murdered Flo. I ask myself, Doi, over and over again, if it was you. Just like I've asked that question of everyone else.'

She shook her knife at him, just to the side of Courtney's nose. 'What's your answer? It wasn't me. You know that, right? If you don't know that you don't know nothing.' Her tone suggested that she had doubts of her own, although she would surely know if she was guilty.

'You're capable,' Cinq-Mars pointed out. He paced within a small quarter, enough movement that she followed him with her eyes, concentrating more on him than on Courtney. 'In a one-on-one battle, in a fair fight, then yes, Flo would have handled you quite easily. You're not light, you're not weak, but you're no match for a brute like Flo. But this was not a fair fight. A garrote around the neck incapacitates a victim very quickly. Oh, there are ways and maneuvers to help yourself, but you need training for that. Flo, as almost everyone would do, brought her hands to her throat to try and take the wire off. The autopsy showed that she got the tip of her right index finger inside the wire. Doing that spelled her doom. It's a common reaction, of course, just not one that does the victim a speck of good. So, you're capable, Doi. Everyone here is. I'm sorry to be crass but you hacked up your daughter in a pique of temper, now you're holding Courtney hostage in a fit of rage, apparently brought on by your anxiety. No longer can you fall back on being a benign older lady who would never do such a thing. You're doing it right now. You're violent right now. So it is possible that you killed Florence.'

'I'm innocent,' Doi maintained meekly. Many in the room sensed that she could as easily confess guilt.

Cinq-Mars opened and closed his palms in a gesture of conciliation. 'I have reason to think so, too, Doi, that you're innocent. Before we consider that part, it's my job to take into account that you were the one who found Flo. I can place no one at the scene of the murder more directly than you. You were there. We know that. The only issue, was Flo already dead or did you kill her? Due to your proximity, you're easily perceived as the guilty one. Due to that one fact I suspect that some people here think that you *are* the guilty one. They could be right. What you're doing today doesn't help change their minds, does it?'

'You fucker, I'm innocent!' Adamant, this time, pointing the knife at him again. 'I'll split open her gut if you say different. I'm sick of this place!'

Cinq-Mars appeared to retreat and took a step back to emphasize his contrition. 'Doi, there's no need to take it out on Courtney. Or me. Remember, I'm walking everyone through this process. You first, that's all. You want to know who the killer is. So do I. We have that in common. Maybe we'll work it out together. Go over the facts. For now, calm down, we have a lot of ground to cover.'

'You said,' Abigail interrupted, and Cinq-Mars gave her a look, but she persisted, 'you said you would tell each person why she might be innocent. How does that apply to Doi?'

This was helpful. Not merely as a reminder to Cinq-Mars to do so, but it showed a measure of solidarity among the inmates for the cause of Doi's innocence. Feeling that she had people on her side might help her stay calm.

'Right you are.' He scratched the back of his neck, as though giving the matter deep thought. 'Doi, let's face it, you come across as a sweet old lady. Old by the standards in here, anyway. The guards are only half your age. I have a sense and also reason to believe that Flo's death was gang-related. I've heard evidence on the outside to that effect. If so, that leaves you out of it, right? Not your milieu. You're high and dry that way.'

Doi nodded aggressively. She liked that explanation.

'Next, continuing clockwise, let's move on to Temple.'

'What about Courtney?' Doi asked.

'I'll go around the room and get to her at the end.'

'Yippee, it's my turn,' Temple jumped in, to help the proceedings along by pushing any objection from Doi aside. 'You want I should say I'm innocent, too?'

'Don't bother. We'll assume everyone's innocent until proven otherwise. Though in lieu of comprehensive proof, I'll accept a confession at any time. How's that?'

'You won't get one of those out of me.'

'I figured as much. But Temple, you must admit, you're a likely candidate.'

'How come?'

'You're a match for Flo physically.'

'Nobody would say that.'

'Closer than anyone else here.'

Heads nodded around the room. Cinq-Mars pressed that advantage. 'Also, you're gang-connected. Flo was close to the Hells. You were, too. But the Hells are undergoing a schism, a split, pending a war that you know about. You've thrown in with the Alliance, which I hear may soon be absorbed into the Rock Machine. The Hells had a score to settle with Flo, for throwing acid on one of their own. You're in the process of being at war with the Hells since you're aiding the Rock Machine to procure guns and explosives. Temple, that's rough trade. Won't help in front of the parole board, you know. Now, if the Rock Machine or the Hells gave you a directive to take out Flo, you'd have trouble refusing that.'

'If,' Temple said in her own defense. '*If.*'

'If,' Cinq-Mars conceded. 'Nevertheless, given your size, your tough background, your gang connections, and the fact that Flo was supposed to spend her time inside intimidating Abigail—'

He paused, as if in deference to the sharp intake of breath he heard go around the room.

'Except,' he continued, 'that didn't happen. Abigail took care of that by befriending Florence, which was confusing to her, which derailed Flo from her intended purpose, something the Hells Angels were not happy about. That made Flo vulnerable to retaliation from her masters. They may have decided that between the acid-throwing incident and being insubordinate by leaving Abigail alone, by being *friendly* with her for God's sake, that she deserved to die. You see, Temple, from my perspective, either section of the gang may have issued the order to terminate Flo and asked you to carry it out. That makes you look awfully guilty to me.'

'Innocent as the driven snow,' she remarked, and smirked.

'We'll see. You admitted to me that Malka was out of your sight from time to time that day, which tells me that you were out of Malka's sight. Others may not have noticed your comings and goings. That gives you opportunity, and I believe that we've established motive.'

'Did you do it, Temple?' Doi asked her.

'No, did you?'

'What sets Temple up as innocent?' Abigail chimed in again.

Cinq-Mars shrugged. 'It can't be said of too many inmates here, but it can be said of Temple. She has no record of violence. She trafficked in weapons, that's true. Not good. But did she ever fire a gun herself, or wield a knife? No. Driven snow, she said. In one sense, she may be right about that part.'

Temple imitated a muscleman pose flexing her biceps, which drew nervous laughter from the other women.

'Next,' Cinq-Mars announced, 'we have Rozlynn.'

iv

'Ah, Rozlynn, it can't be Rozlynn, right? She's First Nations. She's not involved in your white man's bullshit. She's not a gang member. She doesn't get involved with much of anything, stays quiet, keeps to herself, why would she be choking Flo to death? We saw what she did in the yard brawl. Roz wasn't beating people up, she was pulling women off each other. A peacemaker.'

The spiel garnered general acceptance around the room. It couldn't be Roz. Cinq-Mars paced as he spoke, and the eyes of the women, in unison, followed him. Even Rozlynn kept her head up, listening.

Cinq-Mars continued. 'Rozlynn is in prison due to a domestic dispute. She killed her father. Most of you forgive her for that since you assume it was either in self-defense or a retaliation for abuse. It might surprise some of you that she didn't mean to kill her father. In the dark and in the moment, she thought she was killing her uncle. The courts wouldn't care about the difference, so she kept that to herself. But oh yeah, big mistake. Wrong victim.'

The women gazed at Roz to see if this was true. They saw that it was. They returned their focus to the policeman.

'Same difference, mind you. She was both protecting herself from what her uncle might do and retaliating for past abuse. To the court, she confessed without an explanation. She gave no excuses. That was due to her sorrow for what she'd done, for inadvertently killing the father she loved so dearly. What a tragedy. Rozlynn bears the weight of it.'

A few of the women copied Roz in staring at the floor, a palpable sadness in the room. Rozlynn reverted to her withdrawn manner.

'Either way, uncle or dad, murder is murder, and she knew it.'

Several women nodded. They knew that that was inescapable.

'Rozlynn is not connected to the underworld,' Cinq-Mars went on. 'She and Doi were working together when Florence was, you know, garroted. It's difficult to see how they were separated during the time. They sorted out the recycling together, prepared the garbage for examination – you're not permitted to sneak anything *out* of here just like you're not allowed to sneak anything *in* – so it is possible, it's *possible*, for the two of them to have separated during that process. In fact, we know they did, because Doi was not with Roz when she discovered Flo. The opposite could have occurred as well, but no one remembers that. Still, in the main, Doi, you were with Roz. If you didn't do it, did she?'

Doi didn't need to give it much thought. 'I don't think so.'

'There you go.'

'I thought' – Abigail again, as if she was the presiding judge over these proceedings – 'you were supposed to show us how everybody could be innocent *and* guilty.'

Cinq-Mars glanced over his shoulder at her. 'We can look at that, too. Does that seem fair to you, Roz?'

She shrugged.

'Here's a question, then. Out on the trapline with your dad, when an animal was caught in a snare, suffering but not dead, when you didn't want to risk damage to the fur with a bullet and getting up close with a knife could cost you a finger, how did you slaughter the animal? Bear in mind, I've spoken with folks in your community, including the Mounties there.'

Everyone gazed at her in curiosity. What secret could the overly secretive Rozlynn have hidden from them which now might be revealed? Under the intensity of their gaze, Roz looked across at Cinq-Mars in the center of the room. Rather than answer, she brought her fists close together in front of her chest, twisted them over and under each other in a rapid motion, then yanked them a short distance apart, jerking them to a stop.

'Yes. You killed animals with a garrote. A strangulation wire. All of a sudden, you might not be as innocent as most of us, or all of us, have presumed.'

Forever inscrutable, Rozlynn remained a difficult person to penetrate. She betrayed no shift in mood or attitude, although she held her head upright again, defiant. Perhaps she felt a tinge of satisfaction to be included among the others as a suspect now.

Abi was holding a hand up to speak. Cinq-Mars looked at her impatiently. 'What now?'

'She taught us.'

'Excuse me?'

'Roz told us about the trapline. When we had Story Night. She told us about strangling animals. She told us that she used to do that, and we asked her for a lesson on how. So, I guess that keeps us all under suspicion, no?'

Cinq-Mars had not known that detail. 'Who,' he asked, 'prompted Roz to give you the lesson?'

His eyes scanned the room. He checked in on Quinn; she didn't look great, but she nodded to indicate that she was OK. He continued to swing his look around the room – until Jodi's hand slowly lifted. 'Doesn't mean nothing,' she attested.

She was right. If they had all heard the lesson, no one was more implicated than anyone else.

Still, Roz *knew* how, and had experience with the technique. The others knew it only in theory.

'A further issue,' Cinq-Mars continued, 'is motive. No one liked Florence and that's a shame, but it's no reason to kill her. For her, it must have been difficult to bear, having no friends, which may be why she was so vulnerable to the hand of friendship extended by Abigail. Yet Flo, it appears, had a mission. To force Abi to reveal her secrets, such as where she hid stolen loot. Abi, we'll recall, was friends not only with Flo but also with Rozlynn. Motive? Perhaps Roz acted to protect the life – the very life – of her new friend Abi. Also, Roz and Abi possibly had plans to tuck away into the wilderness once they get out of here. Roz, because it's the only life she knows; Abi, because she'll be on the run from dangerous people. Roz, then, may have acted to save her friend from Flo's mission, which was to intimidate her, to get her to talk. So. We have motive.'

'Thanks for pointing that out, boss,' Abigail remarked. 'I mean the wilderness part.'

'Make other plans, Abi. Now, moving on,' Cinq-Mars decreed. He had expected the room to be startled by his revelation about Rozlynn; evidently, that was not the case. The entire circle of inmates was quite subdued, including the woman holding a knife to a young woman's belly.

v

'Speaking of motive,' Cinq-Mars declared as he continued to pace, now around a broader perimeter of their squared-off circle. All eyes were on him. He was testing the limits of Doi's awareness, to determine how close he could get to her before she objected. With his back to Doi, yet stepping closer to her, he stopped within ten feet of her and Courtney. Close to striking distance. 'Our friend Abigail is littered with motive. It's written all over her.'

'Not a pretty picture, Cinq-Mars. Littered? What, am I like a trash can to you now? Rubbish off the street? You don't think I'm cute?'

Always deflecting, always looking for an advantage. The others

found the joust curious and fun. Abigail had their attention now.
She controlled the room.

'Abigail – the oh-so-talented swindler. So much drug money
sliding through the fingers of biker gangs, and on through their
money-laundering schemes. So much of it, she figured she could
rip them off without anyone noticing. Banks would be reluctant to
report the theft, given their own complicity in moving bad money
around. It could have been the perfect scheme. Until the matter got
out of hand. Some say thirty-six million.'

The women had heard such numbers. Most assumed it to be an
inflated figure. Hearing the sum on the lips of a cop somehow
made it feel real, if still unimaginable. Abigail shrugged. As smug
as ever.

'Some folks want their money back. Their greed greater than
their yen for revenge. They want their money first, and then and
only then will they take revenge. They're willing to get to Abigail,
even in here, to make that happen. Abigail figured out upon her
arrival at Joliette that coming here was not her lucky break. How
long did that take you, Abi?'

'Oh, about a nanosecond, give or take.'

'A nanosecond. Bikers calculated that if inmates were in place
before she arrived, she wouldn't finger them to be on any gang's
string. Who, Abigail, was already here waiting to persuade you?'

She shrugged again. 'I really don't want to implicate myself.'

'Flo,' Cinq-Mars suggested, which prompted Abi to shrug again,
a reflex that indicated affirmation. 'Maybe Jodi.'

'Jodi!' Jodi exclaimed.

'Jodi,' Abigail agreed.

'Who else?' Cinq-Mars pressed her.

'You want me to say?'

'Show the people what you got, Abi.'

She mulled it over, then said, 'Isaure.'

Involuntary verbal reactions from every quarter. 'What? Whoa!
Who? Really?' And loud inhalations of breath. The women were
startled. 'Isaure?'

'Yes,' Cinq-Mars confirmed. 'Isaure. Employed by the bikers and
by the SQ, both. Not even a prison guard, not really. Abigail arrived
in good faith but figured out pretty quickly – in approximately a
nanosecond – that she'd been buried in deep shit. Isn't that right?'

'Let's say I caught the aroma. The pungent stench of it,' Abigail concurred.

'So then, for you, motivation includes self-defense. No one can deny that self-preservation can be a strong motive to kill.'

'Flo's a beast. She *was* a beast. How could I kill her without her ripping my head off first?'

Cinq-Mars had imagined exactly that scenario with each individual. 'Your other best friend forever has been Rozlynn,' he pointed out to her. 'Acquire a strangulation wire from her and learn the technique, and with the garrote around Flo's neck she'd be pacified, under your control in about, oh, a nanosecond. Maybe two. You might even induce Roz to do it for you, that's not outside the realm of possibility.'

'In your realm maybe, not mine.' Despite that defense, the women were looking at her more solemnly now, as if she was already swinging with a metaphorical noose around her neck. 'Before I call my lawyer, Cinq-Mars, why don't you tell the girls why I'm the innocent one here, which you promised to do for us all. I presume I'm not an exception to the rule.'

'No. For once in your life, you're not an exception.'

Cinq-Mars moved closer to Abi to lull Doi into being accustomed with his movements forward, back, and around the room. He wanted her to relax as he strolled away to help her so that she'd remain relaxed each time he returned to her proximity. He again made quick eye contact with Quinn and he could tell that she understood what he was doing.

'Throughout your life you've used guile, Abi, not force. You come from a middle-class background. You had advantages, more than most, but you ditched them and made early mistakes. You were snared by evil men, you got entangled in the life, becoming an underage roadhouse stripper. That's one tough gig, Abi, although for a time you probably thought it was cool. We've talked about it in the past.' To the room he explained, 'Abigail chose to rip off the bikers on account of past abuses by gang members. Revenge, more than greed, developed her motivation to steal. Important to keep that in mind. You didn't know I knew that, did you, Abi? This goes back to our previous interrogation sessions.' To the room, he explained, 'When Abigail wanted revenge, she didn't lure a gang member into her bed to slit his throat. She plotted, she gained her victim's trust, she executed a plan to perfection, and got away with it until the deal went south. Money went missing. Let's say it's all of thirty-six million but only one person knows for sure. One of the guys Abi fooled has since landed in a ditch with his legs sawn off, for the crime of being bamboozled by a girl. Imagine what they'd do to the girl who did the bamboozling.'

'Not pretty,' Abigail surmised.

'Damn ugly,' Cinq-Mars concurred. 'It has to keep you awake at night. You can't let your guard drop for a second.'

'Still, my innocence here: I use guile, not force. That proves my innocence in the murder, no?'

'Proves? Your *guile* didn't stop you from getting into a fight with Marie-Philomène, did it? That said, maybe I agree. Not your style, and style means a lot to you. The one thing that's keeping you alive is the interest others have in recovering their lost lucre. Alive, you have the potential to be worth a lot of money. Dead, you're worth less than a dime. Still, you're relying on the patience of your enemies, and you must know that that comes with limits.'

'What I rely on, Brother Émile, is your ability to solve this business and protect me.'

Cinq-Mars smiled. 'As true as that may be, Sister Abi, no one, including me, can ever tell when we're being conned by you. I can't tell right in this moment. I can't declare your innocence too strongly, except to say that it's not your style to kill, nor is it necessary for you. On the other hand, who was working with Flo on that fateful day? Doing up the dishes with her and cleaning up the galley? Mmm. Well, well, that would be you, Abigail. Being with Flo, you might have slipped off to the restroom with her and no one would notice. Flo would trust you, so you could get behind her back, then the wire is slipped around her neck, something you learned from your good friend Roz, and *presto*! Here we are.'

'Not my style,' Abi reiterated and left it at that.

Cinq-Mars looked intently at each woman in turn, so that when he did the same with Quinn no one would notice that his eyes conveyed a message to her.

Malka

Quinn may have received his latest message, or not. Difficult for him to tell. She scrunched her forehead as if to convey confusion. 'Quinn,' Cinq-Mars declared, announcing to the room that she was next on the docket.

'She wasn't here back then,' Temple interrupted.

'She's been here since then,' Cinq-Mars countered. 'She's been living among you. That could be significant. She arrived with no alliances. No enemies. No friends. What has she heard or noticed? Be good to know. What do you think, Quinn? Who killed Flo? Any opinion?'

'No clue.' She winced then and kept a hand on her wounded shoulder. The pallor of her skin no longer seemed healthy to him. His confidence that he could rely on her in an active situation diminished, although he loved the tough chick persona she put on for everyone. She played it well.

'Still, maybe you can help me out,' he postulated. 'Alliances are in play, inside and on the outside, too. Quinn, tell me, have you figured out who's with who yet? And while we're at it, here's another tricky question. Do you have any sense that killing Flo was a joint effort? Answer honestly. If doing so puts you in jeopardy, we'll get you out of here.'

'That cinches it,' Abigail said.

'Cinches what?' Cinq-Mars fired back without looking her way.

Abi shrugged, raised and lowered her eyebrows twice for the others to see. 'Won't say,' was her enigmatic reply. She twisted her lips as though to suppress secret knowledge.

Cinq-Mars elected to ignore her. 'Quinn?' he asked. 'What do you think?'

Put on the spot that way, the undercover officer took her time. She hadn't determined if the detective wanted her to play along with some ruse that she wasn't latching onto, or if he was requesting her honest opinion. Their eyes connected for an instant – they'd been doing well with these silent, covert communications – before she cast her glance elsewhere. Not having cottoned on to his latest gambit, she decided that the man wanted the truth based on an insider's perspective. For some reason he needed only that. She assumed that her opinion might be necessary to knit his conclusions together before he mounted a case against anyone; that a matter sketchy to him depended upon an evaluation from her.

'I don't see how,' she said quietly, which she meant to be interpreted in various ways. 'Did two buds get together, do some shit? Or three or four? Possible. Maybe. But if you mean some sort of gang-type thing, a conspiracy? That I don't buy. I think I'd have sniffed out something like that by now.'

Cinq-Mars nodded, appreciating her contribution, both as an inmate – as others saw her – and as a cop, as only he knew, although he suspected that Abigail was suspicious.

Thoughtfully, Cinq-Mars moved the fist of his left hand against the cupped palm of his right, emulating in a horizontal fashion the action of a pestle in a mortar, or a punch to a jaw. He did that repeatedly until everyone lost interest in his hands and looked only at him. His visage took on an intensity that interested them. Then, as he withdrew his fist from his palm one last time, a finger pointed, for an instant, indicating a direction. That part, Quinn, and Quinn alone, saw very clearly. She nodded back, imperceptible to anyone except Cinq-Mars as they were intent on him.

'Next,' he announced, 'we have Malka.'

ii

A scream.

Brief. Emphatic. Chilling.

Cinq-Mars spun on his heels.

He saw Courtney first, looking stunned, mute.

She was gasping for air.

Who screamed? Not her.

The same woman screamed again.

Doi.

And again.

'Doi! What's wrong?'

What emerged from her lungs and lips mimicked the rage of
a fierce feline, like a jaguar's voracious roar, as if augmented by a
snarling demonic visage geared to intimidate any prey or foe.
Consumed by fury, she looked as though she'd lost her mind. Her
knife perilous on the young woman's chest.

'Take it easy. Easy, Doi. We'll talk it over. It can't be that bad.
What's the matter?'

'*Yes it's that bad!*' she fired back. At least she was still in the
room with them and not in the swirl of a breakdown. 'It's so much
worse! I'll kill this tramp little vixen slut! She's a n'er do well! A
bitch-fucking whore!' Typical language from her days as a mom
got mixed in with words she overheard daily in prison. At least two
women released a giggle over the phrase, 'n'er do well'. Cinq-Mars
got that but recognized the situation as precarious, nonetheless. Doi
was volatile and for anyone to be laughing at her at this moment
accelerated the risk.

'Doi, Doi, look at her. Doi. Please. Just look. She's Courtney.
That's all. A very young woman who needs our sympathy, don't
you think? She needs our care. Look at Courtney. See her. She's
not your daughter.'

'Courtney,' Doi spat out. 'Yeah, this Courtney – she stabbed her
best friend to death. How can somebody do that? Stabbed her for
talking to her boyfriend! That's all!'

Courtney squirmed in Doi's grip and uttered an intelligible moan
that conveyed both fright and utter despair.

'Is that why you punished your daughter? She did more than talk
to her boyfriend. She had sex, probably. It happens, Doi. When we
don't approve of a child's choices we can still be forgiving, don't
you think?'

'What's wrong with them, these girls? They're so crazy. I don't
understand them.'

At least she was talking. 'Doi, you don't know this, but I read
the psychiatrist's report that was prepared for your trial.' Ordinarily,
he might not be permitted such a disclosure, but he was working
at the prison without official designation. He believed he could say
whatever he wanted. 'You were raped as a young woman, Doi,'
Cinq-Mars said, and it seemed that everyone in the room, already
still, stopped breathing.

Doi went quiet, also.

She was gripping Courtney's neck in the crook of her elbow and squeezing her face against her own neck, while her hand with the knife worked menacingly up and down between her breastplate and abdomen as if searching for a vulnerable spot to slice open.

She refused to look at her victim. Couldn't.

'She won't visit,' Doi whispered. 'Why won't she visit? I asked her to visit me. She never comes.'

'Look at Courtney. How afraid she is, Doi. Your daughter's afraid, too. You can show her she has nothing to be afraid of – if you can let Courtney go free.'

'*I'll fucking kill her!*' Doi aimed the point of the blade right on Courtney's cheek, nicking her, drawing blood, and this time it was the girl who uttered an outcry and the prisoners in the room all moved in their places in an involuntary reflex, some as though they wanted to leap forward to intervene while others fell back in fright. A few were halfway erect now, holding the railings at the foot of their beds. Others were halfway prone.

Cinq-Mars put his arms out to indicate to everyone to stay put. He softened his voice even further to address Doi.

'How about we start working on the possibility of your daughter coming in for a visit? It'll take a while. Ultimately, it's her decision. If you release Courtney as a gesture of goodwill, and I know that, in your heart, you are a woman of goodwill, Doi, and if you agree to therapy – we can give you more time than usual with a therapist, you know, and private time, not just group therapy – then the possibility becomes more real. Right?' He spoke quickly to give her little time to think, and no moment to act. 'We can arrange a visit. If you hold up your end, I promise to speak to your daughter myself. Doi, I need to be able to tell her that you have held up your end of the bargain. That you set Courtney free when you were having a hard time. Your daughter will need to hear that story.'

Doi appeared to consider the offer. She seemed calmer while holding her aggressive stance.

Facing her, Cinq-Mars went down on one knee, less like a suitor proposing marriage than a hunter surveying terrain. He continued to speak gently while Doi seemed mesmerized by his position on one knee.

'When I come back around to you, Doi, in a little while like I said, there are two things I will want to find out. Think about those two things while I'm talking about Malka. Then Jodi comes next, then Courtney. Then you. Doi, I will want to know what set you off today. And this, this is very important to me, I will want to know how you got hold of that knife. Think about your honest answer to those two things, and I'll get back to you.'

Doi gave no indication that she was listening or considering his words, yet she seemed to have drifted away from her upset.

'Shall we move on?' Cinq-Mars suggested and didn't really give her time to answer. Intuitively, he did not think she was going to relent, not yet. A step-by-step process. The next step was to relieve her of taking any immediate action, resuming the status quo prior to her outburst. 'Will it be all right with you, Doi, if I continue around the room? It's what you wanted me to do.'

Doi took her time, but soon enough she nodded her acquiescence.

iii

Everyone in the room knew Doi to be volatile. She had not been placated; no one could count on her compliance. Occasionally, a voice spoke up to encourage Courtney to 'Hang in there, doll,' or to assure Doi that, 'It'll be OK, hon, it's all right.' Émile Cinq-Mars was not alone in fearing what might happen in a twinkling in Doi's hyper-state: pretty much anything. But he was equally anxious about Courtney. The younger woman appeared to be close to the end of a frayed rope. For her to freak out might instigate a horrific result. He hoped to relieve the pressure on both Doi and Courtney by diverting their attention, giving each of them time to calm down, so steered the group's scrutiny toward Malka.

To change the atmosphere in the room, he elected to be dramatic with her.

'Malka, as everyone knows, is tall enough and large enough to be considered a threat to Flo. Florence was tougher, meaner, more physically imposing from what I hear. I get that, and we have to bear in mind that Malka worked behind a desk her whole life. She's softer, we can agree there. But something else comes up with Malka taking her husband's life. First, she made him suffer terribly before he died. She's got it in her. She's a killer in a housewife's frock.'

The room concurred that Malka had to be marked down as wicked.

'Except—' Cinq-Mars held up a forefinger for effect.

'Except what?' someone – it was Temple – asked.

'That line is pure malarkey.'

'Pure what?'

Cinq-Mars didn't catch who asked the question, but explained, 'Horseshit, in other words.'

'What's horseshit?' Abigail spoke this time, her curiosity genuine.

'Do you want to tell them or shall I?' Cinq-Mars asked Malka. She scowled back at him, so he carried on. 'Malka poisoned her husband, that's true. Whether or not she should do time for that is a matter of opinion, although a court ruled against her, obviously, because she's doing time in Lady Jail like the rest of you. Her husband was dying a miserable slow death – that's also true – but brought on by cancer, not by Malka.'

No one spoke up, but all eyes were on him, and a few jaws had relaxed. He took a furtive glance at Doi and Courtney and saw that they were more interested in him for the moment than in their own drama.

'Not kidding,' he stated, as though someone had suggested he was. 'He pleaded with his wife to help him out, to end it for him. So Malka did. An act of love, you see. An act of kindness. An act of *mercy*. As far as she was concerned that's what it was, even if society thinks differently. Society will probably change its mind someday, but the point is, she's not the badass killer she pretends to be inside these walls. Her man was suffering, and she committed a mercy-killing. Telling you she poisoned him slowly? That was her way to get along with you badasses. A way to fit in. She wanted to sound tough. Right, Malka? Mere self-defense. Malka's a puffball, just so you know.'

She continued to scowl. This press release was not something she wanted distributed.

'Fuck you, Cinq-Mars,' she muttered under her breath, her only words on the subject.

Courtney broke just then. No rhyme or reason to her sudden collapse. Something shattered inside her. Cinq-Mars had taken his eyes off her for a few seconds. Perhaps Doi had relaxed her grip, or had made a motion to tighten it, but Courtney suddenly erupted in a manic frenzy, putting herself at extreme risk but unable to control herself. Her arms flailed out, her legs kicked up somehow from under her, her body lurched forward and in that wild flailing and lurching Doi's knife flashed and cut her and Doi recoiled from inflicting that injury and the knife seemingly leapt from her hand as she released it and skidded on the floor. It bounced and rattled. A momentary hush. Then bedlam. Not nine but nineteen women it seemed dove for the weapon. They might as well have been ninety. Courtney celebrated her release with a horrendous outcry and a brazen thrashing of her limbs with blood flitting about as though she was fighting off an army. Another voice, unidentified, hollered also. Cinq-Mars was looking for that voice when his right leg buckled. A body slammed into the back of his one upright knee and he toppled forward like a bowling pin. Flattened to the floor with weight on top of him he glimpsed the knife, close enough, and he, too, stretched for it when a foot either intentionally or accidentally kicked it from his reach back the way it had come.

The uproar both strident and plaintive. Someone was moaning strangely. Flattened and pressed to the floor, Cinq-Mars located the panic button in his jacket pocket – he was supposed to protect it in his palm – and considered what to do. Press or not press? When another woman tripped over him – Temple – he dropped it. Someone swore, a screech, an expletive that cut through the fuss and alarm as the chaos of bodies began to disassemble, retreat. When Cinq-Mars was able to raise his head off the floor and as the women around him picked themselves up, he discovered that the knife had apparently skidded right back into Doi's possession again. She wielded it, threatening everyone who was near. This time, in her other hand, she held Jodi by the hair. The young woman squirmed and squiggled and kicked. Then she went tense and still as Doi brought the knife across her throat.

One young victim exchanged for another. She had seized the nearest one at hand.

Nothing personal, although her action may have belied a preference for the young.

Noise was erupting behind him – that moaning – and most women were looking back there now.

Malka was gripping her calf, which bled. She tried to stifle her moans, failing often.

The women fell further back toward their beds, confounded by the conflicting scenes.

At one side, Doi had found a new victim, and near her, her previous victim bled, although not profusely. Opposite that scene, Malka writhed on the floor with a nail protruding from her right calf, and her sudden blood loss was shocking.

Cinq-Mars retrieved his panic button yet decided not to use it. Not yet. He returned it to his jacket pocket. But this time he kept his thumb on it.

'Help her,' he said to the room at large. Courtney was being held and comforted by Temple. They knew he meant Malka.

iv

The women were at a loss. One of their own twitched gently on the floor with a nail in her calf. Someone else had stabbed her with that nail. The culprit was not owning up to the deed and no one knew who she could be. Which cast another level of dread onto their general malaise.

'Help her,' Cinq-Mars instructed a second time as no one had budged. Abigail and Rozlynn responded then, going on to their knees to attend to Malka. Abi held her hand while Roz examined the wound. Looking back at Cinq-Mars, Roz inquired, 'Should I pull it out?'

'Do it. Watch out for a sudden gush of blood. Keep it clean. I brought extra bandages for Quinn. Use those.'

Roz was the right person for the job. While others might have hesitated to pull the nail free of the wound, she managed it, both swiftly and with care. Temple left Courtney who had been squirming anyway and came on to the floor beside her. She passed Roz the gauze, bandages, and wrappings. Roz applied them and pulled the wrappings tight. A virtual triage unit, and an efficient one.

Abigail looked up, though, when Roz was done, and asked, 'Who the hell did this?'

They all wanted to know exactly that.

'How do you feel, Malka?' Cinq-Mars inquired of her.

'It hurts, all right? How do you think I feel? What the fuck happened? Who did it?'

'Who's got nails?' Temple wondered. 'Who's got nails?' She had trafficked in weapons, outside of prison and perhaps inside as well, but she was making it known that she was clueless here.

'We'll do a house search later. If there are any more, we'll find them. But Malka, are you well enough? I can keep going with you?'

She was pale, dismayed, subdued, yet she still had her wits about her. 'Knock yourself out, copper. Just don't fucking stab me in the leg.'

'Let's not have anybody stab anybody, all right? In the leg or anywhere else.' He turned, as he said this, to impose his request upon Doi. She was keeping Jodi close to her through a combination of yanking on hair whenever the younger one tried to pull away, and by flashing her knife. That menacing blade kept her in place and in peril.

Doi acknowledged his imperative by giving Jodi's hair an extra tug, and by jutting out her chin.

'Fine,' Cinq-Mars determined. 'As I was saying, Malka's a puffball. She's not the killer you ladies think she is.'

'She still killed, though, didn't she?' Temple, having quit her nursing job, was returning to her bunk. 'She went through with it. Maybe she got a taste, right? I'm kidding, but still, if she had a reason, she could do it again. She's done it before. Once more for fun, right?'

'We can take that into account,' Cinq-Mars admitted. Truth was, he'd prefer they all chimed in with such remarks, which might spark an alternative outcome. 'I'm not sure if you're defending her or making a point against her, Temple. Which is it?'

'Neither. No skin off my schnoz.'

'Are you sure about that?'

Temple scrunched her forehead, surprised by the implied and abrupt accusation. 'What's that supposed to mean?'

'Hmm.' The policeman's murmur seemed to constitute a reply. The women did seem to believe that something of import had been conveyed, subject to interpretation.

'No, seriously, what's that supposed to mean?' Temple asked again, her dander up.

'I'll get back to you. We're discussing Malka now.'

'Are we?'

'Indeed. We've established that Malka's a puffball who, despite that designation, when the chips were down, had the gumption to poison her own husband. As Temple pointed out. Plus, although we can't hold this part against her, not really, somebody thought it necessary to stab her in the leg with a nail. Who took the trouble? Or was that an accident in the melee? Who knows? Malka's an enigma. A small-town mayor, an upstanding member of society, not your customary criminal. And yet . . .'

'And yet what?' Malka, intrigued, wanted to know when Cinq-Mars appeared to drift off.

'And yet, we've learned today, haven't we, that an older woman who was a mom and a housewife before arriving at Lady Jail can be dangerous with a weapon in her hand.'

'Not my nail, you can take that to the bank,' Malka pointed out.

'I believe you. But was it your garrote? You're large enough, strong enough, a physical threat to Florence. Add in the element of surprise . . . it would be surprising, Malka, if you came up behind anyone intending to kill. I'm not saying otherwise. But give you the right weapon, then you, like everyone else in here, cannot be eliminated as a suspect.'

Malka considered that, then scoffed.

'What?' Cinq-Mars asked her.

'You're forgetting. I'm a puffball. Your words.'

'You poisoned your husband, as Temple said. You did so out of love and mercy. That was your story in court. It can be argued that you've never been part of the criminal element, so you're right. A very big checkmark in your favor. Let's move on, then. Doi! Is that all right with you? Next up is Jodi, and it will really be better if you let her go, you know? How can I talk to the poor girl with your knife at her throat? Not to mention, I'm giving reasons why everyone here has to be considered a suspect, and reasons why not. If I say something untoward about Jodi, how do I know you won't do something rash?'

'You don't,' Doi spat back. 'That doesn't matter. She's staying where she is.'

'No,' Cinq-Mars stipulated. 'Let her go. For God's sake.'

'Please.' The one word, plaintive and sincere, humbly spoken, caught the attention of the room. Cinq-Mars thought that Jodi was begging for a reprieve, but no, it was Courtney speaking up in favor of her pal, and she further entreated Doi. 'Please, don't hurt Jodi. She's my friend. She did nothing wrong. Please don't hurt her.'

Courtney looked so exposed, so bare, down on her knees with blood trickling from her collarbone. The pain, the worry, evident in her tone even caught the attention of Doi herself. She looked at the girl, finally, as Cinq-Mars had been asking her to do, and like the others, she was moved by the young woman's entreaty. Tears broke from the girl then, undoubtedly an effect of her trauma and having been abruptly released, but the knife aimed at Jodi's throat and at other times at her belly prompted both her tears and her intervention.

'Listen to her, Doi,' Cinq-Mars remarked quietly. 'Two young women. You may have a dispute with your daughter – as I said, we will try to help you out with that – but you have no dispute with Jodi or Courtney. Let her go, all right? How can I talk to her, how can I get to the bottom of this, if you're threatening her with a knife? I'll make a deal with you, Doi.'

Doi seemed hardly to notice the young woman in her grip. She did look at Courtney though, and listened to her, too. Anyone in the room might guess that she was suddenly brought up short, made aware of her own transgressions for the first time.

'What deal?' Doi asked Cinq-Mars, her voice barely above a whisper.

'Let Jodi go, but keep the knife. I'll stay far enough away that you can grab somebody else before I can make a move, so you're still in complete control. You're still calling the shots, Doi. But let Jodi relax. Let me talk with her. You're still in charge, but you asked me to find out who killed Flo—'

'Isaure, too,' Doi demanded.

'Isaure, too. But one step at a time. Help me do this, help me identify the killer, which is what you say you want me to do. Just let Jodi go. You grabbed the knife back when you dropped it and we had that mad scramble. I'm proposing something much easier. If anyone makes a move toward you, or if I make a move, just grab hold of somebody else. But let Jodi relax. Let her talk freely. Let her go. Doi? Let her go.'

Doi was thinking about it. The others could tell that, conflicted, she didn't know what to do. She saw sense in the policeman's request, but she didn't want to surrender her perceived advantage. Cinq-Mars gave her something else to think about to tip the argument to his side.

'It's very possible, Doi, that this can be Step One. Let Jodi go. Keep the knife. I'll stay away from you. If, after this talk, there are things that happened today that might land you in solitary, or worse, well, we might find a way to forgive and forget. You know? But take Step One.'

Others thought that that was as good an offer as was likely to come down the pike and encouraged Doi to comply.

'Shut up! The fuck!' she broke out suddenly, perhaps not getting her words in the order they were intended, adding on the expletive in deference to where they were. The room fell silent.

She considered her options. Everyone else waited. Doi dipped her head to whisper in Jodi's ear. Jodi appeared to nod, as much as she could with the knife so near. Jodi then readjusted her body position, getting up off her bottom and on to her knees, then she walked on her knees a short distance forward, arms' length away from Doi. Then remained on her knees, sitting back on her haunches, still captive.

To impress upon them all that she maintained her advantage, Doi warned, 'Come at me anybody, I stab her right in the back. Don't think I won't.'

No one doubted her resolve.

'OK, copper,' Doi invited. 'Talk.'

v

He did.

Jodi & Courtney

'Jodi's in trouble now, isn't she? A knife at her back. Not fun, but, when you think about it, not so unusual for you, is it, Jodi? You've known trouble from the day you were born. You've always had a knife at your back.'

To everyone present, a huge difference existed between a metaphorical knife and one with a tempered steel blade. Nonetheless, he had their attention and they waited for the tale behind his remark. Jodi kept her eyes on him, wary of what might be revealed. Cinq-Mars then appeared to turn reticent, as though emotionally moved by some stray thought and requiring time to recompose himself. That impression was not sustained, for when he spoke next his tone conveyed a confrontational, even a combative, edge.

'Sad, isn't it, how Doi lost her head and attacked her daughter with a hatchet? It's also sad how Courtney went berserk and ambushed her best friend with a butcher knife. Something similar happened to Jodi when she went wild and shot up a convenience store. That's how the story is told, anyway. Funny though, all that blasting away and she only shot a man in his right big toe. She also shot a Corn Flakes box dead center and put a few holes in the walls. Hit a couple of milk cartons. Still, there's another key difference. Neither Doi nor Courtney were ever in trouble with the law prior to going bananas. Jodi, though, poor, innocent Jodi, who was induced by a boyfriend to stand guard while he emptied the till – Jodi has been in trouble with the law, if not from birth, then pretty much from when she learned to walk.'

'Wouldn't say that,' Jodi said, objecting more to the exaggeration than the substance.

'Fine. But I'll say this. From the first day you had the ability to choose between right and wrong, you chose wrong every time.'

She shrugged, no longer disputing the characterization.

'Jodi keeps you laughing. She and Court spend their time giggling at the world. So folks give her a pass – inmates, the guards, me, everybody – we think she's just a kid gone wrong.'

'That's all she is,' Courtney protested.

'Think so? Jodi grew up in a biker family, did you know that? Her parents and siblings have lived outside the law since . . . well, you tell me, Jodi. Can you remember a time when you weren't a petty criminal?'

That shrug again, half-resentful, partially proud.

'Which raises a concern, don't you think? Why she should suddenly lose her shit in a convenience store robbery? It really wasn't that big a deal to her.'

The women looked at each other, then Temple stated what several were thinking. 'Drugs?'

'Not her thing. I'm saying that because I've seen her sheet and her medical screen from when she was admitted here. Blemishes, of course, but nothing to suggest behavior that way.'

'Then what?' Temple asked.

'Here's a clue. Think the opposite of Malka.'

They tried to think what that might mean but no one offered a response.

'Malka, the puffball, pretended to be tough in here. Jodi, tougher than anyone knows, more bitter than anyone knows, more experienced than anyone knows or gives her credit for being, wanted to come across as a crazy girl who lost her head for a minute. But she's cool, our Jodi. She's collected. We've seen her in fights. So that part about going nuts? Pure virgin bullshit. I bet she took dead aim at that Corn Flakes box. Am I right about that, Jodi?'

She was thinking about it, what she should deny, what she might be willing to concede. She began once more with a shrug, then said, 'I've hit a few barn doors in my time.'

'You grew up with a pistol in your hand. You can hit a milk jug at twenty yards, I bet, let alone a Corn Flakes box at ten. A regular Annie Oakley. You can hit a man's big right toe when you're standing next to him. He was wearing sandals, so you could see your target. Thanks for not inflicting more damage on him than that, although that was enough.'

Given the option of denying a compliment or accepting it, she chose to agree that she could shoot.

'I don't get it,' Temple said, which was what most of them, or all of them, were thinking.

'Malka fakes being tough. Jodi's the opposite. She's in here pretending to be a snowflake.'

'How come?'

'Because she was sent here. Isn't that the truth, Jodi? She got arrested on purpose. She's inside on a mission.'

They gazed at her, wondering, putting two-and-two together, adding things up and perplexed that she wasn't denying it, when Cinq-Mars interrupted that chain of thought by saying, 'Doi. Don't even think about doing what you're doing.'

Attention promptly switched to Doi. The older woman relented under their scrutiny. Her torso visibly sagged. An urge to plunge her knife into the young woman's back dissipated.

Courtney spoke. Still in defense of her friend. 'Jodi didn't kill Flo. She couldn't've. Flo would've thrown her through a wall.'

'I'm not saying she did kill her, not yet anyway. Remember, Court, as I've done with everyone else, I'm relating Jodi's dark side first. We can talk about whether she's innocent later. Here's what everybody needs to know about her – and Jodi, correct me if I'm wrong. I've had to guess at this, that, and the other thing.'

The young woman didn't know whether to give him her whole attention or continue worrying about the knife at her back. She kept trying to look over a shoulder at Doi without making her concern obvious. 'Eyes front,' Doi would whisper, her voice threatening, and Jodi would quiver. Knowing well the story of Doi hacking up her daughter redoubled her peril in the moment.

'Can I hold her hand at least?'

Courtney was asking the question, not of Cinq-Mars, but of Doi. The older woman nodded consent. Courtney worked her way over on her knees, then settled in front of Jodi and to one side. Not concerned that her hands were blood-covered from her wounds, she clasped Jodi's left hand in both of hers.

'So what's Jodi's big mission?' Temple asked.

Cinq-Mars shot a glance her way and smiled. 'Interesting that you, of all people, should ask.'

'Oh yeah? How come?'

'She's probably here because you are.'

That befuddled the room, and Temple especially.

'Doi – I need to talk about you for a second, before getting back to Jodi. I don't think you really understand what sets you apart in here.'

'I know what sets me apart.'

'No. You don't. Whatever you think it is, it's not that. It's not being older. Malka's older, too. It's not being someone who harmed a family member. Talk to Roz about that. It's not being someone who's never been involved in a life of crime. Courtney, same deal. So I have a third question for you to think about, because it's important to what we're discussing, to help us get to the bottom of this. It'll help us figure out who killed Florence and perhaps – perhaps even Isaure. Which is what you asked me to do, Doi. I'm hoping you're thinking hard about your answers to my two questions: How did you come across the knife, and what set you off today? Now, we have one more. This: What sets you apart from everyone else in here? I think it's important. It might be a key.'

He wanted, of course, to deflect her inner rage, to deter her instinct to lash out with a knife in her hand. He wanted her to sense that she could depend on him for sympathy, or better yet, depend on his help.

'How can I keep talking about everyone individually,' Cinq-Mars lamented, and walked in circles within a small square, 'when the first thing you do when you arrive here is figure out who's in with you? Who will be your buddies? Who do you guard against? Everybody gave Flo a wide berth, except maybe Abigail. Flo was volatile, and scary, so you can't blame anyone for that. But some people come inside with certain alliances already in place. Some are even under orders. They have a job to do.'

The women glanced around, perhaps assessing their alliances, or readjusting them. What he said was true, they knew that.

'Jodi, for instance, since I'm still on you: I suspect you're the primary source for weapons. In the yard, from the yard, and from time to time into this unit. You're connected to Marie-Philomène since you're both connected to the same gang. Flo, too. A Hells Angels lady. But where the Hells once ruled with impunity, inside and outside, a rival gang is forming. Which side anyone is on – if you were on a side; some of you weren't – is changing underfoot. Allegiances can shift, depending on events on the outside. That's one reason why Jodi, not Temple, is running weapons on the inside.

Temple's satellite gang is now tight with the Rock Machine. That's a change. Jodi's – and remember, with her it's a family business – Jodi's satellite gang, a small, mean one from Ontario, a pack of killers, is connected to the Hells and connected to the young woman who had acid thrown in her face by Florence. An existing grievance there, an existing motivation.'

'I didn't kill Flo,' Jodi reiterated. If she hadn't defended herself, Courtney would have done so on her behalf.

'To be determined, but that's not the issue at the moment. Everyone here makes the same claim – "It wasn't me" – so save your breath. No point repeating it.'

Jodi shrugged. Hers was the hostile shrug of the dispossessed, of the person who disregarded any opinion that differed from her own or was more nuanced. Vehemence was her baseline attitude.

'Weapons have shown up in this unit. The garrote that killed Flo. The knife in Doi's hand today. We have to think about Temple for that, but also Jodi. Just like Temple never killed anybody herself, not that we know of, the same is true for Jodi. It would be out of character for her to kill Flo herself, and certainly a feat beyond what we might expect of her little body tangling with Flo's mass. I know where I'd lay my bet even if Jodi had a garrote. She's not physically capable of taking her on, not by herself. She may have been a target of Flo's. She might be able to make a case for self-defense, although in all my conversations that has never come up. Perhaps Courtney was a target, for sex, violence, or both, and Jodi wanted to protect her friend the same way Courtney is fighting to make the case for Jodi today. The two of them might have done it together. That's slightly more feasible and helps make them each other's alibi. Anything's possible, of course.'

'Then what's the point?' Jodi remarked. 'Anything's possible, so any of us could have done it. If nobody admits to it, you've got nothing. A bunch of stories. Those stories don't tell us who did it, who didn't do it. They don't say I did it any more than anybody else. Add it up and you got nothing.'

Cinq-Mars appeared to agree, but tagged on, 'Except this. There's no way you went berserk on a job. You got arrested on purpose. Violent enough to do time, but you tempered your level of violence to keep the years down. Enough to get into a pen, not enough to be here forever. Then your mob connections worked to see you transferred to Lady Jail. Stranger things have happened. Look at Abigail.'

On cue, everybody looked.

'She was probably transferred in here so that the mob could kill her. But only after they found out where she hid their money. That has to come first.'

ii

Abigail performed a twisting motion with her hand, as if she was working an invisible screwdriver. Cinq-Mars wondered what the action indicated, but it was Quinn who posed the question. 'What's that supposed to mean?'

'I thought he was smarter,' Abi said to her. Then tempered her remark. 'Or better informed.'

'How so?' Cinq-Mars asked.

'Digging in the screws, but you screwed up, Émile.' Others smiled when she called him by his first name. 'Jodi's connected to a gang connected to the Hells. Did you say that or not?'

'I did.'

'Flo was connected to the Hells. Everybody knows that. How can you pin the murder on Jodi when she's in the same gang? She wouldn't dare kill one of her own.'

'You're giving me cause to proclaim her innocence?'

'Keeping it fair is all.'

'Will you let me get back to you on that?'

'You will anyway, if you want. I can't stop you.'

'Thanks. See that, Courtney? Your friend has an advocate who's made a point in favor of her innocence. What do you think?'

Courtney looked at each of them for a moment, then determined, 'I think that's great.'

'Mmm. I hope that helps you to leave her alone, Doi.' He engaged the woman who still held the knife with a steady look, and while no one was certain, most everyone thought they saw her nod in the affirmative. Progress.

Cinq-Mars turned then and winked at Abigail. They both knew that the others were forgetting his original statement, that either gang might have had an interest in knocking off Flo. One gang might have wanted to do so out of revenge, the other because they were frustrated that she was not scaring the hell out of Abigail, then getting her to talk as a result of their intimidation.

'Now. Who's left?'

'Me,' Courtney said.

'I left you alone while you had a knife at your throat. I'm glad that's changed. Maybe now we can talk more freely.'

'I had nothing to do with killing Florence.' She smiled rather sweetly. 'Everybody knows that.'

'But everybody was involved with killing Flo,' Cinq-Mars contradicted her. 'None of you are innocent of that.'

Temple objected to that remark. 'What are you saying? I had nothing to do with killing Flo.'

'Everybody did,' he insisted. 'No one befriended her. The one exception was Abigail, but for her to befriend Flo was literally the kiss of death and Abi—' He paused to think it through. 'Abi probably knew that. For the rest of you, isolating her, always keeping your distance, that left her vulnerable. It made her afraid and for good reason. No wonder she went off to solitary so often. She erupted and did things and went off to solitary partly because she was pissed off with all of you and angry inside, and partly because she couldn't take being so alone, and partly for her own protection. She felt safer in solitary. Imagine that. Nobody ganged up on her there. When you all ignored her, she felt ganged up on.'

'I couldn't be friends with her,' Courtney protested. 'You know why. She might do things.'

'You were afraid. I get that. Still, Abigail proved you wrong. Flo didn't do anything to Abigail except protect her from the rest. At risk to herself, possibly. But this points out where you are perhaps more than complicit, Courtney.'

'How?' She wasn't challenging him. She feared his condemnation too much.

'When you make friends with someone, Court, you let yourself slide under that person's influence. Jodi's been guiding you toward a life of crime. You want Abigail to teach you to be a swindler, but come on, really? No. You don't want that, not really. But you let Jodi think that way because you think that way with Jodi. The point is, if someone wanted to convince you to help kill Flo, you'd probably go along with it. That's what you do. You went along with your boyfriend being unfaithful until you couldn't take it anymore, then broke out in a rampage. Maybe you went after totally the wrong person, but you did what you did, probably because you were trying to express yourself, instead of being somebody's puppet. But inside Lady Jail, you're still somebody's puppet and you still mistake that for real friendship. Until you become your own person, you must be considered a suspect, because you let yourself be influenced by others against your better nature.'

Courtney stared back blankly at him, then slowly withdrew her hand from Jodi's.

'Now cheer her up,' Abigail instructed him.

'What would I do without you?' Cinq-Mars asked, the sarcasm in his tone so over-the-top that many smiled, including Abigail. 'But she's right, Court, I need to cheer you up now. Let's face it. Killing Flo took planning, subterfuge, execution. None of that fits you. Perhaps you were a silent witness, but I don't see you in on the planning, and honestly, not in on the execution, either. Not cold-blooded. If you were to kill, it would have to be part of a rampage.'

He let his words sink in, and the women around the room gazed at the floor, some the ceiling, contemplating all that. When they came back to Cinq-Mars they realized that only one person remained on his agenda. That would be Doi, the one who had sabotaged their routine for the day.

Cinq-Mars, however, had a different plan.

iii

'Will you do something for me, Courtney? The prison reads your letters home before they're mailed. As I said I would, I've read a number of them myself. I don't have any on me, but I imagine you've got one on the go. You're about due. Will you read a bit of your letter to us all.'

'Why?'

'I think it will be educational. Informative.'

'Do I have to? I don't want to.'

'You're a daughter who writes to her mother. I think Doi, who's a mother who hasn't heard from her daughter for quite some time, might like to hear one of your letters.'

Courtney stared back at him as she considered his request, and eventually turned to look at Doi. The woman had held her at knifepoint and threatened her life. She still sat with the dagger in her hands. A communication occurred between them; Courtney could tell that the older woman wanted to hear her read a letter. She disentangled her legs and strode across the room to her bunk. She fished a letter-in-progress out from her books on loan from the prison library, then returned to her previous position on the floor, near Jodi.

She started to read the letter silently to herself at first, perhaps to make sure that she could go through with this.

'Courtney?' Cinq-Mars inquired of her.

She put the letter down and implored him with her gaze to let her off this hook. Instead, he encouraged her to proceed with a gentle nod.

Courtney lifted up her pages again to read from them.

> *Hi, Mom,*
> *I'm good. How are you doing? I guess you know what day*
> *it is.*

She let the pages drop into her lap again, and explained, 'I wrote a few days ago.'

The women of Lady Jail were interested, and they nodded to let her know that they understood. They wanted her to read on. Courtney raised her pages again.

> *Yep, it's my birthday.*

'Oh my God, little girl, Happy Birthday!' Temple exclaimed. The others took up the refrain with varying degrees of enthusiasm, but they all noticed that Courtney was ignoring them. The room fell silent again. Waiting.

> *I didn't tell anybody because I can't stand it. I'm twenty-one*
> *now. When I'm thirty-one I'll still be here. I won't get out*
> *then, either. I know I deserve it but it's hard to imagine. Ten*
> *years ago I was eleven! Eleven! I was still your little girl.*
> *That seems like so long ago I can't count that far back. The*
> *same time is ahead of me and then a bit more and it will all*
> *be the same.*

If I told people, maybe Abigail – you'd like her Mom, she's nice – maybe she'd've baked a cake. She makes good cakes. So yummy. They're the best thing we have in here. But I didn't tell her because I can't stand it, thinking about how many years are left. I should be celebrating my birthday with you. Instead, I make you sad. I make you sad every day because of what I did but I bet you were extra sad on my birthday. I'm so sorry. I say that all the time but I'm so sorry it's like this big gigantic blob inside me, this sorry blob, it's so huge I don't know what to do with it sometimes. Or all the time. I don't know how to live with it, this big sorry blob. Some days it's all I am.

I'm learning, though. I want you to know that. I don't want you to be so sad. I'm a human being who acted like a monster. I'm not a monster though. There's a big difference. I killed Daphne in a wicked way. She's dead now. She always will be. I can't bring her back. I'm so sorry. All I can say is, all I keep saying is, I'll never do nothing like that again. Sorry, again, double negative. I know you hate those. If I could erase it I would, but I can't. I can't erase anything. If I scratch it out it just makes a bigger mess but it's still there. All I can do is promise you that I won't do anything like that again. (There! No double neg!) Not even in here where sometimes a person can get to feel that way. Like killing somebody, I mean. Like the murder in here I told you about. That made you worry, you said. But I'm all right, Mom. Really, I am. I want you to know that. I'm all right, I just can't celebrate – and here comes a double negative on purpose! – I just can't celebrate nothing.

Me and my friend, Jodi, I told you about

Courtney put her pages down. 'Far as I got,' she said.

The room was quite still.

'That was lucky,' Jodi remarked. 'You didn't say nothing bad.'

'Real lucky,' Courtney agreed.

Doi

i

'Doi?'

Cinq-Mars noticed her consternation, directed inward. Her head suddenly jerked from side to side, three times, four, then more, as if she battled a demon in her sleep.

'Doi!' Sharply. Loudly. To call her back to the room from a different locality, to knock her loose from her derangement.

Everyone was watching, both frightened and fascinated, as Doi disintegrated internally before them. Rising from the depths of her diaphragm she disgorged a colossal guttural bellow, a roaring, her mouth stretched to its limits. Her throat warred open and out of that cavity a reflux of caterwaul and moaning overwhelmed their enclosure. Anyone might have expected the walls to splinter, the roof to collapse from the ferocity of her shake and shudder. She took a breath and did it again. A windstorm of rage and torment emitted from a tempest of visceral regret. No one had heard anything similar. Not even those who had struck a blade into another's gut or beaten a face without regard had heard such sound. They had experienced the dreadful outcries of others, the grievous suffering, the jeremiad of pain and fright, of utter despair or of loathing, yet no one had heard remorse bray so profoundly.

They were each struck numb.

Moments passed before anyone noticed that Jodi, with the bellow loud and fearsome at her back, had pitched forward in surprise on to the floor, then rolled halfway over to face her captor. Too shocked to respond further, she looked as stunned as any deer in headlights, as if she had indeed leapt from her skin. Émile Cinq-Mars caught the sudden advantage. He strode forward. Doi was too deep inside her manic trance to notice him step right over Jodi and hover above her. If Doi was going to use her knife now, he feared, it would be on herself, this vociferation of her spleen a prelude to that. He considered a fierce slap but shocked her instead with a hellacious roar of his own. A grizzly's foursquare thundering over her, then her name, again, 'DOI!'

He broke through.

Having stripped herself to the marrow of her own false pretenses and the vast subterfuge she had so long used to ignore both her ruinous life and the atrocity of her actions, and the atrocity of actions committed against her, what remained of her sat still, a tottery shell, as delicate as crystal, as acrid as smoke. She could be snapped with a word or wrecked by a look.

'Doi,' he said, and this time Cinq-Mars summoned the depth of his sympathy to strike the right note.

She turned to him. Gazed up, emerging from her mania. She was returning to herself, to an honest reality, to finally accept that she had indeed taken a furious hatchet to her daughter and landed in prison for it where she deserved to be. A hell of her own devising.

'I think it would be a good thing,' Cinq-Mars suggested, rather than leaping forward and seizing the knife, or her, which he could do now with every chance of success, 'if you would kindly pass the knife to Courtney. We don't forget everyone's wrongdoing, do we? But who knows? Maybe this is how we can start to forgive.'

He didn't expect her to know what he was talking about, but felt that she could respond to his tone, and to the notion that an action could be taken now that could not have been contemplated before. No real logic in it other than a fury's demise. The woman looked exhausted and spent.

Doi passed Courtney the knife. Just like that. The girl took it. Like that.

'Put it down,' Cinq-Mars directed the younger one, 'in the center of the room.' To the others, he said, 'If someone wants to make a dive for it like you did before, go ahead. Just be the person who killed Florence. I'll pin that on you whether you did it or not.'

'The wheels of justice,' Abigail said, but he was no longer giving countenance to her script.

'Dive for it and find out,' he warned her.

She put her hands up, declared, 'Just sitting here. Bump on a log.'

'Good. I hope that holds for the rest of you, too.'

Temple made eye contact with him, received his approval, and went down on her knees next to Doi. Rozlynn went over, too. Each lightly held one of her hands. The older woman half-wept, half-despaired of being able to speak again and uttered a few lines of gibberish. That made the women laugh, and Doi laughed a little, too. She was trembling. Her lips quivered. Cinq-Mars saw in that moment a chance to get through to her.

'Doi, here's an old saying. One that's touched up with a gracious truth. At least some of the time it's true, maybe not every day of the week as Abigail once pointed out to me. *The truth will set you free.* Three questions, Doi. Where'd you get the knife? What set you off today? And what do you think has set you apart from the others in here? You can answer the first two, if you're willing. I can help you out with the last question, if you like. Doi, tell us. Where'd you get the knife?'

'She's still an inmate,' Abigail pointed out.

'Why are you speaking?' Cinq-Mars asked over his shoulder.

'Just saying. The poor woman, what's she's been through just now and you're asking her to be a snitch? The truth can set us free to be killed in here, Detective, if we don't watch out. Not by me. To be perfectly clear. I'm just saying.'

'Won't all of you forgive her?'

'All but one maybe,' Temple said, taking up Abigail's side.

'All but one,' Cinq-Mars noted. She had a point.

'Maybe more,' Abigail tacked on.

'I'll tell you,' Doi piped up. Her voice had lost its impetus, having run its course perhaps and requiring a recharge. She barely spoke above a whisper. She looked around the room and noticed that many heads – most of the other women, in fact – were nodding encouragement.

'Go ahead,' Cinq-Mars said.

She chose silence.

Cinq-Mars tried again. 'When you screamed. I don't mean for Flo. I mean today. Nothing was happening but your scream shocked us. Why did you let loose at that moment? Try to think back. You were holding Courtney, then suddenly something set you off. What?'

She shook her head, as though she didn't know.

'What was I saying, do you remember? Seconds before you screamed.'

She looked at him. She remained silent, but this time he could tell that she knew the answer.

'I said, didn't I, to everyone, to the room, "Next, we have Malka."
I mentioned that I was going to talk about Malka, and you went
around the bend. How come?'

She stared back at him a while. She was looking away when she
finally told them all, quietly, 'I found the knife in Malka's bed.'

'You bitch,' Malka murmured from her place on the floor. 'No
business. You had none.'

'Where did Malka get it, do you think?' Cinq-Mars asked quietly.

Silence for a moment, which Cinq-Mars interpreted to mean that
Doi really didn't know. He looked at Jodi, who rolled her eyes, but
she admitted, 'Yeah, yeah. I gave it to Malka. So what?'

'Fuck you, too, bitch,' Malka said. 'Whose side you on anyhow?'

'Enough with the tough-girl talk,' Cinq-Mars instructed her. 'We
know that's not you.'

'Maybe it is. A nail was stuck in my leg. That's tough-girl shit.'

Cinq-Mars let her stew. He came back to Doi. 'What set you off
today? Before your big scream? In the beginning. Tell us why finding
the knife turned your world inside out and backwards, because that's
what happened.'

She seemed to think about it but once again didn't come up with
anything.

'Try,' he suggested. 'Think back to when you went batty. When
you grabbed Courtney.'

She did. 'When I found the knife in Malka's bed. I sat on it by
accident.'

'I see. You've been friends with Malka. In your mind, the two
of you are not supposed to be here. You're the ladies of the house.
That's how you used to think anyway, until a moment ago. The
ladies in Lady Jail who don't belong here. You know differently
now. Am I right?'

She nodded. Her eyes welled up.

'You attacked your daughter. You belong here. But until now you
haven't thought that way. You and Malka were not only the older
ones in here, Doi, in your head you were also the innocent pair.
Today, you know better. When it hit you that Malka was more like
the others than you knew, that she had a knife, just like any bad
criminal, that maybe she was dangerous, you saw then that you
were alone. You probably thought that she might have killed Flo
if she concealed a weapon in her bed. That left you as the only

innocent one. As the only true lady in jail. Just you. Which meant you now had no support inside. That's when you went a little nuts. You took the knife. Then you grabbed Courtney.'

Doi's nod indicated that that was true.

'I can come up with other considerations that perhaps you missed. Malka might want the knife for her own protection. Why not? Two women have been murdered recently. She may have felt the need to protect herself. Did you think of that?'

Doi shook her head to indicate that she hadn't.

'You may have leapt to the wrong conclusion, Doi. That's something I've tried not to do since I've been here. All of you have given me a lot of practice with that.'

He was able to evoke a small smile or two around the room.

'Doi, the third question I asked has allowed me to solve this case. At least, I think so. What set you apart in here? You believed you didn't belong here. You denied the obvious truth. You were alone in thinking that way. Malka could argue that she killed her husband as an act of mercy. She told you that, didn't she? She confided in you. It's why you were such fast friends. It was true, too. She did do it as an act of mercy.' He gazed at Malka where she lay wounded on the floor, one hand stretched down to clamp a bandage to her calf. 'Except Malka only wanted you to think that she was a nice, suburban lady. She never felt that way herself. She knows that she belongs here, on the inside. Maybe not for mercifully ending her husband's life. But she was the mayor of a midsized town in Ontario that permitted the Hells Angels to have a clubhouse and do their business in the countryside. How many of you knew that?' He awaited a response. Got none at first. Then Jodi tentatively raised her hand. 'Yeah. Jodi knows. She's biker Ontario. When the citizens of Malka's town learned how their mayor helped out the bikers and received their financial support, they kicked Malka out of office. The Hells could not let that stand. They arranged with their money and their intimidation tactics to get her back on council. They needed her there. Right, Malka?'

'Sing me a song, Cinq-Mars. Learn the violin while you're at it.'

Cinq-Mars smiled, which he shared with Doi. 'It won't be a pleasant song. Let me ask you, Malka, how does a woman acquire poison to kill her man? Not as easy as some might think. Not unless you have friends in very low places who can help a pal out with

something like that. And then, of course, they have something over
on you, don't they? Another favor granted is another favor owed,
at least in some quarters. You rose like cream to the top of my list,
Malka, when a biker on the outside mentioned you. He spoke of
your innocence, or maybe he wasn't so sure about your innocence.
He may have suggested that you might be guilty. Either way, why
would he bother when there's no reason on earth for him to ever
have heard of you? How would he know you even exist?'

She twisted her neck as though she wanted to belt someone.

'None of that gets me a stretch in the can, Cinq-Mars. Not past
the time I'm doing now.'

'Killing Flo does.'

The charge created a bustle in the room. He said nothing more,
and Cinq-Mars and Malka stared one another down. Neither moved.
Neither relented. Until Malka did.

She said, 'Blow it out your fancy pink ass, copper. You got no
proof.'

'My opinion? Everyone shares the blame for Flo's murder. All
of you let her grow more isolated. Lonelier. That left her vulnerable.
But one person here – at least one – knows something the others
do not. One person here was so afraid of what she knew, that she
messed up the map I had all of you draw. She didn't want me to
know what she knew so she deliberately messed up her map. Why,
Courtney, did you mess up your map?'

The room went dead quiet again. Women looked around at each
other, and it seemed that they were reaching a consensus, even while
a question, or an issue, or a fear, still hung in the air. They all looked
then at Courtney.

'Perhaps everyone here should decide if you're going to look
after your own lives or let yourselves be led around by men on the
outside. Personally, I wonder if you all don't owe something to Flo.'

Temple and Jodi, an adversarial pair, and Abigail, perpetually an
outsider, worked the matter through and appeared to reach a conclusion amongst themselves without uttering a word. Temple spoke up
for them, 'Go ahead, Court. We got your back.'

Courtney nodded, then quietly attested that, 'Flo went to the
toilet. I was there myself, coming out. I didn't want to say that.
Then Malka went in. I saw her come out. Flo didn't. I saw Doi go
in later. Then Doi started screaming.'

The women appeared to be breathing the news, in and out.

'You see,' Malka pointed out defiantly, 'it could've been me; it could've been Doi. It could've been Courtney, no? No proof. It could've happened before that and nobody noticed. Flo was down at the end. People come in, go out, without seeing her. Not until Doi did.'

Cinq-Mars returned to the center of the room again. He bent low. He picked up the knife by the tip of the stock. 'I believe her. And I hear you. Her testimony won't be enough to get you another prison term, but you probably don't deserve the one you have, so maybe this makes up for that. However, my believing that you did it is enough to get you out of Lady Jail, back into a regular penitentiary. Back into a jumpsuit. People in here want to live in peace.'

He walked across the room toward the exit and placed the knife down on a high shelf by the door. Then turned back.

'Speaking of staying here or going . . . Jodi, you have a long, long way to go to prove that you should stay. Do you want to stay? If so, it won't be easy. Before you answer with your tough girl lip, and we both know that you'll have biker support wherever you go, think about this: You are unlikely to get another chance like this again. A life-changer. It's all or nothing for you, right here, right now.'

She held her head down, thinking about it, then had to look up and face Temple. They were supposed to be mortal enemies, at least on the outside.

'Somebody else's fight,' Temple said, and shrugged.

Jodi agreed. They nodded. They'd work it out.

'I want to stay. But I also want to get out.' The women laughed at that.

'For now, you can stay. Short leash.'

'Got it,' Jodi said, her way of saying thanks.

'What about who fucking stabbed me?' Malka wanted to know. 'Who did that? Does that bitch stay, whoever she was? I want to know who.'

'Yeah, who did that?' Abigail asked.

'That would be me,' Quinn admitted.

'Yeah, why'd you do that?' Cinq-Mars asked her.

'I thought you wanted me to.'

'If things got hot, maybe. It was a backup plan.'

'Seemed pretty hot to me.'

'Is she your girlfriend? This one?' Abigail inquired.

'You know who she is.'

'A cop.'

'And no, she's not my girlfriend.'

Another ruckus and uproar with everyone talking at once, but no one really seemed to mind that Quinn was a cop. They were amazed. A few even regretted that she'd also be leaving Lady Jail.

Borde

Abigail settled into the seat at the table opposite him, slouched down a little. She took her time before looking up as though abruptly distracted by a stray thought. Émile Cinq-Mars motioned the guard at the door with his chin. If looks could kill: the corrections officer settled on a sigh, obeyed and left the room.

'Wish I could do that,' Abi said.

'I wouldn't put it past you.' They shared a grin, then Cinq-Mars said, 'You wanted the meeting, Abi. To break the routine or something serious?'

'What's not serious? My life is on the line, Émile. That's not changed.'

'Mmm,' he murmured.

'Not good enough. If that's all you've got, I'm dead meat.'

'You know the drill, Abi. Show us where you hid the money and police departments across the country will compete to bail you out. If you keep a smidgen for yourself, who'd know? You'd get away with it. No one has an accurate account of how much you stole. No one ever will. You pulled off the perfect crime and all that, until you didn't.'

She seemed to want to respond, but never found the words.

'My guess? You don't have the money,' Cinq-Mars said. He smiled in a way she found curious.

Abigail studied his expression, wondering what he knew to say that or smile that way, or if his words and his look were mere conjecture, a false flag. She finally managed to admit, under her breath, 'Never did.'

He nodded. He added, also under his breath, 'I know.'

'You *know*? What do you know? You don't know squat. You're bluffing.' Her voice remained hushed as though someone in the room might overhear. But they were alone.

'Never bluff a bluffer, as they say. You're a modern day Robin Hood, Abi.'

She went silent then. Her eyes moved around the small room, calculating.

Cinq-Mars pressed his advantage. 'Remember, I studied your process. Best as I was able, anyway, back when we were building a case against you. High finance is not my bailiwick, Abigail, but still, did you really think I put in all that time and found nothing?'

She met his gaze again. 'Of course I did. Are you having me on, Mr Copper-Man?'

He raised his hands and spread them apart for a moment. 'Everyone who investigated you outwitted themselves. Including me. We aided and abetted your own deceptions. We failed to consider your basic motivation. I cottoned on, eventually. I'm not saying you're altruistic to the bone, Abi, but you funneled biker drug money into charities around the world.'

'Oh, did I? That's a wild thought, Émile. You can't prove nothing like that.'

'Sorry, Abi. That jig's been up for a long time. What I think is, you never figured out how to funnel the cash back to yourself. Hitting up foreign accounts where money was being moved at lightning speed and in huge numbers – rapid-fire money laundering on the fly, heady stuff – you figured out how to skip a beat.'

'Skip a beat?' She was trying to put on a brave face although defeat showed around the edges. They'd been adversaries for years; she had never shown signs of being foiled before.

That smile of his again, a mere uptick, difficult to decipher. He explained, 'No one was likely to notice if a chunk here or a chunk there vanished along the way. Chunks always vanish along the way and no one is ever certain of where. It's just expected. Once in a while, somebody gets a bullet to the back of the head, but half the time that bullet was only a crude guess. No one actually knows where all the money went, and not many care as long as most of it arrives on target and close to being on time. Some banks take a cut, it's assumed. They're adept at making money disappear. Your problem, Abi, was where to put it all? Once you opened a funnel, giving the lion's share to yourself was a hurdle too big and a step too far. You might have figured it out one day, that might have been the plan, but you failed to do it in the short term. A whole other problem for you that required more time.'

'Especially if you're not free to travel,' she admitted. 'I had to look like I was on the job.'

'What bank could you hoodwink to store it for you – for you, personally? But charities? They received these odd deposits, raw cash to them, and never looked that gift horse in the eye. Why would they? No need to even issue a tax receipt or say thanks. They had a notion where it was coming from. Probably thought hoodlums the world over were suffering a crisis of conscience to be so generous. By moving it around from one charity to another, no big red flag was raised. Until one was hoisted when the tally really began to add up. Good scheme, Abi. Very smart.'

Her mouth remained slightly agape.

'You knew? Yet said nothing?' She seemed to be accusing him of a crime, and Cinq-Mars accepted that he might be guilty of one or two himself. She was growing wary, for if he had crossed a line to her side of the fence and had something on her, what did he want from her now? That was how her world had always worked.

He folded his arms across his chest. 'Abigail, if people were aware that you never possessed the money you pilfered, that you never hid it away in a secret vault somewhere, you'd be a carcass in a dumpster within the hour, no matter where you're living. Let's keep this one to ourselves. No need to mention it. I haven't. You gave the money away. I'll admit to my failure, take the abuse the department will enjoy heaping on me. I'll claim I couldn't drag it out of you, that you're one stubborn lady.'

'Shit, man. I had no idea.'

'Why so glum?' She did appear to be dismayed.

'If you figured it out, other people will, too.'

Cinq-Mars dismissed the notion. 'I had resources and imagination, both. Other people? They'll assume forever that you took the money for yourself. Who gives it away in this world? They'll keep looking for a stash of cash overseas with your name on it. Money, Abi, is hard to find when and where it doesn't exist anymore. You'll be fine.'

She wasn't so sure. 'In here, for now. I might survive – short term.'

'I'll be working with honest officials. We want to take away the bikers' ability to move prisoners around the system. We'll add security checks specifically with you in mind so that the new regulations cannot be subverted. Very senior people will have to sign off on moving you, and on moving anyone close to you.'

She shook her head in defiance of him. 'Then what? When I get out, bikers will have my skin. I'm not sure I can live without it, Cinq-Mars. I used to strip naked in their clubs, when I was still a kid, but naked with no skin? That's another story.'

'You've been working on that one I know.'

She shot him a glance, confused. 'What do you know? Surprise me again, Cinq-Mars.'

'Your disappearing skin. I'm talking about Rozlynn.'

She sighed. 'More bad news. You figured that one out and this time you told people. I'm burnt toast.'

Cinq-Mars wasn't so sure. 'Before you join her in the Manitoba wilderness, Abi, a biker war will be underway. My prediction? Whoever doesn't die will be imprisoned. But many will die. More than one or two. Probably more than one or two dozen. Some say more than a hundred, although I hope not. You're a concern for bikers now, that's true, but after a bloodbath who will remember you? When all that shakes down, who will still be alive to remember you or give you a second thought after your release?'

She shrugged. Although her nerve endings and her bones were keenly interested.

'No one,' he told her. 'All you have to do is survive your time in Lady Jail, hang out in the wilderness for a few years until you're utterly forgotten, then you'll be home-free. Just don't find your way back to prison, not here, not anywhere, and forget about your old haunts. No nostalgia tour.'

Abi put her elbows on the table and her head in her hands. She held the pose. She broke from it when her survival instincts took hold again. This time she was the one with the ironic smile. 'What do you want, Cinq-Mars?' Life came down to that. She reverted to his surname to show that she was onto him.

He wasn't going to say, initially. An intensity in her eyes changed his mind. She deserved that much, and he could tell that her brooding led her back to distrusting him as she did the rest of the world. 'I followed the money, Abi. When not a single penny was detected, I figured out that it must have been dispersed. You helped a lot of charities. Do I really want to go back to them and demand that the mob's money be returned or that banks who participated in their schemes be compensated?'

She stared back at him.

'A rhetorical question, Abi.'

'Our secret, I hope. But if you don't want the money back, the question still remains. What do you want, motherfucker?'

Cinq-Mars nodded in agreement. 'It's true. I have something on you. So behave.' He put his elbows on the table. 'What I want is to get you out of here, because we both know I probably can't keep you alive if you stay on the inside long term. A year or two will bring the news of your demise.'

'Reality kicks in. Finally. I'm listening.'

'Always. This is what you'll give me. The ways and means. Show us how to disrupt the flow of biker money. Do it now while they are on the brink of an all-out war, when they won't be able to handle the confusion, or stem the outflow. Yes, I know, they'll stick a finger in the dyke. They'll establish a better system next time. But let us jangle their nerves and undermine their structure at the same time that they're self-destructing. Give us the keys to knock down their money-laundering system, even if that's temporary. With that, I can spring you early. I can spring Roz early. You'll both be off to the wilderness and you won't have to come back.'

She seemed to be in a trance, scarcely breathing. Staring at nothing at all. Perhaps not even listening. A grave notion appeared to cross her face, altering her coloring. She took a few breaths. Nodded. Stared him down again. She spoke quietly, the underlying intensity apparent. 'How else could I get to them, Émile? I had to hurt them. I stripped for them as a kid. I was a fucking kid. They passed me around. You can imagine. You don't need the gory details and the truth is, as these things go, compared to others I got off easy. I'm not saying I got over it, but maybe I could let it go a little. I was smart. I could take care of myself. Up to a point. I made my way out from under them. I made myself useful and kept my clothes on. I could handle the paperwork when they needed someone for that, and day-by-day I made myself more important. You know, when the really big money first started coming in, they didn't have a clue. They'd go down to Las Vegas or Atlantic City. They even brought me along sometimes as their play doll. I saw a way out.

They didn't care if they made or lost money at the tables, as long as they came home with clean sparkly cash. I learned how money worked. Made friends with Mafia accountants, got tips. The old men were willing to share stuff with a young chick and they were, I have to admit, generally good to me. Happy to settle for a little flirtation, a kiss on the cheek, a friendly hug. They let me claw my way up the ladder. Still a criminal but left alone. Independent. I taught bikers how to flip real estate deals six ways in Germany for God's sake, give up a small bribe here or there, to exchange dirty money for crinkly cash and piles of it. I learned what banks were willing to comply. What foreign governments were hoping you'd call. You know? I became important. My own person. Then some crooked engineer wanted me as a reward for fixing a job. He'd seen me show up at a job-site with the payroll – another way of cleaning cash – and just like that, the bikers sold me out. They let the guy have me just to put me in my place, to let me know that, never mind my upper class manners – I was born and raised with those – and never mind the job I did for them, I was still their wasted worthless little gutter whore. I could say a word less gentle. That's when I knew I had to hurt them. Really hurt them. I knew how to do that, too.'

'Take their money.'

'That, too.'

'Too?' She had surprised him for a change. 'What else?'

'Put one over on them. Trick them. Fool them. Beat them at their own game. They hate that so much more. That was my revenge. Also, truth be told, my downfall.'

Cinq-Mars felt a tingling, as if a premonition was stirring on his fingertips.

She confirmed what she had alluded to. 'I'm not saying I let them find out what I did. I don't think I'm that stupid. But almost. I left clues. I found ways for them to think that someone, somewhere, was ripping them off. If not for that, nothing would have come back to me. I'd still be supporting charities. I just so much wanted them to know they were being ripped off.'

'What you could have done with your life, Abi,' Cinq-Mars said, and sighed, his tone sympathetic and wistful. He honestly admired her.

'Tell me about it. But never on the cards in this lifetime. Anyway,

I'm past fretting about that. Sergeant-*Dee*-tective Émile Cinq-Mars, what the hell do you want from me?'

The crux of their negotiation, for this was proving to be a negotiation. 'Ways and means, Abi. Ways and means.'

'Then I'm out?'

'By leaps and bounds. Do we have a deal?'

She thought it over. 'Out first. Then the good word?'

'No guarantee on that. I can try.'

'I can offer more than you're asking for. Your bosses' heads will spin.'

'In that case, we can swing it. I've already softened up the interested parties.'

'All right then.'

'Deal?'

'Deal. Now, Émile, let's talk about what I really came here for.'

This time, he was the one confused. 'What's that?'

'Tell me. I need to know.' That sly gaze. 'Million-dollar question. Not, where's the money, but . . . you know how it goes. Us girls, we're starved for good gossip. Even a hardcase chick like me. So, Émile, tell me, tell us all, how's your love life going these days?'

Rather than blow her off, or join in the laugh, Cinq-Mars took the question to heart. He closed his eyes a moment. She wasn't sure if that expression emulated taking a bullet to the chest, or if he was deep in thought. When he opened them again, he confided, 'I've decided. I'm going to ask the lady to marry me.'

'You will! Will you? Émile!' She bounced up in her seat. 'Cinq-Mars! Fantastic. Attaboy!'

He did his best to smile but couldn't hold it. 'I've got a snowball's chance, Abi. She's already been thinking about it. Fair enough. There's lots to think about. She's American. She lives on a farm. I'm a big-city cop in Canada. She's hung around, though. She hasn't beat it home yet. If she's waiting for me to pop the question, maybe she's thought things through. Hard to imagine she'll say yes.'

'Émile Cinq-Mars, you're scared.'

He managed a thin smile. 'Terrified, actually.'

'Good luck with it, Émile. Holy shit!'

'Yeah. Let's hope we both have enough good luck to go around.'

'We'll need it. Cheer up. Hang in there, baby.'

'You, too, Abi. All in all. You, too.'

ii

Before meeting with his next, and he hoped his last, inmate, Cinq-Mars was interrupted by an unexpected visitor. Inspector Gabriel Borde of the Sûreté du Québec stepped into the room shortly after Abigail was led out.

Unexpected, but not surprising. 'What are you doing here, Gabs?'

'Good to see you, too, Émile. How's it hanging out here in the bushes?'

'Sorry. It is good to see you. I didn't know you were still around.'

'I wasn't. I'm not still around. I'm zipping in and I'll zip back out again. This meeting is not happening even though it's official bees' wax. We need to talk, Émile.'

That sounded ominous, and Cinq-Mars indicated the chair opposite his own. 'I'd offer you a beer, but this is a penitentiary. They'd put us both in solitary for that.'

'You may be headed there anyway.'

He was hesitant to ask. 'What's up?'

'You're a tall man, Émile. With big feet and we all know you have a large nose. It's exceptional, in fact. You've been sticking your big beak where it doesn't belong – only according to some, I'll grant you that – and stepping on toes smaller than your own.'

'Meaning?'

'Meaning that in sticking your neck out it's landed in a noose.'

'Aren't you just full of nutty illustrations regarding my physique.'

Borde chuckled. He was the gentlest of men. Thinning prematurely, he had started to wear his hair straight back in recent months and the style suited his visage. He looked as though he might be a friendly face in haberdashery who could pick out a client's suit size in an instant, rather than a detective alert to a gangster's next move. A family man with simple interests; a good cop with an unswerving moral code which is what had brought the two men, from different forces and different agendas, together. They knew there were times when cooperation between departments – given nothing more than lip-service by the higher-ups – was vital to the public's interest. Their liaison was unofficial but fiercely defended between them and included other like-minded cops.

'Sticking with the theme of body parts,' Borde continued, 'the SQ wants to slice your balls off.'

'With a rusty blade, I imagine.'

Borde considered, only for a moment, continuing with the imagery, but he had arrived on a serious mission and wanted to get to it. 'Some will say you've tracked down the money. Some say you're clever enough to keep a slice of that pie for yourself. Some say you've thrown in with the inmates to run your own scheme. They've concluded that that's what's really behind the reforms you want to impose on the prison system, on the chain-of-command. Some say under suspicion and since the brain trust is as dumb as ducks that opinion might fly.'

'They have nothing on me.'

'They don't need anything on you to wreck you. You might still get support in your department but if the SQ sets out to wreck you, they'll just wreck you. They want the money. They want *something* out of this. We have a dead comrade, and this flag you're flying that Isaure Dabrezil was gang-compromised does absolutely nothing for our public relations. You get me?'

'If I'm hearing you correctly, Gabs, we're not talking about the truth or about what's right.'

'That offends the priest in you, I know. We're not talking about justice. We're talking about power and we're talking about politics and we're talking about the one whose head will land upright on a pointy stick. Ah, that will be your head I'm talking about.'

'I thought my neck was in a noose?'

'Whatever works best.'

Sergeant-Detective Émile Cinq-Mars of the Montreal Police Service placed his right forearm on the table between them and gently tapped his palm against it. The incessant tapping annoyed Inspector Borde of the provincial police but he let it go. He waited, hoping that his friend, with all his plans, had also figured a way out for himself. He'd upset the prison bureaucracy in revealing how the gangs could influence the movement of prisoners, and upset the SQ echelon by suggesting that their undercover cop posing as a prison guard was also undercover for the mob. As the gangs splintered into warring factions, Isaure Dabrezil was not quick enough on her feet, knowing too much to suit one side and doing too little to suit the other and probably still a cop, too. She may have thought herself immune from retribution due to her police and prison status. A lesson you don't get a second chance to learn. She had to go, and gone, the SQ was pissed. Meanwhile, his own city police department had been hoping he'd unearth a treasure trove of cash they could announce to the media, then request a bump to their budget in the new year. That these imaginary monies would be returned to previous owners – not rightful owners – was neither here nor there. They wanted and had expected that announcement and that it be theirs, and neither the Mounties' nor the SQs. The mucky-mucks had their private agendas and he was not cooperating.

He finally stopped tapping and looked his friend in the eye.

They needed to pull strings. He explained it. 'First, this is what I need.' He wanted Abigail released. Her sentence had been rigged from the get-go, and their connections in the Mounties could sneak through an early 'conditional' parole. 'Let people think she's being paroled early to give up the money. Any judge will sign off on that. Our friends will know better, but others won't object if they think it's the money.'

'Émile, come on, they'll turn rancid if it isn't. No noose for your neck. You'll be flattened by a freight train. I'm talking a hundred cars long.'

'I love your illustrations, Gabs.'

'Get serious.'

'I'm dead serious.'

'Then get this. I haven't told you, but they're thinking to let Malka Hayer walk on the murder rap. What might come out in trial is too risky, and anyway, they don't think they can convict on the word of a fragile teenaged killer. This is no time to be making demands, Émile.'

'I have more.' He blocked his pal's objection. 'Hear me out.' Cinq-Mars explained that they had to call on their friends in the Mounties for another favor, to force a retrial for Rozlynn, and to spring her on bail in the interim.

'Émile, when does this madness end? Give me something, for God's sake.'

'How about I give you more than something? How about I give you the mother lode.'

'Listening.'

'A biker war is coming.'

'Rumors are rampant, Émile.'

'Horse's mouth, from my side. How would you like to take down their financial money-laundering system, complete with international banks, enablers and subordinates? The prison bureaucrats will be happy because they go undisturbed as long as Abi and Roz are released. Your SQ has an orgasm because they totally rock the bikers' fiscal world. They might pull in some excess cash, too, maybe. The Mounties are delirious because they participate on an international level. They uncloak and reveal. Even my department is happy enough although I will remain a perpetual disappointment to them. But my head stays on my shoulders.'

Borde gazed back at him. While there was admiration in his gaze, another element mixed with that. One that feared for the man's well-being and safety. Not for this time around, perhaps, but over the course of their lives this priestly cop might receive his comeuppance. As though the world of cops and bad guys was too treacherous a path for one of his inclinations.

'Your nose is huge. You do stick it in where it does not belong.'

'Again with the body parts. What else do I get?'

'We're on. Of course. By the way, I've delayed mentioning that two people are waiting for you outside these walls. One a biker I know. The other a rather attractive woman, Émile. The biker introduced me to her. They were talking amicably outside. Both waiting for you to emerge. Is this your life now?'

Borde noticed his friend pale. Cinq-Mars asked, 'Was she packed?'

Borde adapted his tone to convey sympathy. 'Looked like it,' he said.

iii

Rozlynn slumped into the room, her usual recalcitrant self. Cinq-Mars expected to get no reaction out of her and didn't but proceeded to detail his plan anyway. He told her that she deserved a new trial. He had talked to the Mounties on her home reservation and they agreed. She'd been a good kid. They didn't understand why she had killed her dad without ever saying a word in her own defense. They could understand now that mistaken identity might have played a part; they knew the character and record of her intended victim, which brought up the notion of self-defense given the nature of her uncle, and with it the possibility of early parole pending a retrial.

The Mounties were willing to take it up with the public prosecutor. They'd present a compelling argument. Given time served, the circumstances, with any luck Roz could be freed, pending that new trial.

Roz listened. Implacable.

He wasn't sure what freedom meant to her. He assumed that it might be complicated. They had once discussed whom she might kill if freed.

Then she said, 'OK.' A woman of few words.

Cinq-Mars said, 'OK.' They both waited in silence. Then he said, 'You didn't give Malka extra time on how to use a strangulation wire, did you?'

Roz didn't respond at first and stared at the tabletop. After a while she adjusting her posterior, and answered, 'Why would I?'

'I don't know,' he responded. 'But I think I have my answer.'

He had no clue how things might work out with her, but he figured she had the patience to see the matter through. For the time being, she would have to wait without getting her hopes up and she was good at both those things. He kept his own hopes for her high. He was naturally optimistic that way, but at the same time he accepted that challenges lay ahead for her.

iv

Sandra was leaning on the front hood of her two-tone green pickup, an old and dented Ford Ranger, alongside the battered biker, Paul Lagarde. He grinned upon spotting Cinq-Mars emerge from the penitentiary. A grin so broad he looked like a kid again who'd been nabbed playing hooky. Cinq-Mars strolled over. Sandra remained in place, immaculately alluring to him in her jeans and cowgirl boots, leather vest with fringe over a mauve shirt. By comparison, Lagarde resembled a hirsute mannequin dressed in debris rejected by a garbage dump. A look that possessed its own peculiar charm, he had to admit, although Cinq-Mars could do without his Iron Cross that always dangled from an earlobe. He presumed that the accessory was meant to offend, and so, as always, he did his best to ignore it as the man stepped forward to greet him. He focused on his smile.

'Paul.'

'Émile.'

A first name basis with your foe. Merit to that over the long haul.

'In for a visit. Saw your girl waiting for you. Thought I'd hang around to say so long.'

'I'm glad we're on different turf, Paul. May we never meet again.'

'I hear you. But I enjoyed it. Anyway, before we go down different roads, Émile, tell me, what do I need to know?'

'Are we trading?'

'Everything's negotiable, right?'

'Your work here is done, Paul. Airtight and absolute. Nothing for you to see or know or do.'

'That so? Maybe I don't agree. But I'll keep it in mind.'

'You have a war to fight. Stay safe. What's here disappears from view.' He wasn't going to mention names.

Paul Lagarde put his hands on his ample hips to consider the news. 'Could come a time,' he mused, 'middle of a war, when a tip might help us both out. Maybe one less body on the ground.'

'If you expect me to arrest an enemy of yours the info needs to be golden. Nothing fabricated. Otherwise, you become the target yourself.'

'Sure. That's fair. I leave you to your girl. Her, I asked for a favor, Émile. Take her up on it.'

He had no clue what that might mean. Considering the source, he was unnerved. 'OK. I guess. Stay safe.'

Lagarde tilted his head as though to suggest that that was not likely, raised an eyebrow, and moved across to his Harley. By the time Cinq-Mars walked over to where Sandra was standing by her Ford Ranger, the man was on his way. Loudly.

'Lovely fellow,' Sandra said.

'I hope he behaved himself.'

'A perfect gentleman.'

'You're packed,' he said.

'Yeah. Well, you know. Time to get back. You're wrapping up here anyway.'

'That's true. You could, you know, stay awhile. Come back to Montreal for a bit. I could show you around the city. Lots to see.'

'Ah, I dunno. From what you tell me, your apartment is the size of a phone booth. I'll pass.'

He put a hand to the back of his neck, trying to think of

something to alter the course of history. She was packed. She was leaving. Nothing he could do about that. He was dying on the pavement of a parking lot. He wanted to marry her.

Sandra placed a hand on his forearm, forcing him to look up, and she smiled. 'I'm not going to move to Montreal, Émile. Nor to any city.'

'I understand. Of course not,' he acknowledged. Breath felt difficult.

'On the other hand, the local paper is advertising a couple of horse farms for sale. Not that I want to live around this neck of the woods. I don't.'

She had his attention now. He remained mute, waiting.

'Other parts of Quebec though, ones I've visited in the past for horse shows, they might hold out possibilities.'

At the same moment that his heart clogged his throat, despair sullied his disposition. 'I can't afford to buy a horse farm,' he told her. His life atilt, as if he was a kid at the top of a teeter-totter about to be slammed down hard on his butt.

She was trying to get his attention with her eyes. 'I can,' she told him. 'I can make it pay, too. As long as you're willing to drive into the city to do your silly policing, I'll deal with the horses all day. I've been thinking about it. I can't imagine a better life. Can you?'

He honestly couldn't. Obstacles and challenges presented themselves, but none that were persuasive.

'Most men in your situation, Émile, are asked if they're willing to commit. You're only being asked if you're willing to *commute*.'

How could he not love a woman who could turn a phrase that way? How could he resist the sparkle in her eyes? He didn't know how it happened, but her hips were resting against his, his hands encircling the small of her back.

He finally found his voice, and a blithe buoyancy of his own. 'You know, San, I am Roman Catholic, and in my own way, *practicing*. Pretty conservatively, too.'

She quizzed him with her expression. Commented, 'I'm not coming off the pill, if that's what you mean.'

'Not at all what I mean.'

'Then why bring it up?' A light dawned. How could she not love a man who posited these neat little riddles? He was bringing up his religion because he knew she feared the connotations. 'Émile,' she said, 'did you just propose to me?'

'Could be. I do believe in the sanctity of marriage. I'm not into living in sin.' Serious words, although his tone was decidedly tongue-in-cheek.

'Good, because I already invited Paul Lagarde to the wedding. I promised him a dance.'

His eyes scrunched. He looked away. She had the upper hand again. They could make their lives a game of this. He looked at her again, held her gaze, and they were both smiling giddily. 'Wait. Wait. Wait one minute. Are you saying that you told Paul Lagarde about our wedding before you told me?'

'Hey, he was here. You were late.'

She could so easily make him laugh. 'My fellow cops won't know what to think,' he surmised. 'If he's still alive, which will be in doubt, Lagarde can come. You can dance with him, but only if he takes off that damn ornament, or whatever you call it, the one on his ear. If so, I can make that work.'

'Always scheming. So we're on?'

'I'm definitely willing to commute,' he said, to confirm their vow.

She laughed. 'I'll just commit,' she said.

They laughed together. The kiss they both knew was coming was purposefully delayed, a moment too rare to be hurried. Cinq-Mars turned her, and held her with his gaze, and for just that moment it was as though they were dancing by the walls of the Joliette Institution for Women, which some call Lady Jail, by any name a penitentiary.

Afterword

The turf war between the Hells Angels and the Rock Machine arrived as full-blown in 1994 and lasted until 2002. The death toll, primarily among bikers but including innocent victims, would number 162. Scores more were wounded.